Rowanne was not about to let any practiced flirt cause her one more ounce of anguish.

"I am minded to steal another memory to take back with me to cherish," Carey declared.

Rowanne did not want another scene, and she did not want him staring at her with that devilish gleam that made her toes curl in her slippers.

"It's only a kiss I want to steal," he murmured, matching action to words like the military man he was, taking her gently in his arms and bringing their lips together. It was a moment of such bursting radiance that Rowanne forgot her toes, forgot that she was spreading more raspberry stains on his unmentionables where they were touching her body in the most interesting manner.

Only a kiss . . . ?

—from THE LUCK OF THE DEVIL

AN AFFAIR OF INTEREST

♥

THE LUCK OF THE DEVIL

Barbara Metzger

FAWCETT CREST • NEW YORK

A Fawcett Crest Book
Published by The Ballantine Publishing Group
An Affair of Interest copyright © 1991 by Barbara Metzger
The Luck of the Devil copyright © 1991 by Barbara Metzger

http://www.randomhouse.com

Library of Congress Catalog Card Number: 97-94787

ISBN 0-449-00204-7

Manufactured in the United States of America

First Edition: May 1998

10   9   8   7   6   5   4   3   2   1

Contents

An Affair of Interest

This one's for craft-show friends, creative, talented, and *nice* people, especially Barb, John, Russ and Debbie.

1

Money and Matrimony

If love were a loaf of bread, the Lattimore sisters could afford the crust, or perhaps a handful of crumbs. Being one half-pay pension away from poverty, neither Miss Winifred Lattimore nor her younger sister Sydney could afford the luxury of love in a cottage, not when their own cottage needed a new roof. One of them, at least, had to find a wealthy husband.

"But why must it be me?" Winifred poked at the tangled skeins of needlework in her lap. The discussion had been going on for some time, to Miss Lattimore's obvious distress. The needlepoint armrest was not faring much better.

"Why, you are the oldest, Winnie. Of course you must marry first," her sister answered, rescuing the knotted yarns from further mayhem. Heaven knew they needed the new armcover. Sydney plunked herself down in a patch of sun by her grandfather's chair and straightened the blanket over the general's knees before starting to unravel the mess. "Am I not right, Grandfather?"

General Harlan Lattimore, retired, raised one blue-veined, trembling hand to where his youngest granddaughter's single long braid shone red-gold in the sun. He patted her head as if to say she was a good girl, and grunted.

Sydney took that for assent. "You see, Winnie, the general agrees. Gracious, you are twenty years old already. You are like to dwindle into an old maid here in Little Dedham, while I am only eighteen and have ages left before I need think of putting on my caps. Besides, you are prettier."

The general grunted again. He didn't have to agree quite so quickly, Sydney thought, for all it was the truth. Winnie had the fragile blond-haired, blue-eyed beauty so eternally admired, an elegant carriage, the fairest of complexions, and a smile that could have graced a medieval Madonna. Her hair even fell in perfect ringlets from a ribbon-tied twist atop her perfectly formed head. Sydney scowled at the snarled yarns in her lap, considering her own impossible gingery mop that refused to take a curl no matter how many uncomfortable nights she spent in papers. Of course, it had to be matched with a tendency to freckles, she continued her honest appraisal, and nondescript hazel eyes, a complexion more sun-browned than any lady should permit, and a body more sturdy than willowy. No, Winnie stood a much better chance of landing them a nabob. If only she would try.

"You are much more the domestic type anyway, Winnie, teaching Sunday school, visiting the parish poor. You know you couldn't wait for Clara Bristowe to have her new baby so you could hold him."

"Yes, but a rich man with a big fancy house." Winnie fussed with the ribbons of her sash. "I don't know, Sydney. You are a much better manager than I. Think how you have been taking care of us since Mama passed on."

The general nodded. Sydney had done a good job, or at least the best she could, holding household on what His Majesty's government saw fit to award its retired officers. Mama's annuity had expired with her three years earlier, along with her widow's benefits from Papa's military unit. Since the general's seizure shortly after, Sydney had been juggling their meager finances to maintain both the cottage and Grandfather's comfort with just Mrs. Minch as housekeeper and his ex-batman Griffith as man-of-all-work.

"Exactly, Winnie," Sydney declared proudly. The pride may have had more to do with unknotting a particularly tangled skein than her accomplishments as a frugal chatelaine. That last particular skill was one she was hoping to find unnecessary in the future. "And that's precisely why we should bend our efforts to finding you a husband. No man wants a managing-type female, Winnie, they want a sweet, gentle girl." She smiled up at her sister, showing her dimples and her love. "And no one is

6

sweeter or more lovely than you, dearest. Any man would be fortunate to win you for his bride."

Winnie blushed, and the general grunted his concurrence. Then he stroked his other granddaughter's head again and said, "Aargh."

Sydney covered his gnarled hand with her own. "Yes, Grandfather, I know you are fond of me too, even if I am no biddable miss. We'll come about."

The old man smiled, and Sydney couldn't help feeling a trifle guilty that she liked him so much better now than she did when he had all his faculties. He'd made their lives hell, and Mama's, too, before she died, running the house like a military installation. The general had to have the best of everything—food, wine, horseflesh—and instant obedience to his every whim. He issued orders to family, neighbors, and servants alike until no one in the village would work for them and none of their friends would come to call. One day he'd thrown an apoplectic fit over some sheep in his path, falling off his horse into the street. The local men waited a good long while, making sure he wouldn't lay into them with his riding crop, before they picked up the general and carried him home. He had not walked since, nor spoken. For the most part, the Lattimore home was a great deal more peaceful.

The general seemed resigned to his Bath chair, napping in the sun, having his granddaughters read the war news to him, listening to the clacking of the village hens when they came to call, bearing gossip and sharing their good cooking. He'd led a long life, called his own tunes. Now it was time to pass on the command before sounding retreat. But he was worried.

When the general fretted, life in the cottage resembled an army camp under siege. All the other nodcocks rushed around, bringing him things he wouldn't have wanted if he were in his prime. That pretty widgeon of a granddaughter even started blubbering when she couldn't understand the general's agitation. If there was anything General Lattimore couldn't abide, it was a spineless subaltern. Even his man Griffith took to acting out charades as if the general were deaf, blast him. Only Sydney seemed to understand. Too bad she wasn't a lad, the general thought. She'd have made a deuced fine aide-de-camp.

He'd no more leave his men in the field without ammunition than he'd let his family be thrown out in the cold. But, damn, his pension wouldn't last forever. Hell, not even General Harlan Lattimore thought he'd last forever. Of course Sydney knew what worried him; she was worried, too. That's why they were having this discussion, to convince Winnie that she had to make a marriage of convenience, for all of their sakes.

Winifred wiped her eyes with a mangled scrap of lace. "But, but, Sydney, what if I cannot like him?"

Sydney jumped up, tossing the yarns into an even worse pile. "Silly goose," she said, hugging her sister, "that's the best part. I'm fussy and crabby, but you like everybody!"

The next question, naturally, was where to find the paragon good enough for their Winnie. He first had to be rich, but Sydney vowed she would insist on a cultured gentleman. She was not tossing her gentle sister to any caper-merchant hoping to better his standing in the social world. He should be handsome, too, this husband Winnie would be facing over the breakfast dishes for the rest of her life. And kind, Winnie put in. Most of all, he had to be generous enough to accept a bride with a houseful of dependents and a dowry slightly better than that of a milkmaid.

The answer to the question of locating this most eligible of *partis* was, of course, London. He could be lurking anywhere, in truth, anywhere but Little Dedham, that is, since the local bachelors—sheep farmers, squires' sons, tutors, and linen-drapers—had been coming round the cottage for years. None had fulfilled Winifred's romantic dreams or Sydney's mercenary ones.

Winnie laughed, a gay, tinkling sound. "London, Sydney? Now who is dreaming? You know Aunt Harriet would never invite us."

"And I shan't ask her, the old cat!" Sydney did not look the least contrite, speaking thus of their maternal relation, not even at her sister's gasp. "Well, you know it's true, Winnie. Telling us the strain of Cousin Trixie's come-out was too much for her to undertake presenting another debutante! It's not as if she doesn't still have that platter-faced chit on her hands this Season, and dragging two girls from party to party cannot be any more exhausting than one. Before that it was firing off Cousin Sophy, or measles in the nursery party, or the general's ill health, though why she thought two of us were required to attend Grandfather at home is beyond me. You could have gone anytime these past years if she weren't afraid of your casting Trixie in the shade."

"She did invite us to Sophy's wedding," Winifred put forth, trying to be fair.

"Yes, and sat you with that tongue-tied young curate for both the dinner before and the breakfast after."

"He was very shy."

"He was poorer than his own church mice, and had less countenance! That was better than my treatment, at any rate. I got put in charge of cataloguing the wedding gifts, for Sophy's thank-yous."

"Aunt knows how very organized and capable you are, dearest," Winnie said, her soft tones trying to soothe her sister's indignation.

It did not work. Sydney had been seething for years over Lady Harriet Windham's slights to her family. "Aunt Harriet knows how to get the most from unpaid servants."

"But you couldn't join the company, Syd, you were not out yet."

"And never will be if left to Aunt Harriet." Sydney took to striding around the small parlor. Winifred hastily wheeled the general into a corner, out of the younger girl's way. "Face it, Winnie, getting blood from a stone would be easier than wringing the least drop of human kindness from Aunt Harriet, and getting her to part with a brass farthing on our behalf would be even harder, the old nip-cheese."

"Sydney!" Winifred's scold was drowned out by the general's chuckle. He'd never liked Lady Harriet Windham either, and he wasn't even related to the harpy. She was connected to the girls by marriage, and it was a marriage of which she had never approved. Lord Windham's younger sister Elizabeth's running off to follow the drum with a lieutenant in the Dragoons did not suit her notions of proper behavior. Geoffrey

Lattimore's leaving Elizabeth a widow with two small girls and no money suited her even less. Lord Windham's own demise saw the end of any but the most grudging assistance from that quarter, and good riddance, the general thought at the time. Lattimore was a fine old name, with a tradition of serving King and country for generations. There was no getting around the fact, though, that nary a Lattimore put any effort into settling on the land or gathering a fortune or making friends in high places. The Windhams had, blast the parsimonious old trout. The general banged his fist on the chair's armrest. That's why they needed so many new covers.

Sydney retrieved the needlework and set to untangling the mess again. She smiled sunnily at her family, the angry storm over as quickly as it had come. "I have a plan," she announced.

Winnie groaned, but her sister ignored her.

"I do. We're going to London on our own. We'll rent a house of our own and make connections of our own. We won't ask Aunt Harriet, so she cannot say us nay. Once we are there, she shall have to introduce us around, of course, and at least invite us to Trixie's ball. She'd look no-account to her friends in the ton if she ignored her own relatives, and you know how much appearances count to Aunt Harriet. Besides, perhaps she'll feel more kindly to us when she sees we don't mean to hang on her coatsleeves or ask for money."

Winnie's pretty brows were knitted in doubt. "But, Sydney, if we don't ask her for the money, however shall we go?"

Sydney kept her eyes on the embroidery and mumbled something.

The general made noises in his throat, and Winnie asked, "What was that, dear?"

"I said, I have been saving money from the household accounts for a year now." She hurried on. The general had always said to get over rough ground as quickly as possible. "Yes, from our dress allowance." Winnie fingered the skirt of her sprigged muslin gown washed so many times no one could recall what color the little flowers had been. She hadn't had a new dress since—

The general was sounding like a dog with a bone in its

mouth, faced with a bigger dog. "And your wines, Grand-father. You know the doctor said spirits were no good for your health. Furthermore, all the port and cognac and fancy brandies you used to drink are being smuggled into the country without excise stamps. You yourself used to say how that was sending money straight to Napoleon to use against our troops."

Winnie's rosebud mouth hung open to think of her sister's daring. Still, a few dress lengths, some bottles of wine, fewer fires, and less candles could never see their way through a Season. She started to speak, but Sydney was already continuing.

"You know how Mama always said I had a good head for figures? Well, I started helping old Mr. Finkle keep track of his profits from the sheep shearing after his boy moved away, in exchange for mutton. Then some of the other sheepherders asked me to help them figure expenses and such, so they wouldn't be cheated when they got to market. They started setting aside a tiny portion from each sale, a lamb here, a ewe pelt there. Now I have a tidy sum in the bank, enough to rent us a modest house. I know, for I've been checking the London papers' advertisements."

Winifred had no head for figures whatsoever. The general did; he shook his head angrily. It wasn't enough blunt by half.

"I know, but there's more. I didn't want to say anything until I was sure, but the Clarkes' daughter-in-law is increasing again, and there's no room down at the mill. They are building a house, but they have agreed to rent our cottage for a few months until it's ready. So we have all that, and Grandfather's pension . . . and my dowry."

The general almost tore the arm off the chair with his good right hand and Winnie cried out, "Oh, no!"

Sydney stood, tossed her thick braid over her shoulder, and crossed her arms, looking like a small, defiant warrior-goddess from some heathen mythology. "Why not? That pittance won't do me any good in Little Dedham, for I *won't* marry a man who cannot add his columns."

"What about Mr. Milke? You know he has always admired you."

"The apothecary?" Sydney grimaced. "He's already supporting his invalidish mother. Besides, he smells of the shop. No, I don't mean to be a snob. He truly does, smell of the shop, that is. Asafoetida drops and camphor and oil of this and tincture of that. I cannot stand next to the man without thinking of *Macbeth*'s witches."

Winifred smiled, as Sydney knew she would. "Very well," Winnie said, "then we'll use my dowry, too." The idea was instantly overthrown.

"No," Sydney insisted, "you shan't go to your handsome hero as any beggar maid. We Lattimores have our pride, too. And you must not worry, nor you either, Grandfather. Winnie is sure to attract the finest, most well-to-pass gentleman in all of London! He'll be so smitten, he's bound to open his wine cellars to you and his pockets to me. I'll be so well-dowered, I'll have to watch out for fortune hunters."

And then, Sydney said, but only to herself, she could even marry a poor man if she loved him. Winnie would make a grand marriage, but Sydney vowed she'd become a paid housekeeper rather than wed without love.

Winnie was dancing around the room, wheeling the general's chair to an imaginary waltz. They would get to London after all, with parties and pretty gowns and handsome beaux. Sydney could do anything!

Sydney could do *almost* everything. She could outfit her housekeeper's twin sons, the Minch boys, as footmen and send them off to London to find lodgings. She could move the family, bag and baggage and grouchy general, to the perfect little house on Park Lane. They were on the fringes of Mayfair, but still thoroughly respectable. She could even face down Aunt Harriet, managing to convince that imposing dowager that the Lattimore sisters would be an asset: as eligible men flocked toward Winifred's beauty, they were bound to notice Trixie's . . . ? What? The girl had no charms to recommend her. Lady Windham saw only what she wanted to see though, and was sure the town beaux would recognize her Beatrix's better breeding, especially when compared to Sydney's harum-scarum ways. The rackety gel even refused to wear corsets!

Sydney actually did the near impossible. She improved Trixie's personality, if only by example, showing the brow-beaten chit that lightning wouldn't blast from the sky if Mama was contradicted. Trixie blossomed, if one could consider a horse laugh better than a genteel, coy simper.

What Sydney could not do, unfortunately, was make a pence into a pound, nor make one shilling do the work of five or ten. London was expensive. No matter how she figured, no matter how many lists she made or corners she cut, there was not enough money.

They had small expenses, like having calling cards printed, and subscribing to the fashion journals so they could study the latest styles. And medium expenses, like purchasing fine wines to offer the gentlemen who began to call, renting opera boxes, and hiring hackney carriages. In Little Dedham one could walk everywhere. And there were big expenses Sydney had not counted on, like all the dresses considered *de rigueur* for a London miss. She had figured on a new wardrobe for Winnie but, never having been through a London Season, Sydney had not realized exactly how many different functions a popular young lady—and her sister, at Winnie's insistence—was expected to attend. It would not do to wear the same gown too often either.

Sydney certainly never anticipated her own need for fash-ionable ensembles, nor that she would ever be too busy to sew her own gowns, as she and Winnie had done their entire lives. She surely never budgeted for an abigail to take care of their burgeoning wardrobes. And there was Aunt Harriet, yammer-ing on about Sydney employing a paid companion to act as chaperone for the girls, as if the general and their de-voted Minch-brother footmen were not enough protection—or expense.

But it was worth every groat. Sydney was thrilled at the feel of silks and fine muslins and, best of all, Winifred had caught the eye of Baron Scoville. He was perfect for Winnie, pleasant-featured, always courteous, well-respected in the ton, of an age to settle—and rich as Croesus! If he seemed a trifle starchy to Sydney's taste, correct to a fault, she was quick to forgive this minor handicap in favor of the rancor in Lady Windham's breast. Aunt Harriet had been measuring the baron for Trixie, and now he was paying particular attention to Winifred. What more could Sydney ask?

Of course the regard of such a social prize brought its own complications. The baron took his position as seriously as Aunt Harriet took her purse. He would never go beyond the line, and his associates must also be beyond reproof. His bride would have to be pretty and prettily behaved, an ornament to Scoville's title. There could be no hint of straightened circumstances or hanging out for a fortune, no irregular behavior or questionable reputations, no running back to Little Dedham!

Sydney just had to get the money somewhere!

2

Rights and Responsibilities

*I*f love were a loaf of bread, Forrest Mainwaring, Viscount Mayne, would resume his naval commission and eat sea biscuits for the rest of his life. He'd take the acres of his father's holdings under his management out of grains and he'd plant mangel-wurzels instead. Love was a bore and a pestilence that would choke the very life out of a man. If he let it.

"They'll never get us, eh, Nelson?" The viscount nudged his companion, a scruffy one-eyed hound. Nelson rolled over and went back to sleep at Lord Mayne's feet.

"You're no better than Spottswood," his lordship complained, thinking of the latest of his friends to turn benedict. Old Spotty used to be the best of good fellows, eager for a run down to Newmarket for the races or a night of cards. And now? Now Spotty was content to sit by the fire with his blushing bride. Mayne would blush, too, if he had so little conversation. Gads, Spotty was as dull as . . . a dog.

Then there was Haverstoke, another one-time friend. Six months he'd been leg-shackled. Six months, by Jupiter, and he was already afraid of turning his back on the lightskirt he'd wed lest she plant horns on his head. "She would, too," Forrest told the sleeping dog. "She's tried to catch me alone often enough."

Nigel Thompson had wed a Diamond. Now he was bankrupting his estate to keep the shrew in emeralds and ermine. The viscount poured himself another brandy and settled back in his worn leather chair. "Females . . ."

Just then a plaintive howl echoed through the night. Nelson's nose twitched. His ears quivered. Squire Beck's setter bitch! The old dog was through the library window before his master could complete the thought: "Bah."

Forrest was not quite the misogynist his father purported to be; the duke would expound on his pet theory at the drop of an aged cognac. Hamilton Mainwaring believed, so he said, that since women's bones were lighter, their bodies less well-muscled, and their skulls smaller, they couldn't possibly think as well as men. On the other hand, the Duke of Mayne would relate to his cronies at Whites, their brains were so stuffed with frills and furbelows, it was no wonder they made no sense. No one ever asked the duchess's opinion.

The viscount did not share his father's views, not entirely. He had great respect for his mother, Sondra, Duchess of Mayne. He even felt affection for his two flighty sisters, more so now that they were married and living at opposite ends of England. He also had a connoisseur's appreciation for womanhood in general, and several discrete widows, a few high-born ladies with lower instincts, and the occasional select demimondaine in particular. Forrest Mainwaring was not a monk. Neither was he a womanizer. At twenty-nine, he was considered by the ton to be worldly, and too wise to be caught in the parson's mousetrap. The viscount was a true nonpareil, one of the most attractive men in town, with extensive understanding and accomplishments in the fields of business, agriculture, the arts, and athletics. In addition, he was wealthy in his own right. Lord Mayne would have made a prime prize on the marriage mart if his views on the subject were not so well known. Zeus, he thought without conceit, he'd be hunted down like a rabid dog if the grasping mamas thought he could be cornered.

He couldn't. The Duke of Mayne was in rude good health, and Forrest's younger brother, Brennan, provided a more than adequate heir. His sisters were busy filling their nurseries, so the succession was assured. Forrest saw no other reason for him to submit to the ties that bind.

Bind, hell, the viscount considered, taking another sip of his glass. Bind, choke, strangle, fetter, hobble, maim. He shook his head, disarranging the dark curls. He liked women well enough; it was marriage, or the double yoke of love and marriage, that had this decorated hero quaking in his Hessians.

The viscount did not need his friends' experiences to set him against the state of matrimony and the toils of love. He'd had enough examples aboard ship, when his fellow officers would discover their sweethearts had found someone else or, worse, their wives had. And the lovesick young ensigns, sighing like mooncalves over some heartless charmer, had Lieutenant Mainwaring feeling all the symptoms of *mal de mer*. No, even those reminders came too late; he'd learned his lessons far earlier, at his parents' knees. His mother's in Sussex, his father's in London.

To say the Duke and Duchess of Mayne were estranged was gilding the lily. They were strange. They hardly spoke, seldom visited, and continued through years of separation to send each other tender greetings of affection—via their sons. And what a legendary love match theirs had been!

Hamilton and Sondra were neighbors, he the heir to a fortune and a trusted place at court, she the only child of a land-rich squire. They were too young, and from far different backgrounds and stations in life, so both sets of parents disapproved of the match. Naturally the young people eloped.

The early years proved them right. They were deliriously happy, spreading their time between travel on the Continent, joining the London swirl at the highest ranks, and riding for days over their lush fields, reveling in nature's bounty. Then Hamilton ascended to his father's dignities and, soon after, Sondra's father's acreage. Sondra started breeding, and the foundation of their marriage started cracking, along with every dish and piece of bric-a-brac in one castle, three mansions, and two hunting boxes.

Sondra wanted a nest; Hamilton wanted a foreign legation. The duchess loved the peace of the estates; the duke craved the excitement of court. She wanted a country squire; he wanted a political hostess. Mr. Spode had a standing order.

Children only aggravated the situation. Wet nurses versus mother's milk, home tutors versus boarding schools, pinafores for the boys, ponies for the girls—everything was a bone of contention, and more crockery would fly. Finally the duke did accept an ambassadorship.

"If you leave the country, I shall never speak to you again," Lady Mayne swore.

"Is that a promise?" Lord Mayne replied, already packing. "Well, if you don't come with me, I shall never speak to *you* again," he countered.

He went, she didn't, and they enclosed loving messages in their children's letters. The senior Lord Mayne returned often enough to toss a china shepherdess or two and drag his children into the tug-of-war. Forrest should be groomed for political life by running for a seat in the Commons, the duke decided. The duchess thought he should pursue further studies, as befitted a man with vast holdings to overlook, since his father neglected those duties. The young viscount bought himself a commission and ran away to sea. The French blockade was more peaceful than life between the Maynes. That was some years earlier, and now they were arguing, through the mails of course, about Brennan's future. At twenty-two Bren should have been making his own decisions, but his mother swore she would die of a broken heart if another son went off to war, and his father was holding out all the glitter of the City to keep the boy from turning into a country bumpkin.

So Mother raised dogs and roses in Sussex and the governor raised votes and issues in Parliament and the privy council.

Brennan raised hell in London like every well-breeched young greenheaded sprig before him ... and Forrest Mainwaring, Viscount Mayne, raised his glass.

It was his lot, though the Lord knew what he'd done to deserve the task, to look out for all of them. He moved between estates and far-flung holdings in the country, banking institutions and bawdy houses in the city, trying to safeguard the family investments and Brennan's family jewels. He managed Mayne Chance, the ducal seat, and struggled to keep staff on at Mainwaring House in Grosvenor Square. The turnover in servants was not surprising considering the duke's penchant for tossing the tableware; it was just difficult for his son.

Life in the country was not noticeably easier. Mother filled the castle with dogs: tiny, tawny, repulsive Pekingese, with their curling tongues, pop eyes, and shrill yips. Lady Mayne said raising the creatures was more satisfying than raising children. A man could not walk without fear of tripping over one of the ugly little blighters nor sit down without finding that gingery hair all over his superfines. Worse, a man could not even bring his own pet, his own (sometimes) loyal dog, Nelson, into the house. On the hound's last, unsanctioned visit, Nelson had caught one glimpse of the little rodents in fur coats and, knowing that no real dog was fluffed and perfumed and beribboned, he did his level one-eyed best to rid Mayne Chance of such vermin. Banished, he was, and his master with him.

Viscount Mayne sat alone and lonely amongst the holland covers in the dower house library, still cold despite the new-laid fire. His hair was mussed, his broad shoulders were bent with the weight of the world—and the Mainwarings—on them, and he'd have a devilish headache in the morning. He should have stayed in the navy, Forrest thought as he contemplated the most recent missives from his loving parents.

My dearest son, his mother wrote from ten minutes away, *How I miss you.* The viscount almost laughed. She'd most likely have moved Princess Pennyfeather and the bitch's latest litter into his bedroom by now. Forrest skimmed over the body of the letter—gads, he'd been gone only a day and a half. Whipslade's prize bull Fred got into Widow Lang's garden again, a tile was loose on the south wing, Reverend Jamison thought the tower bell might have a crack in it, and the Albertsons were coming to dinner tomorrow. The viscount would see to the first three in the morning, and see that he was otherwise engaged by the evening. Lady Mayne wanted grandsons or revenge, Forrest never knew which. The Albertsons had a daughter.

I am worried about your brother, the letter continued in the duchess's delicate copperplate. Not Brennan, but your brother. That meant trouble. Lady Mayne had a network of information gatherers spread through the ton which would put Napoleon's secret police to shame. Bren's larks usually flew home in the next post, where the duchess could cheerfully shred his character to bits and lay the pieces at his father's door. Of course the duke was to blame for *his* son's peccadillos; the boy was always properly behaved in the country. When Brennan became Forrest's brother, she wanted the viscount to handle the bumblebroth. Dash it, Lord Mayne cursed, he wasn't the lad's keeper. He didn't have time to rush off to London to tear the cawker out of some doxie's talons, no matter how homely the Albertsons' daughter was. For once, though, there was no mention of a female anywhere in his mother's enumeration of Brennan's misdeeds and character flaws, not even between the lines. Usually she would refer to "persons about whose existence a lady is supposed to have no knowledge." This epistle was filled with basket scramblers, gallows bait, the ivory tuners instead. Those were some of the fonder epithets she was tossing at her youngest child's head. No, the viscount realized when he reread the rambling paragraph, sure he'd find a Paphian in there somewhere; the basket scramblers, gallows bait, et al., were the villains of the piece. Brennan, for once, was an innocent lamb being led to the slaughter through his father's neglect. Someone, she wrote, would have to save her baby from the wolves.

"She must mean you, old fellow," the viscount told Nelson

when the hound vaulted back in through the window, leaving muddy footprints on the carpet. " 'Cause I ain't going."

When you get to London, Her Grace concluded, not if, but when, *give your dear father my fondest regards and tell him I wish he were here by my side.*

The viscount shook his head and scratched behind the hound's ears. Nelson drooled on his master's boots, radiating affection and the mixed aroma of swamp and stable. Now there was a man's dog.

The duke's writing was firm and bold; his letter was short and succinct, the antithesis of his lady wife's style, naturally. *Forrest, Your brother*—they seemed to have something in common, after all—*is in a spot of trouble, but do not let the duchess hear of it lest she worry. The doctor says he'll be fine. You might suggest your mother come to London for the beginning of the Season. Tell her I miss the waltzes we used to share. P.S. We need a new butler.*

"Dash it, Father, why couldn't you have thrown the inkwell at your new secretary instead of at Potts? Educated young fellows are as common as fleas on a dog, but a good butler . . ."

The duke was looking hopefully out to the carriage, where a footman was carrying in Forrest's bags. The light seemed to go out of his eyes when the coach proved empty.

"She did send you her best wishes," the viscount hurried on, "and some apples from the west orchard. She remembered they were your favorites, Your Grace."

"What's that? Oh, yes, apples. No, I must get back to Whitehall straightaway. Did I tell you we might get passage of the Madden-Oates Bill finally?" A second footman stood ready to hand the duke his hat and cane.

"But what about Brennan?"

"No, I don't think he'd like any apples either. Loose teeth, don't you know."

His Grace departed and Forrest temporarily promoted the sturdiest-looking footman. Then he went upstairs.

Forrest almost did not recognize the man in the bed. The viscount was even more alarmed when he considered that

Brennan was usually his own mirror image, less a few years and worry lines. Like peas in a pod, they shared the same dark curls and square jaw, the same clear blue eyes and the authoritative Mainwaring nose. They used to anyway.

His lordship's next thought, after vowing mayhem to whoever had done this to his brother, was to thank the heavens the duchess hadn't come to London after all. If the idea of Bren's putting on a uniform sent Lady Mayne into spasms, he could not imagine her reaction to the sorry specimen between the sheets.

"What in bloody hell happened to you, you gossoon?"

Bren opened one eye, the one not swollen closed and discolored. He tried to smile without moving his jaw, winced, and gave up on the effort. He raised one linen-swathed hand in greeting. "The governor send for you?" he asked.

"No, His Grace merely needed a new butler."

Bren sighed. "I suppose it was Mother who sent in the big guns."

"It was either London or the brig on hardtack and bilge water." Forrest dragged a chair closer to the bed and carefully pulled the covers over his brother's bandaged chest.

"I can handle it," Bren said, looking away.

"I can see that."

The younger man flushed, not an attractive addition to the yellow and purple blotches. He cleared his throat and Forrest held a glass to his cut lip so he could drink. "Thank you. Ah, how is Mother?"

"In alt. Princess Pennyfeather had four pups, all that coppery color she's been after. Of course I wasn't permitted to see the new additions. I might disturb the princess, don't you know."

"She's daft when it comes to those dogs, ain't she?"

"My dear Brennan, anyone else would have been committed to Bedlam long since. Mother is a duchess, however, so she is merely eccentric." Forrest picked a speck of lint off his fawn breeches. Then he inspected his Hessians for travel dust.

"You ain't going to be happy."

"I'm already overjoyed, bantling."

"I didn't ask you to get involved."

Viscount Mayne stood to his full six foot height, his legs spread and his arms crossed over his chest. Men had been known to tremble before Lieutenant Mainwaring in his quarterdeck command. "Cut line, mister. I am here and I am not leaving. I'd go after anyone who treated a dog this way. Perhaps not one of Mother's rug rats, but my own brother? They must have loosened a few spokes in your wheel if you think I'll just walk away. No one, I repeat, no one, harms one of mine."

"Well, there was this woman . . ."

"I knew it!"

3

Might and Mayne

*T*he woman was not to blame. Not that a pretty little red-headed opera dancer wouldn't have taken Brennan's money and laid him low; she just hadn't—yet.

"They were giving a benefit performance after the regular show that night, so I had a lot of hours to kill before I could meet Mademoiselle Rochelle."

"A French *artiste. Je comprende.*"

"I'm not such a green 'un as all that. Roxy's no more French than I am. She's not even much of a dancer, and I found out straightaway she sure as hell ain't a natural redhead. Still . . ." He shrugged, as much as two strapped ribs would allow.

"Still, you had a lot of hours to kill."

"So I had a few drinks with Tolly before he went on to Lady Bessborough's. He needed it; she's his godmother and has her niece in mind for him. So I toddled off to White's."

"And had a few drinks there."

"Dash it, Forrest, that ain't the point. I can hold my liquor."

The viscount studied his manicure. His brother swallowed hard before going on. "White's was as quiet as a tomb. You know, the governor's cronies nodding over their newspapers. I decided to step over to the Cocoa Tree. Don't raise your eyebrow at me, I know the play gets too deep for my pockets there. I just had a glass or two of Daffy and watched Martindale lose his watch fob, his diamond stick pin, and his new curricle and pair to Delverson."

"Dare I hope it was an illuminating experience?"

"What's that? Oh, d'you mean did I learn anything? Sure. I'll never game against Delverson. Fellow's got the devil's own luck. Anyway," he continued over his brother's sigh of exasperation, "Martindale knew of a place where the stakes weren't so high and drinks were free. Since I still had a few hours before I could go back to the theater, I went along. I know what you're going to say. I ought to, by George, you've said it often enough: Don't play where you don't know the table. But the place looked respectable enough—not first stare, don't you know—and I recognized some of the fellows at the tables. The long and the short of it is, we sat down to play."

"And had a few drinks?"

"And had a few drinks. They were serving Blue Ruin. I think now that it may have been tampered with."

"Undoubtedly, but do go on, Bren, you're finally beginning to get interesting. Or wise."

"You ain't making this any easier, you know. Anyway, the stakes weren't real high, and I wasn't laying out much of the ready, 'cause I needed it for later and, ah, Roxy. Martindale lost his ring and decided his luck was out, so he quit and went home. I should have left with him."

"But you still had a few hours to fill."

"And credit in the bank, with the quarter nearly over and next quarter's allowance due. So I stayed, won a little, lost a little. Fellow by the name of Chester was holding the bank. Otto Chester. He seemed a gentleman. You know, clean hands, clean linen. Wouldn't have seemed out of place at White's. I signed over a couple of vouchers to him, nothing big, mind, and then I went home."

The viscount was up and pacing, having reached the ends of even his copious patience. "What do you mean, then you went home? Then you were set on by a pack of footpads? Then you were mowed down by a runaway carriage?"

"Then I went home. My head was too heavy for my neck and my eyes didn't fit in their sockets. My insides felt like I'd swallowed a live eel. I didn't think I was so castaway; I just thought it must have been from mixing my drinks all night. Anyway, I wasn't going to be much good to Roxy, and I was afraid I'd embarrass myself by casting up accounts on her shoes or something, so I sent her a note and took a hackney home."

Forrest ran his fingers through his hair, wondering whether he'd pull it all out or turn gray before this tale was told. He frowned at his brother and told him, "You know, you take after Mother."

"And when you knot your eyebrows together like that and start shouting, you remind me of the governor. Just don't throw anything 'cause I can't duck right now. There's not much more to tell anyway.

"The next morning I woke up late, stopped by the bank to withdraw the balance, and at Rundell's to pick out a trinket for Roxy. Then I called on Mr. Chester at the address on his card, to redeem my vowels. Only he didn't have them. Said he had expenses of his own, gambling losses he had to meet, so he'd sold *my* notes to a moneylender to get money to pay off *his* debts. Have you ever heard the like? A gentleman would have given a chap to the end of the week, at least. Well, I told him what I thought of such a scurvy move, in no uncertain terms, you can be sure."

"I bet you threatened to call him out."

Brennan smiled, and a tiny glimmer of the blue spark showed in his one good eye. "Worse. I swore never to play with him again. At any rate, I went to the new address, somebody Randall, an Irish Shylock. I introduce myself, tell him I want to settle up—and damned if this Randall says I don't owe hundreds, I owe thousands! With interest building every day. He shows me chits that look like my hand, but they couldn't be. I don't have that kind of blunt and I didn't play that deep, I swear."

"I believe you, cawker," Forrest said. He rested his hand on his brother's shoulder. "So what happened? You went after Randall?"

Brennan cursed in disgust. "I didn't even get the chance. He whistles and this ogre as big as a house lurches out of a side room. Next thing I know, I'm lying in the gutter. They've got my purse, my watch, and Roxy's bracelet. Goliath is grinning and the bastard Irishman is claiming I still owe a thousand pounds. Says he'll go to the governor if I don't pay up in a week, or send his bully to call to remind me." He winced. "As if I could forget."

"You can. Just rest now, I'll take care of it."

All of it. The bogus debt, the bone crusher, the bloodsucker, and the cardsharp.

Forrest Mainwaring really was an even-tempered, mild-mannered gentleman to the dignified core. He was tolerant, temperate, thoughtful, and slow to anger. He waited till after luncheon.

First he sent a note to his mother, assuring her of Brennan's welfare and, out of habit, his father's continuing devotion. Then he checked some of the accounts, sent a note round to a new hiring agency, and made an excellent meal of turbot in oyster sauce, veal Marsala, a taste of rarebit, tomatoes in aspic, and cherry trifle.

Viscount Mayne proceeded methodically down his list. His first stop was the bank, his second Rundell and Bridges, the jewelers. After consulting their sales records, the store's manager was able to find a duplicate of Mademoiselle Rochelle's erstwhile gift. Forrest matched the simple bracelet to a necklace set with emeralds—a redhead, *n'est-ce pas?*—and dangling earbobs.

"Coo-ee," Bren's *chérie* exclaimed in perfect cockney. "If those ain't the dabbest sparklers Oi ever seen!" Having seen a bit of the world herself, she knew the meaning of such a generous gift. " 'E's not comin' back, then, your love of a brother?"

"His illness is more than a trifling indisposition, he regrets. He did not want you to wait."

"Ain't that a real gentleman." She was admiring the effect of her new possessions in a smoky glass over a dressing table littered with bottles and jars and powders. She suddenly spun around to face His Lordship, eyes wide with concern. " 'Tain't nothin' catchy-like, is it?"

Forrest's lips curved in a slow smile. "Nothing he won't outgrow."

"That's all right, then." Roxy considered that smile, and the viscount's well-muscled figure leaning nonchalantly against the door frame. "Oi don't suppose you'd . . . ?"

Lord Mayne's head shook, but his smile widened, showing even white teeth.

Roxy turned back to her reflection. "Well, you can't blame a girl for tryin'."

"*Au contraire, chérie*, I am honored." He raised her hands to his lips in farewell. *"Enchanté, mademoiselle."*

"Enchant-tea to you, too, ducky."

The proprietor of the gaming rooms on King Street recognized the crest on the carriage. It was Alf Sniddon's business to know such things. He made sure his doorman told Viscount Mayne the place was closed till evening. The doorman made sure he'd stay alive till evening instead, and was therefore richer by a handsome tip besides. The place was open for business, but not for long, it seemed, unless Mr. Sniddon changed his policy.

"But I don't make the bets or take the young gentlemen's vouchers, my lord."

"No, you take only a hefty cut of the winnings. Let me put it this way, Sniddon: How long would you stay in business if word went out in the clubs that you ran a crooked table, plucking young pigeons with drugged wine?"

Sniddon calculated how long it would take to find new quarters, change the name of the establishment, change *his* name, establish a new clientele. It was cheaper to change policies.

"Right-o, cash on the barrel it is, my lord, for all young gentlemen."

"There, I knew we could agree. And who knows, you might just set a new style, an honest gaming hell. I'd be tempted to stop in myself."

Sniddon recognized Mayne's soft-spoken words for the mixed blessing they were: a threat that the powerful lord would be monitoring Sniddon's compliance, and a promise of reward, for where the handsome viscount led, his well-heeled Corinthian set followed. Sniddon nodded. He'd try it the nob's way a while, then move if he had to. It wouldn't be the first time.

So much for business. The viscount tapped his cane on the coach roof to signal his driver on to the next destination. It was time for pleasure.

Otto Chester lived in rooms at 13 Jermyn Street, where accommodations were cheap because of foolish superstitions. Such imbecilic notions meant little to a man used to making his own luck with marked decks and loaded dice. Today his luck was out. Otto Chester wished he'd been out, too. Instead, he was in the act of setting the folds in his neckcloth when Lord Forrest Mainwaring strode into the room without waiting to be announced. Fate seldom makes an appointment.

Chester was a jackal dressed in gentlemen's togs. He was everything Viscount Mayne despised: pale, weak, preying on the unwary like a back-biting cur. In short, he was a coward, not even attempting to regain his feet after Forrest's first hard right.

"But—" he gulped around the rock-hard fist that was embedded in the material of his neckcloth, dragging him up and holding his feet off the ground. He batted ineffectively at the viscount's steely right arm with an effete left. "But I had notes of my own. You know, debts of honor, play and pay."

Forrest sneered in disgust. There wasn't any satisfaction in darkening the dirty dealer's daylights; the paltry fellow was already quaking in his boots. On second thought, he reflected, there might be a modicum of satisfaction in cramming the muckworm's mockery of the gentleman's credo down his scrawny throat. "You wouldn't recognize honor if it hit you on the nose," he growled, following through with a cross punch to said protuberance. "Now you will."

Lord Mayne tossed the offal aside like a pile of rags and wiped his hands on a fresh neckcloth waiting in reserve on a nearby chair back. He threw it to the sniveling scum in the corner. "Here, fix yourself up. We're going for a ride."

4

Debt and Dishonor

The office of O. Randall and Associates, Financial Consultants, was located on Fleet Street in convenient view of the debtors' prison. Randall himself was a small, stocky man a few years older than Forrest, he guessed, with carroty hair, a soft Irish brogue, and hard, calculating eyes. Those eyes shifted from his distinguished caller sitting at ease across the desk to the sorry lumpkin huddled in an uncomfortable wooden chair in the shadows. As far away from his lordship as the room would allow, Chester dabbed an already-crimson neckcloth to his broken nose. Randall's gaze quickly left the gory sight and returned to the viscount.

"And may I pour ye a bit of Ireland's best, me lord?" he offered. "No? Well, 'tis a wise man who knows his limits. That's what I tried to tell the lad, I did. A fine boy, young Mainwaring, an' the spit an' image of yourself, b'gorn. 'Twas sorry I was to see him in a mite of trouble."

"We were all sorry. That's why I am here."

Randall poured himself a drink. "Ah, family feeling. 'Tis a fine thing indeed." He shot a dark look toward Chester's corner. "Never had a brother o' me heart m'self. Never regretted it more than today."

For all his relaxed manner, Lord Mayne had no desire to discuss his family with any loan shark. He reached to his inside pocket and retrieved a leather purse. Tossing it to the desk with a satisfying thud and the jangle of heavy coins, he announced, "There's your thousand pounds. You can count it if you wish, but the Mainwarings always pay their debts. *Always.*"

Randall missed the danger in the viscount's silky "always," too busy scheming. His eyes on the sack, he sipped his drink and licked his thick lips. "Well now, a thousand pounds was the figure two days ago. Ye do ken the nature o' me business, would ye now?"

Slowly, with careful deliberation, Forrest removed his pigskin gloves while he addressed the third man in the room. "What do you think, Mr. Chester?"

Chester clutched the stained cravat to his nose as if to hold all his remaining courage inside. Wild-eyed over the cloth, he babbled, "I fink a fousand pounds is fine."

Lord Mayne smiled. Randall didn't like the smile, and the leather purse *had* played his favorite tune. He nodded and reached out for the gold. The viscount's iron grip was around his wrist before Randall could say *compound interest*. "The chits?"

"For sure an' we're all bein' reasonable men conductin' a little business." Randall pulled a chain with a ring of keys out of his pocket, selected one, and opened the top drawer of his desk. Then he used another key to open a side drawer. Glancing quickly back and forth between Forrest and the pouch, he withdrew a stack of papers. He slid them across to the viscount, keeping one hand close to the open top drawer.

Forrest checked the signatures. They were a good enough forgery to pass for Brennan's. He nudged the leather purse toward the Irishman, who put both hands on the desk to draw it closer.

The viscount proceeded to rip up the vouchers. When that chore was finished to his satisfaction, with small, narrow pieces, he started to move around the desk, prepared to rip up the Irishman.

There was that smile again, and a glimmer of anticipation in Mayne's blue eyes. The moneylender finally realized he'd been petting a panther instead of a lapcat. He pursed his lips to whistle but, instead of a breath of air, he suddenly found a fist in his mouth.

It was hard to whistle with a mouthful of blood, so Randall went for the gun in the top drawer. That was an error. The viscount dove headfirst across the desk, reaching for the weapon. He flung Randall's arm up at the height of his lunge, then crashed to the ground with Randall under him. The pistol discharged its one ball, wounding the ceiling grievously, sending plaster down on all of them.

Forrest stood up, brushing at the white dust in his hair. Randall managed to get to his knees, where he tried to whistle again. This proved an impossibility with his two front teeth gone missing. So he reached down for the knife in his boot.

The viscount was grinning. "Thanks for evening the odds. I hate to maul a smaller man. It's not gentlemanly, but you wouldn't know about that, would you?" He removed his coat and wrapped it about his left arm, all the while keeping an eye on the little man.

Now, Lord Mayne had his superb physical condition from working alongside his laborers in the country, and his boxing science from sparring with Gentleman Jackson himself whenever he was in town, but he had his gutter instincts from his naval days. Dark quays and stench-ridden harbors were excellent school yards for dirty fighting, where there was nothing to keep a pack a cutthroats from your wallet but your fists and your wits. In the dark you didn't wait to see if your opponent was giving you fair odds. He never was.

Randall was shouting, "Whithtle, Chethter, whithtle," as he lost his knife to a well-placed kick. Then he lost the use of his hand to a vicious chop. Then he lost his lunch to a fist in the breadbasket.

Between Randall's retches and moans, Chester asked "Wha?"

Forrest wasn't even breathing hard. He looked at the man, still in his corner, still nursing his broken nose. "He means 'whistle.' "

"Whiddle?"

"Yes, man, whistle. Go on, do it."

If Forrest had said "fly," Chester would likely have tried flapping his arms. He puckered his lips and tweeted—the opening bars of *la Marseillaise*!

Forrest shook his head. "Spineless and a traitor to boot. Here, man, let me do it." He put two fingers in his mouth and let loose a piercing shrill that almost always brought Nelson to heel.

Sam Odum was as big as Brennan had said, and twice as ugly. Bald, scarred, and snaggle-toothed, he lumbered into the room swinging a piece of kindling. Odum's kindling was more like a medium-size tree, but who was going to quibble with him about starting a fire? The ape paused in the middle of the room, looking around in confusion.

"Your employer is on the floor behind the desk," Forrest pointed out helpfully. "We've had a small disagreement. The gentleman with the interesting headpiece"—nodding in Chester's direction—"has wisely selected a neutral corner. Have you any opinions on the matter?"

Sam Odum scratched his head, then his crotch. "Huh?"

Randall spat out, "Kill him," along with another tooth, so Sam Odum hefted his club and plodded in Chester's direction.

"Not him, you ath! The thwell!"

Sam Odum was confused again, not an unusual occurrence, it seemed. Gentleman that he was, Mainwaring decided to help the poor bastard identify his intended victim. He tossed a chair at him. It missed, but the hard right that followed didn't. Sam staggered, but came back swinging the bat. Forrest was ready with the other chair. He used it as a shield to parry a blow that could have decapitated him, then followed by smashing the chair over the mammoth's head. The chair broke, and Sam Odum just staggered a little more. And kept swinging that blasted tree trunk. Forrest kept ducking, getting in punches where he could, getting battered when he couldn't.

There were no more chairs except the one Chester crouched behind. Forrest backed toward the desk and swept the papers, all those little shreds, into Odum's ugly phiz. While the ogre was distracted, the viscount finally managed to land a kick and a punch and a jab and another punch. Odum still stood, but at least the club had come dislodged from his hamlike fist. Now Forrest could close in for some real boxing.

No human could stand that kind of punishment. Sam Odum wasn't human. "Oh, hell," Lord Mayne swore, then took the small pistol from his boot. He turned it around and whacked the bruiser alongside the head.

That brought him to his knees. Forrest threw all his remaining strength into a blow to Odum's chin, then grabbed him by both ears and banged his head into the floor.

"Now that I have your attention"—wham!—"this is for my brother." Wham. "And this"—wham!—"is for kicking him while he was down." There was now a considerable dent in the floor, to say nothing of Sam Odum's head. He stayed put when Forrest took his hands away.

The viscount looked around to see if anyone else was offering further entertainment. Randall was still moaning and Chester appeared to be praying. Forrest pocketed the pistol and Randall's knife, out of temptation's way. He didn't think he'd be tempted to skewer either of the muckworms, but one never knew. He hauled the unconscious bully to the doorway and shoved him down the outside stairs.

"Take him to the docks," he ordered his driver and waiting footmen, "and find the recruiting officer. Give my name and tell him I said Mr. Sam Odum is dying to join the navy."

"Well, gentlemen, now that I've introduced myself, shall we discuss *my* terms?"

The question was entirely rhetorical; Chester and Randall sat bound and gagged on the floor in front of the desk. On Forrest's return from disposing of the late debt-collector, he'd found Randall creeping toward Sam Odum's tiny "office" and the small arsenal stashed there. "How convenient," the viscount murmured, gently tapping the Irishman's fingers with a length of lead pipe. He swept all but two pieces of rope into a carpetbag nearby for later removal. The two associates wouldn't be needing weapons. He tied Randall for safety's sake, "So you don't hurt yourself during our little talk," and stuffed the man's neckcloth in his mouth to stop his foul curses. He did the same to the taller man, whose whining pleas were embarrassing both of them, then took his seat in what was left of Randall's chair.

"Where were we? Oh, yes, terms. You can keep the thousand pounds—it was worth every shilling—and your lives. Of course, that's assuming I never see either of you again or hear my family name mentioned in connection with you or your filth.

"As for you," he said, fixing Otto Chester in his blue-dagger gaze. Chester cringed back as far as his bonds would permit. "You are finished in London. You'll never be admitted to the better clubs for being a Captain Sharp, and word will be sent to even the lowest dives that you're not particularly good at it. I should think that if I passed on my doubts as to your loyalty to the Crown, to say nothing of your manhood, you'd have a hard enough time in this city finding flats to gull. You might do better on the Continent. Am I understood?"

Chester nodded vigorously, which disturbed a small cloud of plaster dust that had fallen from the ceiling into his hair. He looked like one of the tiny snowmen in a crystal dome, a child's plaything.

There was nothing so innocuous about O. Randall. Venom flowed from him in near-tangible waves.

"I could bring charges against you, you know," the viscount told him. "Usury, extortion, forgery, paying someone to assault a nobleman, threatening violence to a peer of the realm. I could make the charges stick, even if Uncle Donald weren't Lord High Magistrate. But trash like you isn't worth my time or effort. I'd prefer you to slink off to find some other rock to hide behind. Let us just see how many others would miss you if you go."

He started to go through the drawers, tossing another pistol and a wicked stiletto into the carpetbag near his side of the desk. His eye caught on a tray of calling cards.

"Otto Randall," he read aloud. "How curious, considering the only other Otto I knew was a Prussian, and now there are two in the same room and almost the same profession." Forrest looked from Otto Randall to Otto Chester and shrugged, returning to the drawers. When he reached the files with the moneylender's receipts, he began separating the chits into three piles. One stack was for men who could afford to play deep, or those so bitten by the gambling fever they would only find another source of money to support their habit. One fairly notorious courtesan had a folder of her own. No wonder she'd been sending billets-doux to half the well-heeled coves in town. Let her pay Randall back in trade, he decided grimly; that would be enough of a lesson. The second stack was of names unknown to the viscount, or men whose circumstances were not broadcast in the clubs. Half of these he ripped into shreds, calling it the luck of the draw. The other half he added to the first pile. The third and largest collection of chits belonged to young men like his brother, young scholars and country squires without town bronze to protect them, or other innocents up River Tick. He frowned over four slips with one name, a friend who should have known better. Then again, Manfrey's wife was a virago; it was no wonder he stayed out late gambling. Lord Mayne added two of Manfrey's vouchers to the first pile and added the other two to the third stack. These he tucked into a pocket of his coat, now draped across the back of his chair.

"Consider this batch of debts canceled. I'll see to them." He straightened the remaining papers and nodded toward Randall. "This is your share. You ought to be able to settle up with these loose screws in a week. After that you are out of business and out of town. There will be a warrant for your arrest and one very conscientious citizen to see that the warrant is served. You don't want that, do you?"

Before Randall could give answer, grunt, nod, or whatever choice was open to him, a knock sounded on the door. Forrest cursed softly and waited to hear the footsteps recede down the outer stairs. He did not want to be bothered with someone creating a public scene or calling the watch; he still had to interview butlers that afternoon.

He quickly dragged both Ottos into Sam Odum's cubby and shoved them to the rank palette on the floor. "And Father thought politics made strange bedfellows," he mused as the tall, pale Englishman sank thankfully into the ticking while the banty, red-faced Irishman still struggled against his ropes. Forrest was trying to close the door around their jutting legs when the knock was repeated with more force.

"Damn. Some poor bastard can't wait to sell his soul to these two bankers from hell."

5

Hair and There

Cravats were handy items with myriad uses: bandages, gags, nose wipes, napkins, white flags of surrender. And a decorative essential to a gentleman's haberdashery. Forrest's once precision-folded Oriental was now a limp, mangled, blood-spattered bit of evidence to recent events. He removed it on his way to the door and dabbed at a cut on his lip. He could only hope the bruise on his jaw, where Odum's club had connected, was not already discolored. At least no one could tell that his ribs were aching.

He opened the outer door and looked up, and up, then silently groaned. No one else might know, but Forrest's body was telling him it was in no condition to handle another belligerent behemoth. And this blond fellow in the doorway was big, way taller than the viscount's own six feet, and broad.

And solidly built. And young. If he was in Randall's employ . . . It was too late to run like hell, so Forrest did the next best thing. He smiled.

The caller hesitated, still uncertain of what *he* confronted, then nodded. "My employer," he said, indicating a waiting hackney, "requests an interview with Mr. Otto Randall." He held out a calling card with the corner turned down to show the visitor had come in person.

Forrest belatedly noted the man's neat livery uniform, a footman of some sort, then, and glanced quickly at the card. He didn't recognize the name *Sydney Lattimore*, in fancy script, but he could guess the type. He'd be a nervous, effeminate man-milliner, judging by the curlicues surrounding his name, afraid to venture into a den of iniquity by himself, hence the sturdy bodyguard. He was no man-about-town—Mayne would have made his acquaintance otherwise—nor was he among the other debtors in Randall's file. Forrest surmised he was a young sprig who'd tipped the dibs and punted on tick. The least Forrest could do for the muttonhead was play Good Samaritan with some good advice.

"Tell your employer that he doesn't want anything to do with moneylenders. He should stay out of gaming parlors if he can't make the ante, and away from his tailor if he can't pay the shot, if that's his weakness. Tell him that his pride can stand a bout with honest employment better than it can a sentence in the Fleet, which is where he'll end up, dealing with the sharks."

The footman nodded sagely, tugged at the tight collar of his uniform, and started back down the stairs. Halfway toward the waiting carriage he remembered he had a job to do. "But, Mr. Randall, sir . . ."

Gads, that anyone would think he was one of the Ottos! That's what came of playing at guardian angel. Damnation, what kind of angel had his shirt half torn and his knuckles scraped and plaster dust trickling down his neck? Angry, Forrest shouted loudly enough to be heard from the carriage: "This establishment is closed, shut down, out of business. Thank your lucky stars and stay away from the bloodsuckers before you get bled dry."

He slammed the door and went back to get his coat and the satchel.

"Damn." He couldn't get his deuced coat on without skewing his ribs—and there was another blasted knock on the door. This benighted place saw as much traffic as Harriet Wilson's! He threw the door open.

"Double damn." Just what he needed, a woman. He looked down at the card he still held and noted what he'd missed the first time. *Miss* Sydney Lattimore. "Bloody hell." And a lady, judging by the shocked gasp from behind the black veil, the volume of concealing black swathes and shrouds, and the imperious way she brushed past him as if he were an upper servant, despite her small stature. She motioned the blond footman to wait outside. Now Forrest's day was complete: a little old spinster lady in mourning—she had enough crepe about her to mourn the entire British losses at Trafalgar—and her lapdog. She walked with teetery, unsure steps and kept trembly, black-gloved hands wrapped round the handle of a basket containing a miserable midget mutt. By Jupiter, Forrest would recognize that brassy Pekingese color in one of his nightmares. Fiend seize it, this *was* one of his nightmares. A friend of his mother's! The viscount could only wish Sam Odum back from the briny.

"No, ma'am," he began. "No, no, and no, whatever it is you want. The establishment is closed, the association disbanded. The Ottos are leaving town." He couldn't see behind the veil, but the old bat wasn't moving. "If you've swallowed a spider, go pop your ice."

A thin voice came to him weakly through the black drapery. "Spider? Ice?"

Of course she didn't understand cant. How could she, when the hag most likely hadn't been out of the house in ten years? Twenty, from the smell of mothballs about her withered, shrunken person. Lord Mayne took a deep breath, which his battered ribs protested, and started again. It just was not in his makeup to be rude to little old ladies. He'd likely be wasting his time with a rational explanation, but he had to try.

"Madam, if you have outrun the bailiff, you know, spent more than your pin money, I strongly urge you to retrench until your allowance comes due. Throw yourself on your relatives' mercy or confess to your trustees. You could pawn your valuables if you haven't already. Anything is preferable to dealing with the cents-per-centers. This office in particular is pulling in its shingle, and the profession in general is no fit association for a lady. It's a nasty, lowlife business, and borrowing will only bring you more grief than the money is worth. Please, please, ma'am, go home."

There, he'd tried. The little lady did not reply. Lord Mayne shrugged, turned to retrieve his coat and finally get out of there.

Sydney's jaws were glued shut in fear. Her legs were cemented to the floor with terror, but her knees wouldn't support her weight even if she did convince her feet to move. Dear heaven, what had she gotten herself into? This was even worse than her imaginings, which had been bad enough. She had spent a week getting her courage to the sticking point to approach this place, without her thinking she might have to face a half-naked savage shouting rough or incomprehensible language, a sack full of guns and knives, blood everywhere. Now she did not think she had enough courage left to make it down the stairs. On the other, shaking hand was *two* weeks of persuading herself that visiting a moneylender was her only choice. It still was. Sydney was determined to make the general proud. If he did not take another fit at what she was doing.

She swallowed—that was a start—and through sheer determination forced words past her dry lips. In a pitiful little voice she herself hardly recognized, Sydney asked, "Please, sir, could you tell me where else to go?"

She could go to Hades for all he cared! Botheration, hadn't the woman listened to a word he'd said? He dragged a hand through his hair in exasperation. "Miss L—" He remembered that the door to the anteroom was not quite shut. "Miss, I am trying to help you. Go home."

Sydney was fascinated by the white particles sifting from his hair, wondering what bizarre activities were conducted in these chambers. At least the humanizing gesture served to reassure her that the ruffian did not mean her bodily harm. She touched the basket's contents as if for confidence and, in tones more like her own, she informed him, "My need is great, sir, so I would appreciate the direction of one of your colleagues. In the ordinary course of events I wouldn't think of asking you to divulge a competitor, as it were, but since you seem reluctant to pursue your trade and my business is pressing . . ."

Reluctant? He was growing less and less reluctant about shoving the old hen down the stairs. If the witch wasn't already a friend of his mother's, she should be. They'd get along like cats and cream with that certainty of getting their own way and the mule-stubborn refusal to listen to logic.

". . . And I had a hard enough time getting your name and address."

"And how did you get, ah, my direction, if I might ask?" The viscount was stalling for time and inspiration, wondering if his conscience would permit him to make his escape and leave her with Chester and Randall. No, they'd had a bad enough day.

Sydney *really* wished he would offer her a seat before her knees gave way altogether, but she answered with still more assurance. "My abigail's former employer was Lady Motthaven. Her husband was a trifle behindtimes, and he borrowed to settle his debts. My maid recalled where he went for the loan."

"And did the abigail report that Motthaven repaid the loan easily?" The viscount knew he hadn't; the chit was on the desk. His words were measured, as if to a child.

Sydney looked down, shifted the basket from hand to hand. "They fled to the Continent. That's why the maid needed a new position."

"And did you not consider how Lord Motthaven's experience might relate to your own situation?" Hardened seamen would have sunk through the fo'castle deck at those silky tones. Sydney's chin came up.

"Yes, sir, I considered myself fortunate to acquire the services of an experienced lady's maid."

Sydney could not like the expression on Mr. Randall's face. He might have been an uncommonly attractive man but for the disfiguring bruises and the unfortunate continual scowl. Right now his eyes were narrowed and his mouth was pursed and

Sydney thought she'd be more comfortable back in her carriage after all.

"Well, sir, I shall be going, then, seeing that you are determined to be unaccommodating. Far be it from me to tell you how to conduct your business, but I should wonder at your making a living at all, turning customers away." The moneylender growled. Yes, Sydney was sure that sound came from him. She edged closer to the door. Then she recalled her desperate need and the basket in her hand. She held it out. "Do you think, that is, if you could . . . ?"

Take her dog in pawn? The female must be queer in the attics for sure! The viscount backed away lest she put the plaguey thing in his hands. Only the desk kept him from backing through the wall.

"If you won't direct me to another moneylender, could you help me find someone who buys hair?"

"Hair? The dog is your hair? I mean, you have your hair in the basket?" Lord Mayne knew he was blathering. He couldn't help himself. That glorious red-gold shade, that sunkissed honey fire, was her hair? He collapsed unawares into the chair. Brassy Pekingese? What addlepate thought that?

Sydney took the chair opposite, ignoring its missing arm and her host's lack of courtesy in not offering her a seat. One had to make allowances for the lower orders. After all, one should not expect polished manners from a usurer, nor from a madman for that matter. So far Sydney could not decide which he was, hostile barbarian or befuddled lack-wit, sitting there now with his mouth hanging open. At least he seemed more disposed to assist her. Subtly, she thought, she used her foot to nudge the bag of weapons closer to her side of the desk, then started to lift her veil. "May I?" she asked.

"Oh, please do." The viscount gave himself a mental shake to recall his surroundings. "That is, suit yourself." Still, he held his breath. That gorgeous, vibrant mane could not belong to a shriveled old hag. Life could not be so cruel.

"You're . . . you're . . ." He couldn't say *exquisite*, he couldn't say *ravishing*. One simply didn't to a young lady one hadn't even been introduced to. Hell, he couldn't have said anything at all, not past the lump in his throat. Forrest thought of how she would have looked with a cloud of that hair floating over her warm, glowing skin, highlighting the golden flecks in her greenish eyes, and he nearly moaned out loud. Enough for a small dog, the hair would have come well over her shoulders, maybe to her waist, veiling her—oh, God. Not that she wasn't adorable as she was, with shaggy curls like a halo framing her lovely face. The curls gave her a pixieish look, a fresh, young innocence. "My God, you're a child!"

Sydney raised her chin. "I am eighteen, Mr. Randall."

"Eighteen?" Now the viscount did groan. "At eighteen females who look like you shouldn't be allowed out of the house without an armed guard! And where do you go, missy, leaving your sturdy footman outside, but into a nest of thieves?"

Oh, dear, Sydney thought, he was getting angry again. "Please, Mr. Randall, I only need—"

"You need a better haircut." Forrest almost bit his tongue for saying that. What he was going to say was "You need a spanking," which only sent his rattled brain reeling in another direction. He compromised with: "You need a keeper. And I am not Randall, for heaven's sake."

"Oh, I am sorry." And Sydney was sorry their conversation had to end; she was finding this man a fascinating study, almost like a new species. "Could I speak with Mr. Randall?"

"He's, ah, tied up at the moment. I'm Mayne."

Sydney bowed slightly in her seat. "How do you do, Mr. Mean, er, Mayne. I am Miss—"

He held his hand up. "No names, please. The walls have ears, you know." He also knew that deuced door was partly open.

Sydney nodded wisely, humoring the man. He was obviously dicked in the nob. She could hear grunts and thuds coming from the connecting room as well as he.

"Newlyweds next door." He shrugged, then almost blushed at her blank look. Gads, he wasn't used to such innocence. Which reminded him again of the hobble the chit had nearly landed in, a little lamb prancing into the wolves' lair. "Miss, ah, miss, I am sure you think your situation is dire, but coming here is not the solution."

Sydney was confused. "If you can't go to a moneylender for a loan, were can you go?"

Forrest dragged his hands through his hair again. He vowed never to introduce this featherbrain to his mother. "Let us start over again, shall we? Has no one warned you that moneylenders are unscrupulous?"

She nodded, and he looked pleased. "Has no one warned you that you end up paying, and paying again, far more than you borrow?"

She nodded once more. Mr. Mayne seemed almost pleasant now. "And finally, has no one warned you that moneylenders are the last resort of even hardened gamblers?" He was positively grinning, a lovely boyish grin despite the rumpled, battered look. He had nice eyes, too, she thought, May-sky blue and not the least bit shifty. Why had no one warned her that moneylenders could be such handsome rogues?

6

Cads and Collateral

"*B*ut I only need a thousand pounds, Mr. Mayne."

He didn't think to correct her about his title. The determined little baggage must be the only female in London not conversant with his office, income, and expectations, and some devil in him wished to keep her that way. As infuriatingly pigheaded as the chit was, at least she wasn't simpering and toadying up to him. Besides, there were more important misconceptions to remedy. He thought he could depend on the stalwart-seeming footman to see they were not interrupted.

"A thousand pounds? That's a great deal of money, you

know." It fairly boggled his mind to consider what she could have done to require such a sum. Unfortunately, simply by being where she was the wench proved nothing was too preposterous for Miss Sydney Lattimore. Ridiculous name for a girl anyway. But "A thousand pounds?"

"I really wish you would stop treating me like a wayward child, Mr. Mayne. I do know what I am about." His raised brows expressed skepticism. "I haven't undertaken this move lightly, I can assure you," she went on, determined to erase that patronizing half smile. "I do know it's not at all the thing for a young female to conduct such business, and I did have sense enough to wear Mama's old mourning clothes so no one would recognize me. But my circumstances absolutely require such funds."

"And you couldn't go to your father or brother or banker for aid, like any proper female?"

"I do not have any of those," she said quietly, bravely, bringing a pang of . . . something to the viscount's heart. He prayed it wasn't knight-errantry.

"You must have some family, someone."

"Of course I do, that's why I need the loan. I have a plan."

The viscount didn't doubt it for a moment. He steepled his hands and prepared to be entertained. Miss Lattimore didn't disappoint him. Her plan was no more mercenary than that of any mama planning to fire her darling off in society, hoping to land a prize in the marriage mart.

"So you see, if Winnie weds Baron Scoville—oh, no names. If my sister marries a certain warm gentleman, then we can repay the loan and not have to worry about the future."

So it was Scoville the sisters had in their sights. The baron was rich and wellborn, a worthy target, the viscount believed, if too proper by half for his, Forrest's, own liking. The self-righteous prig was never going to ally himself to any penniless nobody from a havey-cavey household though; he held his own value too dear. "Barons can generally look as high as they wish for a bride, you know," Forrest said, trying to be polite.

Sydney lifted her straight little nose anyway. "The La—we are not to be despised, sir. Mother's brother was an earl and my grandfather is a very well-respected military gentleman. We do have some connections; what we don't have is the wherewithal to take advantage of them. Besides, the baron has already paid my sister particular attention."

General Lattimore, by George. So the chit was quality. She just might pull it off. Especially if . . . "Is your sister as pretty as you?"

Sydney laughed, showing enchanting dimples. "Me? Oh, no, Winifred is beautiful! And she is sweet and kind and always behaves properly and knows just what to say even to the most boring curate. She does exquisite needlework and has a pleasing voice. We've never had a pianoforte, but I am certain Winnie would excel at it. She's—"

"A perfect paragon," the viscount interrupted, "who would make a delightful wife for any man, especially a rich one. You have convinced me. How do you propose to convince the mark—er, the man?"

Miss Lattimore did not need to reflect on the matter; she had it all worked out. She smiled again, and something about those dimples and the sparkle in her eyes made Forrest forget to listen to her rambling recitation about dresses and receptions and music lessons. "For the polite world seems to feel a lady should be musical. I do not see why myself, if she has so many other accomplishments, but the baron never fails to compliment my cousins on their playing. I am certain Winnie can do as well."

Sydney was satisfied that she had presented her case in a reasonable, mature fashion. She would have been furious to know the viscount hadn't heard a word. He was too worried about his own urge to go slay all of Miss Lattimore's dragons. No, that kind of chivalry was dead and well-buried. He would not get involved, not past warning the maiden to stay out of the paths of firebreathers.

"Have you considered what would happen if you borrow the money, rig your sister out like a fashion plate, and still do not bring the baron up to scratch? How would you repay the loan, considering it will be far higher than when you started, due to the exorbitant interest rates?"

Sydney chewed on her lower lip, adorably. The viscount bit his. "You are still thinking about the Motthavens," she said.

He wasn't, not at all. "The, ah, cents-per-centers feel strongly about getting their blunt back."

"Of course you do, you couldn't stay in business else. I do have other strings to my bow. There are other men, of course. They might not have as deep pockets as the baron, but I feel certain they would repay the debt to have Winnie as their bride. Moreover, I do not intend to use the full thousand pounds on Winnie's clothes. It would hardly cover a court dress, for one thing, though we do not aim so high. Naturally you wouldn't know about such matters."

The viscount knew all too well about dressmakers' bills and the costs of entertaining. A thousand pounds was not nearly enough for a chit's presentation Season. His sisters' balls had each cost more than that for one night's show. He passed over Miss Lattimore's assumption of his ignorance of the ton and focused on the convolutions of her great plan. "So that I might be clear on all the details," he asked, "precisely how, then, do you intend to outfit the sacrificial virgin?"

Sydney resented his sneering expression and high-handed tones. "My good man," she replied in Aunt Harriet's most haughty manner, "I shall use a portion of the money on *my sister*, and invest the rest. My earnings shall be enough to see us through the Season, and yes, even repay the loan if Winnie cannot like any of her suitors. There is no question of a sacrifice."

The chit continued to amaze him. "Do you mean," he practically shouted, "that you intend to borrow money at twenty percent or higher and invest it in what? Consols or such? At less than five? No one could be so crack-brained!"

"I'll have you know that I have ways of doubling my money, sirrah. That is fifty percent!"

"It is a hundred percent, you widgeon! That's why women should never handle money. You—"

"You made me nervous by shouting," she said quietly, accusingly.

Damn. She wasn't the only one rattled, if he could yell at a slip of a girl. "I apologize. Pray tell, though, if you have such a sure way to capitalize on an investment, why don't you take it to a bank? They are always eager for new ventures. They give fair rates of interest and plenty of advice."

She did not sound quite as smug. "It is not that kind of investment. I intend to wager on an exhibition of fisticuffs."

Sam Odum's club must have done more damage than the viscount knew; this had to be a fevered dream wherein a budding incomparable could spout the most skitter-witted nonsense with the serene confidence of a duchess. He really tried not to shout this time. His voice came out more a hoarse croak: "You're going to gamble your future on a mill?"

"Put like that, it does sound foolish, but it's not just any mill, er, match. There is a boxer, a Hollander, who has established a certain reputation and therefore high odds. My footman, Wally, is scheduled to take him on in a few weeks, and we have every confidence of Wally's victory." Sydney was on firm ground now that she had the usurer's attention. She should have saved her breath about Winnie and the baron and gone right to the boxing with a man like Mr. Mayne. One look at him, his broad shoulders and well-muscled legs, should have told her he'd be more absorbed in fisticuffs than fashion. Perhaps his line of business even required a degree of skill in the sport. "No one in Little—where we live has ever been able to beat Wally, and he's been training especially hard now. He'll win."

Viscount Mayne was indeed a follower of the Fancy. "Do you mean the Dutch champion they call the Oak? I heard he was to fight again soon. And Wally's the big fellow outside? He might have a chance if he's as good as you say. The Oak has gone to fat, I've heard."

"No, that's Willy outside, Wally's twin. Willy can't box; he has a glass jaw."

Forrest sighed. "Don't you know anything about defense? The fellow is there to protect you; you don't tell the enemy about his weaknesses."

"Oh. I didn't know you were my enemy. I thought we were simply discussing a loan."

"Right, the loan. Well, Miss, ah, miss, what would you put down as collateral?"

"Collateral?"

"Yes, you know, as guarantee for the loan. Loans are often secured with a mortgage, the title to a piece of property, a race-horse or even a piece of jewelry. Something of equal value that the lender gets to keep if the loan is not satisfied."

"Oh, but I intend to repay every farthing."

"They all do, the pigeons Randall plucks. You see, no one is going to issue an unsecured loan to a schoolgirl."

"I am *not* a schoolgirl! And that's gammon, for my maid Annemarie said gentlemen write out vouchers all the time for loans, on their word of honor alone."

"Precisely. Gentlemen. On their word of honor."

Instead of becoming discouraged, Miss Lattimore got angry. "I have as much honor as any man. I'll have you know my family name has never been touched by ignominy, and it never shall in my lifetime. I resent any implication to the contrary, Mr. Mayne, especially coming from one in your position. Why, I'd sooner trust my word to repay a loan than I would yours not to cheat me on the terms. So there." And she pounded the chair arm for emphasis the way the general did, and nearly fell off her seat when the arm wasn't there. The dastard was grinning.

"You have definitely made your point, Miss, ah, Lamb. I—"

"And I resent your comparing me to that notorious female. I am trying to help my family in the only way I know how. I am not trying to make a spectacle of myself."

The viscount stroked his chin. "I rather had in mind one of those cute, curly little creatures who gambol into quicksand."

Sydney fingered her uneven curls. "I did it myself."

"I never would have guessed. But I cannot keep calling you Miss Ah if we are going to be partners."

"Partners? We are?" Sydney didn't care if he called her Misbegotten, if he would lend her the money! "Oh, thank you!"

Lend it he would, and most likely was always going to. The viscount was acting against all of his better judgment . . . and bowing to the inevitable. Giving her the blunt was the only way to keep the minx out of— "Yes, Mischief, I am going to give you the money, but with conditions."

Sydney eagerly drew a pencil and a scrap of paper out of her reticule. "Yes, sir, what is the rate? Shall you want payment in installments or one lump sum? I can figure out a schedule, or reinvest from the dress allowance or—"

"Hold, Mischief. I said *give*. Consider it a parting gift from O. Randall and Associates." He ignored the louder thumps from the other room and pushed the leather purse with the thousand pounds over to her. "That way neither of us is ensnared. You know, 'neither a borrower nor a lender be.' "

She shook her head, sending curls every which way. The devil was quoting Scripture again. "And you say women have no head for business. You cannot just give away a sack of gold to a stranger."

"Why not? It's mine. My brother had some gaming debts."

"And you collected from your own brother?"

The viscount didn't bother refuting fustian. He pushed the purse a little closer.

Sydney could almost feel the weight of the coins, but she could not reach out those few inches for the sack. "I do not mean any offense, Mr. Mayne, but a lady cannot accept such a gift. There are certain standards of which you may not be aware, but it would be highly improper. Flowers, perhaps, but a thousand pounds?"

The viscount laughed out loud, even though it hurt his sore jaw and disturbed his ribs. "Doing it too brown, my girl. If you can dress up in your mother's clothes and go to the Greeks, talking about boxing matches like they were afternoon teas, then you can take the money. It's too late to stand on your uppers, Mischief." He got up and put the sack in her lap. "Besides, I have a secret to tell you. I am not really a moneylender."

Sydney looked at the bag of money in her lap, the rumpled man with the lopsided grin, the shambles of an office with the sign on the door. She nodded. She had the money; she could humor the Bedlamite.

"I am a viscount."

"And I am the queen of Persia. Therefore I shall have no problem repaying you by the end of the Season." She stood to leave.

"But you haven't heard my conditions yet."

He was standing quite close to her, still wearing that devilish smile. Sydney sat down. "Of course, the rates."

He waved that aside. "I said you needn't repay the deuced loan; I certainly would not make profit on it. Even we viscounts have some standards. But here are my terms: the first is that you never, ever try to contact another loan shark. You contact me and only me if you find yourself in difficulty again." He scrawled his Grosvenor Square address on her piece of paper. "Next, you never return here, no matter how many musclebound footmen you have. Promise me on your honor, Mischief, and your family name that you prize so highly."

He was no longer grinning. Sydney solemnly swore and he smiled like the sun coming out again. "Good. And finally, I get to keep the hair."

"As collateral? But it's not worth nearly enough."

It was to him.

Sydney stood by the door, cradling a sack of currency instead of a basket of hair, and vowing again to repay the reckoning. Up close, Forrest got a hint of lavender mixed with the camphor and he could almost count the freckles across the bridge of her nose.

"You know, my dear," he said, keeping his voice low, "if you have trouble meeting the obligation, I am sure we could find some mutually satisfying way of settling accounts."

There was that wide-eyed stare of muddled incomprehension. Miss Lattimore hadn't the faintest idea of what he was shamefully suggesting. So he showed her. Tenderly, he placed his lips on hers and softly kissed her.

Oddly enough, Sydney was not frightened. It was all of a piece for this incredible afternoon. In fact, it was quite enjoyable, being held in a man's arms and sweetly kissed. All the other men of her acquaintance—not many, to be sure, and more boys than men—smelled of bay rum or talc, soap or sandalwood. This one smelled of . . . sweat. And the smell was as wild as the man, disturbing and exciting and—a cad! Sydney struggled and he released her immediately. Smiling.

"You ... you," she sputtered. "You were right. Money-lenders *are* vermin." And she slapped him.

Sydney was horrified. She'd never struck a man before. Then again, she'd never been kissed before, nor been offered a slip on the shoulder. She knew she was partially to blame for being where no lady should be. Of course a gentleman would not have taken advantage of a lady no matter what the circumstances, but Mr. Mayne, or whoever he was, was not a gentleman. She should not have expected him to act like one, nor reacted so violently when he did not. Sydney was prepared to apologize, when the door burst open.

Willy shoved his way in, ready to do battle after the noises he'd heard. He saw his mistress looking irresolute, saw the five-fingered calling card she'd left on the handsome devil's grinning face. He shook his head. "I told you and told you, Missy, not with your open hand." He smashed his fist right in the viscount's eye with enough force to ensure a spectacular shiner.

Forrest raised his hands in submission. He knew he was wrong to steal the kiss, but it was well worth it. He smiled, remembering.

"And if that don't work," Willy continued, "we taught you what to do." He kneed the viscount in the groin.

Miss Lattimore stepped over his lordship daintily, swearing to have the money back and wishing him good day.

Forrest groaned. Women.

7

Fils et Frères

*T*he Lattimore sisters were in funds and the Mainwaring brothers were nearly identical again.

Before leaving the Fleet Street premises, Viscount Mayne staggered to the doorway of the adjacent room and told the occupants: "Listen up, you bounders. I just made a donation to a worthy cause on your behalf. A thousand pounds of charity ought to buy you a better seat on the boat to hell. Unless you want that lucky day to come soon, you bastards best remember everything I said, and forget everything you heard."

Then he gathered his coat—London would just have to see the immaculate viscount in his shirttails for once—and his misused cravat. He picked up the carpetbag of weaponry and Miss Lattimore's basket. On reflection he decided he was going to look enough like a bobbingblock without a little wicker handle slung over his arm. Removing the mound of hair, he carefully wrapped it in that vastly utilitarian item, his soiled neckcloth.

Forrest entered Mainwaring House through the rear door. One of the scullery maids dropped a bowl of beans, the turnspit dog growled, and Cook threw her apron over her head, wailing.

The viscount slunk off to the study, where he penned out notes to accompany the canceled IOUs. *This matter has been attended to,* he wrote. *Best wishes for your future, Yrs., etc. Vct. Mayne.* He did not feel he owed the flats any further explanation, nor did he think they would pay attention to any advice he might give about the folly of dipping too deep. He placed the notes with a footman, then finally placed himself in the hands of his father's toplofty valet. That worthy's already pasty complexion took on a greenish cast when confronted with this latest Mainwaring casualty. Heavens, Findley thought. Did they never win?

After a long soak in a hot tub, a nourishing meal, and half a bottle of the duke's Burgundy, the viscount took to his bed for a long night's rest. He awoke—and instantly declared that was miracle enough for the day. He felt, and looked, worse than he had since a cannonball sent him flying off the HMS *Fairwind*'s deck, ending his naval career.

He couldn't bear to stay inside, where the housemaids tiptoed around him, their eyes averted. He didn't dare go outside, where children could get nightmares from a look at his face, horses might bolt, ladies swoon. He had to get out of the London fishbowl.

As soon as his brother was declared fit to travel, Forrest bundled Brennan into the coach for the ride to Sussex. He and Bren would be better off recuperating in the country under their mother's tender care. There would be fewer questions, at any rate. They could give out that there had been a carriage accident. Or two.

Two beefsteaks for Wally every morning, for his training. Three cases of the general's favorite port. Enough macaroons and almond tarts and seed cakes for the legions of morning callers and afternoon teas. A small dinner party for Lord Scoville? No, that would be too coming. Besides, she'd have to invite Aunt Harriet.

Sydney was making lists and spending money. What joy! She and her sister had already been to the Pantheon Bazaar where, Annemarie the maid informed them, they could get the best bargains on ribbons and lace and gloves and stockings. The Lattimore ladies had patronized fabric warehouses, plumassiers, milliners, and shoemakers. They had *not* visited a single dressmaker, saving money as fast as they spent it. Annemarie's émigré connections could whip up the most fetching outfits, *à la mode* and meticulously crafted, for a quarter of the price of a haughty Bond Street modiste. Annemarie herself was a wizard with a needle, changing a trimming here, a mesh overskirt there. She removed ribbons and sewed on spangles, making each of the girls' gowns appear as many.

At Sydney's insistence, most of the attention and expense was devoted to her sister's wardrobe. No one noticed the little sister anyway, when Miss Lattimore was such a beauty. Winifred went out more, too. She did not seem to mind interminable visits with Aunt Harriet and Trixie, while Sydney preferred to stay home, reading the newspapers to the general and reveling in every gossip column's mention of the new star rising on the social horizon.

Sydney did allow herself to be persuaded to purchase a dress length of jonquil muslin, which then required the most dashing bonnet she'd ever owned: a cottage straw with a bouquet of yellow silk daisies peeping from under the brim, two russet feathers a shade darker than her hair curling along her cheek, and green streamers trailing down her back and under her chin. It looked elegant, sophisticated, alluring—more so once she had her ragged locks trimmed by a professional coiffeur.

"Oh, Sydney, your beautiful hair," Winifred cried. "And you did it for me!"

Sydney thought that cutting her hair was the least of what she'd done. She would never discuss her visit to Fleet Street with her sensitive sister, though, especially not this afternoon, when Winnie was due to go for a drive in the park with Baron Scoville. Sydney couldn't trust the watering pot not to have a *crise de nerfs* right in front of him.

"Hush, you peagoose," Sydney teased. "We can't have the baron see you with swollen eyes and a red nose. He might think you the kind of woman to be enacting him scenes all the time. No gentleman would like that." She did not add, *Especially one so concerned with his consequence as the baron.* Winnie seemed pleased by the attention of the self-important peer; far be it from Sydney to disparage such a well-breeched gentleman.

"Besides," she said, "I did not cut my hair for you. I always hated that impossible mop. It weighed down my head and would never take a curl. Now I couldn't make it lay flat if I wanted to, and I feel free of all that heaviness and constant

53

bother. Look at me. I am almost fashionable! You better be careful I don't steal all of your beaux away!"

"You could have all the admirers you want, dearest, if you would just go out and about more. Why, the gentlemen will flock to your feet when they see you in your new bonnet. You can have your pick!" Winnie giggled, her spirits restored. "Maybe one of the Bond Street fribbles will catch your fancy."

Sydney didn't think so.

The Duchess of Mayne was a student of breeding. She had intricate charts of the bloodlines of her dogs, their conformations, colors, temperaments. When she selected a mating pair, she was fairly certain of the results. Hers was the most noted establishment for Pekingese dogs in the kingdom. Lady Mayne was proud of her dogs.

She herself collected seeds from the best blossoms in her garden, for next year's blooms. Her gardens were mentioned in guidebooks. She was proud of her flowers.

She should have stopped there.

In the middle years of her marriage, when Lady Mayne still discussed her marriage at all, she used to boast that her husband could accuse her of many things, but never infidelity. All four of her children had his dark hair and the Mainwaring nose. (Fortunately the girls had pleasing personalities and large dowries.) She used to say that blood would tell, that breeding was all. She used to be proud of her sons, tall and straight, darkly handsome, like two peas in a pod.

Like two peas in a pod that had been left on the vine too long, stepped on by the farmer's hobnail boots, then run over by the farm cart.

"This is why I sent you to London? This is how you help your brother and keep the family name from the tattle-mongers? This is how you were raised to behave?"

If Forrest had expected loving kindness and tender sympathy from his mother, he was disabused of that notion as soon as he helped Brennan past the front door. The duchess didn't even wait for the servants to retreat before lighting into her eldest offspring.

"This is what comes from letting you go off to the navy.

You did not learn violence with your mother's milk! It's all that man's fault, I swear. There has never been so much as a soldier in my family. The Mainwarings were ever a belligerent lot, so proud of tracing their roots to William the Conqueror. Merciful heavens, who wants to be related to a bloodthirsty conqueror? And all of those kings' men and cavalry officers your father's always nattering on about, that's where you got this streak of brutality. And you are supposed to be the sane and sober one, the heir. Heir to your father's lackwits, I'd say. A diplomat, he calls himself. Hah! If he was ever around to teach his sons diplomacy, they wouldn't behave like barroom brawlers and look like spoiled cabbages!"

"Thank you, Your Grace," Forrest teased, trying to coax her into better humor. His mother hadn't been in a rant like this since last Christmas, when the governor came down to visit. "I am pleased to be home, too."

Brennan was grinning as best he could around the sticking plaster, since it was his brother under fire. Then the duchess turned that fond maternal eye, and scathing tongue, in his direction.

"You!" she screamed as if a slimy toad had arrived in her entry hall. "You are nothing but a womanizer. A drunkard. A gambler. Up to every tomfoolery it has been mankind's sin to invent! You are even more harebrained than your brother, associating with such riffraff. You"—her voice rose an octave—"inherited your father's dissipations."

Bren tried to reason with the duchess; Forrest could have told his brother he was making a mistake, but he'd suffered enough pulling Bren's chestnuts out of the fire. Let the stripling dig himself in deeper. "Cut line, Mother," Brennan started. "You know the governor ain't in the petticoat line, never has been. And he don't play more than a hand or two of whist or drink overmuch. Gout won't let him. Besides, this last scrape wasn't all my fault."

"Of course not, you're too stupid to get into so much trouble on your own! I know exactly who is to blame. When I get my hands on that—"

"As a matter of fact, Mother, none of it would have happened if you had let me join the army as I wanted."

"Are you saying it is *my* fault?"

Forrest moved to stand in front of the buhl table; he'd always admired that Sèvres vase on it.

"Of course not, Mother. It's just that, well, London's full of chances to drink and gamble and, yes, meet that kind of woman. There's nothing much else to do."

"My dogs have better sense. You are supposed to spend your time in town at parties and museums and plays and picnics, meeting the *right* kind of woman. And as for the army, you lobcock, you can't even keep yourself in one piece in London! Imagine what might happen to you in Spain. Go to your room."

"Go to my room? You cannot send me to the nursery like a child, Mother. I am twenty-two."

"And you can come down to dinner when you act it."

Bren wasn't in shape to put on the formal clothes the duchess required at her table, nor make the long trek up and down the arched stairways. Still, to be dismissed like a schoolboy in short pants rankled. "But, Mother . . ."

The duchess picked up a potted fern from the sidetable. Bren left.

Lady Mayne turned to her eldest. "I'm going, I'm going," he surrendered, starting for the stairs to help Brennan.

"And I," she pronounced, still holding the plant, "am going to the greenhouse."

Forrest spun around and dashed down the hall after her. "Not the greenhouse, Mother! Not all that glass!"

A few hours later the duchess relented. Maybe she had been too hard on Forrest. He had brought Brennan home, after all. She decided to forgive him and listen to the whole story, perhaps hearing some news of the duke. She would even bring Forrest a cup of one of her special brews of tea. The poor boy looked like he needed it.

When the duchess knocked on Forrest's door and received no answer, she thought he might be sleeping. She turned the handle and tiptoed in to check. The bed was empty, so he must be feeling better. She'd just go along to Brennan's room to see how he was faring.

On her way out, the duchess chanced to catch sight of a foul piece of linen on her son's otherwise immaculate dresser. She knew that new valet of his was a slacker! Not in her house, Lady Mayne swore, yanking on the bellpull. She went to pick up the offending cloth, to demand its immediate removal, and that of the person responsible. Sweet mercy, the linen was bloodstained, and wrapped around . . .

If Forrest thought going down to Sussex would have stopped the talk in London, he was wrong. The duchess's shriek could have been heard in Hyde Park. If he thought his injuries would heal quicker in the country, he was wrong. Flying up those stairs did not do his ribs any good. Taking a flying teacup on the ear did not do his face any good. Listening to his mother berate him in front of his valet, the butler, two footmen, a housemaid, and his grinning brother did not do his composure any good.

And that was *after* the duchess realized the bundle was a woman's hair and not a Pekingese pelt.

"Well, old boy," the viscount told Nelson in the cold dower house library, "it's just you and me again." And a bottle of Madeira. "You're the wastrel and I'm the womanizer. No, I'm the ruffian and the rake. You're just the rat catcher."

Tarnation, how could his own mother think he'd ever take up the life of a libertine? Gads, that's the last vice he'd pick. Of course, he'd never met a woman like Mischief before. She was an exasperating little chit, he recalled with a smile, but pluck to the backbone and loyal to a fault. And a beauty. He'd like to get a look at the sister, Forrest mused. Maybe he would, if Scoville dropped the handkerchief. Forrest didn't travel in the same circles as the baron, but sooner or later he would meet the peer's bride.

He doubted he would ever meet Miss Sydney again. She'd move heaven and earth to get the money back to Mainwaring House, he was sure, but he wouldn't be there. And he never went to debutante balls or such, so that was that.

He shut the book on Miss Sydney Lattimore and he shut his eyes, but he couldn't get those silly coppery curls out of his mind, or her quicksilver dimples or the way she nibbled on her lip before saying something outrageous. Zeus, she was always saying something outrageous. Forrest poured out another glass of wine and spilled some in a dish for Nelson. The viscount didn't like to drink alone.

What was going to happen to the widgeon? he pondered. She'd make micefeet of her Season for certain, landing in some scandalbroth or other. It would be a miracle, in fact, if Sydney's rackety ways didn't scare off that fop Scoville. On the other hand, maybe there was an intelligent *parti* not looking to rivet himself to a milk-and-water miss. He'd snap up Sydney Lattimore before she could say "I have a plan," debts and dowry or not.

What a dance she'd lead the poor sod. Forrest took another sip. Nelson belched. "You're right. We're a lot better off out of it," he told the hound. "We'll never see her after this anyway."

Wrong again.

8

By-blows and Blackmail

$\mathcal{V}$iscount Mayne had also been wrong when he called the Ottos bastards. Only one was. The other was his legitimate half-brother. Otto Chester, the ivory tuner, was actually the natural son of one Lord Winchester Whitlaw and his cook at the time, Mrs. Bella Boggs. No one knew the whereabouts of Mr. Boggs. Lady Whitlaw was less than pleased. Since his wife held both the reins and the purse strings in that marriage, Lord Whitlaw watched as Bella was tossed out in the cold on her *enceinte* ear. Before she got *too* cold, though, Lord Whitlaw sent her to his Irish estate, where Lady Whitlaw never visited. Before Bella grew too big with child, Whitlaw married her off to Padraic O'Toole, his Irish estate manager.

The infant was named Chester O'Toole. He took after his father, being pale and thin and feckless. He also inherited his father's left-handedness, to Paddy O'Toole's bile at the continual reminder. The boy was sent to England at his father's expense, to receive an education befitting the son of a lord. Being weak and puny and a bastard, he quickly learned cowardice and subterfuge.

Randy O'Toole was Chester's legitimate half-brother, born on the right side of the blanket. Presently using the name of Otto Randall, financial consultant, Randy was also presently bound and gagged in his side office, next to Chester.

The younger O'Toole resembled *his* father, with the same red hair, stocky stature, and vile temper. (The Duchess of Mayne would have been pleased with this true breeding of bloodlines.) Randy was also well educated at Lord Whitlaw's—unwitting—expense, thanks to Paddy's fancy work with the estate books. Randy turned out to have his sire's flair for figures. The crookeder the better.

Bella never had life so good, there in Ireland. For the first time in her life she did not have to work. Indeed, as the manager's wife, she could lord it over the lesser employees and socialize far above her station. She had two sons with futures, a husband who provided well, a cozy kitchen all her own. And she owed everything to Lord Whitlaw.

So grateful was Bella, in fact, that she bore his lordship another child, another colorless, stringy left-hander. This child was a girl, who now plied a trade on the streets of Dublin, lest her mother's heritage be forsaken.

Paddy was furious, but what could he do? His job paid too well to leave and his wife was too well liked by the boss to beat. Paddy took to drink. He also took more and more money out of Lord Whitlaw's share of the estate and added it to his own account. Bella was better off, but not feeling as well blessed, with a surly, jug-bitten Irishman at her hearth.

Life went on. The children grew to young men and fallen woman. Bella grew stouter on her own cooking and Paddy grew meaner and the estate grew poorer, all of which may have contributed to his lordship's less frequent visits.

When he did chance to come north one fall for the hunting, Paddy followed him closer than his shadow, waiting for Whitlaw to come near Bella. More for loyalty's sake and the comfort of familiarity than anything else, Whitlaw did approach O'Toole's wife. In the stables, in the back parlor, on the kitchen table. That last was too much for Paddy. He challenged Lord Whitlaw to a duel.

Whitlaw refused. A gentleman did not duel with his social inferiors. Especially not if they were better shots. Then bare fists, Paddy insisted. Whitlaw turned craven—not a far turn at that—and threatened to call in the sheriff.

Now what could Paddy do? The estate was bled dry and Bella was free to anyone who wanted the immoral sow, for all Paddy cared. He shot Lord Whitlaw.

Paddy hung, of course. No low Irish land agent could get away with the hot-blooded murder of an English lord. Bella and the boys fled to England with the money before anyone thought to look into the estate books. O'Toole not being a good name to bear right then, neither in Ireland nor England, Bella took back her maiden name, Bumpers. The boys became Otto Chester and Otto Randall, since Bella determined that no one would suspect them of being brothers if they had the same first name. Also, it was easier to remember.

Bella used Lord Whitlaw's—unknown—bequest to establish herself as a respectable widow in Chelsea. Her sons went into business, O. Randall and Associates, Financial Consultants. Cardsharps and loansharks, limited.

Among certain circles, Lord Forrest Mayne was considered to be of careful intellect, a thoughtful man who brought his not inconsiderable powers of ratiocination to bear before forming a judgment. Among other circles he was simply called a "knowing 'un," and respected as such. One could only wonder what was going on in his mind for this downy cove to make so many false assumptions. He'd thought to bask under his mother's solace; he really should have known better. He concluded she was the most unnatural parent a grown man could have; he hadn't met Bella Bumpers. At least the duchess never kicked him while he was trussed up like a Christmas goose.

"My babies," Bella wailed when she entered the office on Fleet Street and found her sons tied and gagged. "My precious boys! How did this happen? How many cutthroats jumped on you?"

She got Chester's neckcloth out of his mouth first. "Mayne," he gasped.

"Mayne?" Bella's face turned red and her nostrils flared. Her chest swelled like a pouter pigeon's. Then she started kicking at Chester and beating him about the head with her reticule, which contained, as usual, a small pistol.

"Bud, Ma," Chester whimpered, trying to drag himself out of her way.

"Don't you 'ma' me, you gutless clunch. I don't want to be your ma anymore. I *never* wanted to be your ma. I even changed my name so I could pretend I wasn't your ma. I told you and told you to leave the little lordlings be. Pick on country grapeseeds, I said, new-blooming tulips, or raw army recruits. So what pigeon do you find to pluck, huh? Young Mainwaring, that's who! With big brother right here to protect him, like any jackstraw could have told you!

"And you," she screeched, aiming her next kicks at Randall, "you couldn't leave well enough alone. No, you had to set your bully-boy on the sprig. Where is that dung heap anyway? I'll tear him limb from limb for this!"

Bella hadn't taken the gag from Randy, so Chester tried to answer: "Mayne had him pred-ganged."

"What's wrong with you?" Bella's beady little eyes narrowed.

"I fing my node id broke."

"Oh, yeah?" She screwed his head around toward a better angle, squinting at the questionable fixture. "Yeah, it is." She put her knee on Chester's chest and wrapped her fat fingers around his nose. Then she yanked. "Now it ain't. Bad enough you look like some corpse without you sniffing at your ear for the rest of your life."

While Chester was unconscious, she untied Randall, after getting in a few more kicks. "So what did he do to you, fleabrain?"

Randy wouldn't say. He just shook his head.

"What's the matter, runt? Cat got your tongue?" Bella cackled, then peered at him. "Nah, Mayne's known for a gentleman. He'd never carve a man up like that, not even a little maggot like you."

"My teeth are mithing. I thwear I'll kill the bathtard."

"That ain't no way to talk about your brother. 'Sides, he just gulled the flat. The duke would of coughed up the reckoning. You're the one what ordered him worked over, not Chester."

"Not Chethter. Forretht Mayne. I'm going to thee him dead."

"I always said your bark was bigger'n your bite. Ha-ha!" Sympathy was not one of Bella's strong points. "You're just lucky they didn't set the magistrate on us for what you done."

"The deuthed codth head threatened to do jutht that. That'th why I—"

"Oh, shut up already. You sound just like your father at his last prayers."

Since Padraic O'Toole's last prayers were spoken through a hood with a noose around his neck, Randy shut up.

Bella was shaking her head. "You two together have about as much brains as the average pullet. All that schooling, and you didn't even learn to listen to your ma. I told you time and time again about quality and family. You know, how some of them watch out for kinfolk just the way we look after each other."

A few days later the same little group was gathered at Bella's row house in Chelsea.

"Stop looking over your shoulder, Chester. Swells like Mayne hardly set foot out of Mayfair. 'Sides, he wouldn't recognize you anyways. I hardly do myself and I'm your mother. I ain't happy about that neither, but I can live with it."

"But, Ma, what are we going to do? We can't just stay here. I say we take what we have and set up on the Continent."

"Shut up, you pudding heart, we ain't running," his brother said.

Randy had false front teeth by now, fancy ivory ones taken from some dead nabob by the undertakers next door. They hurt like hell, which did not do much for his temper. The top set stuck out over his bottom lip, not doing much for his appearance either. "I still say we kill Mayne. Then we don't even have to relocate."

"That's the most harebrained idea I ever heard. Get that? Harebrained, rabbit-toothed?" Bella nearly fell off her chair, laughing so hard. When she stopped laughing she boxed Randy's ears until the false teeth flew out. "You got your father's same nasty temper. You want to end like him, too? Like as not you will, but you ain't making gallows' bait out of me and Chester. Didn't you learn anything from your father? No one can kill a titled nob less'n he's got a higher title. They call that a fair fight. Or if he's got more money. They call that justice."

"And what about the money, Ma?" Chester asked. "How are we going to collect without Sam?"

"We've got enough of the ready for now. As for the slips His Nibs left us, a solicitor's letter with them big words like 'debtors' prison' ought to be just as encouraging as a visit from Sam."

"And what about that thousand pounds he gave away?" Randy wanted to know.

Bella's pudgy arms waved that aside. "We'll get the blunt back easy enough. But this ain't about money, you blockheads. It's about revenge."

Chester started shaking but Randy smiled, looking more like a rabid rodent than anything else.

Bella's plan was simple: hit 'em where it hurt. Mayne's pockets were so deep, he wouldn't even feel the loss. His pride was another matter.

"We can get the money from that dandy Scoville anyway. Soon as he announces the engagement and can't back down from the wedding, we threaten to go to the gossip rags with word that his bride's family ain't all it should be. Shady deal-ings in backstreet offices and all. He'll pay quick enough to keep that quiet."

"But how are we going to know if he picks the right girl?" Chester was nervous. Chester was already packed. "We don't have the chit's name. Even if Mayne wouldn't kill me on sight, you know I'm not fit enough to go to the clubs to listen to the gossip."

"You're not fearless enough, you mean," Bella taunted. "Don't worry, chicken-liver, we won't ask you to go outside yet. We just have to read the gossip columns ourselves. If that pompous ass Scoville is sniffing 'round some filly, the papers'll know it. If not, you just have to follow the footman home from that prizefight to see where he goes."

"Me?"

"Well, Rabbit-face sticks out like a sore thumb, don't he?"

"I want to know about Mayne." Randy wanted to change the subject.

"Oh, we get to him through the other wench, the one with gumption. My kind of female, from what you say, conniving and crafty. Imagine if your sister'd had that kind of bottom. B'gad, she could have been some rich man's mistress by now. No matter, we find out who that little baggage is and wait till she's got her name on everybody's lips, which I misdoubt will take too long. If she don't do it herself, we help her along, like mentioning her betting on the mill. Then we shout it loud and clear that the high and mighty Viscount Mayne has ruined her. He compromised her all right and tight. A gentlebred innocent what's blotted her copybook. Either he'll have to marry the hobbledehoy brat and be miserable the rest of his life, or he'll see his name dragged through the mud along with hers. That won't sit well with him, not with his notions of family honor and all. Of course, if none of that works . . ."

"We kill him."

"And run to the Continent."

9

Mills and Masquerades

"*I* swear I'm sick of this petticoat tyranny, Forrest. You've got to do something!"

Brennan stormed into his brother's study, interrupting to no one's displeasure an uncomfortable meeting between the viscount and one of his tenants. The farmer touched his brim and nodded to the younger lord on his way out.

"What was that about?" Bren asked, flopping into the chair just vacated.

"It was about the proper handling of randy young bulls. Whipslade can't seem to keep that Fred penned in, so I said I'd castrate him myself the next time he got into trouble." Forrest grinned. "Now, what was your complaint, little bull, er, brother?"

Bren got the hint. "But dash it all, Forrest, there's nothing to do!"

Forrest had plenty to keep him occupied, overseeing the vast Mainwaring holdings, to say nothing of checking all the London dailies for mention of acquaintances. Brennan's cracked ribs had kept him more confined to the house and his mother's carping, and he was fretting to be gone. He would have returned to London a se'night past, in fact, had the duchess not given strict orders to the stables forbidding him horse or carriage. No way was she letting him go back to the fleshpots of the city . . . or his father's house.

"You've got to talk to her, Forrest, convince her she's wrong about London."

"Dear boy, do I look that paper-skulled? I'd rather be keel-hauled than tell the duchess she's wrong, thank you."

"Then the grooms. They will listen to you, Forrest," Brennan begged. "Deuces, they can't deny you your own cattle, can they? I know you wouldn't let me have the bays, but surely you'll lend me Old Gigi and the pony trap? The dog cart? How about a ride to the nearest posting house?"

For Brennan's sake, the viscount decided to make a short excursion to town. For Brennan's sake, he planned some harmless diversions, like a drive out to a prizefight at Islington two days later. They weren't doing *The Merchant of Venice* at Drury Lane, and he had to keep the boy entertained and out of trouble, didn't he?

They took the viscount's phaeton to Islington, with his matchless bays and his tiger Todd. Brennan half jokingly wondered why, if this was supposed to be his treat, he couldn't handle the ribbons. Todd nearly fell off his perch on the back, laughing.

They left town early to set an easy pace on account of Brennan's ribs—and the viscount's sworn word to his mother. As it turned out, they were none too early and had no chance of springing the pair with the roadway so clogged. All the sporting bloods were on their way to Islington, along with every other buck in town who was game for a wager. The upcoming bout had caught the attention and imagination of the entire male population of London, it seemed, and they were all on the road at once.

The Dutch champion was not called the Oak just because no one could pronounce his name. He had stood unbent through years of matches, never once being knocked to the canvas. Few men were corkbrained enough to meet him these days, so an exhibition of fisticuffs by the near legend was not to be missed. No one except the viscount knew much about the challenger, one Walter Minch. The word was he was undefeated in some shire or other, a young lad with size if no sense. Some claimed they'd seen him in training and he stripped to advantage. "Minch the Cinch" they dubbed him, hoping for better odds. Others swore he had to be a sacrificial shill for the bout's promoters. They weren't betting on his winning or losing, just on how long he stayed standing.

The viscount, of course, would have gone to the grave without divulging any foreknowledge of any footman's brother. He hoped and prayed Miss Lattimore's connection never came to light, much less his own. Not even his brother knew it was a servant named Willy who'd darkened Forrest's daylights, not the bloodsucker's hired killer. The viscount's eye was still sore; Wally stood a deuced good chance.

There were shouts, wagers, and rumors all along the slow drive. The clamor grew worse near the actual meeting grounds, naturally, as the drivers tried to thread their vehicles through the crowds to good vantage points. Todd jumped down to clear a path, and the viscount slid the bays between a racing curricle and a gig, with at least an inch to spare on either side. Then there were greetings and fresh odds, and everyone wanting to know the viscount's opinion, since he was known to be a follower of the Fancy himself.

Forrest smiled and told his eager listeners that since he'd never seen the man box, he couldn't make a fair guess. That's what they were all there for, wasn't it?

Anyone wishing an expert's advice before making his own wagers would have been wiser to follow the viscount around when he climbed down from the phaeton, leaving Todd at the horses' heads and Brennan with an ale in his hand.

Forrest greeted his friends, smiled at casual acquaintances, and ignored would-be hangers-on. The crowd was a mix of London gents, local gentry, neighborhood workingmen, pickpockets, and other riffraff. The viscount strolled about the grounds with no fixed purpose in sight, placing a wager here, making a bet there. He never put his name down for a lot of money, always denied knowing the new boxer. He shrugged good-naturedly about rooting for the underdog and took the long odds. The longer the better. If he'd staked all his blunt with one bookmaker, the odds would have swung considerably, with less profit for him—and Miss Lattimore.

Content, he ambled back across the field toward his phaeton, from whose high perch he'd have a clear view of the roped-off square. He was so satisfied with his transactions that he tossed a coin to an odd-looking clergyman standing on the perimeter of the crowd, clasping his Bible. "Say a prayer for Minch, Reverend," Forrest called over his shoulder.

The minister appeared as if St. Peter had just called his name off the rolls, but he hoarsely answered to the viscount's back: "Bless you, my son."

He was the last person you'd expect to see at a place like this, a holy man at a mill, and this was the last place Reverend Cheswick wanted to be. But if Cheswick had to be there—and Bella seemed adamant about that—then Chester was going in disguise. Randy tried to tell him that his own wishy-washy phiz with its newly bloated nose was the best camouflage, but Chester went out and got himself a bagwig, thick spectacles, and a moldy frock coat from the same source as Randy's choppers. The mortuary workers threw the Bible in free. Chester's identity was well hidden, in the one disguise guaranteed to draw attention to himself. He stuck out among the other men like a sore . . . nose. And wasn't it just his luck that the bastard who broke his nose had to be so bloody charitable? First Mayne gave away their thousand pounds and now he went out of his way to toss a golden boy to a man of the cloth. Chester supposed he was the type to encourage beggars with handouts, too.

At least the worst was over. His disguise passed the test and now he could go home. He didn't have the information Bella wanted about where the footman lived or who he worked for, but she would have to understand. His pants were wet.

"Who was that rum touch you were talking to?" Brennan wanted to know.

"Who? Oh, the old quiz? Most likely some missionary come to save our souls. Why?"

"Something about him just looked familiar."

"I doubt you meet many religious sorts in the circles you travel," his brother noted dryly, passing over the hamper of food they'd brought from town.

Before they could do justice to the cold chicken and sliced ham and Scotch eggs and crusty bread, a roar went up from the crowd. The champion was coming. The Oak strode to the clearing. The ground almost shook with his every step. The spectators cheered themselves hoarse, then they passed around the bottles and flasks again.

The Oak waved to the crowd, turning toward all four compass points while his seconds set a footstool in his corner. His cape swirled around his massive frame. Next he removed the cloak and slowly repeated the move so they could all appreciate his naked upper torso. They did, howling and stamping their feet as muscle rippled over muscle every time he raised an arm.

The viscount held his looking glass to his eye. "The Dutchman seems heavier than the last time I saw him fight. I wonder if it's all muscle or if the weight might slow him down."

"Care to hazard your blunt on it?" Bren asked, forgetting he'd sworn off wagering, at least for the remainder of this quarter.

Since Forrest was already financing the chub until his next allowance, he declined. "But I'll take you up on the bet anyway. If the Dutchman wins, you get to drive the bays home."

"And if the Oak loses?" Brennan asked suspiciously.

"Then you go to Almacks like Mother's good little boy and do the pretty."

Bren looked at the sleek pair in front of him, then at the mighty boxer in the ring. He couldn't lose. "Done."

It was the contender's turn to enter the ring. The mob hooted and whistled. Lord Mayne focused his glass on the young blond giant and nodded his satisfaction. She hadn't said identical twin, but the challenger could have been Willy of the glass jaw—and the strong right. Wally handed his coat to his second, the butter-stamp Willy, and the audience took on a new frenzy. There was not an ounce of fat on Walter Minch, just taut muscle. In addition, he and his twin were right handsome English lads, not foreigners. Bets were changed, notes passed across carriages.

"How are you at the quadrille?" Forrest laughed at his brother's look of dismay, then turned his glass back to where

Willy and the waterboy were arranging towels and buckets and—

The smile faded from the viscount's lips, to be replaced by the most colorful string of curses heard outside a navy brigantine. Brennan would have been impressed if he didn't fear for his brother.

"Are you hurt? Did someone toss something at the bays? Should I send for a doctor, Forry? Do you want to go home? Do you want to change your bet?"

"Shut up, you rattlepate, you're drawing attention. And if you ever call me Forry again, I'll use your guts for garters."

Attention? Bren looked around. Everyone else was watching the referee giving instructions. Brennan didn't know whether to fear for his brother's sanity or for his own life. The curses were lower now, more mumbled than spoken, and seemed to be mixed with smoke. Bren could pick out expressions like "sons of rutting sea serpents" and "flogging around the fleet."

Life with his parents having taught Bren much about the Mainwaring tempers, he thought he just might get down and visit with some friends from town. "A little closer view, don't you know?"

The viscount did not know about his brother's painful climb down from the high-perch phaeton, nor Bren's worried backward glance as he limped toward a rowdy pair of bucks in a racing curricle. He didn't pay any attention to the shouted rules of the match, and he did not notice when his looking glass slipped through numb fingers to the ground far below. All he noticed—and the image would be etched in his mind's eye forever, magnified or not—was the waterboy. A slight, scruffy lad he was, dressed in a loose smock and baggy britches tied up with rope. His face was dirty, as though someone had rubbed his nose in the mud, and a greasy woolen cap was pulled low over his curls. His bright coppery curls.

He was going to kill her. There was no question in Forrest's mind. He was going to take her pretty little neck in his two hands and wring it. After the bout. Then he'd deliver some home-brewed to Willy's glass jaw—he owed him that anyway—and he'd shatter whichever of Wally's bones the

Oak left in one piece. After the bout. To act before would not be prudent, and the viscount was always discreet. To smash his way through the crowds the way he wanted to with a raging Red Indian war cry, to tear the threesome limb from limb starting with the bogus waterboy, just might draw a tad of attention to Miss Sydney Lattimore. Murdering her was his fondest desire; protecting her reputation had to come first.

If one hint, one inkling of her presence here reached the tattle-mongers, she would not have to worry about dresses or dowries. She'd never be received anywhere in London and no man could think of offering for her. A woman in britches? Fast didn't begin to describe the names she would be called, and her precious sister would be tarred with the same brush.

And if Sydney didn't know what could happen if this horde of drunks found out she was a woman, then Wally and Willy should have known. They were supposed to protect her, weren't they? Hell, he only kissed her, and look what it got him. The twins couldn't be stupid enough to bring her unless they were sharing one brain between the two of them; he'd find out if he had to tear their skulls open.

Sydney must have twisted them around her thumb, Forrest decided, the same way she wheedled the loan out of him when he had no intention of giving it. Damn and blast, how could she have been so mutton-headed as to jeopardize her life and her entire future this way, and after giving her word, too?

That wasn't quite true, he conceded. She'd sworn only to stay away from the cents-per-centers, not boxing matches or congregations of castaways. The viscount cursed himself for not getting the little fool's promise to *pretend* to be a lady. Then he cursed himself for getting involved in the first place.

10

Riot and Rescue

Her whole life and future depended on this match, and Sydney could not watch it. While the viscount seethed about her presence there, chewing the inside of his mouth raw, not the least of his aggravation stemmed from the fact of Sydney's viewing men's bare chests. Blister it, the only bare chest she should ever see was his—her husband's, he meant. He need not have worried. For the most part her eyes were closed. When she had to open them to perform her duties, Sydney was still oblivious to everything but the screaming, shouting men, the fumes from pipes, cigars, and spilled ale, the appalling sound of fist meeting flesh. The blood.

"Let's go home," she whispered in Wally's ear after the first round. He gave her a big grin and pulled the cap down lower over her eyes. The bout went on.

The match was being fought under the new boxing rules with twenty-five timed rounds, short rests between, and judges to make the final ruling of victory or defeat. The old-style contests saw no break and no finish until only one man stood. The only decision was on the part of the loser, deciding when to stay down.

The innovations sought to make boxing less a gory contest of brute strength, more a test of skills and science. The new format appealed most to gentlemen like the viscount, who sparred himself and appreciated neat footwork and clever defense as well as carefully aimed blows. The nearer elements of the crowd, however, those on foot surrounding the canvas ring, had come to see mayhem committed. These bloodthirsty masses did not appreciate the finesse of a fencing match. They booed and hissed at each rest period and pressed closer to where Sydney stood, nearly paralyzed, along the ropes.

In the early rounds, the boxers were evenly matched. Wally had more cunning and quicker timing. He could dance out of danger, watching for openings and getting in some solid blows of his own. The Dutchman had the advantage in reach and devastating power behind even a glancing blow from those massive fists. Wally kept moving; the Oak kept missing. When the Dutchman connected, he did more damage. Wally's blows barely rocked the Oak, though he got in twice as many of them.

Wally collapsed in his corner at the rests while Willy and Sydney wiped his face and ladled out cool water and advice. The Oak just stood and glowered. The crowd loved him.

In the middle rounds, Wally took a blow that sent him to the canvas. He valiantly got back to his feet, blood streaming from his nose, and the crowd started cheering for him for putting on a good show. The odds shifted again, and more wagers were recorded in the betting books. Those who'd bet on Wally to go ten rounds were happily collecting. Sydney clutched her bucket.

Wally got in a solid right in the very next round, then a left before he danced out of range. He quickly ducked back in under a flailing windmill to land another one-two combination, and still a third, to the mob's joy, spilling the Oak's claret for him, too.

By the nineteenth round, both fighters were slowed with exhaustion. Wally had visible bruises on his face and body and a swollen gash over one eye that was restricting his vision. He was still game, despite Sydney's pleas that he not get up the next time he went down. The Oak was using the breaks to catch his own breath. He'd never had to go so long with a challenger, and his lack of conditioning was showing in the labored breathing. His worried seconds advised him to end the match soon.

The Hollander opened the twentieth round with a surprise roundhouse punch that caught Wally flat-footed. Now Wally's other eyebrow was cut open and blood poured down his face. There was a vehement disagreement in the corner when

Sydney tried to wrench the towel out of Willy's hands to throw it in the ring. The mob howled, to think they would be deprived of the bloodletting.

"What's going on, for pete's sake?" Bren asked, starting to climb back up to the phaeton's seat so he could see better. He was almost knocked to the ground by his brother's hurried descent.

"The waterboy's trying to stop the fight," Forrest shouted over the crowd's roar as he pushed and pummeled his way toward the ring.

"My God, they'll kill him," Bren called, automatically following in his brother's wake.

"No, they won't," Forrest said through gritted teeth. "That's my job."

The gong finally ended the round.

"Enough, Wally. I'm going to end the match."

"No, Missy," yelled Wally, and "You can't, Miss Sydney," bellowed Willy. At least the noise of the rabble masked her name.

"We have to, Wally! You can't see and you can hardly stand. You can't get out of his way, and that's slaughter! Give me the dratted towel!"

She reached for it, where Willy was using the cloth to staunch the blood. Wally was furious and adamant. "No!" he shouted, throwing his arms up.

Sydney should have listened to Wally the first time, for he certainly had strength left. Enough strength for one of those arms to catch Willy on his all too susceptible jaw. Willy collapsed at Sydney's feet like a house of cards.

Sydney was in a near panic, trying to decide what to do. Wally was half blind and his senses pain-dulled. Willy was out for the count. Crude voices were screaming at her and rough hands were reaching through the ropes. Heaven help us, she prayed.

Then strong arms grabbed her from behind and plucked her out of the ring. Sydney started to scream until she heard a gruff voice close to her ear say, "Stow it, Mischief."

74

She had never been so happy to see anyone in her life, and neither had the crowd. Mayne himself taking a part in a great contest was just about the icing on the cake. Their angry shouts turned into cheers. Sydney couldn't understand any of it, nor why her devout Christian prayers had been answered by a raging pagan war god breathing thunder, but she was content to let him take charge. She never doubted for a moment that Mr. Mayne was at home in Purgatory. She watched as he cleared Wally's vision with a few deft strokes and whispered some words of encouragement, like "I'll kill you myself if you don't get back out there." Wally grinned and met the bell. Barely taking his eyes off the fight, Mayne grabbed Sydney's bucket and tossed its contents over Willy.

Willy lifted his head, saw who was above him, mumbled, "Aw, gov, this ain't the time for revenge," and passed out again.

Mayne grabbed Sydney by the collar, giving her a good shake while he was at it, before thrusting the empty bucket into her hands. "Go fill it," he ordered. She ran.

A stupefied Bren reached the corner just as Willy opened his eyes again. "Uh, Forrest," Bren said, helping the twin to his feet, "mind if I ask a foolish question?"

"You've always done so before," his brother answered, his gaze fixed on the fighters. Wally was circling and dodging, wearing the Oak down even if he wasn't landing any blows.

"Uh, what are we doing here?"

"I thought that was obvious. We're watching a prizefight."

"But do you *know* these people?" he asked in disbelief.

"Thanks to you, dear brother, only thanks to you. Now you can repay the favor by taking my bays and getting the waterboy out of here. Send Todd back to me."

Now Brennan was even more convinced that his brother had brain fever. "The bays? That guttersnipe?"

Willy was more alert. He knew what he'd seen the last time this angry cove was near his mistress. "You can't take her! I won't let you carry Miss—" Thanks to Sydney, Lord Mayne knew just where to hit the footman to stop his protests.

The multitudes cheered. Now they had two mills to watch! Brennan just gaped.

As soon as Sydney returned with the full bucket, she found herself thrust against another chest. Mayne made the introductions. "This is my nodcock of a brother Brennan, and this," he said with a sneer, "is Sydney."

Brennan could tell, even through the strips still binding his ribs, that the waterboy didn't feel right. "But he's a—" he started to say.

Forrest grabbed his shoulder. "That's right," he ground out close to Brennan's ear, "she's a lady. Now get her the hell out of here before anyone else notices!"

A lady? Should he then try to hand this ragamuffin up to the carriage? Brennan stood indecisive by the phaeton.

"You'll give the whole thing away, you looby," Sydney hissed at him. "You wouldn't help a boy to mount, would you?" Once she had clambered up and Sydney realized how well she could see, she declared her intention of staying to watch.

Brennan sent Todd back to help the viscount and took up the reins, muttering about totty-headed females, if she thought *he* was going to cross his brother. Sydney poked him in the ribs.

"Ow." Then Bren had to concentrate on backing the bays out of the narrow spot, answering the shouts of the amazed neighboring spectators with information that the boy was a runaway and he was taking him off before they lost sight of him again. "Relative of of Mayne's tenants. The mother is frantic. M'brother's always watching out for his people, don't you know."

Sydney waited for Bren to complete the delicate maneuvering and reach the nearly deserted roadway before ripping up at him. "How dare you carry me off against my will when I should be helping my friends, and then tell your friends I'm a truant schoolboy or something?"

Bren's attention was fixed on the horses. "Well, I had to tell them something; it was the first thing I could think of, other than telling them Forrest was saving the bacon for a ramshackle miss. And I can't see where you were doing your friends much good. Better to leave things in Forrest's hands. It usually is."

Sydney had no answer. She sat quietly, worrying at her lower lip.

"You ain't going to cry, are you, brat?" he asked after giving her a quick look.

"Of course not, you nimwit." She sat up straighter. "You really are as unpleasant as your brother."

"Uh, just out of curiosity, none of my business, don't you know, but how exactly do you know m'brother?"

If he didn't know about the loan of his own blood money, Sydney wasn't going to tell him. "He did me a favor" was all she said.

Bren nodded, relieved. "That explains it, then. Best of good fellows, like I said." When she made a very unladylike snorting sound, he continued. "Made no sense otherwise. You're not in his usual style. Forrest don't go near debs, and you"—taking in her dirty face and stablehand's clothes, from the smell of her—"ain't some expensive high flyer."

Wouldn't he just be surprised at his brother's infamous offer to her, Sydney thought indignantly, not that she wanted to be considered a barque of frailty, of course. And as innocent as she might be, she could not imagine a thousand pounds being an inconsequential payment for a lady's favors. At least the rake put a high value on her charms, as opposed to the opinion of this paltry gamester. Sydney tilted her nose in the air and told him, "I'll have you know I wouldn't care to be your brother's usual anything, Mr. Mayne."

"Oh, I ain't Mayne. That's Forrest's title, not his name. I thought you knew." In fact Brennan could not imagine anyone not knowing. "I'm Mainwaring," he added.

"Then he wasn't lying and he really is a viscount? How sad."

Bren was confused enough. "I always thought being a viscount was a good thing. Not that I envied him, you know. Wouldn't want all those headaches."

Sydney meant it was sad that a noble family was so come down in the world that one son was a wastrel and the heir was reduced to earning a far from honorable living among low company. He must be successful at it, she considered, judging from the horses and fancy carriage. Unless he'd claimed them from some poor loan defaulter. That was even sadder.

"Hungry?" her companion asked, interrupting Sydney's contemplations.

"Famished. I couldn't eat breakfast, I was so nervous, and of course luncheon was out of the question."

Brennan nodded toward the basket at their feet; he still wasn't taking his eyes off the cattle for more than an instant. Sydney eagerly rummaged through the contents, coming up with some cold chicken, but no fork. She shrugged and picked up the drumstick in her hands. "Thank you," she said between bites, earning her a quick half smile.

It was a very pleasant smile, Sydney reflected, remarkably similar to his brother's. Appraising him over the chicken bones, she realized how alike the two really were. Brennan was not quite as handsome as Mr.—no, *Lord* Mayne. He would do very well, she thought, with a little more attention to his appearance than the simple Belcher necktie and loose-fitting coat he wore. Now that she had the leisure to think back, she recalled that Lord Mayne was dressed bang up to the nines, as Willy would have said. Most likely Brennan couldn't play the dandy because all of his money went to pay gaming debts. She was sorry that an otherwise nice young man should have such a fatal flaw as the gambling fever. Perhaps he only gambled to recoup the family fortune, the same way she did. Sydney smiled in understanding, and wiped her hands on her grimy breeches.

He grinned back. "I've surely never met another young lady like you."

"Of course not, if you only keep low company in gaming hells."

Brennan laughed outright. "I can see you know m'brother better than I thought."

Since he was in such a good mood, Sydney asked if she could drive. Bren almost dropped the reins and needed a few moments to bring the bays back under control. "Then again, maybe you don't know him at all. He'd kill me."

Nodding thoughtfully, Sydney agreed. "Yes, I did note he

had a violent nature. I can see where you would be afraid of him."

"Afraid? Of my own brother? You really are an addlepate. They're his cattle, by George. Uh, can you drive?"

"No," Sydney answered happily, "but I've always wanted to try."

On his brother's high-bred pair? Brennan groaned. "You'd better ask Forrest to teach you. Of course," he added lest she get her hopes up, "he's never let a woman take the ribbons yet that I know of." Then again, after Forrest's fantastical behavior today, who could tell?

11

Reunions and Reckonings

"*Let* me off here, you clunch. I don't want to be seen with you."

"Well, you ain't doing my consequence any good either, I'll have you know." Brennan sniffed disdainfully. "But I have my orders."

"And do you always obey your brother's dictates?" Sydney met him sneer for sneer.

"I do when I'm driving his horses!"

Whatever amity the two had found evaporated when they reached the environs of the city. Brennan's brother had told him to take the chit home, and home he would take her, not set her down like some loose fish halfway across town to make her own way back.

"Don't you think the neighbors might wonder at this fancy

rig outside my house and watch to see who is getting out? Let me off at the corner, at least, and I'll run around to the back."

"Now who's being the clunch? I can't just leave the horses standing to see you in, and I ain't leaving till I see you through the door myself. What kind of gentleman do you take me for?"

"None, if you must know. A gentleman would have let me stay at the mill. And a gentleman would not make nasty comments about my appearance, and a gentleman—"

Brennan thought he should do his brother a favor and drown the female while he had the chance, but he had his orders. He kept driving, keeping to side streets and back alleys, until he arrived at the mews behind Mainwaring House. He pulled up before reaching the stable block and told her to get down and wait there. He looked at her suspiciously, then said, "If you think Forrest was angry before, you cannot begin to imagine how he'll be when he gets to Park Lane and you ain't there. He did tell you he was coming, remember?"

Sydney remembered. She waited. She told herself it was only because she didn't know her way around London yet and she was afraid of getting lost.

Bren took the phaeton to the stables and put the bays into the hands of the head groom, who was flummoxed to see the rig and no master, no tiger. "They'll be along presently," was all Bren could think to say, practically running down the mews. "Carry on."

He bundled Sydney into a hackney—at least he didn't have to make any explanations to the driver, no matter how many curious looks they received—and they did not speak until the coach reached the corner near her home. Trying to act as nonchalant as they could considering that they looked like a pair of housebreakers casing the neighborhood, they finally reached Sydney's back door.

"I suppose I should thank you for seeing me home safely," she said, which sounded rag-mannered even to Sydney, so she grudgingly invited Bren in for refreshment. He was looking peaky after their convoluted journey. She guessed a night creature like Mr. Mainwaring would not take proper care of his health.

Brennan accepted, more out of hope of seeing the scene between his brother and this little hellcat than anything else. Knowing Forrest's opinion of the weaker sex, he thought it might be better than any Drury Lane farce. Because she set a plate of his favorite macaroons in front of him on the kitchen table while she put the tea kettle on, he felt generous. "You just might want to put your skirts on before m'brother gets here," he volunteered. "You do have skirts, don't you?"

"Heavens, you're right. Here," she said, thrusting an oven mitt at him as if he knew what to do with the thing.

"Uh, don't you have any servants, Miss Sydney?" he asked before she could fly away.

"By all that's holy, who did you think was boxing? Their mother is our housekeeper and she's waiting at the inn near Islington. Poor Mrs. Minch will be so worried. I should have gone to her."

"You should have *been* with her, you mean."

"And poor Wally," she went on, ignoring his remark. "Oh, how could I have left?"

"He'll be fine," Brennan reassured her. "Forrest wouldn't let him continue if he wasn't up to snuff. Knowledgeable, don't you know . . . I wonder how long before he gets back?"

Sydney disappeared with a hurried "You stay right here."

In keeping with the rest of the day, he didn't. When Sydney ran down the stairs, wearing her new jonquil muslin to give her confidence, she heard voices from the front parlor. "Oh, no," she murmured. "What else could go wrong?"

Between Wally getting walloped and a visit from the unpredictably tempered Lord Mayne to look forward to, plenty.

Sydney forced her feet to the parlor door, already knowing what she would see. Sure enough, there was Mr. Mainwaring laughing and chatting, telling the general how honored he was to meet such a great man, and about his hopes to join the army someday. Brennan didn't seem to mind that the general never answered, and Grandfather didn't seem to notice that the young gentleman's eyes never left Winifred. And there was Winnie, sitting demure and rosy-cheeked in the white dimity frock that made her look like an angel, golden curls trailing

81

artlessly down one shoulder. And she, the peagoose, was gazing back at the handsome scamp with that same look of wonder.

Sydney almost searched the little room for blind Cupid and his darts. No, she amended, love wasn't blind. It was stupid and mean. If that wasn't just what Sydney wanted to see, her beautiful sister throwing her cap over the windmill for a ne'er-do-well gamester, the brother of a rake and worse, who did not even have enough blunt to buy himself a commission. She had a vision of delicate Winnie following the drum as the wife of an enlisted man while he gambled away the pittance a private was paid.

Sydney was so upset at the idea, in fact, that when she reached across to take her tea from Winnie, she spilled the cup. On Mr. Mainwaring's legs. "Oh, I am *so* sorry you have to leave us now."

"You're home! Oh, Wally, I'm so happy to see you! Are you all right? Shall I send for a physician? Here's Willy, thank goodness. You don't look so bad. No, don't try to talk. Just give me a hug. And you too, Mrs. Minch. Don't cry, please don't. Wally's safe and Willy's safe and I'm home safe."

They were all in the little kitchen, with Sydney needing to touch each of her friends to reassure herself they were really there. Mrs. Minch was blubbering into the apron she quickly donned, meanwhile putting pots on the stove. Willy held a damp cloth to his jaw, but Wally kept bouncing around the room in boxer's stance.

"You should have seen him, Missy. Why, the big oaf couldn't get his hands up to save himself. Just stood there breathing so hard he nearly sucked up the canvas they put down. Never laid a glove on me after you left, he didn't."

"That's the nicest news I could ever have!" Sydney danced a circuit with him, then made him promise to go rest. "And you, too, Willy. Go find Griff to help you get cleaned up. He'll know what to do and can get the doctor if you need. And don't either of you worry about chores or anything. We'll talk tomorrow."

She gave Wally a final pat, embraced Willy, squeezed what

she could of Mrs. Minch's ample form—and walked into the viscount's open arms. She jumped as if she'd just hugged an octopus. "My lord."

"Miss Sydney." He nodded back, grinning. "May I have a moment of your time?"

"Of course, sir. I need to thank you for seeing my people home."

He waved that aside and pointedly stared around the kitchen. Willy was busy at the pump and Mrs. Minch bustled with dinner preparations. "Elsewhere."

"I'm sorry, my lord, but Grandfather is resting now and my sister has gone visiting." There, that should keep her from being alone with him. He was still smiling, but . . .

"I should be honored to meet your family—another time. For now, your own company will suffice."

"But, my lord, I have no other chaperone, and it would not be at all the thing for me to—"

"Flummery, my girl. You cannot claim propriety, not after this day's work. Now, come." He held out his arm and raised his eyebrow. Sydney remembered how he'd lifted her out of the boxing ring as if she weighed no more than a footstool. She didn't doubt he'd resort to such tactics again. Really, the man was a savage. She ignored his arm and led the way to the front parlor, the "company" room. On the way there, however, she decided that she did not need another lecture, especially from him. Especially when he was ruining all of her careful plans. Besides, Grandfather had always said the best defense was a good offense. She put her hands on her hips and turned to face him.

"Before you say one word, my lord, I should like to thank you, and then thank you to get out of my life. My grandfather is ill and he would be terribly upset to think that someone of your type was in the house, or that a wastrel was trifling with my sister. You should know better than to scrape up acquaintance with proper people."

The viscount was astounded. He'd been prepared to be gentle, firm but not overbearing. After all, he'd had the entire afternoon to put a check on his temper. She was only a green girl, he'd rationalized, perhaps she didn't know better. He would just explain the error of her ways, then go about his own business. Somehow his best intentions flew out the window whenever he was near her. Now, when she was looking as appetizing as a bonbon in a stylish yellow frock with a ribbon in her hair, when she didn't smell of attic or stable—now she was back to hurling idiotic insults. He took a deep breath.

"Miss Sydney, I am not a mushroom trying to climb the social ladder; I am not trifling with your sister. Indeed, I have never met the young lady and, if she is anything like you, only pray that I may never do so."

"Not you, you jobbernowl. That wastrel brother of yours was here setting out lures for Winnie, and I won't have it, I tell you! Just being seen with him will ruin her chances!"

"My *brother* could ruin her chances, miss, while it is permissible for you to dress up in boys' clothing? My presence in the house could upset your grandfather, but your presence at a mill couldn't? Do you know what could have happened to you out there today? Some of those men were so foxed, they were beyond manners or morals; some of them never had either to start. How would your ailing grandfather have felt when your raped and ravished body was brought home? You tell me what your precious sister would have done then, Miss High-and-Mighty, if she is too good to associate with a mere second son?"

So much for firm but gentle. Sydney was ashen, trembling. Forrest felt like the lowest blackguard on earth. He pushed her into a seat and found a decanter on a side table. He sniffed and then poured a tiny amount into one of the glasses. "Here," he offered, putting it into her hand. "I am sorry for speaking so harshly. It's just that I tend to get a little protective of those I feel responsible for. I was concerned for you, that's all."

Sydney stood to her full five feet three inches. Her voice was flat, nearly expressionless when she said, "Yes, I see. I'll go get you the money."

"Money? What does money have to do with anything?"

"The money I owe you. The thousand pounds. I'll just go get it from Willy and then I will not be in your debt and you need not feel responsible for me any longer. I was so excited when they first came home, I forgot all about the winnings."

The viscount poured more brandy into her glass, up to the brim this time, and held it out. "There are no winnings. The bout went five extra rounds and was declared a draw. No winner. No payoff."

Sydney took the glass and drank down the whole thing. Then she coughed and sputtered and turned an odd shade. Seasick green did not look attractive next to the jonquil gown. The viscount pounded her back and shouted at her to breathe, damn it.

"If you kill me," she gasped when she could, "then you'll never get your money back."

"Hang the money, Mischief, it might be worth it anyway." Then he smiled and touched her cheek as lightly as a butterfly's touch. "I'm sorry."

"But it's true, about the money? We didn't win anything?"

"Unless you were clever enough to bet on Wally by the round, or how long he would last."

"Of course not," she answered indignantly. "That would have been disloyal." Then she sighed. "At least we didn't lose any. I can pay you back that part of the sum now anyway."

"Dash it, Sydney, forget about the money. I know it's hard, but try for once to believe me: I am a viscount, not a moneylender."

She finally smiled, showing those dimples that flashed in his dreams. "And I am a lady, but here you've proof that I'm a shameless hoyden. So we are neither what we seem and we are both trying to fool the ton."

Gads, she still did not believe him! A man may as well talk to the wall as reason with a woman! "No matter what you think, I do not need the money."

She was still smiling. "Of course you do. Then you can wash your hands of me and my problems, and I can make sure neither you nor your brother come near us again." If her goosish sister found Brennan half as attractive as Sydney was finding the viscount, despite knowing his rakehell ways, Winifred was in deep trouble. These Mainwarings were disturbing creatures.

Forrest could feel the heat rising again. He didn't know about Bren, but he did not like being made to feel unwelcome somewhere he hadn't wanted to be in the first place! "Devil take it, will you leave my brother out of this!"

"Of course, if you promise to keep him away from Winnie."

"I'll do my damnedest to warn him away from this lunatic asylum, madam, but I shan't mandate my brother's social life. And let me tell you a few other home truths. I herewith do not care about your reputation. If you do not, why should I? Furthermore, I no longer consider you any kind of responsibility of mine, and I pity the poor man whose concern you do become. His best chance at sanity would be to beat you regularly. And finally, for the last time, I do not want the bloody money!"

Sydney refilled the glass and handed it to him. "You really should not get so excited, you know," she said sweetly. "I believe that's what brought on Grandfather's last seizure. And don't worry, I'll still be able to repay you by the end of the Season."

Forrest took a deep swallow. He should get up and leave, he really should. Better, he should hold that tapestry cushion over her pixie face. Instead he asked, "Just as an observer, mind, not that I intend to get involved, but how do you expect to come into funds? Are you planning another boxing match? Frankly, Mischief, I don't think you have the stomach to watch another, thank goodness."

"No, I won't let Wally take any more challenges. It was his idea, you know. He and Willy have ambitions of their own, to open up an inn if they can just earn enough for the down payment. They're not actually footmen."

"Really? I thought you embraced all your servants."

Even in her naiveté Sydney could recognize his lordship's sarcasm as jealousy. She giggled to think this rogue and rake was jealous of her, Sydney Lattimore, who hadn't even had a come-out Season in town. Then again, maybe she giggled because of the unaccustomed brandy. "Mrs. Minch was my mother's nanny," she explained. "She came to us as housekeeper after Mr. Minch died, so I have known the twins forever, almost like cousins. When I decided to come to London,

86

they wouldn't think of being left behind, so here we all are, trying to better ourselves. Now we'll have to try something else. But don't worry, I have another plan."

The viscount had another drink.

12

Beaux and Bonbons

*W*innie was a Toast. It was official, announced in the *on dit* columns. She was the darling of the *belle monde*. Her beauty was unsurpassed, according to the papers, her manners all that was pleasing. She was sweet and well-spoken, suitably if not grandly connected. The meager dowry was unfortunate, but no matter; she had the most famous footmen in London!

In a few days after the fight, when Willy and Wally were able to accompany the Lattimore sisters on their rounds, they were instantly recognized. What other set of twins was tall, blond, and battered? Aunt Harriet confirmed the fact to a few of her cronies, which meant that all of London knew within hours that the pretty Lattimore chit employed prizefighters as footmen. Instead of redounding to Winnie's discredit, however, as Lady Windham intended, the situation was deemed irregular but not improper by those at the highest ranks of the polite world, some of whose husbands had made a tidy bundle at the match. Winnie was an overnight sensation, especially when she blushingly declined any knowledge of the match.

"Oh, no," she told her admirers, a hint of moisture on her lashes like morning dewdrops. "I . . . I couldn't bear to think of anyone getting hurt, you know, so they did not tell me about it until the next day."

Such tender emotions could only raise her stock with the doyennes of society. Vouchers for Almacks were promised. Winnie's success was guaranteed.

Sydney still preferred walks in the park, making sure she was accompanied by Annemarie, to making those tedious morning visits. She still preferred to stay home with the general, reading and concocting plans, rather than wait endless hours outside another crush just to curtsy to her hostess, dance once or twice with some spotty clothhead Aunt Harriet dragged over to her, then wait another hour for the carriage.

Sydney's position was equivocal at best. She was not formally Out, she was not as beautiful as her sister, she did not have the extensive wardrobe that Winnie did—and she was terrified that she might do or say something to ruin Winnie's chances. So the ton saw her, when they saw her at all, as a shy, retiring sort of girl, content to stay at home.

These days, home was as crowded as the average rout.

Sporting gentlemen came, ostensibly to call on Winnie, but more likely to pass a few minutes with Willy or Wally when they opened the door and took the visitors' hats and gloves. These gents did not much care which twin greeted them—they could not tell the difference anyway—they just wanted to be the first to know if another bout was scheduled. A coin pressed into the footman's hand should guarantee inside knowledge, or a bit of boxing wisdom.

The Tulip set came to Park Lane, at first just to be seen where the fashion was. They came back when they realized what an adornment Miss Lattimore would be on their arms, her golden beauty surely a reflection of their good taste. They wrote odes to her eyebrows and filled the rooms with bouquets, tipping the footman to make sure their offering took precedence.

Military gentlemen arrived in droves to pay their respects to the general's granddaughters. Or to hear a recounting of the match.

The Minch brothers were going to make their down payment one way or another.

With such a wealth of easy pickings, the vultures soon came too: every mama with a marriageable daughter found her way to the Lattimores' teas. The mothers catalogued the gentlemen for future reference; the debs blushed and giggled over the least glimpse of Willy or Wally.

The Dowager Countess Windham was the worst harpy of the lot, in Sydney's estimation. Aunt Harriet made sure Trixie was on view in the Lattimores' parlor every afternoon, displaying the family wealth in gems and laces for all the eligibles, and just in case Lord Mayne came to call. Everyone knew of his extraordinary affiliation with the footmen at Islington; they were waiting to see if the elusive viscount expanded the association here in London.

How should she know? Winifred asked in confusion when pumped for information by Aunt Harriet. She never met the man. He was most likely just another eccentric they were better off not knowing, Sydney added, firmly believing her own words.

The viscount did not call, neither did his brother.

"I don't understand," Winnie fretted. "He said he would call the next day."

Sydney understood perfectly. She'd ordered the general's man Griffith, standing in for the footmen right after the fight, to deny Lord Mainwaring the house. By the time Wally and Willy were back tending the door, Sydney had turned her sister's mind against the good-looking makebait.

"He most likely heard about your tiny dowry. A man like that cannot afford a poor wife, so he wouldn't waste his time."

"Do . . . do you mean he's a fortune hunter?" Winnie clutched a tiny scrap of lace to her cheek. "I knew he was a second son, but . . ." Sarah Siddons could not have portrayed Virtue Distressed better.

"I have it on the best of authorities"—his own brother, though she wouldn't tell Winnie—"that his character is unsteady. I know for a fact that his closest associates are of low morals. And," she intoned, "there is gambling." As in leprosy. "Think of the hand-to-mouth existence his unfortunate wife would lead, after he went through all of her money, of course."

"Oh, the poor thing." Winnie wept. The next time Lord Brennan Mainwaring did call, he was cheerfully admitted by

Willy, who would have done anything for Lord Mayne or his younger brother. Winnie turned her back on him and let some fop in yellow Cossack trousers read a poem to her rosebud lips. Brennan left, and did not come back.

There was one other worry furrowing Winnie's brow, to Sydney's horror. "Stop that, you'll make wrinkles! Worrying is my job!"

"But Lord Scoville doesn't like all the attention we're getting, Sydney. He doesn't think it's proper."

"Oh, pooh, he just wants you all to himself. Besides, there will be something else to steal the public eye next week. Some debutante will run off with a junior officer, or some basket-scrambler will lose his fortune at the baize tables. As long as our names aren't mentioned in either instance," she warned, not so subtly, "Scoville will get over his pet."

"He thinks we should dismiss the twins."

"Why, that prosy, top-lofty bore. How dare he—that is, I'm sure he didn't realize we consider the Minches as family."

"Oh, yes, he did. He doesn't think that's proper either. 'Ladies should not become overfamiliar with the servants,' he says."

Sydney hoped the pompous windbag became overfamiliar with Willy's fist one day, but for now he was their best paddle to row them out of River Tick.

Everyone in London seemed to know the way to their door, including a past visitor to Little Dedham. Mrs. Ott was not actually an acquaintance, being more a relation to the vicar's wife's dead brother, who used to visit there. The girls must have been too young then, but Mrs. Ott recalled meeting the general once or twice. If the general recalled the rather plump woman in darkest crepe, he did not say.

Mrs. Ott was calling, she told Sydney, because Mrs. Vicar Asquith had written that her dear friends were coming to town, and could Bella help make them feel more at home. So there she was, bringing a plum cake, just like folks did in the country.

Sydney would have been suspicious of anyone trying to scrape up a connection like that, but Mrs. Ott did not seem to want anything more from the family than their friendship. She had no daughter to marry off, no son to introduce. She did not wish introductions or invitations, for she went out seldom, still being in mourning.

"Dear Lady Bedford keeps urging me to attend one of her dos, but I cannot enjoy myself knowing my dear Major Ott is no longer with me." Mrs. Ott had to stifle a sob in her handkerchief. "I am a poor army widow like your dear mama," she told Sydney with another sniffle for the departed. "That is, I ain't poor. My husband had other income than his regular pay." Paddy O'Toole certainly had.

So Sydney welcomed the quaint grieving widow even if she could not quite recall Mrs. Asquith's mention of a relation in London, and Mrs. Ott's speech was broader than she was used to. But those were country manners, she excused, and they were not altogether unwelcome after the starchy *grandes dames* of London. Besides, the plum cake was delicious.

"Oh, that's just a hobby of mine, don't you know. For when Mon-shure Pierre has his half days off. Here, try another piece, dearie, and why don't you call me Bella? I can tell we're going to be friends. You just call on me whenever you need anything."

"Do you like to read, Mrs. Ott?" Sydney asked. "The reason I inquire is that my sister is really not interested, and I should like to visit the lending libraries more. I wouldn't think of going by myself, but my sister often needs our abigail, and I hate to take the household staff away from their tasks. I thought that perhaps if you were ever going, that is, if you do not think I am too forward . . ."

"Not at all, dearie, not at all. Why, I said you could count on old Bella Bu—Ott for anything. And I love to read. Ain't that a coincidence? It's my favorite thing, right after cooking. Lawks-a-mercy, I haven't had a good read since I don't know when. Why don't we go right now? I have the carriage outside, with m'driver and footman."

"Oh, no, I couldn't impose," Sydney said, but she was glad to be refuted. She was delighted that this new colleague not only shared her interests but could quiet Aunt Harriet's carping about a chaperone. A respectable older widow with servants and all ought to satisfy the strictest notions of propriety. Even the outré Lord Mayne would be satisfied that her reputation was well protected.

The servants weren't quite what Sydney would have selected for a genteel household.

"Just ignore 'em," Bella advised as she saw Sydney pause at the doorstep. "I try to. You might say my husband left them to me. Their names are Chessman and Rand, but I call 'em Cheeseface and Rarebit. You can see why."

Chessman held the carriage door. Actually he hid behind the carriage door and Bella had to shout to him to close it once they were inside. He had a powdered wig and a lead-whitened face, and his livery had a large sash around his thin middle. (The undertaker reported that the dead footman had been caught in his master's bedroom.)

The coachman did have rabbity teeth hanging over his lower lip; otherwise he was bundled head to toe in coat, boots, cape, hat, and muffler. Sydney could not even tell what color hair the man had, and he was so small she wondered if he had the strength to manage the horses. Oh, well, she thought, they were going only a few blocks.

Actually, they were going to Bella's house in Chelsea. Since Sydney had not been condemned in the ton for her part in the prizefight—and the Ottos never knew how big her part was—and Lord Scoville seemed to be cooling off toward the sister, Bella'd had the knacky notion of kidnapping the chit. Everyone knew Mayne stood by her servants through the boxing match; he was certain to ransom the gel.

"I ain't going to hire no witness to drive the coach," Bella said, "so which of you is going to do it, the runt or the milksop?"

The milksop won, the runt drove . . . for the first time in fifteen years, and badly. In a few blocks of the lending library, Randy scraped the side of a standing carriage, ran over a small delivery wagon, and wrapped one of the wheels around a lamppost. Sydney suggested they get out and walk. There was nothing for it but to acquiesce, so Bella got down and informed the driver that she would take a hackney home, dear boy, not to worry. As soon as Sydney's back was turned, Bella buried her reticule about an inch deep in Randy's scalp.

"Coming, dear," she called, grabbing Chester's sleeve before he could shab off, now that the day's plan was abandoned. "And you better stick like glue, pudding-heart," she spat at him. "Someone's got to pick out my damn books."

The trip could not be counted a success by anyone, especially Bella Bumpers Ott. If Sydney thought her new friend a trifle odd, Bella's reading tastes confirmed the supposition. Sydney found Miss Austen's latest work and her favorite Scott ballads while Mrs. Ott checked out *A Gentleman's Guide to Rome* and *Statistical Configurations of Probabilities*. And Sydney would rather spend the rest of her days inside the house than put one foot inside the carriage again.

The next time Mrs. Ott called, with a poppy seed cake and an invitation to visit the Tower, Sydney refused, though she would dearly have liked to go. Winifred never wanted to accompany her; she feared the place would give her nightmares.

Trying to salve Mrs. Ott's feelings, for she could see the older woman was screwing her face up to cry, Sydney offered a box of chocolates, each piece wrapped in silver paper. "Please, ma'am, will you do me the favor of tasting one of these candies? I ask because you are such a fine cook; and I value your judgment. You see, this is an old recipe from Little Dedham. The church ladies make them for Twelfth Night. Perhaps you've had them before? No? How strange. Anyway, my housekeeper and her sons are thinking of going into the confectionery business, and I thought I would help them along by soliciting an expert opinion. Not that I intend to have anything to do with the sales, of course."

Of course. Sydney had the profit margin figured to the ha'penny, a list of every sweet shop in London and the outskirts, a plan to promote them through the ton, and a schedule whereby she and the Minches could produce enough bonbons and still see Winifred through the Season.

"Delicious," Mrs. Ott pronounced. "What's that in the center, eh? Blackberry cordial, you say? Clever, but I think it could use a drop more, maybe a smidgen of rum. Do you think your friends would accept my help? I love to putter in the kitchen, and I *do* like to see the lower orders improve themselves."

The next few days were busy ones, experimenting and tasting. Sydney fell into bed each night, more exhausted than she would have thought, but at least she no longer dreamed of blue eyes that raged like a wild sea and smiled like a placid lake.

The general's man, Griffith, was the designated sales force. The Minch brothers were too recognizable; no one must suspect the Lattimores were in trade. Griff brought free samples to some of the shops and chatted with the proprietors while they tasted. He, too, couldn't wait to reach his pallet.

Sworn to secrecy, Trixie took some home to Lady Windham, who declared she hadn't had such a good night's rest in years, and ordered a dozen boxes from her favorite tart shop to give to her friends.

In no time at all Sydney was up to her dimples in orders. Mrs. Ott mixed the rum-flavored chocolate. Willy and Wally poured the heavy vats into molds. Mrs. Minch filled the centers with the blackberry cordial syrup. Sydney and Trixie wrapped each piece in its silver twist. Winifred lettered signs to go with each package: CHURCHLADIES' CORDIAL COMFITS AND COMPOSERS. Griff delivered the boxes. Sydney did the books. She figured they would start to see a profit over the initial outlay for materials in a week or two.

The candies kept selling, the money kept coming in, and Bella kept pouring more and more laudanum into the vats.

13

The Marriage Mart

"*W*hat do you mean, I have to go to Almacks? The match was a draw, remember? All bets were off."

Forrest admired the high shine on his Hessians. "Didn't you drive my bays?"

"But, but, you asked me to!" Bren sputtered.

"And now I am asking you to go to Almacks. Think how happy the duchess will be. Furthermore, they are saying in the clubs that Miss Lattimore will be making her debut appearance there tonight. Surely that's incentive enough to suffer knee smalls for one evening."

Bren wore a long face. "She don't like me. She ain't even home most of the time, at least not to me. When she is, she's sighing over some drooling mooncalf and his mawky rhymes. I thought we were getting along fine at first."

"So I deduced," the viscount replied dryly, having been forced to sit through his brother's rhapsodies on Miss Lattimore's infinite charms. Bren had not *quite* drooled. "I see Miss Sydney's fine hand at work there. She wants better for her sister."

"I suppose you mean Scoville," Bren conceded disconsolately.

"Not just that. I, ah, may have mentioned to Miss Sydney your difficulties with those gambling debts." He held up his hand to still Bren's protests. "I didn't know I'd ever see her again, or that she'd take my ill-advised words so much to heart. I'm afraid Miss Sydney thinks you are a hardened gamester." Forrest wasn't about to tell his brother what she thought of himself!

"But it was only that one time! Well, maybe a time or two

before, but that coil wasn't my fault. I've hardly wagered since!"

"Try convincing Miss Sydney of that." Forrest's cynicism came from long experience.

"Well, she don't think much of you either."

"Miss Sydney's mind is particularly tenacious. She's a difficult female to reason with. In fact," he went on with a frown of reminiscence, "she's a difficult female altogether. Nevertheless, it is also her first time at Almacks, and I would appreciate your making her feel comfortable."

"She's more like to spill the punch bowl over my head. If you care so much, why don't you go do the pretty with the girl?"

Forrest grimaced. "Can you imagine what would happen if I had even one dance with her? The gossipmongers would have the banns read! That's why I haven't called in Park Lane myself."

"And I'm not quite the social lion, so it's fine to sacrifice me, right? Hang it, Forrest, the chit's got less sense than a carp. She's just as liable to tie her garters in public or wear the general's uniform."

"Or dance with the servants. That's why I want you to go and look after her."

Brennan considered his options, then nodded. "I bet she dances like an angel."

"Mischief? I mean Sydney?" Forrest briefly imagined the heaven of having her in his arms.

"No, Miss Winifred Lattimore. I'd be surprised if your scapegrace even knows how to dance. Well, I think I'll toddle over to Park Lane this morning and see if Miss Winifred will speak to me. If she'll give me a dance or two, I'll go. Otherwise, bro, you'll just have to face the music yourself. Literally."

The man Griffith turned Bren away at the door with a surly "The ladies are not at home this morning." Having come this long way, Bren decided to step around back to the kitchen—he knew the way well enough—and check on Wally and Willy.

The place looked like some mad scientist's laboratory. A

large order had come just this morning, of all days, when they needed to get ready for Almacks! The girls were so sleepy, Mrs. Minch insisted they all had to rest that afternoon so they would be at the top of their form for the big evening. Even Sydney was ordered to nap.

Sydney had not wanted to go, naturally, to face another evening of sitting in little gilt chairs along the wall, pretending she didn't care. The assembly also promised a gathering of society's most exacting hostesses. One foot wrong and a girl might as well join a nunnery. Sydney was so tired she couldn't possibly remember all the rules Aunt Harriet had been drumming into her head. For once Sydney and her aunt agreed on something: the fear that Sydney would land them all in the briars. Lady Windham decreed, however, that the Almacks patronesses would take Sydney's refusal as a personal affront.

"So you'll attend, girl. You'll sit still and keep your mouth shut. You'll wear white like every other debutante and you won't complain about the music or the refreshments or the partners found for you."

Now, that was an evening to look forward to! First Sydney had to rush them through this latest order, if they had enough boxes and Trixie didn't eat all the profits, claiming she was just checking to ensure consistent quality. Everyone else was working double time, and thank goodness for Mrs. Ott, who was keeping those vats of chocolate coming. One more batch and they could all—

"Oh, no, not you! Get out! Don't look!" Sydney shouted. Mrs. Minch tried to hide the molds with her wide body, and Winifred turned as white as the huge apron she wore. Trixie giggled.

"Too late, brat," Lord Mainwaring announced, stepping farther into the kitchen. "If you didn't want anyone to see, you should have kept the door closed. 'Sides, I didn't cry rope on you over the Islington fiasco, so you should know I'll keep mum. It looks like fun. Can I help?"

He was right, it was too late. Winifred was already offering him a candy and showing him her neatly lettered signs.

"Perfection!" he declared, and everyone but Sydney cheered. She wasn't sure if he meant the bonbon or Winnie.

"And if they are good for the nerves," he went on, "I'll send some home to my mother, who could certainly use a composer. She'll tell her friends and you'll have a whole new market." Then he happily took his place next to Trixie, wrapping the candies in their silver paper.

Trixie licked her fingers and giggled again. She was giddy with Mrs. Ott's whispered suggestion that she take some boxes into Almacks, where the food was so scarce; she was thrilled to be doing something her mother would hate; she was in alt at sitting beside Lord Mainwaring. She was drunk.

Almacks was supposed to be dull, but this was absurd! Everyone sat around yawning. Aunt Harriet was dozing in a corner with some of her friends, leaving her daughter Sophy, Lady Royce, to watch out for the younger ladies. Sophy had long decided that her status as a young matron entitled her to a degree of license unknown while she was under her mama's thumb. She further considered her freedoms doubled since her husband was abroad with the Foreign Office. Tonight she was more concerned with disappearing to the balcony with hard-eyed older gentlemen than in finding partners for her sister Beatrix or her cousin Sydney. Winifred's card, as a matter of course, was filled within minutes of their entry to the hallowed rooms on King Street.

Lady Royce was too busy pursuing her latest dalliance to stop Trixie from accepting a waltz without permission from one of the patronesses, but no matter. The lady patronesses were just as logy and disinterested in platter-faced chits as Aunt Harriet. Her good friend Lady Drummond-Burrell was actually snoring. Without the doyennes and dowagers pushing them to their duty, the younger men formed groups of their own on the sidelines or in the refreshments room, discussing the latest curricle race to Bath.

So Sydney sat in her white dress until Winnie brought over one or another of her surplus coxcombs, or some young buck took the chance she might know something about boxing. Sydney fervently declared it the most barbaric sport imaginable, which ended those conversations fairly quickly.

Now that her dragon of a mama wasn't guarding her, every

gentleman with pockets to let asked Trixie to dance. She went off gaily, more often to the refreshments room than to the dance floor, leaving Sydney alone and uncomfortable. By the time the doors closed at eleven o'clock, though, Trixie hardly knew her name, much less the figures of the quadrille. Proper manners forced the fortune hunters to ask Sydney to dance in default, to no one's benefit or pleasure.

Trixie's doughy complexion was taking on a grayish cast, and she kept trying to rest her head on Sydney's shoulder. Embarrassed and concerned, Sydney tried to catch Sophy's eye. They may as well go home anyway, for all the notice Lady Jersey, et al., were taking of them. Contrarily, Lady Royce was finding the place unusually stimulating. She sent one of her cicisbei off to fetch a restorative lemonade for Trixie and chided Sydney for not being more accommodating.

"Why, you were positively snappish to Lord Dunne, and he's worth ten thousand a year."

"Not to me, he's not," Sydney replied, "not when he keeps squeezing my hand in that oily way of his. And I truly do have the headache, Sophy. Can't we go— Good heavens, what's he doing here?"

All eyes—all that were open anyway—were turned to the door. Standing framed by candlelight in the hush between dances was Lord Mayne, magnificent in black and white evening formals. The only dash of color from his curly black hair to his shiny black pumps was a blue sapphire in his perfect cravat. His blue eyes would be gleaming to match, Sydney knew, though she could not see from so far away.

He looked like a true nonesuch, but she knew better. Sydney's opinion of this supposedly exclusive club fell another notch. "You mean they let in people like him?" she asked in disgust.

Trixie drawled back, "La, you silly cabbage, Almacks *exists* for people like him."

She was right. All the languorous mamas pushed their daughters forward; the torpid patronesses bestirred themselves to have their hands kissed; matrons like Sophy, not the least bit sleepy, tugged down the necklines of their gowns and licked their lips.

Sheep, Sydney thought, they were all sheep. The ninny-hammers thought that since he had a title and a pleasant face—all right, a heart-stoppingly handsome face—then he must be worth knowing. Hah! You could dress your cat up in a lace bib and sit him at the table; he would still put his face in the food. Just look at Lord Mayne smiling at those boring old dowagers, when she knew what little patience the foul-tempered peer had. Look at him making his bows to several giggly young chits, when she knew the rake could send them fleeing to their mothers' skirts with an improper suggestion. And look at him kissing Cousin Sophy's hand! Why, that—

"Lady Royce, how charmingly you look tonight. No, I should say how particularly lovely, for you are always in looks." Sophy tapped his arm with her fan and pushed her chest out. If she took another deep breath, Sydney seethed, Almacks would truly be enlivened. Then he turned to Sydney and bowed. She gritted her teeth and curtsied, almost low enough for royalty, just out of spite. She could behave like a lady, so there.

Sophy's fan hit the floor. "You mean you actually know the chit? I mean, the gossip and rumors and all, but I never dreamed . . . Why, Sydney, you sly thing."

Lord Mayne smoothly interrupted: "We've never been formally introduced, actually. I was hoping you could do the honors. You see," he went on, not exactly lying, "my mother asked me to look up the daughters of an old friend of hers." Sydney noted that the silver-tongued devil did not mention what old friend.

Sophy performed her part before reluctantly leaving on the arm of her next partner. A fine chaperone she was, Sydney stewed, leaving an unfledged deb alone with a shifty character who was grinning at her discomfort, blast him. And everyone else was staring! She tried to kick Trixie into escort duty, but the caperwit actually winked at the viscount before putting her head down on Sydney's seat. He raised an eyebrow.

"She was, ah, tired out from all the dancing."

Forrest raised his quizzing glass and surveyed the room in what Sydney considered a horribly foppish manner. "There seems to be a great deal of that going around."

"I always understood Almacks to be quite staid. I can't imagine what would bring a man like you here."

"Can't you, Mischief?" he asked with that lopsided smile. Sydney looked around to make sure no one heard him. "I came to dance with your sister."

For a moment she felt her heart sink to her slippers, then outrage took over. "Well, I wish you wouldn't. You'll ruin everything! I imagine one dance with you would label her fast. Lord Scoville would have a kittenfit if he saw her in such company."

"Is that really what you think, Mischief?" He flipped open a cloisonné box and took a pinch of snuff, one-handedly.

No, she really thought Winifred would fall in love with the rake and follow his blandishments right down the garden path! Out loud she said, "Don't call me that," forcing herself not to stamp her foot. "And you need not persist in these dandified affectations for my sake. You might humbug the ton, but I know you for what you are, and I do not want you near my sister."

"I am continually amazed at what you know and what you don't. Nevertheless, my dear, I am going to have the next dance with her. My brother was promised a set with Miss Lattimore, but fell too ill to attend. He was devastated that she might take umbrage at his defection, so I gave my word to deliver his regrets. I always keep my word. Like now, I'll promise not to eat the gel if you'll stop scowling for all the *haute monde* to see. After all, I do have *my* reputation to consider."

Sydney smiled, although she was even more worried for Winnie if he was going to be charming. "I hope nothing serious ails Lord Mainwaring. He seemed fine this morning."

Lord Mayne was watching the dancers, a slight frown on his face. "No, something about overindulging in a box of candies he purchased for our mother. Some new chocolates that were all the crack, he said, and my other mission was to have another box sent on to Sussex for the duchess."

"Did he, ah, say anything else about them? Where he got them, perhaps?" Sydney bit her lip.

"No, but most confectioners seem to carry them suddenly. I

even thought I recognized a box or two in the refreshments room here, if you'd like to try one."

"No, I, ah, have a few in my reticule, as a matter of fact. I was told they served only stale cake, you see." Sydney looked at Trixie slumped in her chair, snoring. Aunt Harriet and her friends were in no better frame, the ones who hadn't already left on the arms of their footmen. Sophy was now doing the stately Galliard as if it were a galop. And she herself had the headache. "Did you say Lord Mainwaring got sick from them?"

"I can't be sure. He couldn't wake up enough to describe the symptoms. I had to leave him in the hands of my father's valet before they closed the doors here. Perhaps I'll taste one of these new sensations after my dance with your sister."

"Please do. I'd like to hear your opinion." Her headache was getting worse every second.

14

Waltzes and Woes

"We talked about his mother," Sydney said for about the hundredth time. One would think the man some kind of oracle the way the other girls on the sidelines wanted to know his every word. "No, I was only introduced to him tonight and, yes, I do think Lord Mayne and Winifred make an attractive couple."

Lord Mayne and Sally Jersey also made an attractive couple, as did Lord Mayne and Lady Delverson, Lord Mayne and Lady Stanhope, Lord Mayne and Miss Beckwith. Sydney finally escaped to the ladies' withdrawing room, sick and tired of hearing the wretch's name on everyone's lips. Which reminded her that she was also sick and tired. The chocolates!

She hurried to the refreshments room, which was nearly deserted now. Sydney had no doubt everyone stayed in the dancing area to watch Lord Mayne. The gentlemen were wagering on his next partner or trying to figure out the new arrangement of his neckcloth. The ladies were hoping to be that next partner, or admiring his graceful leg. Prinny himself wouldn't have drawn more attention from the gudgeons. Sydney had more important matters to consider.

Drat Trixie! She said she was taking some boxes to her mother in lieu of stopping at a sweetshop for them, but here they were. Sydney counted three empty boxes and another half filled, hidden behind a fern. She stuffed candies into her reticule until it looked as if she had a small cannonball in it, then dug around in the fern, burying the rest. That's where he found her.

He looked at her dirty glove through his quizzing glass and muttered something suspiciously like, "I knew I shouldn't have taken my eyes off you for a minute." Sydney blushed and felt her face grow even hotter when he asked, "You do not dance, *petite?*"

She was not about to admit that no one asked her. Then the strains of the next number started and she could thankfully claim, "It's a waltz, my lord. I have not been given permission."

"Then perhaps you'll take a turn about the room with me," he offered, placing her hand in the crook of his elbow.

Sydney couldn't refuse without making a scene, for a flock of gawkers had followed him to the refreshments room. She could see tongues wagging everywhere. She wanted to ask him why he was doing this thing, making a byword of her, but there were too many interruptions. Gentlemen kept shaking his hand, telling him how glad they were to see him in town and inviting him for dinner, cards, morning rides. Ladies of all ages nodded and smiled and batted their eyelashes at him, while the prominent hostesses begged him to attend their next affairs. Or *affaires*, Sydney thought maliciously. Finally she blurted out, "They like you."

He stopped walking and looked around. "I never thought about it in those terms. I have known many of these people my entire life and value their respect. I hold some in affection, and believe my regard is returned. I don't see a single soul here whom I have wronged, so yes, I suppose you could say they like me."

"But, but why? I mean, how could they when you—"

He laughed. "Ah, Mischief, your candor delights me. Much more so than your buffle-headed reasoning." He patted her arm on his and started walking again. "They like me," he told her, "because I really am a fine fellow. Honest, polite, helpful, even-tempered." He lightly tapped her fingers with his quizzing glass when she started to giggle. "I know everybody and treat them equally, no matter rank or fortune; I try not to abuse the privileges my title and wealth give me."

Sydney was giggling even harder. "O ye of little faith," he chided, mock-frowning at the gamin grin she gave him. "You doubt my power? What if I said I could bring you into fashion with just one dance?"

Sydney laughed. "Gammon, my lord, no one could do that."

"Just watch, and keep smiling."

He was gone a few moments, only till the end of the set. When the music next began, he returned, bowed, and held his arms out to her, his blue eyes dancing with deviltry.

Sydney looked around uncertainly. It seemed all eyes in the place were on her. "But . . ."

"Chin up, little one. Didn't your grandfather tell you that good soldiers never back down under fire?"

"But it's a waltz." She looked over to where the patronesses stood, the ones who were lively enough to stand. Lady Jersey nodded and waved her hand.

"Sally likes me," was his simple comment.

"But they just played a waltz."

"The orchestra likes me." He dropped his hands. "You do know how to waltz, don't you?"

She nodded. "I practiced with the twins."

He laughed that Brennan was right: Mischief did dance

with the servants. Then he swept her onto the floor the way no cousinly footman ever had.

Sydney's head was spinning. It must be the headache coming back, she decided, but she no longer felt the least bit tired. Her feet were as light as soap bubbles, and her hand where he clasped it tingled as if from cold. But she wasn't cold, not at all. He smiled down at her and she could only gaze back, her eyes drawn to his like magnets, and she smiled. Her heart was beating in waltz tempo and her thoughts were swirling like clouds in a kaleidoscope. Heavens, what had they put in those chocolates?

She realized the dance was over when Lord Mayne raised her hand and, turning it over, kissed her wrist. Of course, she thought, her fingers were dirty. He winked and said, "Now watch."

One gentleman after another asked to put his name on her dance card. They tripped over each other to fetch her lemonade. And these were not callow youths who were busy digging in all the ferns, at any rate. They were Mayne's friends and contemporaries, men of means and influence and taste—just like him, she was forced to concede. These gentlemen spoke of books and politics and her grandfather's renowned career. They were interesting and interested in her, and did not seem to mind when she gave her own opinions about anything and everything. She felt more alive than she had in days.

Sydney tried to rouse Trixie between sets, but her cousin only stirred enough to visit the room set aside for the ladies, where she had earlier stashed the other three boxes of Church-ladies' Cordial Comfits. Sydney was too busy enjoying her new popularity to notice Trixie passing the treats around to her girlfriends and bringing a box over to her mother. Lady Windham was staring confusedly in Sydney's direction, wondering if her two nieces had changed identities.

A few dances later, *he* was back, piercing Sydney's euphoria with a dagger look. "It is time to go home, Miss Sydney" was all he said through his clenched jaw. He took her arm, none too gently, when she protested that it was early yet and she was having the best time ever, thanks to him. "There will be other balls," he ground out, then added, "with any luck."

Lord Mayne stuffed Lady Windham and her daughters into their carriage. Trixie offered him a chocolate while Lady Windham and Sophy tittered over his well-filled stockings. He tossed the candy to the ground in disgust and ordered the driver to move on.

Sydney was content that she and Winnie were to travel in Lord Mayne's more elegant coach, until he followed them into the carriage. She supposed he was going to spoil everything now with his thundercloud expression, just to prove he could do that, too. She stared out the window, not talking.

Winifred was used to her sister's sitting mum-chance in company and knew it was her responsibility to fill the silence with polite conversation. She tried. "Did I thank you for the dance, my lord?"

"Twice."

"Ah, did I ask you to send my sympathy to Lord Mainwaring?"

"At least that many times."

"And to thank your mother for her interest?"

"Yes."

"Then could you stop the carriage, my lord?" she asked in that same sweet tone. "I think I am going to be sick."

"Whatever made you cockleheads think you could cook, much less measure?" Lord Mayne was shouting. Sydney sat at the kitchen table, miserably huddled over her third cup of black coffee. Forrest was waiting with the fourth, and she didn't even like coffee. Winifred was suffering in the hands of their abigail, but Sydney was not going to be permitted such an easy death.

"You are the most blithering idiot it's ever been my misfortune to meet." His lordship was in full spate. "It wasn't enough for you to threaten your whole family with scandal by going into trade, not you! You had to try to poison the whole ton! And at Almacks of all places!"

Sydney did not blame Trixie for that particular lunacy; she

106

knew the girl was jingle-brained and should have watched her. It was all her fault. She just sat, feeling more blue-deviled.

Wally tried to exonerate them. "We didn't set out to poison anyone. It must have been a bad batch."

"And I suppose you didn't sample every one?" He could tell by the guilty looks and mottled complexions that they had. He poured the twins more coffee. "Damn if you two haven't taken too many punches to the head! And you, miss, should have been left out at birth for the wolves."

"I was," she sniffed through gathering tears. "The wolves threw me back." Then she was crying in earnest. "Do you think . . . that is, will they send me to jail?"

Forrest cursed and handed her his handkerchief. "Coventry maybe, brat, not jail. Who exactly knows that you were responsible?"

"Everyone in the house except Grandfather and—"

Willy shook his head. "The general enjoyed the bonbons so well, I told him we made 'em. He won't talk."

"—And Annemarie."

Wally shook *his* head. "She kept smelling the chocolate, so I showed her the molds. But she's sweet on me. She won't peach on us."

Forrest was tearing his hands through his hair. "Who else?"

"Trixie, but she can't say anything. She's the one who brought them to Almacks. And even if she tells her mama, Aunt Harriet cannot tell, for she handed them around to all her friends."

"Anyone else?"

Sydney started to weep again. Through the folds of the viscount's handkerchief she whimpered, "An old friend from home . . . and your brother was here this morning, helping."

There was a moment of silence. Sydney began to think she might live through the night. Then she had to grab for the coffee cup as his fist came down on the table, rattling the china. "Well, I told you to keep him away," Sydney cried into the cloth.

"To protect your sister's reputation, fiend seize it, not his! You didn't warn me you'd involve him in your hen-witted schemes, or try to kill him with your concoctions! I should have shipped him to the front lines. He'd be safer."

"I'm sorry," she said, "and you can be sure that I won't mention his name if they bring me in front of the assizes. And I promise not to tell them that you lent me the money to start the business."

"Hell and damnation!" Then he took a look at Sydney, so woebegone, so wretched, her hazel eyes swimming in tears, and his anger melted. "Don't worry, Mischief, I'll try to fix it."

She brightened immediately. "Oh, can you? I'll be in your debt forever. How silly, I'm already in your debt. But what shall you do?"

The viscount sighed and got up to leave. "Forget about the damned money, Mischief, and go to bed."

She followed him to the door. "But maybe I can help."

"That's the last thing I need," he teased, just to see her dimples. Then he wiped a tear away from her cheek with his finger. "I'll see you in the morning. Wear that pretty yellow dress."

Embarrassed, she twitched at the folds of her white lace gown. "I know it's not becoming on me, but Aunt Harriet said I had to wear white."

"And you always follow Aunt Harriet's rules?"

She chuckled and answered, "Only when I am playing her game."

There was nothing Forrest could do that night, beyond shooting his own brother, that is. And he was too restless for bed, disturbed more than he ever wanted to be by Sydney's unhappiness. Her eyes should never be dimmed with woe; they should have stars in them, as they had when she looked up at him during the waltz. Her mouth was never meant for drooping sorrow; those full lips were meant for laughing, or kissing. And her body—

He went to visit his current mistress.

Forrest did not own the little house in Kensington, but he was presently paying the rent, so he let himself in despite the near darkness of the place. Lighting a candle, he found his way to Ava's bedchamber. There she lay, fast asleep, propped up on a mound of frothy pillows. Her filmy negligee was open invitingly, but her mouth was open too, trailing a thread of drool and issuing raspy snores. An open box of bonbons, each wrapped in silver paper, rested by her side.

The viscount shrugged. He wasn't in the mood anyway. He wrote a check and left it on the dresser. She would find it in the morning and know he wasn't coming back. Forrest left, feeling relieved, and not just because she hadn't fallen asleep while he was making love to her.

15

Double Trouble

*M*orning came too early. Sydney groaned and went back to bed. Minutes later, it seemed, Annemarie was shaking her awake. Certain the authorities must have come for her, Sydney hid under the bedclothes. "No, I won't go!"

"But, mademoiselle, the handsome *vicomte* waits downstairs."

"That's even worse." Sydney burrowed deeper.

Forrest had been up before daybreak, buying all the unsold boxes of comfits in the stores. He made sure the shopkeepers believed the supply was for a personage of the highest rank. This unidentified gentleman with the large sweet tooth was also hiring the confection's creator, so there would be no more of the candies forthcoming. And no diplomatic way of complaining about their ingredients.

He drove the carriageload of boxes to the naval hospital, where a doctor friend of his gladly accepted the donation. A heavy hand with rum and laudanum would not come amiss there.

Then Forrest went to the park, greeted several friends, and listened to gossip of foxed females at the bastion of propriety, Almacks. He even added a rumor of his own, wondering if some young blades had poured Blue Ruin into the punch bowl. If the Lattimores' names were mentioned at all, it was with a partial compliment, such as "Lovely girls, aren't they?" Such hesitancy he correctly interpreted as an inquiry to his own interest in the sisters. He carefully showed very little. "Quite charming if you like sweet schoolroom misses. Connection of my mother's, don't you know?"

He repeated his taradiddles in the clubs, convincing everyone that his relationship was the most casual, so the Lattimores were fair game. Of course the girls were not to be trifled with, it was understood, without incurring the Duchess of Mayne's disfavor, which indubitably meant facing the viscount.

Satisfied with the morning's work and wondering if he had ever told so many lies before, his lordship went to Park Lane. Sydney was anything but a sweet schoolgirl, and he almost regretted bringing her to the attention of the more observant members of the ton. But how could anyone have swallowed that Banbury tale? he wondered. Forrest thought of Mischief as a freckled moppet in red-gold pigtails doing her sums on a slate, and chuckled. She was most likely figuring percentage points from the cradle! She didn't even have a schoolgirl's shape, but he had lost enough sleep thinking of her rounded figure in his arms. Ah, well, he told himself, her feet were firmly planted in the marriage market now, and it was better that way. He could go home to Sussex with a clear conscience as soon as he delivered his messages.

"The young ladies are still abed," Willy—or Wally—told him.

"Get her" was all Forrest said. He didn't have to specify which sister he wished to see, nor that he dashed well would go fetch her himself if he had to.

Forrest chatted with the general about the war news while he waited. This was more satisfying than such conversations tended to be with his own father, who threw newspapers around whenever anyone disagreed with him. The general merely pounded his armchair a few times.

Then Sydney arrived, dressed in a peach-colored round gown that highlighted the warm tones of her skin. He wasn't surprised that she didn't wear the yellow gown, in defiance of his wishes, nor that she sat on the stool near her grandfather's feet, as if for protection. He wasn't even surprised at how heavy-eyed and tousled she looked, only at his body's reaction to seeing her like a woman who had just been made love to. A schoolgirl, hah!

Griffith came and wheeled the general away, over Sydney's protests. Forrest smiled and jingled some coins in his pocket. Griff liked him, too.

"I'm sorry I cannot stay and visit with you, my lord, but I have to see Mrs. Minch about the day's menus."

"I'm sure whatever she selects will be fine, as long as you don't have a hand in the cooking. Don't you want to hear how your adventure turned out?"

"I already know; I haven't been arrested yet." She waved her hand around at the flowers on the buhl table, on the mantel, in the hall. "Some of them are even for me, according to Annemarie, so we're not even to be ostracized. And no, I do not want another lecture. Please."

"Poor poppet, does your head still ache? I'll keep you only a moment, so you'll know what stories are being told. The servants' grapevine has a lot of headaches like yours but nothing worse among the ladies, who are swearing off sweets. The Almacks hostesses are investigating the punch bowls for signs of tampering. The shopkeepers consider the candies a national treasure, and the Lattimore sisters are a great success. Oh, and the Churchladies' Confectioners are out of business."

"We are? A success, I mean. I know we're out of business. I would never use that recipe again, you can be sure. I can close the books as soon as I collect on the last deliveries."

The viscount idly swung the tassels on his Hessians. "The books are closed. I packed up all the inventory, vats, molds, and supplies, and I bought all remaining stock at the stores. As I said, you are out of business."

Sydney was too drained to grow irate. Anger never seemed to get her anywhere with him anyway. "But that was my business. You had no right."

"No? I seem to recall a certain gift that I wished to give you. You kept insisting it was a loan, remember? In effect I bought the Churchladies' business from you in exchange for the debt. Now we are even."

Sydney's brows were furrowed as she thought about that. Either her brain was still drugged or his reasoning was as suspect as his character. "That doesn't make sense. I started the business with your money. Then you ended the business and saved my neck, with your money. The way I see it, I not only owe you my gratitude, I owe you twice as much money!"

"Dash it, Sydney, you can't still believe I make my living by collecting a pound of flesh!"

"Well, no," she conceded, "but you were there, and you did give me the gold."

"And I should have told you right away. All right. My brother was cheated and I went to retrieve his vouchers from the dastards. The thousand pounds I gave you was the payment for his misbegotten debt."

Sydney jumped up. "Then I owe the real moneylenders the money?" she squeaked. "And they are charging me interest while you sit here and blather on about punch bowls and patronesses?"

He stood too, and brushed a wayward curl off her forehead. "I don't blather, Mischief, and no, you don't have to worry about the Ottos. They are out of business, also. Out of the country, if they know what's good for them. So will you forget about the money once and for all?"

Sydney wished she could. Oh, how she would like to be unbeholden, especially to this man who kept her in such a flutter. But, "I cannot," she said. "I borrowed it in good faith, and swore to repay it on my honor. If I do not, then I shall have no honor. But don't worry," she told him in a brighter tone, "the Season is not yet over."

"And you have a plan. Now, where have I heard that before? But, sweetheart, a few more such schemes and you will owe me your soul." She was still looking soft and dreamy, so he couldn't help adding, "Just how much is your virtue worth?"

Her mouth opened to give him the setdown he deserved—so he kissed her.

Sydney was lost, and never more at home. Her toes curled in her slippers, and her hands reached up to touch his face, to feel his skin. Every church bell that ever rang in every steeple was chiming in her heart—or were those fire alarms clanging in her fuddled mind? What was she doing, enjoying herself in this shameful manner? Winifred still needed to make a good marriage, and Lord Scoville would be horrified. Heavens, Sydney thought, *she* would be horrified! She bit down hard where the tip of his tongue happened to be playing on her lips. He jumped back, cursing, and waited for the slap.

It never came. Sydney felt as much to fault because she hadn't pushed him away before, though she sensed he would have released her at the first hint of reluctance. She had stayed, sharing the kiss and thrilling to his nearness. She was disappointed in herself, and in him.

"You may not be a moneylender, but you are not a gentleman. I was right, wasn't I? You're still a rake."

The viscount was trying to rid his mouth of the taste of blood and his blood of the taste of her mouth. That's how well he was thinking. "I am not a rake," he declared firmly, then surprised himself by amending, "except where you are concerned."

"Why?"

"Why except for you? Because I am not interested in marriage but, God help me, I am interested in you. And why you? The devil only knows. You're the most wayward, troublesome female I've ever known. You're too young, too impetuous, too independent. And I can't seem to keep my hands off you."

That could almost be a compliment. Sydney grinned. "I think you are nice too, sometimes."

He lightly kissed the top of her nose and then smiled. "Didn't I tell you everyone likes me? At any rate, I have business in Sussex, so I'll be out of your hair for a while. Before I go, though, I want you to make me a promise." He was beginning to recognize her stubborn look, so he addressed her as he would a seaman contemplating mutiny: "By your own say-so, miss, you are in my debt. Therefore *I* name the terms, *I* call the play. You will promise to stay out of trouble, period. Nothing illegal, dangerous, or scandalous. Is that understood?"

Sydney was tempted to salute and say "Aye, aye," but she did not think he would be amused. She also did not think he would understand that she mightn't be able to keep such an oath. She compromised with the truth: "My next idea is none of those."

He was two blocks away before he realized she hadn't promised at all.

Aunt Harriet bustled over the next morning, top o'er trees at her nieces' success. "Lord Mayne, my dears. Just think!" Sydney did, and thought how shallow the *beau monde* was, that it could admire such a man. If they only knew what a libertine he was! Then again, if they only knew what a wanton *she* was, for welcoming the liberties he took, she'd be back in Little Dedham before the cat could lick its ear.

Lady Windham, however, deemed his lordship worth her paying the Lattimores' admission to Vauxhall, in case he was there. Naturally Sydney did not inform her aunt that the viscount was in the country; she wanted to see the fireworks. Unhappily Lord Mainwaring had stayed in town and Lady Windham invited him to make up one of the company in their box.

"I wish you would not encourage him to dangle after Winifred, Aunt Harriet," she said. "I do not believe he is at all the thing. He may even run away to join the army or something."

"Nonsense, his mother would never allow it. If he does put on a uniform, I'm sure she'll see it's a general's." Furthermore, Lord Scoville's nose was out of joint at being cut out in Winnie's affections by a green boy. He was paying *his* attention to Beatrix, so Lady Windham was not about to dampen Lord Mainwaring's ardor. "Whatever can you be thinking of, Sydney? We wouldn't want to do anything to offend Lord Mayne."

Sydney almost choked on her arrack punch. Everything she did seemed to offend the man!

Lady Windham was carried away with dreams of finally getting Trixie off her hands. If she threw the young people together often enough, Scoville would see his case with Winifred was hopeless. He was bound to settle on Beatrix with her better breeding and larger dowry. It was just a matter of planning some small entertainments, picnics and such, where he wouldn't be distracted by yet another pretty face. Nothing too extravagant, mind. And of course Sydney could help send out the invitations and plan the menus.

"What was that, Aunt Harriet? I'm sorry, I must have been wool-gathering. No, I'm afraid I won't be able to help with your plans for an excursion to Richmond, although I would love to go if I have the time. You see, I am going to be busy with a project of my own which already has Lord Mayne's approval. We wouldn't want to offend him, would we?"

16

The Pen and the Sword

Grandfather was a famous general. Everyone wanted to hear his adventures. Sydney happened to have reams and reams of closely written pages the general had penned right after his retirement and before his last seizure. She put the two together and came up with the answer to her difficulties. She'd sell the general's memoirs and they would all become rich.

Sydney had not read past the first pages, which concerned themselves with the background history of the Mahratta Wars, geographical details and catalogs of the various artillery and troops. She recalled bedtime stories from her childhood, however, tales of elephant hunts and native uprisings, towns under seige and man-eating tigers. She had been spellbound at the time—it was a miracle she did not have nightmares to this day—and was positive others would be equally as fascinated with the general's heroic account. Even his descriptions of the odd customs and religious practices were sure to capture the imaginations of any who read them, especially if they were like Sydney, who itched to see foreign lands. *Narratives of a Military Man* simply could not fail; it was only a matter of finding the publisher who would pay the most.

Sydney was very methodical about her quest. The general would have been proud at how she first scouted the terrain. She visited the lending library and studied all the titles in the history section. She copied down the names of a few publishers who seemed to specialize in past wars. Then she surveyed the biographical works, noting which companies produced volumes with the most elaborate embossing on the covers or the most gold leaf. She reasoned that these denoted a solvent operation. Furthermore, she firmly believed that an attractive cover had a great deal to do with a book's sales. Combining the two lists produced Sydney's primary targets.

Then she armed herself. She was not parading off to battle dressed like a pastel ingenue at Drury Lane. She and Annemarie designed a fashionable walking gown of forest-green cambric, with tight-fighting spenser to match. Not unintentionally, the short jacket had military-style buttons and epaulets on the shoulders. She wore a small green bonnet with gold braid trim and a wisp of net veiling which, Winifred assured her, added at least two years of maturity.

The campaign began. Sydney marched to the office of Watkins and Waters, Publishers. Her escort convoy, Wally, was two steps behind, proudly bearing the precious manuscript like a standard.

Sydney introduced herself to the clerk and told him she wished to inquire about the publication of a book. When he stopped ogling her, the flunky replied that if she made sure her name and direction were on the package, he would see that

someone looked at it and returned the manuscript to her with a decision, in a month or two.

"I am sorry, sir, but you do not understand. I need a decision"—she needed a check—"long before then."

The clerk laughed and pointed to the area behind him. Manuscripts, some bound with string, some in leather portfolios like hers, some in cloth satchels, were stacked from the floor to above her height, several rows deep, across the width of the room.

The general's granddaughter was not to be defeated at the first skirmish. She withdrew one of her calling cards and insisted the clerk bring it to the instant attention of Mr. Watkins.

"Dead."

"Then Mr. Waters."

"Dead."

"Then whoever *is* in charge."

"That'd be Mr. Wynn, but he doesn't see anybody."

"He'll see me. You tell him that I am General Harlan Lattimore's granddaughter and ... and a friend of Viscount Mayne's."

Whether due to her glowing account of the general's adventures or her inspired use of the viscount's name, Mr. Wynn agreed to look at the memoirs himself.

"But we do not have a great deal of time," she prompted him. Mr. Wynn took that to mean the general was soon to join Mr. Watkins and Mr. Waters, and he vowed to read the pages that very evening.

Sydney was able to enjoy her afternoon's outing to the British Museum with Lord Thorpe even more, with victory in sight.

True to his word, Mr. Wynn had the package delivered to Park Lane the very next day. Unfortunately, he also sent his regrets that he was not able to offer to publish such an unfinished work. Since he understood time to be a critical factor, he could only wish her luck with the worthwhile venture.

"How dare the man call your writing unfinished!" Sydney fumed, sharing the note with her grandfather. He pounded his chair. "What did he expect from a military man anyway,

Byron's deathless prose? Well, I am sure there are other publishers with a better sense of what readers want. If they wanted poetry, they would not be buying a war memoir in the first place."

Once more into the fray marched the troops. Hardened by her first battle, Sydney did not waste time with the clerk; she invoked Grandfather's rank and Lord Mayne's title. She was ushered into the senior partner's office at once and promised a quick reading.

Within days the hefty tome was returned, this time with a polite disclaimer: although the first chapter was as intriguing as Miss Lattimore had indicated, they would need to speak with the general in person before committing themselves to the project.

If the general could speak, he'd be out there trying to sell the blasted book himself. "Impertinent snobs!" Sydney raged. The general grunted and grred.

In no time at all Sydney hated all publishers, hated the green dress, and hated those polite notes of rejection worst.

Only one publisher, the noted Mr. Murray, came in person. He asked for an interview with the general. Willy, minding the door that day, sent for Sydney.

Seeing tooled-leather volumes and pound notes dance in her head, Sydney hurried into the drawing room. "I'm so sorry," she temporized, "but my grandfather is resting. May I offer you tea?"

While she poured she nervously eyed the ominous package on the sofa beside the publisher. "What did you think of the memoirs?" she finally asked.

"I think they have great possibilities, Miss Lattimore, although they need a great deal more work, naturally. I understand the general is something of an invalid. Do you think he is up to so much more writing?"

Sydney knew for a fact he wasn't. He could barely hold a pen, much less dictate. She gnashed her teeth and promised to discuss Mr. Murray's suggestions with the general. She thanked the publisher for his time—and kicked the door after he left.

As she told her friend the next morning, those publishers and editors were all just disappointed writers who thought they could do better.

Mrs. Bella Ott nodded her head sagely and agreed.

Sydney had not seen as much of Mrs. Ott as during the candy-making days. She was out most times when Bella called, on her rounds of publishers or enjoying her new popularity. In addition, she could not feel easy with the woman after the mingle-mangle with the chocolate. Bella was the experienced cook; she should have noticed something was wrong with the recipe. No matter, she was a willing ear on this gray day of despond. A cold rain blew from the north, and there would be no gentlemen calling and no walks in the park. There were no more publishers for Sydney to try.

"Hogwash, dearie, you've just been going about it arsy-varsy. Did you offer them cash?"

"Money? Of course not. That's not the way it works. . . . Is it?"

"Girly, stop acting like you were born yesterday. That's the way everything works. New writers pay the publishers to get their books in print. You don't think book dealers are going to gamble their precious blunt on an unknown, do you? Not those cautious chaps. Didn't that poet fellow Byron have to scrape up enough to publish the first scribbles himself before his name became an instant seller? That's how it goes. Subsidies, it's called. A writer or his family or a friend of his, a patron-like, puts up the ready. I bet that Mr. Murray was sitting here sipping your tea, waiting for you to flash a golden boy or two. Instead, you give him another sticky bun."

"I never thought. Uh, how much money do you think it would cost?"

Bella hefted the packaged memoirs. "Big book like that, I reckon thousands."

"Thousands! But then how could we make any money?"

"You really are a green 'un. It's the publishers who make the money. Good thing Mrs. Alquith wrote me about you."

"Mrs. Asquith," Sydney corrected her absently, pondering

this new dimension to her own ignorance. "We could never afford even one thousand, not after the loss on the confectionery business."

Bella did not want to talk about the candy venture. Hell, no one wanted to, it seemed. She and her boys had tried their best to get the rumor mills grinding. Granted the boys' best wasn't any great shakes, but no one would listen. Viscount Mayne had his story battened down so right and tight, no whispers were going to shake it. One of the scandal sheets even had the nerve to ask for proof that a parcel of chits had tried to drug the ton. Proof? Since when had truth ever had tuppence to do with what they published? Since one of the most powerful noblemen in the land got involved, they told her, that's when. Slander was one thing, they said, suicide was another.

There were other roads out of London, as the saying went. Things weren't hopeless yet, not by a long margin. She patted Sydney's hand. "Things ain't hopeless yet, my dear. Bella's here."

Bella knew a man. Among her wide acquaintance was the nephew of Lady Peaswell. ("No, she don't attend Almacks; she raises cats in Yarmouth.") Bella looked after this young man the same as she looked after Mrs. Asquith's young friends. She even cooked for him sometimes. It just so happened that this enterprising young man, of good family but needing to support himself, was just starting a printing and publishing business. All of his capital had gone for the equipment and rental for his new shop, so he was looking for material to publish—by subscription. He just might be willing to share the expenses with Sydney, and the profits, of course. It would only cost her, oh, maybe five hundred pounds, Bella thought, especially for friends. But Sydney would still see vastly more income if the book sold well than the pittance an established publisher would pay. Sydney needed a publisher and Bella's young friend needed a best-seller to get him started. So what did dear Miss Sydney think? Sydney thought she couldn't wait to meet this enterprising, innovative young entrepreneur.

"Fine, fine. Why don't we go visit his office? You can get a look-see at the place and show him the pages. That way he can get the presses rolling, ha-ha."

"Right now, in the rain?" Sydney wouldn't get in Bella's carriage with that impossible coachman on a clear day. She surely would not trust his driving on slippery roads with bad visibility. "I, ah, felt a tickle in my throat and thought I should stay inside today, the weather being so foul and all."

"Right you are, dearie. 'Sides, if I take the book to him on my way home, you'll have a decision that much sooner. And if Mr. Murray can call in person, so can Mr. Chesterton."

Mr. Oliver Chesterton was not quite what Sydney had expected in her daring new partner. Then again, he certainly was dressed creatively.

Chester refused to wear his own clothes when Bella insisted he had to look ink-stained, and the only chap his size to die that week was a Macaroni who'd succumbed to wet pavement and high heels. They managed to get the wheel marks off the checkered Cossack trousers. So there Chester was for his appointment with Miss Lattimore and her five hundred pounds, in black and white trousers, a puce coat, and cherry-striped waist. He had a huge boutonniere and shirt collars starched so high he could barely turn his head. His thin hair was slicked back with pomatum, and a rat-brown mustache was affixed under his nose. The false hair tickled, so he'd kept trimming it until the thing looked more like a rattail on his lip. He wore thick spectacles to make him look more bookish. Like Bella said, now he could stop looking for Lord Mayne behind every bush; he couldn't see the bush.

Before he left, Randy had spattered him with ink and then dipped each of his fingers in the pot. Everyone knew printers had ink under their fingernails, he said. Bella said he looked more like an acrobat she saw at a fair once, who walked on his hands right through the cow-judging tent.

If it weren't for the glasses, the ink, and Mrs. Ott's recommendation, Sydney would have thought him a park saunterer at best, a cardsharp at worst. She supposed his nasal accent

was from Yarmouth, and his reed-thin frame a result of invest-
ing his life's savings in his business. He was assuredly not a
reference for Bella's cooking.

Bella made the introductions and Mr. Chesterton reached
out to shake her hand, curiously with his left. When that awkward moment was past and Mr. Chesterton found his seat, he
got down to business. For a thousand pounds he would publish the book and she would keep all profits. For five hundred,
they would split the earnings.

"I do think the manuscript has great possibilities, Miss Lattimore, so I would be willing to gamble," Mr. Chesterton
offered. Mrs. Ott snorted into her tea. "But I do need the
money in advance, you realize. I need to buy tickets—I mean,
typefaces."

This was a big decision. For once in her life Sydney wasn't
eager to leap headfirst into unknown waters. Perhaps the fact
of Chesterton leaving ink stains like pawprints on her mama's
good china had something to do with it. Perhaps Lord
Mayne's lectures had finally paid off. Then again, perhaps she
only needed more time to decide between the five-hundred or
thousand-pound arrangement.

Sydney told her guests that since it was such a major investment, she would have to consult the general and, no, she did
not feel the need to inspect the premises.

"Thank you for coming in person, Mr. Chesterton," she told
him, holding out her hand. She held out her left hand, assuming there must be something amiss with his right.

Chester never saw her hand at all. "I won't need to call
again, will I? I mean, you can just send a check. Unless you
change your mind about visiting us. Ma—Madam Ott can
bring you."

17

Trust and Treachery

The general did not like any of the choices. Either that or he had something stuck in his throat. Wally, on duty that day, did not like the cut of Chesterton's jib. And Winifred did not understand the dilemma at all.

"But, Sydney, if we do not have enough money for the rest of the Season, why don't we just go home?"

"Because we would never have the chance to leave home again. Because Grandfather's pension will not be ours forever, and because you have the opportunity to make a good alliance."

"But what if I do not want to make a fine marriage, Syd? What if I thought being an officer's wife would suit me better, or a gentleman farmer's?"

A pox on both the Mainwaring brothers, Sydney thought, ripping up another note to the viscount. Drat the smooth-talking rake who could turn a girl's head, and drat his younger brother, too.

She tried another sheet of stationery. She couldn't even decide on the salutation! *Dear Lord Mayne,* or *My dear Lord Mayne*? Stuff! Where was the cursed man when she needed him? Brennan said he was back in town. Wasn't it just typical of the contrary cad to make her write to ask his advice, when *he* was the one always mouthing propriety at her? Even Sydney knew it was totally improper for a young lady to be writing to a gentleman's residence. And heavens, she did not want to write this letter!

It was humiliating enough that she needed his money, and worse that she needed his name for entry to the publishers.

Now she needed his advice as a man about town, and swallowing all the pages she had shredded would be easier than swallowing her pride. It wasn't that she wanted to see him, she told herself, just that she needed to see him. And he hadn't called.

She started again: *Your Lordship*.

Forrest Mainwaring despised gossip. He hated it worse when his name was mentioned. He was not in town over two hours when the gossip caught up to him. Something about his protégé, Miss Lattimore, of course, but how much of a hubble-bubble could even Sydney get into with the general's memoirs? He needed another day to track his friend Murray through the coffee shops before he had his answer. A partial answer anyway.

The next morning he went for a hard ride on a half-broken stallion. Later he worked out at Gentleman Jackson's. After luncheon at White's he took on Brennan in a fencing match at Deauville's. Now, he felt, he was ready to face Miss Sydney Lattimore. He was too physically and mentally drained to lose either his temper or his self-control.

He hadn't counted on the joy written on her face when she flew down the stairs to greet him, wearing a Pomona green muslin gown that swirled close to her rounded limbs. His traitorous body overcame exhaustion and rose to the occasion.

"You came!" She beamed, for she never had gotten around to posting a note. "You must have known I needed your advice."

Her smile made him feel like a slug for putting the visit off so long. Hell, he would have put it off for a lifetime rather than tie himself in knots like this. Nevertheless, he flicked a speck of lint off his sleeve and drawled at his most blasé, "Never tell me the indomitable Miss Lattimore has at last recognized the need to consult wiser heads about something."

She giggled at his affected manner, and his resolve to keep his distance fled. Ignoring her chaperone, the general fast asleep in his Bath chair across the room, Forrest sat on the sofa next to her instead of the chair opposite. He draped his arm across the back, where he just might touch the nape of her perfect, graceful neck. What was lower than a slug? He sighed, got up, and moved his seat. Polishing his quizzing glass, he wondered, "This mightn't have anything to do with a certain manuscript, would it?"

"Yes. You see, I've had this wonderful offer, but it is not quite wonderful, I think, and I thought—" But she never wrote the note, asking him to call. Uncertain, she asked, "That is, how did you know? I suppose my pea-wit of a sister mentioned it to Lord Mainwaring."

"She may have, but that's not how. I merely had to visit my club to hear your name—and mine—on everyone's lips."

Sydney felt the need to inspect her kid half-boots. "I, ah, didn't think you'd care. That is, no one would speak to me otherwise, and you said how much influence you have, and it was not dangerous, illegal, or scandalous, so I cannot see why you mind."

"It's not so much that I mind, poppet, as I do not understand what you were trying to do. No one does."

The "no one" was ominous. Sydney rushed on. "What is so difficult? I was trying to get the general's memoirs published, and received nothing but insults at first, your name or not. If certain persons were so quick to inform you I was trading on our acquaintance, for which I do apologize since you don't seem best pleased—but then, you never are, are you?—they should also have mentioned the poor treatment I received. Why, if they wanted money, those publishing gentlemen should have been aboveboard about it like Mr. Chesterton, instead of maligning the general's work."

As usual when dealing with Miss Sydney Lattimore, the viscount felt he was missing something crucial. Perhaps he'd been watching her lips too carefully and hadn't heard an important fact. Then again, he'd always believed she was the one missing something important, in her brain box.

"Hold, Mischief. I spoke to Murray and he had only high praise for the general's writing."

"You know Mr. Murray?"

"Yes, he's a good friend. He was eager to ask me about the manuscript, knowing I had an interest in this quarter. He was most desirous of talking to the general or finding out if there were any notes, or anyone else who might be able to finish the work."

"F-finish it?" The color had left Sydney's face, leaving a row of freckles across her nose.

"Do you mean you never read it, you goosecap? You were trying to peddle a book you never read?"

"I—I read the first few pages. There wasn't time, and I knew all the adventures anyway. The first chapter was full of dry-as-dust details."

"Then you would not have liked the rest of the book any better, Mischief, for they were all the same chapter! According to Murray, some gave more attention to the battles, some to other generals' viewpoints. But they were all the same chapter!"

Sydney did not understand. She was worrying her lip in that way she had of driving him to distraction. Forrest got up and turned his back on her to inspect a Dresden shepherdess on the mantel. "The general was a perfectionist, it seems, not a writer. He could never get the facts to come out like the exciting stories he used to tell his granddaughter, but he kept trying. Over and over. Murray says he would have done fine with a little guidance. It's too late now, isn't it?" he asked quietly.

Sydney just nodded.

"I'm sorry, Mischief," Forrest said, returning to her side, and she believed him.

She forced a tremulous smile. "It was a good plan, though, wasn't it?"

He raised her hand to his lips. "One of your best, sweetheart."

Sydney felt a glow spread through her—and then a raging inferno. She snatched her hand away and jumped to her feet. "Why, that miserable, contemptible, low-down—"

"Murray? I swear he didn't—"

"No, Mr. Chesterton, the publisher! He liked the book! He said it was sure to be a best-seller. He was going to print it with brown calf bindings and little gold corners—with my money! Why, that mawworm was trying to diddle me out of my whole bank account! He must have heard how green I was from those other publishers, the bounder. Wait till I see him again. I'll—"

"Chesterton? You don't mean Otto Chester, do you? Pale, thin, nervous-looking chap?"

"He was pale and thin, but his name was definitely Oliver Chesterton. Why? Who is Otto Chester?"

Now the viscount was up and pacing. "An insect that I should have squashed when I had the chance! He's the associate in O. Randall and Associates. You remember, the backroom banker. Otto Chester is the double-dealer who cheated Bren, then handed his forged markers to Randall for collection. I never thought he'd have the guts or the gumption to—"

"To come after me for the money you stole from them!" Sydney screamed.

"I did not steal the bloody money," he shouted back. "I told you, they got it dishonestly, so they were not entitled to the blunt!"

"Well, I'll just inform them of that fact the next time they come to tea!"

The general jerked awake and looked around to see if they were under attack. Sydney tucked the blankets back around his knees and turned his chair so he could look out the window. She grabbed Forrest's sleeve and dragged him to the other side of the room.

The viscount pried her fingers loose before his superfine was damaged beyond repair. "They are not coming anywhere near you. I'll see to that! And they'll be dashed sorry they ever tried, too."

Sydney clutched her hands together to keep from wringing them like a tragedy queen. "Couldn't I just give the money back? If I had it to give, I mean. What I haven't spent? Maybe they would go away then."

The viscount took on the expression a cat might wear once it has the mouse between its paws. "They'll be going away for a very long time."

Sydney laughed nervously. "Here I thought they were your partners. Can you imagine?"

"Don't start that again, Mischief. Fiend seize it, do I look like an Otto?"

Healthy, tanned, strong, and confident, he did not resemble Mr. Chesterton in the least. She shook her head and smiled up at him.

He brushed the back of his fingers across her cheek. "Thanks, sweetheart. Now, listen, I do not want you even to think about contacting this dirty dish or giving him a groat. I'll track him down and take care of everything. You don't have to worry. Trust me."

Trust me. Isn't that what the snake said to Eve? Besides, how could she trust a man who was branded a rake by his own lips? By his own lips on hers, if she needed more proof! She still was not sure he wouldn't hold her to personal repayment of the loan—very personal. She wasn't even sure she would refuse!

Of course she would, Sydney told herself firmly. On the other hand, it would be far better if she could dissolve the worrisome debt and never let the question come up. She wondered, alone in her room, what might happen if she were independent and able to meet Forrest more as a social equal. Not that Miss Lattimore from Little Dedham could ever be the equal of the lofty Lord Mayne, but a girl could dream, couldn't she? She'd once tamed some wild kittens. How much harder could it be to reform a rake?

It still came down to the money. Whether she owed a hardened libertine or hardened criminals, she was in one hard place. She was never going to be safe, one way or t'other, unless she paid them all back. But how?

Lord Mayne placed guards around Sydney's house, alerted the twins, and made sure his brother accompanied the young ladies whenever he could at night. Forrest had his men out searching for Randall, and he himself haunted low dives and gaming hells looking for Chester.

He was never going to find Chester, not unless he crawled under every bed in every row house in Chelsea.

"He can't be an outlaw," Bella gasped as Sydney waved the vinaigrette under her nose. "He's Lady Peaswell's nephew."

Sydney poured tea to calm the older woman's nerves after her attack of the vapors. "I'm sorry, Mrs. Ott, but for all your town bronze, you were taken in the same as I was. The man is a charlatan, a professional gambler, and a cheat."

"Poor, poor Lady Peaswell," Bella blubbered into her handkerchief.

"Yes, well, even noble families have their black sheep. You must not let titles and such affect your good judgment."

Bella thought of Lord Whitlaw, Chester's father, and blubbered some more. "How true, how true. And how foolish I have been, my dear, me with my simple, trusting nature. I fed the boy, took him to my hearth, introduced him to my friends! Oh, how could I have been so blind? And how can I ever make it up to you, dear Sydney? Tell Bella what I can do so you'll forgive me for bringing a viper to your nest."

"Well, I have this plan. . . ."

18

Hell and Beyond

$\mathcal{A}$ polite hell was not one in which the sinners helped lace each other's ice skates. *That* was a cold day in hell, which was about when Miss Sydney Lattimore should have attended Lady Ambercroft's salon.

Lady Ambercroft was a young widow making a splash in the ton and a small fortune for herself by turning her home into a genteel gaming establishment. A lady could play silver loo or dip into her pin money at the roulette table without rubbing elbows with the lower orders or sharing the table with her husband's mistress. (Unless that mistress was another woman of birth and breeding on Lady Ambercroft's select list of invitees.) There was, supposedly, no drinking to excess, rowdy behavior, or wagering beyond the house limits.

The elegant premises were visited by much of society—even Aunt Harriet considered going when she heard refreshments were free—and gossiped about by the rest.

Lady Ambercroft herself was a lively, attractive woman who had married a foul-breathed old man for his money, then celebrated his demise by spending her hard-earned inheritance. She still had her looks, she still had the house, she was still celebrating. She was also still on all but the highest sticklers' guest lists, so Sydney had met her. Over braised duck at the Hopkins-Jones buffet two evenings before, Sydney asked Lady Ambercroft if she could attend one of her game nights. The widow had laughed gaily and said of course, whenever Miss Lattimore's Aunt Harriet brought her. Which was right back to when hell froze over.

Sydney chose to consider that an invitation, as long as she was well chaperoned. She chose to accept. Lady Ambercroft was making money, she was not ruined in polite society, and, best of all, she lived right around the corner from the Lattimores!

Sydney had no problem feigning illness to cry off Aunt Harriet's musical entertainment planned for that evening; listening to Trixie and her friends torture the pianoforte and harp always gave her the headache. She just claimed one in advance.

Sydney had a little trouble convincing Mrs. Ott. "If you want to play cards, dearie, we can just go to my digs. That'll be more the thing, don't you know. My coach is right outside."

It might be more *convenable*, but it would not serve Sydney's purpose at all. It would serve Bella's even less to see her thousand pounds slide into some other woman's purse. She tried again: "His lordship ain't going to like it."

"He won't know. We can slip out the back door and walk the half block. I intend to stay for only an hour."

Bella revised her plans. In an hour even a cabbagehead like

this gel would have rough going to lose a thousand pounds, but she sure as sin could lose her reputation.

As soon as Winifred left with Lord Mainwaring and Wally, and Annemarie as duenna, Sydney hurried into her most sophisticated evening gown, an amber silk with a lower neckline than usual and little puffed sleeves. She put a black domino over that, and pulled the hood up to cover her easily identifiable hair.

Ten minutes later she realized her mistake. She recognized no one in the place, she was by far the youngest female, the play was intense, and Lady Ambercroft was not happy to see her. The merry widow was not best pleased to see an unfledged deb in her establishment. Word that she was gulling innocents could ruin her. The old quiz with Miss Lattimore looked more like a procuress than a chaperone, furthermore, and Lady Ambercroft was having none of that type of thing in her house. Except in her own bedroom, of course.

She gave Bella a dirty look and pulled Sydney's hood back up.

The rooms were fairly thin of company this early in the evening, so there were a lot of dark corners for Sydney to stand in to watch the play. Bella took a seat at the *vingt et un* table, whispering that Lady Ambercroft would get in more of a pucker if they didn't drop a little blunt her way. Sydney drifted from room to room, counting the number of tables, checking the spread at the refreshments area, noting how many servants waited on the players. Some of the men at the craps table began to notice her, elbowing each other and pointing to the "phantom lady." She moved on. At the roulette wheel she received suggestions that she stand behind this man or that to bring him luck. She shook her head and continued her survey, thankfully not understanding half of the comments that followed her.

In a short while Sydney felt she had all the information she needed. The only thing she was not sure of was whether the dealers were paid employees or guests. Foolishly, she asked the man standing next to her at the faro table. He threw his head back and brayed, reminding her of Old Jeb's donkey back home, yellow teeth and all.

"The little lady don't know the first thing about gaming, gents. What say we teach her?"

A weasel-faced man whose teeth were filed to sharp points grinned at her and got up so she could take his seat.

"No, no, I am only here to watch, gentlemen. My friend—"

"If your friend is that fat old beldam who was playing *vingt et un*, she took a fainting fit and got sent home in a hackney."

Sydney jerked around. "Poor Bella, I have to—"

"She's long gone. Message was, your footman would see you home."

"But I didn't bring a—" Sydney looked around at the leering faces. Oh, Lord, she was in the suds again "—a heavy purse."

"That's no problem, ghost lady," an obese, sweating man wheezed at her. "I'll stake you." He pushed a column of colored chips her way.

"No, I'm sorry, I cannot—" she tried to say, tried to go. But a dark-skinned man with a scar under his eye said she had to play one round, it was a house rule. Donkey-laugh stood behind her so she could not run, and a scrawny old woman in a powdered wig from the last century put a hand on her shoulder and pushed her into the chair. Sydney tried to smile. She only had to wait for Lady Ambercroft to come into the room after all, or for Bella to send one of the Minch brothers back for her. "Very well, gentlemen, my lady. One round it is."

Someone placed a drink in Sydney's hand. She sipped, then pushed the glass aside. Whatever that was, she did not need it now. She needed some warm milk in her own kitchen.

Play began. Sydney did not know the rules or the worth of her markers. She didn't know a shoe from a shovel, as far as cards went. Not to worry, her new associates were quick to reassure, they'd teach her fast enough. She tried to sort out the instructions, then decided it was wiser just to follow what the fat man did, since he had the highest columns of colored chips.

By the time the shoe or dealing box came her way, Sydney had a better idea what she was about, she thought. At least her stack of markers and coins had grown. Weasel kept leering at her, but Marie Antoinette was scowling. Her pile was dwindling, as was Scarface's. Sydney did not want to upset these people by taking their money, not when she was a rank amateur, so she stood to leave.

"Surely one round has passed, and I really must be going." She pushed the winnings in Fat Man's direction. "Your stake, my lord, and thank you. It's been an, ah, education."

"Not so fast, Lady Incognita, not when you have all our blunt." Scarface smiled at her, a horrid, twisted thing. She shuddered. Someone else, she could not tell who, said, "That's not sporting," and a third voice called, "That's the rules of the house." The old lady laid a clawlike hand on Sydney's shoulder. Dear heaven, where was Willy? Sydney prayed. Where was Lady Ambercroft?

Lady Ambercroft was upstairs. Shortly after the unfortunate episode with Miss Lattimore's dragon, a small, long-toothed gentleman with red hair entered the premises. Lady Ambercroft did not know him, but his credentials gleamed in the candlelight: rings, fobs, a diamond stickpin. Lord Othric Randolph, wearing the late Lord Winchester Whitlaw's final bequest, looked around the rooms, nodded in satisfaction, then offered his hostess a private highstakes game upstairs. One she couldn't lose.

Willy was at home in the butler's pantry, throwing dice with Lord Mayne's hired house-watcher. Lord Mayne was not happy about that either. Restless and edgy that no one had spotted Chester or Randall, the viscount had driven through a cold mist to Park Lane on his way to the clubs.

"Don't fatch yourself, milord," his paid guard told him, tossing the cubes from hand to hand. "I'm inside 'cause it came on to drizzle, and the little lady's safe as houses. Her and the sister went off with your brother"—a nod to Willy—"and your brother, milord, to her auntie's. Be back around midnight, I 'spect."

Willy shook his head. "No, that was Annemarie who went

with Miss Winifred and Wally. Miss Sydney is upstairs with the headache."

Now the guard scratched his bald pate. "Iffen it was the maid who went with the others, who was it in the black cape what walked down the block with the old neighbor lady?"

A quick search had the viscount cursing and stomping around the entry hall. Willy tried to convince him that Miss Sydney had a good head on her shoulders; she'd do fine.

"Fine? She hasn't done fine since I've known her! This time I am finished. Good riddance to bad baggage, I say. I told her, nothing dangerous, illegal, or scandalous. So what does she do? She skips off in the middle of the night going the devil knows where—for what? To rob the crown jewels, for all I know! To think I put a guard on the house to keep her safe! I should have chained the wench to the bed." He crammed his beaver hat down on his head. "Well, no more. She can come home looking like butter wouldn't melt in her mouth and those greenish eyes as innocent as a babe's. It won't work this time. I'm gone."

He turned back when the guard chuckled. "And you're fired. Pick up your check when you bring word that she's home safe."

His club was nearly empty. Some older types were playing whist, and a group of dandies were tasting each other's snuff mixtures in the bow window.

"Where is everybody?" Forrest asked a solitary gentleman sprawled in one of the leather chairs with a bottle by his side.

"Those who couldn't avoid it are at Lady Windham's musicale. Bunch of others are at the new production at Covent Garden. New chorus girls." He poured himself another drink. "And those whose dibs are in tune," he said with a grimace for the sneezes from across the room and the state of his own finances, "are at that new hell of Lady Ambercroft's that's all the rage."

Now that was more the thing, the viscount decided, smiling fondly at memory of a romantic interlude with Rosalyn Ambercroft. Lady Ros was just what he needed to rid his mind of

Sydney Lattimore once and for all, even if it meant going out into the damp night again.

Lady Ambercroft was unavailable, the butler informed him when he took the viscount's hat, gloves, and cane. Perhaps if Lord Mayne visited the card rooms, her ladyship might be free later, the servant suggested with a wink.

And perhaps pigs would fly before Viscount Mayne stood in line for a doxie's favor, no matter how highborn. Ah, well, he was already here. Forrest thought he may as well have a drink or two of Rosalyn's fine cognac just to take the chill off, and see if there was any interesting play going on.

He put a coin down on red, even, at the wheel, then strolled away, not waiting to see if he won. He played a hand or two of *vingt et un*, decided he did not like the dealer's lace cuffs, and moved on.

There seemed to be a stir around the faro table, so the viscount headed in that direction, stopping at the dice game to bet on his friend Collingwood's nicking the main. Forrest jingled his winnings in one hand as he made his way to the faro table.

All seats were taken and spectators were two deep behind the players. The viscount moved around the side, where his height would let him view the action. He idly reached for another drink from a waiter's tray, then turned back.

Coins rolled unnoticed to the thick carpet. The glass slipped through Lord Mayne's fingers, spilling wine on his white Persian satin breeches. "Oh, hell."

19

Reputation Roulette

It was dark, her hood was up. He couldn't be sure. Then she turned and one of those blasted Pekingese-colored curls glimmered in the candlelight.

The viscount was going to walk away. This time he really was. If Miss Lattimore wanted to play ducks and drakes with her good name, that was her business, none of his.

"Please, gentlemen," he heard her say as he walked past, a quaver in her voice, "I really do not want to play anymore. See? I have no money left. You've won it all back, so you cannot say I was a poor sport." The viscount's feet refused to take another step, no matter what his head ordered.

A sharp-featured man said they'd take her vowels, and that fat old court-card Bishop Nugee claimed she owed him twenty pounds, for his stake. Lord Mayne was prepared to let Sydney stew a while, to teach her a lesson. Then he saw someone put his hand on her shoulder. Then he saw red.

The viscount brushed the spectators aside like flies.

"No, I did not owe anyone," Sydney declared. "I won't take any of your money or your advice. I am going home." She did not know if these scoundrels would let her; she did not know if her legs would carry her. She did not even want to think about walking out of there on her own, in the dark, with no one beside her. Grandfather always said never show fear, so she raised her chin. "I do not think you play fair." Just then someone tossed a roll of coins over Sydney's shoulder toward the bishop. She turned to refuse before she was in deeper water, if that was possible. Or if it mattered, now that she was drowning anyway. "I didn't . . ." The words faded when she saw who stood behind her chair.

The breath she did not know she was holding for the last hour or so whooshed out of her. Safe! Like dry land to a ship-wrecked sailor, like a sip of water to a sun-drenched jungle wanderer, rescue was at hand. Sydney almost jumped up and hugged her savior, until she got a better look at Lord Mayne's granite face and saw the whitened knuckles clenched around the rungs of her chair back. Like a shark to the shipwrecked sailor, like a tribe of cannibals to the soul lost in the jungle, some fates were worse than death.

Sydney fumbled in her reticule for the few shillings she carried there. "On second thought, I think I shall play a bit more."

Another roll of coins landed on the table, this time right in front of her. "New cards," she heard him call like the sound of doom. "The lady deals."

Sydney did not have to concentrate on the rules or the cards or her bets. The viscount tapped his quizzing glass on the card he wanted her to play, and just as silently indicated how much she should wager. No one else spoke, for the gamblers had to look to their own hands rather than count on a rigged game to pluck the little pigeon of every feather she had. Now the dark lady held the deal and Mayne's reputation kept them honest. No one dared to mark the cards or switch them. It was a fair game.

There were no more ribald comments and no taunts aimed at flustering Sydney, which would have been too late by half anyway. Her hands made the motions of passing cards from the shoe to the players, pushing forward the coins and markers, collecting the winnings. As the pile in front of her grew, so did her trepidation at the unnatural silence. She thought they must all hear her knees tapping together or the frantic pounding of her heart or the drops of nervous perspiration slipping down her back. She had to wipe her hands on her cloak to keep the cards from sticking to them.

"Please." She turned to beg when it seemed the game would go on for another lifetime. "Please may I go home now?"

The viscount gestured to a hovering servant who immediately produced a silk purse, into which he scraped the winnings. The rattle of the coins was the only sound. The viscount pushed some of the markers aside for the house share and some for the servants, then nodded for one of the dealers to exchange the rest for cash. Only then did he pull back Sydney's chair and help her to rise with a hand under her elbow. He kept it there as he guided her out of the hushed room. She could hear the whispers start behind them, but Lord Mayne kept walking at a measured pace, not hurrying. And not talking. He nodded to some of his friends, cut others who tried to catch his attention. Sydney hadn't realized the rooms were five miles long!

Finally they reached the entryway, which was empty except for the butler and some footmen. Forrest merely had to dip his head for his cane, hat, and gloves to be handed over, his carriage sent for, the winnings carried to him.

That sack of coins seemed to loose the flood of words he'd been striving to contain until they were alone. Shoving it into Sydney's hands, too furious to care who heard, he growled: "Here, madam. I hope the gold was worth this night's cost. You have gambled away your reputation, gambled away your sister's future, all to repay a debt no one wanted."

"But, my honor—"

"Your honor be damned. There was no dishonor in accepting a gift when you needed it, only a blow to your stubborn pride. And what is honor but your good name? You have done everything in your power to see yours dragged through the mud, blast you."

Sydney was trembling, his arm the only thing keeping her standing. Still, she had to make him understand. "But the household was counting on me! What else could I do when they all depend on me?"

"You can bloody well let me take care of you!" he shouted for the edification of the servants, the gamblers who were crowded in the doorway to watch, the butler who stood holding the door, and the three carriages passing by.

Scarlet-faced, Sydney shook off his arm. "Thank you, my lord. Now we can *all* be assured my ruination is complete." She loosened the strings of the purse and tipped it over, coins spilling at his feet and rolling across the marble foyer, pound notes fluttering in the breeze from the still-open door. One footman maintained his pretense of invisibility; the other scurried crabwise along the floor to collect the bills and change.

"And as for the winnings, my lord, I do not want anything from either you or this foul place. I did not earn it, I shall not earn it, and I would not take it—or you—if I were starving. If my sister was forced to take in washing," she shouted as she ran through the open door, past the open-mouthed butler. "If Grandfather had to reenlist. If Wally had to wrestle bears. If Willy had to . . ." Her voice faded as she was swallowed up in the dark, rainy night.

"That's not what I meant," the viscount murmured, but only the footman handing him the refilled purse heard. Lord Mayne absently handed him a coin, then he looked at the crowd gathered in the hallway and repeated so they could all hear: "That's not what I meant." The bishop nodded and held his finger alongside his nose. The rest of them leered and winked. "Blast. Very well, let me put it this way: Nothing untoward occurred tonight. Anyone who believes differently had better be prepared to meet me. Likewise anyone who might feel the need to mention the lady's name, if you know it, had best be ready to feel cold steel. Swords, pistols, fists, it matters not. And now good night, gentlemen."

Forrest called her name and Sydney walked faster. He caught up with her before she reached the corner of Park Lane and did not stop to argue. He scooped her up and tossed her and the silk purse into his carriage. Before getting in, he ordered the driver to go once around the park before returning Miss Lattimore to her home. Then he took the seat across from her, his arms crossed on his chest.

Sydney pulled her cloak about her. She was damp, chilled, and shaken, now that her anger was not heating her blood. For sure she was not going to receive any warmth or comfort from Lord Mayne, sitting there like a marble sculpture, handsome and cold. The streetlights showed the muscle in his jaw pulsing from being clenched so tightly.

"I won't take it," Sydney said quietly, moving the purse to his side. "It would make me feel soiled." He nodded. She continued: "And I shall repay the loan, for I do not wish to be beholden to you."

He nodded again. "So I surmised. But tell me, did you really intend to finance the rest of your sister's Season, support your household, and reimburse me, by gambling? Not even you could be so addled to think that. Don't you know the house always wins? You would only end up more in debt, losing what you had to start."

Sydney gathered some dignity around her—it was more rumpled than her sodden cloak—and pulled a small notebook from her pocket. "I have never been the wantwit you consider me, my lord. I did not go there to gamble, but to observe. I wanted to know how such an enterprise was run. See? I made note of the staff and the rooms and tables. I thought that if things got desperate, we could turn the ground floor of our house into a gaming parlor, for invited guests only, of course."

The viscount's lip was twitching. "Of course."

"Don't patronize me, Lord Mayne. I was led to believe that only the highest ton were invited there. I admit I was wrong, but the principle is sound. As you said, the house always wins. I could see that Lady Ambercroft is making a fortune, and maybe I could, too. She is providing for herself and she is still accepted everywhere."

Forrest was not about to discuss all the ways Lady Ros was earning her bread. "Lady Ambercroft is a widow, not a young deb. Furthermore, she is accepted, not necessarily welcomed, and that more for her husband's title and despite her present occupation. And finally, one of the places where she is not accepted and never will be is the marriage market. Gentlemen like Baron Scoville do not countenance their prospective brides shuffling pasteboards in smoky rooms. They don't even like to be related to in-laws in trade, Mischief, much less a sister who runs a gaming den."

"Oh, pooh, I scratched Baron Scoville off my list ages ago. I never liked him anyway, and Winnie seems determined on your brother. I thought we could use him as a dealer, since he is familiar with such places. That way we could save money on the staff and give him a respectable income so he doesn't have to make the army his career."

"A respectable—" He was laughing too hard to continue. "Mischief, your mind certainly works in mysterious ways. Bren has two small estates of his own and will come into a moderate fortune from our mother. The only reason he has not bought himself a commission, indeed why neither I nor my father has seen to it for him, is that Mother threatens to go into a decline if he signs up. She would purchase his cornetcy herself, however, rather than see him become a knight of the baize tables. But thank you, poppet, for worrying about my brother's reformation. As a croupier!"

While he was laughing again, Sydney thought about her plan to reform Forrest Mainwaring as well as Brennan. She could see her strategy needed more refining, especially since she could not resist laughing with him.

Lord Mayne moved over to her side of the carriage and put his arm around her. "Listen, Mischief, we are partners, more or less, aren't we?" Sydney allowed as how they might be. "Then I get to have a say in how the money is spent. That's fair, isn't it?" She nodded her head, dislodging the hood. He brushed the damp curls off her cheek. "Then I absolutely, categorically, forbid our blunt being used to set up a gambling den, no matter how polite. Is that understood?"

"You needn't worry, Lord Mayne, after tonight I would never consider such a thing."

"That's Forrest, sweetheart. I really think we are on familiar enough terms to stop my-lording and my-ladying each other."

Sydney felt they were on quite too familiar terms, her cheek tingling from his touch. She trembled and inched as far away from him as she could on the leather seat.

Forrest was not entirely convinced that she had abandoned her latest scheme. Reliving the horror of finding her in such a place, he said gruffly, "You know, having his granddaughter set herself up as a child of fortune would break the general's heart."

"Having a granddaughter instead of a grandson already

broke his heart. I thought I'd let him operate the roulette table," she said with a giggle. "No one could accuse him of stopping the wheel with his foot under the table."

Forrest did not think she was taking his warning seriously enough. "I swear, Mischief, if you ever mention starting such a place, if you so much as set foot in such a place, I'll turn you over my knee and beat some sense into you, which should have been done years ago. As a matter of fact, it's not too late." Seeing that she was shivering—from his threats or the cold—Forrest reached out to pull her onto his lap. Sydney screamed until he stopped her mouth with his.

Whatever sense she ever had flew right away, for she let him kiss her and hold her and touch her. And she kissed him and held him and touched him back, and enjoyed it mightily.

Such a heavenly embrace might have led heaven knew where, but they were home, and Willy—or Wally—was opening the door, looking mad as fire to find Missy sitting in his lordship's lap. The footman plucked her out like a kitten from a basket and stood glaring at the viscount. Forrest could not tell whether it was the twin with the glass jaw or not, and did not feel like finding out the hard way. He tapped his cane on the carriage roof and left, smiling.

The guard outside, his own paid watchman, called after the coach: "Lordy, you never said I was supposed to keep her safe from you!"

20

High Ton, High Toby

Sydney had a cold, and cold feet about meeting the ton. As soon as word spread that the younger Miss Lattimore was afflicted with a chill, however, even more bouquets of flowers arrived at Park Lane from suitors, along with baskets of fruit from well-wishers and pet restoratives from various dowagers. By some miracle—or Lord Mayne—Sydney had squeaked through another scrape with her reputation intact. She was too miserable to care.

Her nose was stuffed, her plans had gone awry, her heart was in turmoil, and her wits had gone begging. How could it be, she asked herself, that of all the men in London, she was attracted to one with no principles? How could it be that whenever she was with him she forgot her own? As for his taking care of her, he could do that when cows gave chocolate milk! Sydney blew her nose and pulled the covers over her head.

She refused to see any of the callers, except for one. Winifred came upstairs to beg her sister to grant Mrs. Ott an interview. "For you must know she is downstairs weeping and moaning about how it is all her fault that you are ill. I do not know how that could be since you were already feeling poorly before she came. Nevertheless, she refused to leave until she sees with her own two eyes that you are recovering. Grandfather is becoming a trifle overset at the commotion, Syd, and you know I hate it when he makes those noises."

Bella was indeed beating her breast, and the general was beating his fist on the arm of his chair when Sydney dressed and went down. She set Winnie to reading Grandfather the newspapers while she took Bella off to the front parlor for a glass of sherry and a cose.

"Oh, my dear, I am so ashamed! What you must think of poor Bella, going off and leaving you like that. But my nerves! You know I haven't been the same since the major passed on. It was that place what did it, the gambling, the men. Why, a man next to me lost twenty bob right there at one turn of the card, then said the game was as crooked as a goat's hind leg! My stars! My very heart took to palpitating. I knew we should leave. That was no place for ladies like us, I could see straight off."

"Yes," Sydney agreed, "we were sadly misinformed. I think there must not be such a thing as a polite hell. But why did you not come get me when you realized, especially if you were feeling ill?"

"I tried, dearie, Lord knows I tried. I was on my way to find you when a man pinched me! I won't call him a gentleman, I won't, but can you believe that?"

In the usual course of things, Sydney wouldn't. Bella was more pillowy than willowy. In her widow's weeds she looked like raw dough in a sack, puffy face dotted with raisin eyes. And for all her troubles, no one had taken such liberties with Sydney's person until the ride home, of course. Still, as she told Bella, refilling the other woman's glass, she was willing to believe anything was possible at Lady Ambercroft's.

Bella frowned, but went on. "Well, my heart started going *ga-thump, ga-thump, ga-thump*. I could hear it in my ears, I could! Then a black cloud passed right over my eyes. Like the time you told me that publisher chap was a sneakthief."

"Perhaps you should see a physician?"

"Oh, I have, dearie, I have." Or the next best thing, tipping a jug with the mortician next door. "He says emotional turmoil carries away a lot of folks. Anyways, next thing I know, Lady Ambercroft's man is calling for a hackney. But what about Miss Lattimore, I says? I can't just go leave the lamb. She says she'll look after you till I send your footman back to see you home. So I give the jarvey my address, and tell him to go by Park Lane so I can leave a message, and then—oh, I am too ashamed to tell!" She started striking herself on the chest again.

No wonder her heart went *ga-thump*, Sydney thought, if she kept pounding on it that way. "Please, Bella, please calm yourself. Remember what the doctor said. Just tell me what happened."

"A mouse."

"A mouse?"

"Recall how it was raining that night? The jarvey put down a fresh layer of straw to keep his coach clean from the wet boots and such. And I heard it, I swear."

"The mouse?"

"It's foolish, I know, but I am mortal afraid of mice, dearie. Why, my husband used to call me a chicken-hearted maid." (Paddy's actual words were "cheating-hearted jade," or worse.)

"I am sure he did not mean anything terrible by that. . . ."

"But it's true, and I failed you, lovey, through being weak. I heard the mouse. Right at my feet, it was. And I couldn't help myself, I start screaming for the driver and jumping on the seat, and all the time my heart going *ga-thump, ga-thump*, and then that black curtain comes down again. Next thing I know, I'm in my own parlor, with m'footman burning feathers under my nose. Then I remembered! I never got that there message to your house! Well, I almost went off again, let me tell you. But before I did, before I even took a sip of spirits to settle my nerves, I sent my man round with a note. Tell me, dearie, tell Bella so I can stop worrying, he got there in time, didn't he, before anyone could insult you or"—her whole body quivered—"make improper advances."

"As you can see, I am perfectly fine," Sydney told her, somehow not comfortable repeating the evening's true events. "Willy got your message and was there in no time flat. Why, it seemed like just a few minutes after you left." Sydney was already on her way home with the viscount, though, and those were the longest few minutes of her life. There was no reason to disturb poor Mrs. Ott any more, however, so Sydney merely told her, "It was an unfortunate night, but we are neither much the worse for it, except for this wretched cold, so if you would excuse me. . . ?"

"Of course, of course, dearie." Bella heaved herself out of the chair and ground her teeth. "We wouldn't want you to get an inflammation of the lungs or anything. But tell me, what of your plan to open a card parlor?"

"Oh, I can see that would be totally ineligible. In fact, I am surprised you didn't warn— No matter, I have decided to stop worrying about money and let tomorrow take care of itself."

Bella had never heard such tripe in her born days, no, not even from Chester. What else was a body supposed to worry about, if not having enough blunt for the future?

Happiness, that's what. Sydney realized she'd been putting her own pride in front of her sister's happiness, her own desire to avoid a loveless marriage ahead of Winnie's comfort. Facing the prosy Lord Scoville across the coffee cups for the rest of one's life would curdle anyone's cream. No, if Winnie wanted to marry Brennan Mainwaring, Sydney would not stand in their way.

When Brennan applied to the general for Winnie's hand, a conversation bound to be memorable, Sydney would have to be the one to take him aside and discuss settlements. If he truly had two estates, surely he could not object if Sydney and the general occupied one. In exchange, she would be the best aunt ever to his and Winnie's offspring, Sydney swore to herself. Nor should Mainwaring balk at repaying his own brother the funds that kept Winnie in muslins and lace, if he was as warm as the viscount claimed. Lord Mayne could return it as a wedding gift and they would all be satisfied.

Everyone but Sydney. The thought of spending the rest of her life in the country tending to someone else's blue-eyed, black-haired babes, even Winnie's, was so depressing she took to her bed for another day.

After twenty-four hours of hot chocolate and purple prose from the lending library Sydney felt much better. Happily not well enough for Almacks, bless King George and the Minerva Press.

Forrest stayed away for two days. His absence may have defused some of the rumors connecting his name and Sydney's, but it did nothing for his peace of mind. He couldn't keep that mind off the impossible chit. The devil, he still couldn't keep his hands off her. He was besotted, he admitted it, a grievous state indeed. Lord Mayne tried to treat this affliction like any other illness or injury: wrap it up, drown it in spirits, and sleep it off, or else forget about it and get on with one's business. None of those remedies worked. He was neglecting his correspondence, relegating estate matters to the stewards, delaying financial decisions. And all for worrying over what bumble-bath Mischief would fall into next.

Tarnation, the only way to keep the minx out of trouble was to keep her by his side. The idea of Sydney's tempests and tumults cutting up his well-ordered life on a daily basis was enough to make him shudder. Then he realized she was already doing it, driving him to distraction. Every day with Sydney? No, he shouted inside his own head, he did not want a wife! Especially not one who was impetuous, mercurial, and illogical, everything he held in low esteem. He had Brennan; he did not need a wife. He had a full and rich, satisfying existence; he did not need chaos in his life.

But every night with Sydney? *That,* perhaps, was exactly what he needed to cure this ailment.

It was Wednesday, it was Almacks. Why wasn't she here? Forrest surveyed the assembly hall through his quizzing glass, very well aware that he himself was the object of nearly every other eye. Blast, he thought, he'd done his best to see her vouchers to the boring place were not rescinded; the least she could do was not offend the patronesses by bowing out. Gads, if he could suffer being stared at and toadied to, fawned on and flirted with, discussed from his income to his unmentionables, then she could be there to waltz with him.

He waltzed with Sally Jersey instead. Her privileged position gave her the right to ask questions instead of speculating behind his back. Or so she believed.

"You would not be looking for anyone in particular, would you, darling?"

"Why would I, when I already have the loveliest lady here in my arms?"

"But twice in one month to the marriage mart? A lady might think you were on the lookout for a bride."

He twirled her in an elegant loop, ending the dance with a flourish. "My dear Silence, ladies should never think." He bowed and walked to where his brother was leading Winifred Lattimore off the floor.

"Miss Lattimore," he said, bowing over her hand with his usual easy grace. "You are as beautiful as ever. Parliament should send your portrait to the troops on the Peninsula to remind them what they are fighting for. I'll mention it to my father."

Instead of saying "oh, la," batting her eyelashes at him, or rapping him coyly with her fan, Winnie blushed and said, "Thank you, but I am sure those brave men need no reminding. Sydney says they would do better with sturdier boots, however, if you wish to pass that on."

Forrest could just imagine the duke's reaction to Sydney's well-founded suggestion that the war was not being efficiently managed. Not even the Ming vase would be safe. Then he considered how refreshing it was that neither of the Lattimore ladies flirted. He hoped the Season and the adulation would not change her—them.

"Miss Sydney keeps up with the war news, Forrest," Bren told him, "reading to the general. Well-informed, don't you know. She thinks I should reconsider wanting to join up. The war's liable to be over too soon for me to make a difference, she says."

If Forrest thought it curious that his heygomad brother listened to Sydney instead of his mother, father, and brother, he refrained from commenting. Instead, he remarked, "I must remember to thank Miss Lattimore, then. I, ah, do not see her among the gathering."

"No, she was too ill to join us," Winifred said. "She came down with an ague the night of Aunt Harriet's musicale. She should be recovered by tomorrow. Shall I tell her you asked for her?"

"Please." His heart sinking while he mouthed polite expressions of sympathy, Forrest turned to his brother. He remembered the last time Sydney cried off an engagement. She was

148

too sick for Lady Windham's, but well enough for Lady Ambercroft's.

Bren was reassuring. "You should have seen her, nose all red, eyes kind of glassy—ow." Winnie kicked him. "Uh, right. Lady and all, always in looks."

It was an odd infatuation when a gentleman was relieved to find the object of his affections ailing. Forrest smiled. A broken leg would have kept her out of trouble longer; a cold was good enough for now.

Forrest swung Miss Winifred into a *contre danse*, cheerfully cutting out Baron Scoville, whose name was on her card. Then he left, causing more of a buzz that he danced with only one young lady and grinned the whole time.

Lord Mayne went to White's, where he could relax in a male enclave, smoke a cheroot, sip a brandy, play a hand or two of piquet, all without a single worry to ruffle his feathers. He did keep his ears tuned to the flow of gossip, just in case Sydney's last hobble was mentioned. Nothing. He sighed with contentment and ordered his supper before the place got crowded.

When he returned from the dining room the club was in a frenzy with the latest tidings. Knowing Sydney was home safe in bed let the viscount stroll casually toward a knot of gentlemen who were shouting, waving their hands, and demanding action.

"The war?" he inquired of his friend Castleberry.

"No, highwaymen. Where have you been that you haven't heard? Last night five carriages were held up on Hounslow Heath. Three already tonight. It's all anyone can talk of."

"I don't see why. The authorities will have the gentlemen of the road under lock and key in jig time."

"But that's just it, Mayne. This new bunch is a gang of three: two men and a female!"

Talk swirled around the viscount, chatter about what was the proper term for the female robber: Highwaywoman? Footpadess? High Tabby? That dull dog Scoville arrived and surprised them all with a particularly vulgar expression to do with the bridle lay.

But Viscount Mayne was back in his chair, holding his head

in his hands. He was closer to despair than at any time since his navy days. He knew precisely what you called a female out on the roads at night, robbing carriages. You called her Sydney.

21

Low Road, Low Blow

The viscount went home and put on his oldest coat and buckskin breeches. He took out his wallet and identifying cards lest he be held to ransom. Leaving only a few pounds in his pocket, he stuck two pistols in his waistband and called for his fastest horse. He rode out to Hounslow Heath through another dark, damp mist.

He was promptly arrested.

Two nights it took, and two days. Two nights in rat-infested, stinking cells with unwashed drunks and felons. Two days of loutish deputies, ignorant, sadistic sheriffs, pompous magistrates. Forty-eight hours he spent, with no sleep lest his boots and coat be stolen, and food he would not feed to swine. Then he was given the opportunity to make a total ass of himself before one of his father's political cronies, explaining why a notable peer of the realm was playing at highwayman.

He did not stop at his own home to rest, to eat, to change his foul clothes, or to shave. He did not stop when Griffith tried to shut the front door in his savage face.

Bren jumped up from the parlor. "What happened to you, Forrest, and where the deuce have you been? I've been frantic."

Forrest looked toward the couch, where a blushing Winifred was attempting to repin her hair. "So I see," he said dryly.

Brennan bent to retrieve a missing hairpin. "It, ah, ain't what you think, Forrest. Chaperoned and all, don't you know." He jerked his head toward the general, half asleep in the corner.

Forrest knew the slowtop's goose was cooked. He did not care. "Where's Sydney?"

"She's out making calls. But don't worry," he added when he saw his brother's face go even more rigid," she's got both of the twins with her."

Boiling in oil was too good for them. Being stretched on the rack was—

The general pounded on his chair. When he had Lord Mayne's attention he raised his trembling hand and pointed toward the rear of the house.

"Thank you, sir," Forrest said, bowing smartly. Only Mrs. Minch was in the kitchen, scouring a pot. She took one look at his lordship's stormy face and nodded toward the back door. Then she grabbed up the bottle of cooking wine and locked herself in the pantry.

In the rear courtyard, where a tiny walled garden used to be, was a gathering of liveried servants, footmen, and grooms. Forrest did not see them. Willy and Wally sat on one side of an old trestle table in their shirtsleeves; he barely registered their presence. He had eyes only for Sydney, eyes that narrowed to hardened slits when he got a good look at her.

Miss Lattimore was wearing her stable boy's outfit, wide smock, breeches, knitted hat. She was sitting on a barrel, smiling, laughing . . . and counting the stacks of coins and bills in front of her on an overturned crate.

The viscount roared and lunged for her, knocking aside the table, the crate, and the barrel. He yanked her up by the collar of her loose shirt and shook her like a rat.

Wally jumped to his feet, forming his huge hands into fists. Willy grabbed a loose tree branch.

"You stay back, both of you, and wait your turn," Forrest raged, still dangling Sydney in the air. "I'm looking forward to you for dessert. And don't worry, I'm not going to kill the little snirp. I'll leave that to the hangman."

They grinned and righted the table, leaving Sydney to her fate. She kicked out, trying to get free. "Put me down, you barbarian!" she screamed.

He did, only to clamp her shoulders in a viselike grip and shake her some more. "What . . . in bloody hell . . . do you think . . . you are doing?"

Sydney aimed her wooden-soled work boot at his shin, but missed. He squeezed harder. She would have marks for weeks, as if he cared. He hadn't even come to see her when she was ill. She tried to kick him again. "For your information, you brute, the boys and I have found a new source of income. We're taking on all comers at arm-wrestling. I am the bank."

His arms fell. "You're the . . ."

"The odds-maker and scorekeeper and timer. And I am quite good at it, too. And you can just stop breathing fire at me, my lord bully, because I never left these premises, and all of these men are friends. Besides, I had to find something to do when I looked too horrid to go to parties with my nose all red, and *no one* came to visit."

Her nose was indeed pinkish and puffy. She was indignant that he stayed away, an astounding enough discovery. "Did you really miss me?" he asked, and stepped back from another swipe of her boot.

"Then you weren't out on Hounslow Heath?"

"Of course not, there's a band of robbers out— Why you, you dastard! You thought I was holding up carriages! You thought I would *steal* for money! You, you . . ." She couldn't think of words bad enough.

The viscount held up his hands. "Well, you kept thinking I was a loan merchant and a rake."

"You were, and you are!" she yelled, trying one last kick. This one connected quite nicely with his kneecap. She limped into the house while Willy tipped up the barrel and Wally helped the viscount to it.

"So what'll it be, gov, apple dumplings or rum pudding?" Willy asked, enjoying himself immensely.

Forrest grimaced. "Humble pie, I suppose."

Only one of the other men snickered. The rest were in sympathy for the toff who'd been rolled, horse, boots, and saddle, by a slip of a girl. The brotherhood of man went deeper than class lines.

Wally scratched his head. "You insulted her good this time, gov. She won't be getting over this one half quick."

One of the other footmen called out, "Aw, some posies're all it'd take. You can see she's daft for 'im."

"Nah," a groom disagreed, spitting tobacco to the side, "she's got half the swells in London sendin' her boo-kets. Ain't I delivered a dozen here myself? It'll take a lot more'n that to win 'er back."

"G'wan, wotta you know? You ain't had a pretty gal smile at you in dog's years. A little slap and tickle, that's all it takes to get 'em eatin' out o' your hands like birds."

"You English, what do you know about *amour*?" the French valet from across the street put in. "It is the sweet words, the pretty compliments a mademoiselle craves."

"But Mischief ain't like other girls."

"What did you say?" Now the viscount was willing to allow a ragtag group of servants to discuss his personal life. At least until his knee stopped throbbing enough for him to walk away without falling on his face. In his current disheveled state, most of the men did not even recognize him. "What did you call her?" he demanded.

Willy answered. "You wouldn't want anybody here using her real name, would you? And we couldn't go calling the bet-recorder 'my lady,' could we? 'Sides, Mischief seemed to fit."

"You don't have to worry, gov," Wally added, "no one here'll squeak beef on her neither, not if they know what's good for them."

The other men were quick to swear their mummers were dubbed. A little gossip in the tap room wasn't worth facing the Minch brothers. 'Sides, Mischief was a real goer, a prime 'un. They wished her the best. If this rumpled cove with the beard-shadowed face was the best, well, she wasn't like other fillies.

Only one of the workingmen in the courtyard did not pledge his silence. This fellow, the same one who snickered before, was edging his way to the rear gate before the viscount took a closer look at the company. Willy saw the bloke creeping away and stopped him with a "Hey, where do you think you're going?"

Wally snagged the little man by the muffler he had wound around his head and neck. The runt made a dash for the gate, leaving his scarf in Wally's hands, but Willy tackled him, sat on him, and punched those rabbity teeth, and a few others, back down his throat. "That was just in case you thought of talking to anybody about any of this," Willy warned. "And it looks better, too."

He tossed Randy over the garden wall like a jar of slops, then wiped his hands.

"Who was that?" Lord Mayne asked.

"Just the driver for that old bat who comes every once in a while. He won't be bothering no one hereabouts again, that's for sure."

The other men lost interest as soon as the squatty fellow went down. They were back to discussing the gentry cove's chances with Mischief and placing bets on the outcome. It was just like White's, Forrest realized, for speculating on another's privacy and gambling on someone else's misfortune. As the debate went on as if he weren't there, Forrest also decided that clothes definitely made the man; he was certainly not getting his usual respect, here in this disheveled rig.

"Oi still say if she wants 'im, it don't matter what 'e does. And if she don't want 'im, it still don't matter what 'e does."

"Nah, Missy's got bottom, she'll give a chap a chance to prove hisself. She won't be fooled by no pretty words 'n trinkets. Man's sincere, she'll know."

"Pshaw, they ain't mind readers, you looby. Gent's got to prove hisself, all right. An' the only way a female's ever been convinced is with a ring."

A hush fell over the enclosed space. Those were serious words, fighting words, church words almost. It was one thing to tease a man when he was bowed and bloodied, but a life sentence? It was bad luck even to talk about. Half the men spit over their right shoulders. The French valet crossed himself. The viscount groaned.

Willy and Wally looked at him and grinned. The viscount

did not have to be a mind reader, either, to know what they were thinking. He groaned again. Wouldn't Sydney make one hell of a duchess?

22

The Duchess Decides

Surrender did not come easily to an ex-navy officer. Faced with overwhelming odds, though, the viscount gave up. He did what any brave man would when conditions got so far beyond his control; he sent for his mother. On Bren's behalf.

Now, Lady Mayne may have had the finest network of information gathering outside the War Office, but she was itching for first-hand reconnaissance. She heard all about the encroaching females who were hovering on the edge of scandal, clinging to respectability by her son's fingers and her own name as social passport. She would have believed any tales of Brennan's havey-cavey doings, but Forrest's? Schoolroom chits no better than they ought to be? This she had to see for herself. And she would have done just that, showed up in London bag and baggage two weeks ago . . . if it weren't for that jackass of a duke she was married to.

He never came to her except for Christmas, and she wouldn't go to him except for coronations. He hated her devotion to her dogs; she hated his absorption in politics. Neither would budge. Now there were higher ideals that could not wait for a royal summons. Now mother love had to supplant pride. Now she was too eager to interfere in her sons' lives to let that whopstraw get in her way.

Her Grace traveled in state. Two coaches carried her,

her dogs, her dresser, and a maid. Three more coaches bore every insult she could heap on His Grace's household: her own sheets, towels, and pillows, prepared dishes from her own kitchens, her own butler and footmen, her own houseplants. The fourgon followed with her wardrobe, although she had every intention of charging a fortune in modistes' bills to the twiddlepoop while she was in town.

Lady Mayne planned her journey to a nicety, timing her arrival to coincide with the duke's after-luncheon rest period. The hour of silence was considered sacrosanct in his household, she knew, interrupted on pain of dismissal or dishware. The duke was accustomed to retreat to his study, where he reviewed the morning's meetings and speeches, prepared for the afternoon session, and sometimes took a nap, the old rasher of wind.

Hamilton Mainwaring, Duke of Mayne, was dreaming of the brilliant speech he would give, if he ever kept a secretary long enough to write it. That's when his wife descended on Mainwaring House with her dogs, servants, and trunks. There were servants carrying trunks, servants carrying dogs, servants directing other servants. And more dogs. The duchess couldn't very well leave any home, certainly not Pennyfeather's new puppies. They were all in the hall, yipping and yapping and tripping over each other and the London staff.

The duke's bellow of outrage warmed the cockles of his lady's heart; the sound of crockery smashing was worth every jolt and rattle of the last hurried miles. His thundering footsteps down the hall brought a smile to her lips as she gaily called out, "Hello, darling, I'm home. Aren't you pleased?"

Hostilities recommenced after tea, when the duke realized his Sondra's visit was not a concession, just a tactical maneuver. He discovered quickly enough that she had not concluded at long last that her place was by her husband's side. She was not staying in London to be his hostess and helpmate, and everything from the dust on the chandeliers to the war with Napoleon was All His Fault.

Brennan recalled a previous engagement. Forrest had calculated his mother's timing even closer than she had. He was out for the day, dining at his club, promised for the evening. No matter, Lady Mayne had not come to see him anyway.

"Then what the devil *are* you here for, madam, if a poor husband may be permitted to ask?"

Lady Mayne made sure the tea things were wheeled out before she told him. She was partial to the Wedgwood. "I am here, husband, because you have made micefeet of my sons' lives."

"I have?" he blustered. "I have, when it's you who keeps them tied to your apron strings? You have Forrest hopping back and forth like some deuced yo-yo, and you won't let Brennan take the colors like every lad dreams of doing. And *I* am ruining their lives?"

"Yes, you. You live here, don't you? You have eyes to see what is around you, ears to hear that the Mainwaring name is on everybody's lips. And what have you done? Nothing. You are letting your own sons fall into the clutches of penniless nobodies, underbred adventuresses, fortune-hunting hoydens!"

"Well, they ain't nobodies, for one thing. General Lattimore's a fine man, well respected and all that."

"He was a vile-tempered, hard-drinking curmudgeon twenty years ago. I don't fancy he's changed."

The duke cleared his throat. "You can't say they have no breeding either, no matter if it is your hobbyhorse. They are Windhams on the mother's side. Nothing to be ashamed of there."

"Just long noses and a tendency to die early! Thin blood they have, all of them. I met the mother, and a weak, puny thing she was. I was not surprised she cocked up her heels so young. No stamina."

The duke rather thought he recalled Mrs. Lattimore had died in a carriage accident; he was too cagey a fish to be drawn to that fly, though, and too relieved. "So you really do know the family. I couldn't imagine why the boy put it about that you had an interest there."

The duchess pursed her lips. "Couldn't you? He was thinking with his inexpressibles, that's why. The little climbers must have put him up to it, to smooth their way up the social ladder. I met the mother once, as I said. Elizabeth Windham

157

was much younger, don't you know, and we were traveling then. My cousin Trevor was bowled over by her. She had that fragile beauty men seem to admire. But Elizabeth tossed him over for a uniform, ran off with young Lattimore and broke my cousin's heart. He died soon after, so I ain't likely to take her chicks under my wing."

The duke knew for a fact Trevor died of a weakness of the lungs. That's when Sondra started wrapping her own boys in cotton. He was not about to mention that tidbit either, having learned early on that facts only slowed his lady's flow of thought, never diverted it or dammed it. "Well, I don't think you need worry about them hanging on your sleeves. That Harriet Windham's managed to get them on all the right guest lists."

"I always supposed that nipcheese was behind this whole thing, trying to snabble rich husbands for her nieces. Heaven knows what she hopes to do for her own whey-faced chit, but she's not going to snag my sons!"

"I hear the elder Miss Lattimore is a real beauty," the duke offered.

His lady waved that aside. "I hope a Mainwaring has too much sense to fall for a pretty face. Those empty-headed belles make poor— What do you mean, you *hear* she's a beauty? Haven't you seen her for yourself, this harpy with her claws in your own son? Didn't you care sufficiently to take your head out of that dreary office long enough to check, you pettifogging excuse for a father?"

"I care, blast it, I care!" The duke was shouting, growing red in the face.

The duchess ran to the mantel and handed him the ormolu clock there. "Here, throw this," she said. "Your aunt Lydia sent it as a wedding gift. I always hated it."

The duke carefully placed the ornate thing back in its spot. "I know, that's why I always kept it." Then he turned to her and grinned. "Ah, Sondra, my sunshine, how I have missed you."

The duchess colored prettily, and at her age! "Sussex is not so far away, you know."

"But would I find welcome there, or would a dog be sleeping in my bed like last time, when I had to take a guest room?"

"Are you trying to change the subject, Hamilton? It won't wash. What about the boys?"

"Dash it, Sondra, they are men, not boys, and I do care. I care enough to let them make their own mistakes, the same way we did."

"And look where it got us!" she retorted.

"I am," was all he said, and she was glad she had on her new lilac gown, the way he was staring at her with that special gleam in his eye.

"Humph! First we'll see about those upstarts, then we'll see about *that*."

The duchess took her battle to the enemy camp. The duke hurried out to buy a new corset.

Lady Mayne was not surprised to find Harriet Windham at the Lattimores' for tea, she was only surprised how much she still disliked the woman after all these years. Trust that lickpenny to eat anyone else's food but her own and to thrust her own fubsy daughter into a prettier girl's orbit. The duchess could not like how Lady Windham rushed to greet her at the door, neatly stepping in front of the pretty gal and pinching the other chit when she started to say something. Now the toad-eater was ordering the Misses Lattimore to tend to less noble guests, including the duchess's son Brennan, while Harriet fawned over the most exalted. Gads, if she had wanted a chat with the squeeze-farthing, Her Grace would have called at Windham House, not Park Lane. And she would have eaten more first. The almond tarts she was generously being offered here—by the daughters of the house, not servants, she noted—were quite good.

She delicately wiped a crumb from her lip and fired her first salvo: "My dear Harriet, I know it has been ages, but you must not let me keep you from the rest of your calls."

"Don't think anything of it, Your Grace. Beatrix and I have nowhere better—"

Second round: "I am sure, I would like to get to know Elizabeth's charming daughters, however."

"How kind you are to take an interest. Perhaps I should plan a dinner—"

The broadside: "Alone. Now."

Brennan came to her side after the Windhams left. "Masterful, Your Grace," he applauded. "May I stay, or am I *de trop* also?"

"You may bring me that attractive young woman you were drooling over, then take yourself off."

"Attractive? Mother, she's the most beautiful girl in the world. And the sweetest. And just wait till you see her on a horse."

"What, that porcelain doll?"

Bren grinned, reminding her of his father when they met. "She's naught but a country girl, Mother. She knows all about flowers and things. I can't wait to show her your gardens at the Chance, and see what she thinks about that old property of Uncle Homer's." The duchess sighed. She was too late.

She was also delighted with Winifred, who truly was as lovely as she was pretty. She was unspoiled and unaffected, only slightly in awe of meeting Bren's august parent. This last impressed the duchess most, for she remembered her first meeting with the dowager. Her knees might show bruises to this day from knocking together so hard. Lady Mayne also noted how Winifred kept looking to make sure the other sister took care of the general and the rest of the company. If her conversation wasn't brilliant, well, even his doting mother never considered Brennan a mental giant. Incredible as it seemed, the chawbacon seemed to have found himself a pearl. And without his mother's help. She waved the chit off to save him from a boring conversation with a Tulip in a bottle-green suit.

Before the duchess could spot her next quarry, the girl was curtsying to her, and winking! "Did she pass muster, Your Grace?" the brazen young woman was asking with a grin that showed perfect dimples under dancing eyes and curls that— ah, so that explained the bundle her son carried from place to place. Well, it did not really, so the duchess asked.

"My, ah, hair? I am sorry, Your Grace, but I really cannot explain that. I mean, I could, but I don't think I should. I was somewhere I should not have been and Lord Mayne—the viscount, that is, not the duke—was there, too. And he helped. Oh, but you mustn't think poorly of him for being there or, or for acting not quite the gentleman. About the hair, that is."

Not quite the gentleman, her oh-so-proper son Forrest? The duchess was intrigued by the girl's artlessness, and how she did not even seem aware that she was under scrutiny the same as her sister. "My dear," the duchess said, patting her hand, "you have been without a mother too long if you think I could believe ill of my son. It is always some other mother's progeny who is to blame."

Sydney grinned again. "Do you know, your son feels the same way! Whenever he gets himself in a snit or a fit of the sullens, it always seems to be my fault."

Tempers? Moods? The duchess wondered if they were speaking of the same person. Forrest was the most unprovokable man of her experience, and she had been trying for years. Oh, this was a chit after her own heart. "Miss Lattimore, do you like dogs?"

The duchess returned home to inform the duke that he'd done just what he ought, and found their sons the perfect brides.

"Brilliant, my dear, brilliant," she congratulated him over their pre-dinner sherry.

"I thought they didn't have a feather to fly with."

"Pooh, who's talking about money? Of course nothing's settled yet, so I might have to stay on in town to take a hand in matters after all."

The duke pretended to study his ancestor's portrait on the wall. "Might you, my dear?"

"Of course, I would need an escort sometimes, you know, to show we both countenanced the match. If that would not pull you away from your duties terribly."

His Grace tossed back his wine and held out his arm to lead her in to dinner. "Family support is worth the sacrifice. You can count on me, my dear," he said with a bow. His new corsets creaked only a little.

23

Miss Lattimore . . . or Less

$\mathcal{V}$iscount Mayne did not usually peek into the breakfast room before entering, but with the duchess in town, forewarned was forearmed. He'd rather go without his kippers and eggs than have his hair combed with a bowl of porridge so early in the morning. The duchess was smiling, though, and humming over her chocolate and some lists she was writing. He entered, careful to watch for the furry little beggars one always found lapping up crumbs in Her Grace's breakfast parlor.

"Good morning, Mother," he said, dropping a kiss on her bent head before helping himself at the sideboard. "I see you are keeping country hours. Did you sleep well or did the London noise awaken you?"

Oddly, she blushed. "I slept very well, thank you. I wished to speak with your father this morning before he left for his office." The viscount looked around for pottery shards. "And you before you went on your usual ride." Or escape hatches.

"I think I'll just send for some fresh coffee," he said, moving to the bellpull.

"It's fresh, dearest. And so are the eggs, done just the way you like them. Sit. Oh, no, Forrest, I did not mean you. Pumpkin was trying to steal Prince Charlie's bacon."

Forrest excused himself. He was not particularly hungry any longer.

"But you cannot go until we've talked about my dinner party."

"Are you staying in town long enough to throw a party, then? Father will be pleased." He hoped so. He himself was planning on being busy that night, whichever night she chose.

Lady Mayne's London circle was the worst bunch of character assassins he ever met, meddlers and intriguers all. Now that the duchess was in London to look after Bren, perhaps Forrest could return to the peace and quiet of the countryside.

"Yes, I thought I would host a small gathering to introduce Miss Lattimore to our closest friends."

He sat down in a hurry. Sydney at the mercy of those gossipmongers? Heaven knew what she would do if he wasn't there to look after her. "Brennan told me you visited at Park Lane. So you mean to take them up?"

The duchess looked up from her lists. "Of course. That's what you intended when you wrote me, wasn't it? They'd be quite ruined if I were to cut the connection now, after the mull you made of introducing them. A friend of their mother's, indeed! Lucky for you I even knew the peahen."

Forrest waved that aside. "Then you don't mind that Miss Lattimore hasn't a feather to fly with?"

Lady Mayne set down her pencil. "I hope I have not raised my sons to think that money can buy happiness, for it cannot. Then, too, Brennan shall have an adequate income to provide for any number of wives."

"And their families. You don't think they could be fortune hunters, do you?"

"Stuff and nonsense. How could you look at that sweet girl and stay so cynical?" She frowned at him as if the idea never entered her mind. "I think she and her sister have done the best they could to keep themselves above oars, considering all the help they got from that cheeseparing aunt. Why, she has a houseful of underpaid servants, and her own nieces fetch and carry like maids. She must have a barn full of equipages, and they travel about in hired carriages! It's the outside of enough, and I have already taken steps to see things changed. See how Lady Windham likes the ton knowing a near stranger has to frank her relations. The duke agrees."

Forrest choked on a piece of toast. Now, that was a first, the Mainwarings agreeing about anything. Forrest could not help wondering how Sydney felt about his mother's largess, with her prickly pride.

"I was *not* high-handed, Forrest. I let Bren manage it. She's his intended, after all."

"And you are reconciled to the match even though it is not a brilliant one?"

"Who says it is not? She is going to keep him happy and safe at home. What more could I want? And can you imagine what beautiful children they will have? I cannot wait to see if they are dark like Brennan or fair like Winifred."

Forrest had a second helping of eggs. "I am relieved you found her so charming, Mother. I thought you would."

"Yes, and I don't even mind that she is an independent thinker and an original, either."

"Independent? Winnie? If the girl had two thoughts to rub together, I never heard them."

"Who said I was talking about Miss Lattimore? I am speaking of your Miss Sydney, who does not have more hair than wit. And if you did not send for me to get your ducks in a row with that refreshing young miss, I'll eat my best bonnet."

"She's not refreshing, she's exhausting. She is a walking disaster who is forever on the verge of some scandal. *That's* why I sent for you, before she could ruin Winnie's chances, too. Sydney is infuriating and devious and always up to her pretty little neck in mischief."

"Yes, dear," his mother said, bending over her lists, "that's why you are top-over-trees in love with her."

The fork hit the plate. "Me? In love with Sydney? Fustian! Who said anything about love? She's a wild young filly who will never be broke to bridle, and I am too old to try."

"Of course. That's why you carry her hair from London to Sussex and back again."

The viscount couldn't keep his eyes from flashing upward. "Never tell me you check my rooms, Your Grace."

"I don't have to, dear. You just told me."

"I thought the hair upset you at the manor," he said, praying that the warmth he felt was not showing as red on his face. "That's all there is to it, by George."

"Don't swear, Forrest. You've been around your father too much. And don't worry over being so blind you cannot recognize what your own heart is telling you. Your father never believed he loved me either until I told him. Just don't wait too long, Forrest, for royalty won't be too high for Miss Sydney when I am through."

The coffee was bitter and the eggs were cold. Forrest put his plate on the floor for the dogs to squabble over and excused himself. "I am sure you and the housekeeper can work out all the details for your dinner party. Father's new secretary seems a capable sort, too, but feel free to call on me if I can be of assistance."

She was back at her lists before he reached the door. "Oh, by the way, Forrest," she called when his hand touched the knob, "I gave Sydney a dog."

The viscount's hand fell to his side and his head struck the door. "Do you really hate me that much, Mother?"

Did he love her? Not which horse should he ride, which route should he take to the park, just: Did he love her? Forrest controlled his mount through the traffic, galloped down the usual rides, cooled the chestnut gelding on tree-shaded pathways, all without noticing the other men also exercising their cattle or the nursemaids with their charges or the old ladies feeding the pigeons. He was lost in the center of London, lost in his thoughts.

He supposed he did love her. He surely had all the attics-to-let symptoms of a mooncalf in love. But could he live with Sydney Lattimore? Hell, could he live without her?

He had yet another concern: Did she love him? He knew from her kisses that she was not altogether unresponsive to him, but she also resented him, sometimes despised him, and never respected him. More often than not, she looked at him as if he were queerer than Dick's hatband. Maybe he was, to care what she thought. Hang it, he'd had more kicks than kisses from the wench!

His mother thought Sydney loved him, for what the opinion of another totty-headed, illogical female was worth. Plenty, most likely, he thought as he picked up the horse's pace again. Now, there was another woman he never hoped to understand. The duke said you'd end up cross-eyed if you tried, anyway. But the duchess had always preached propriety, breeding, duty to the family name. Now she was pleased to consider one of the devil's own imps as her successor. He shuddered at the thought. Sydney as duchess meant Sydney as his wife.

Confused by the mixed signals it was receiving, the chestnut reared. Forest brought it back under control with a firm hand and a pat on the neck. "Sorry, old fellow. My fault for wool-gathering. I don't suppose you have any advice?" The horse shook its head and resumed the center. "No, gelding is not the answer."

He set his mind to the matter at hand, looking out for other riders and strollers now that the park was getting more crowded. When they reached another shaded alleyway, however, Forrest let the horse pick their way while he searched his mind for answers.

If he loved Sydney, he should marry her. If she loved him, she would marry him. He did not think for a moment that she would wed for convenience, not his Sydney with her fiery emotions. And there was no longer a reason for her to make a cream-pot marriage, not with Winnie's future guaranteed. She had to know Brennan would look after her, and the general as well. Forrest would see to the settlements himself, ensuring she never had to concoct any more bubble-headed schemes, even if she did not marry him.

But she would marry him if she loved him. If he asked, Zeus, what if she refused? What if a slip of a girl with less sense than God gave a duck refused the Viscount of Mayne, one of the most eligible bachelors in London? He'd never recover, that's what. She'd be a fool to turn down his title, wealth, and prospects, but he would be shattered.

And the duchess would know. She always did. Gads, he'd have to listen to her taunts whenever he was at home, unless she told all her friends. Then he'd be a laughingstock everywhere he went. He may as well move to the Colonies, for all the joy he'd find in England.

He reined the horse to a standstill, tipping his hat to a family of geese crossing the path to the Serpentine. The gossip did not matter any more than the honking of the geese. There would be no joy without Sydney, period.

Such being the case, he acknowledged, kneeing the horse

onward, still at a walk, there was nothing for it but to put his luck to the touch. He had to ask. But when? His mother had both girls so hedged about with callers and servants, he'd never get to see Sydney alone now. The duchess was not leaving the rumor hounds a whiff of scandal. Forrest was glad, for no one with baser desires could reach the Lattimores either. He had not forgotten about the moneylending scum and still had men watching the house and scouring London for Randall and Chester. His men had turned up the information that they were brothers, as unlikely as it seemed, by the name of O'Toole. Bow Street was also extremely interested in their whereabouts.

Let Bow Street worry about the blackguards, Forrest decided. The best way to keep Sydney safe was to keep her by his side. Which, he thought with a frown, his own mother was preventing. He might get her alone the night of the betrothal dinner his mother was hosting for Brennan and Winifred. He could suggest showing Sydney the family portrait gallery. No, he would feel all those eyes were watching him play the fool. Perhaps a visit to the jade collection in the Adams Room, he mused. No, the locked cabinets reminded him of his parents' stormy relationship.

As he went on a mental tour of Mainwaring House, the viscount discovered a new romantical quirk to his thinking. He wanted Sydney where no one could disturb them, in daylight when he could see the emotions flicker in her hazel eyes. He wanted to ask her to live with him at Mayne Chance, *at* Mayne Chance.

They were all coming to Sussex for the holidays, after the Season. The wedding would be held there after the new year, he understood from Bren, in the family chapel.

Yes, the Chance was the perfect place to take his own chance. The holidays added a special excitement anyway, with parties throughout the neighborhood, mistletoe, kissing boughs, and the whole castle decorated in greenery. With excursions to gather the holly and the yule log, to deliver baskets to the tenants and flowers to the church, he would surely find the ideal opportunity. Maybe there would be snow, with sleigh rides, long walks, ice skating, and snowball fights with his sisters' children. Forrest found he couldn't wait to show Sydney his home, his heritage, her future.

His mother was wrong; there was no rush. Forrest could wait for the perfect time, the perfect place. He smiled and set the gelding to a measured trot. "Time to go home, boy."

Suddenly his mount reared. Then it bucked and crow-hopped and tossed its head. Forrest managed to stay on by sheer luck and ingrained good horsemanship, for he hadn't been paying attention this time either, visions of Sydney with snowflakes falling on rosy cheeks obscuring his view of Rotten Row.

He collected the Thoroughbred and was straightening his disordered neckcloth when he noticed that the chestnut had flecks of blood on its head. Holding the reins firmly, Forrest dismounted.

"What the deuce?" The gelding's ear appeared to have a clean slice partway through. Forrest looked around and saw no one. Still holding the reins, he murmured soothing words to the horse and led it back to where his beaver hat lay on the path. He kept looking behind him, in the trees, through the shrubbery. Damn, there were a million places an ambusher could hide. Then his eye caught the glint of metal and he tugged the still-nervous animal off the tanbark. A knife was embedded in a tree trunk at just about the height of his head when astride. "Hell and damnation," he cursed under his breath at his own stupidity.

Figuring the assailant to be long gone, Forrest pocketed the knife and remounted. He retraced their path, keeping his wits about him this time. The only person he saw was a bent old woman with a cane and a shawl over her head, sitting on a stone bench. A flock of pigeons pecked at the grass near her feet.

"Good day, Grandmother," the viscount called. "Did you see anyone come after me on the path?"

The old hag raised her head. "Whatch that, sonny?" she asked through bare gums, her mouth caved in around missing teeth.

"I said, did you see someone following me? Anybody suspicious?"

"No, and no." The crone shook her head sadly. "M'eyesight ain't what it used to be."

Forrest tossed her a coin and rode away. The old woman cursed and tore the shawl off her head, leaving a crop of red hair. Then she threw her spectacles on the ground and jumped on them. Then she kicked a pigeon or two. Randy hadn't listened to his mother either.

24

Sydney and Sensibilities

Something was wrong. Circumstances were at their best, yet Sydney felt her worst. She was thrilled at Winifred's good fortune, truly she was. Winnie's slippers had not touched the ground since the duchess nodded her approval. Sydney's sister would be wrapped round with love and happiness, tied with a golden future like the most wonderful, glittering Christmas gift. And Sydney was not satisfied.

They had no more worries about squeezing the general's pension so hard it cried, and Sydney's own dowry was to be restored with all debts—unspecified—absorbed under the terms of the settlements. Sydney and the general were invited to make their homes with Bren and Winnie in Hampshire when they went, or with the duke and duchess in London and Sussex. So there was nothing to get in a pother about.

But it wasn't enough, Sydney knew. She did not want to be a charity case, even if she were the only one who considered herself in that light. She did not want to be a poor relation, hanging on her sister's coattails, the bridesmaid going along on the honeymoon. As much as she liked and admired the duchess, she did not think she would be happy in another woman's household either, especially not one where the china had an uncertain future and the eldest son was likely to bring home a bride of his own at any time. No, she would not think of that.

What she did think of, what kept her chewing on her lip, was that she had not met her goals. She had not satisfied her honor. With the best of intentions and far better results than she could have attained, the Mainwarings were taking over her responsibilities. They were making decisions for her, providing for her, caring for her. She even rode in one of their carriages. Sydney was back to being the little sister, and she did not care for it one whit.

There was a big hole in her life, not filled by all the picnics and parties and fittings and fussing over clothes the duchess insisted on, nor by the maids and grooms and errand boys the duchess deemed necessary for Winnie's consequence. The hole was where her plans and schemes, daydreams and fancies, used to occupy her thoughts. She used to feel excitement, anticipation, the sense that she was doing something worthwhile, something for herself and her loved ones. Now she felt . . . nothing.

There was a bigger emptiness in her heart. He never came except on polite, twenty-minute calls with his mother. He never asked for more than one dance at any of the balls, and he never held her hand longer than necessary. He no longer ordered her about, threatened her, or shouted at her. He did not curse or call her names, and he never, ever made her indecent proposals.

Sydney did not really expect Forrest to continue his atrocious behavior, not with all the maids and chaperones the duchess stacked like a fence around her and Winnie's virtue. And she did not really expect him to repeat his outrageous offer, not with his mother in town.

Well, yes, she did. He was a rake, and no rake would let a few old aunties or abigails get in his way. He'd never been bothered about speaking his mind in front of Willy or Wally. And no rake in any of the Minerva Press romances ever even *had* a mother, much less pussyfooted around her feelings. The duchess said he was dull and always had been. Sydney knew better. He just didn't care anymore.

So Sydney wouldn't care either, so there. It did not matter anyway, she told herself; her dog loved her. Princess Penny-fleur was a delight. Sydney called her Puff for short, since all of the Duchess's Princess dogs answered to Penny, and Puff was so special she deserved a name of her own. The little dog was always happy, wearing that silly Pekingese grin that made Sydney smile. She was always ready to romp and play or go for a walk, or just sit quietly next to Sydney while she read. Puff wasn't like any unreliable male, blowing hot, then cold.

Even the general enjoyed the little dog. He held her in his lap, stroking her silky head for hours when Sydney was out in the evenings. Griffith thought the general's hand was growing stronger from all the exercise. Puff was wise enough to jump down if the general grew agitated, before he started pounding on anything.

They made quite a stir in the park, too, just as the duchess predicted. Traffic at the fashionable hour came to a halt when Sydney walked by with her coppery curls and her matching dog curled like a muff in her arms or trotting at her heels. It was a picture for Lawrence or Reynolds, or Bella Bumpers.

"We gotta nab her in the park. It's the only place she ain't cheek-to-jowls with an army of flunkies. She don't have time for me no more, and they've got a carriage of their own now, not that she would get back into the carriage after that time with you at the reins, Fido."

Randy had a new set of teeth. Actually, he had half of a new set, the bottoms. These ivories, from a blacksmith who had been kicked in the mouth once too often, were again too big for Randy, so his lower jaw jutted out over the upper, giving him the appearance of a bulldog. He blamed the viscount for that, too, setting Bow Street on their tail. Now neither of the brothers dared show his own face outdoors long enough for Randy to visit a real denture-maker. He never admitted to Bella that the footmen smashed the first set, not the viscount, so the grudge was a heavier weight on her back, too.

They were holding their latest planning session in the base-ment at their house in Chelsea, the only place Chester felt secure.

"I'm not going to do it, Mama," he whimpered now. "It's not safe. We've got to get out of London. To hell with the money, I say."

"You'd say you were mad King George if you thought it would save your skin, pigeon-heart. 'Sides, we're all packed. We just have to snag the gel and catch the packet at Dover. We'll have it all. First he'll pay, then we give out her suicide note saying he ruined her. He'll be finished. It's perfect."

Chester lost what color he had. "We're not going to kill the girl, Mama. You promised."

"Nah, Chester, we're going to let the wench swim back to England and fit us for hemp neckties." Randy was practicing his knife-throwing. One landed a shiver's distance from Chester's foot.

"I'm not going, then. I'm not having anything to do with murder. Mayne would find us at the ends of the earth. Besides, she's seen me too many times. The footman, then that fellow Chesterton. She'll recognize me for sure. It won't work. I won't—yeow!"

Chester was going, only now he'd limp.

Leaves crunching under her feet, not even Sydney could be in the doldrums on such a pretty fall day. She had on a forest-green pelisse with the hood up, with Puff on a green ribbon leash scampering at her side. Brennan and Winnie walked just ahead, since there was room for only two abreast on this less frequented path they chose. Sydney slowed her steps to give them some quiet time alone. They must be feeling the lack of privacy even more than she was.

Wally and Annemarie followed after, but they were dis-cussing their own futures. If the Minch brothers stayed with Sydney and the general, how could Annemarie go off to Hampshire with Winifred? But it was a better position, and Wally might never be able to afford that inn, or a wife. No one would arm-wrestle with him anymore, and he'd promised his mother, Sydney, and Annemarie not to enter another prizefight. So involved were they in their conversation, and the pretty maid's anguish which needed to be assuaged behind a concealing tree, that they did not notice Sydney was no longer with her sister and Lord Mainwaring. She could have been beaten, drugged, and stuffed in a sack before they noticed she was gone, which was Bella's intention, except for the sack.

"Help, miss, oh, help!" the bent old woman cried as she used her cane to clear a way through some bushes to the path where Sydney walked. "We've been set on by footpads! My little girl is hurt! Oh, help!" She grabbed on to Sydney's arm with a surprisingly strong grip for one so ancient and frail, and tried to drag her back off the path with her. "My Chessie, my baby. Oh, please come help, kind lady."

The woman had an overbite like Puff's, though not as attractive, and bits of red hair sticking out from her turban. Her voice was a shrill whisper of distress.

"I'll get my footman, ma'am; he'll send for the watch," Sydney offered, trying to turn back.

"Mama," came a screeching falsetto from behind the bushes.

"They're long gone," the old lady told her, pulling Sydney forward. "And I just need you to help me get my little girl Chessie back to the coach. Do you have any vinaigrette? Hartshorn?"

"No, but my maid is right behind me. She must have something." Sydney looked back, wondering just where Annemarie and Wally were. She knew she should not get out of their sight, but a lady in such dire straits . . .

"Don't worry, dear, I'm Mrs. Otis. Everyone knows me. Your maid will find you, but we can have poor Chessie in the carriage by then. It's her foot, you see."

And indeed another female was limping toward them, crying into a large handkerchief. Her cheeks looked rouged and her dress was not quite the thing either, being a coliquet-striped silk with cherry ribbons. The female's hair, under a bonnet with three ostrich feathers, was an improbable yellow shade. All in all, Sydney realized this was not a person she should know.

The outfit had not been to Chester's taste either, but Bella's short, wide black dresses did not fit his tall, thin frame, and he was not about to go outside to shop the second-hand stalls. The only business next door this week was a Covent Garden street-walker who'd died of the French disease. The mortician swore on his mother's grave Chester couldn't catch the pox by wearing her dress. Of course the mortician's mother didn't have a grave; he'd sold her body to the anatomy college. Chester did not know that, so he stuffed some more stockings in the bodice, crying the whole time anyway. He limped effectively, too, with his weight on Sydney so she had to keep moving toward the coach she saw ahead.

"But, but it's a hearse!" Sydney exclaimed when she got a better look at the vehicle with its black curtains, black horses, and casket sticking out of the back.

"Yes, isn't it a shame?" the old woman lamented. "Here we are, on our way to bury Chessie's husband, and she felt the need to get out and compose herself in the serenity of nature. Then what should happen but three ruffians jumped on us! They robbed the money to pay the grave diggers, can you imagine? Then they knocked down poor Chessie and stole her wedding ring. What is this world coming to?"

Sydney didn't know, when the driver with his black top hat and weepers didn't get down to help two women in obvious distress, and when a bereft wife dressed more like bachelor fare than grieving widow. "What is this world coming to, indeed?" she echoed.

By the time they finally reached the carriage, Sydney was breathing hard. Mrs. Otis opened the door and stood back for Sydney to help Chessie up . . . with the weighted handle of her cane poised near Sydney's head. The coffin lid creaked open a crack so Bella could breathe inside it without being knocked out by the ether-dipped cloth in her hand. And Chessie wept. Sydney put one foot on the carriage steps and hauled Chessie up. Then a dog barked.

"Puff!" Sydney shouted. "I forgot all about my little dog! Here, Puff, here I am." She pushed right past the unprepared Mrs. Otis, leaving Chester to teeter on the steps. They could hear the dog barking and, getting closer, Wally's voice calling

"Miss Sydney." Brennan Mainwaring shouted from the other direction.

Chester couldn't catch her, not with his foot bandaged like a mummy, and Bella couldn't get out of the coffin in time. Randy bent to throw the knife in his boot, then recalled he wasn't wearing boots. "Bloody hell," Randy cursed, "let's get out of here." So he shoved Chester through the door, smack into the ether-sopped rag, and sprang in after him. Bella pushed the coffin lid aside, hard, right through Randy's new choppers. The coach was already moving.

When Sydney brought her friends back to the clearing to see if they could be of further assistance, no one and nothing was there, except some ivory dentures Puff found. Bottoms.

25

Plans and Provisions

The duchess could well understand Sydney's megrims. Forrest's intransigence was enough to make a saint blue-deviled. Lady Mayne asked him over and over, and all the close-mouthed churl answered was that the time wasn't right. Stuff, he'd be cutting up chickens and consulting stargazers next. What was worse, she could not even discuss it with Sydney to reassure the poor girl. The duchess didn't want to get the lass's hopes up, in case her war-hero son never gathered enough courage to come up to scratch. Moreover, the duke threatened mayhem if she meddled. With all their friends coming to dinner in two weeks, she could not chance the monogrammed dishes.

Then there was the matter of that loan, the one not spelled

out in the settlements. The duke vowed he knew nothing about it, and Forrest was as quiet as a clam. It would have been beyond the pale to question Sydney, and useless to subject Bren to an inquisition, for he was more in awe of his brother than of his mother. But the duchess knew about the hair and she knew about pride, better than most.

"You know, Sydney," she casually remarked as they wrote out invitations one afternoon, "it occurred to me that you might think me an interfering old biddy, sending you servants, ordering your life about."

"Never, Your Grace." Sydney jumped up to get more cards to address and kissed the older woman's cheek. "Aunt Harriet is an interfering old biddy, you are an interfering old dear. You are kind and generous and have only Winifred's best interests at heart. I would be cloddish in the extreme not to be grateful."

"Yes, but gratitude can be wearing on one," the duchess persisted. "I do not want you to feel the least bit indebted, especially not to my son."

"I shall always be thankful to Lord Mainwaring for the care he takes of Winnie and the general," Sydney answered hesitantly, not sure she liked the trend of this conversation. The duchess was charming, and as sneaky as she could dare.

"I didn't mean Brennan, my dear."

"Did he tell you? That villain! He swore the loan was forgotten, that he wouldn't take the money back under any conditions! Why, I'll—"

The duchess moved the ink pot, from long practice. "No, my dear, Forrest would never be so ungentlemanly." Ignoring the snort of derision from her young friend, she went on. "You must know Forrest would not go back on his word. No, I just got a hint of a loan, from little snippets of information. And no, I am not prying into the details. Of course, if you should wish to confide in me ... No, well, as I was saying, I do not wish to intrude, but I cannot help noticing a degree of constraint between you two. I would not wish you to be—" She almost started to say that she did not wish Sydney and Forrest to begin their married life with a molehill between them; marriage provided enough mountains to climb. She caught herself in time. "I do not wish you two proud people to be at odds."

Sydney laughed. "I suppose I do have a surfeit of pride, Your Grace, for I should dearly love to pay him back, but I could never find the money and he would never take it. For that matter, I would love to throw a ball for Winnie's engagement, to repay all the hostesses who have invited us throughout the Season, and I cannot do that either. I thought Aunt Harriet might, being the bride's family and all." Now it was Her Grace's turn to make rude noises. "But Winnie does not mind, so I shall have to swallow more of my damnable pride. And please," she said before the duchess could say anything, "do *not* offer me the funds, because then I would be offended."

"You wouldn't let me . . . ?"

"You have already done so much, why, I wish I could do something for you!"

"You can, dear girl, you can." You can shake my stodgy son from his cave of complacency, she thought, and out into the sunshine and moonlight.

The duchess had a plan, a great and glorious plan, making Sydney's schemes look like child's play. Best of all, the enterprise was neither dangerous, scandalous, nor illegal. It was perfect. Sydney was going to throw a ball!

"But, ma'am, you cannot have thought. The money, the space, all the expenses . . ."

"Stuff and nonsense, child, think. We're both country girls, so tell me: If the church needs a new roof, what do the parishioners do?"

Sydney giggled. "They dun the richest man in the neighborhood. Is that what I should do?"

"Don't be impertinent, miss. If the local nabob does not choose to buy his place in heaven, what then? What if a farmer's barn burns down? Don't tell me things are so different in Little Dedham. Now use that pretty brain box of yours."

"Why, the villagers would all donate what they could to the church, and they would all get together to help rebuild the barn. Sometimes they would hold a potluck supper, or an auction to raise money. And sometimes," Sydney said, excitement building in her voice, "they would throw a subscription dance, where everyone paid an entry fee and the money went to charity!"

"Exactly! We'll make the guests pay for the pleasure of your ball."

"But that's countryfolk," Sydney said uncertainly. "Not the quality here in London."

"Fustian. Pick a worthy charity and they'll come. There's nothing the wealthy like better than getting something back for their money. You'll help them feel generous without getting their hands dirty. That way you can reciprocate your invitations and show off your sister with all the pomp and glory you want."

The pride of the Lattimores, Sydney thought fondly, but they could never afford it.

"Goose, you tell the guests beforehand that the *profits* are going to a good cause, so they know the expenses are being deducted. You don't need much for the original outlay; most merchants are used to getting paid months later. I shall underwrite the refreshments, and I'll take great pleasure in seeing that Lady Windham pays for the orchestra. I'd make her pay for the food, but I fear we'd be served only tea and toast."

Sydney was laughing now; it really was fun to let one's daydreams take flight, even if they could never come home to roost. "Your Grace, I am sorry to disappoint you when your scheme is so lovely, but there is not even a ballroom in the house. Indeed, our whole house could fit in some ballrooms I've seen. And if we hold the ball at Mainwaring House, as I can see you are going to suggest, then it will not be the Lattimore ball."

"No such thing. We'll hire the Argyle Rooms. They cannot say no if it's for charity. And I'll make sure we get a deuced good price, too."

Sydney thought a good many people must find it hard to say no to the duchess. Out loud she voiced more objections. The duchess had an answer for each.

"Flowers are very expensive."

"So we'll call it a holly ball. There's acres of the stuff growing at Mayne Chance, and armies of gardeners doing nothing this time of year. You'll have to make arrangements out of the stuff, of course, you and Winifred and that platter-faced cousin of yours. Everyone will have a share of the expenses, a share of the work."

"You're forgetting that Winnie and I are just young girls. I never heard of two females hosting a ball."

"I do not forget anything but my birthday, Sydney. And you are forgetting the general. About time the ton honored one of its heroes. Lattimore will be the host. Be good for the old codger to get out more anyway. Now, what else are you going to nitpick over?"

Sydney had a hard time putting her last objection into words without insulting the duchess. "The, ah, worthy cause, and the, uh, loan from the Viscount of Mayne. You weren't thinking that I should tell everyone the ball was for charity, and then give him the money, were you?"

"Lud, infant, where do you get your notions? You know Forrest won't take your money. He certainly won't take money out of the mouths of babes, or whatever. But if you were to give the money in his name, say, or let him give it to that veterans' group he supports, then I daresay he'd be proud to accept."

And Sydney dared hope he'd smile at her again.

Sydney refused to go one step further with the plans until she consulted the viscount, even if she had to suffer Lady Mayne's knowing looks.

"It's not that I care so much for his approval," she lied, blushing. "I need to confirm which charity he prefers."

So that evening at the Conklins' ball, during their one dance, a waltz, Sydney waited for the usual empty pleasantries to pass. She was looking lovely; he was feeling well. He did not say that she looked like a dancing flame in her gold gown, that her warmth kindled his blood. She did not mention that she thought him the most handsome man she'd ever seen in his formal clothes, that she blushed to think of him out of them.

She appreciated last night's opera; he enjoyed his morning ride. Neither said how much they wished the other had been there to share the pleasure. They danced at just the proper distance apart, in spite of their bodies' aching to touch. They kept the proper social smiles on their faces. Until Sydney mentioned money.

"My lord," Sydney began.

"Forrest."

She nodded. "My lord Forrest, I have been thinking about the thousand pounds you lent me."

His hand tightened on her fingers and closed on her waist. Trying to maintain a smile with his teeth clenched, the viscount ground out, "Don't."

"But your mother agrees with me."

For the first time in ten years the viscount missed his step and trod on his partner's toes. "Sorry." Then Sydney found herself being twirled and swirled across the dance floor and right out the balcony doors. Forrest led her to the farthest, darkest corner. With any luck no one would find her body until the servants came to clean up in the morning.

"You haven't even heard our idea," Sydney complained as his fearsome grip moved to her shoulders. She was glad the shadows hid his scowl.

"Ma'am, every time you get an idea in that pretty little head of yours, I am slapped or kicked or beaten or poisoned. I am always out of pocket and out of temper. Add my mother into the brew and I may as well stick my spoon in the wall now." But his fingers had relaxed on her shoulders. Actually he was now caressing her skin where the gold tissue gown left her bare, almost as if he were unaware of what his fingers were doing. Sydney was very aware.

Her breath coming faster than her thoughts, she stumbled through an explanation of the ball. Farmers' roofs and family pride mixed with wine-merchants' bills and Winifred's betrothal. "But it's really for you, Forrest, so I can give you the money and you can give it to a noble cause. What do you think?"

"I think," he said, pulling her to his chest, where she filled his arms perfectly, "that you are the most impossible, pig-headed, pea-brained female of my experience. And the most wonderful."

He moved to tip her chin up for his kiss, but she was already raising her face toward him in answer, an answer to all of his questions.

Just as their lips were a breath apart, someone coughed loudly. Forrest was tired of watching her glide around with every fop and sweaty-palmed sprig. No more. She was his and he was not going to give her up, not even for a dance. He turned to scare the insolent puppy away. The fellow could come back in a year or two, maybe.

The insolent puppy, however, was the Duke of Mayne, and he was grinning. Forrest decided he liked his father better when he stayed in his office.

"I've come for my dance with the prettiest gal here," the duke declared, winking at Sydney.

She chuckled softly, reaching up to straighten the tiara of daisies in her hair. "Spanish coin, Your Grace. There are hundreds of prettier girls here."

"Yes, but they all agree with everything I say. You don't. Just like my Sondra. That's true beauty. Did I ever tell you about . . ."

The viscount opened the hand that had held Sydney's in parting. He smiled when he saw the daisy there in his palm and nodded when he brought it to his lips. She was his. He could wait.

26

Bella of the Ball

It was going to be the best ball of the Season, or Sydney would die trying. She'd likely kill everyone else in the household, too, working so hard on decorations, foodstuffs, guest

181

lists, the millions of details an undertaking of this proportion required. Sydney was in her element. The rest of her friends and family were in dismay.

Finally the invitations were all printed and delivered. General Harlan Lattimore, Ret., was proud to invite the world, they indicated, to witness the betrothal of his granddaughter Winifred to Brennan, son of, etc., on such a date. The engagement would be celebrated at a benefit ball, the proceeds enriching the War Veterans' Widows and Orphans Fund, with paid admission at the door and other donations gratefully accepted.

The invitations went out under the general's name, in Winifred's copperplate, with the duke's frank, at Sydney's instigation, according to the duchess. Nearly everyone accepted, even the Prince Regent, who declared it a novel idea and Sydney an original.

Sydney did not have time to be anything but an organizer. There were measurements and fittings—for the rooms as well as the girls. Lists of guests, lists of supplies, lists of lists. Sydney met with musicians, caterers, hiring agencies. She heard out Aunt Harriet and took Lady Mayne's advice. The duchess was delighted, not just that she was preferred over that clutch-fisted Lady Windham, but that Sydney had such an aptitude. The minx would make a worthy duchess, if that scrod of a son of hers would get on with it.

The duchess had high hopes for the ball. There was nothing like the excitement of a fancy affair to bring a sparkle to a maiden's eyes, and nothing like seeing how popular a chit was to make a man take notice. Like her dogs with their toys, a favorite ball could lie untouched for days, but let one dog play with it, they all had to have it. Men were no different. Nothing would make a male claim possession quicker than others sniffing around his chosen mate. And the duchess intended them to sit up and howl. Her own dressmaker was in charge of the Lattimores' gowns; that was to be her betrothal gift. Winifred's dress was a delicate shell pink with a lace overskirt, selected to set off the ruby pendant the duchess knew Brennan intended to give her. But Sydney's dress was not going to be any sweet pastel or wedding-cake froth. It was a simple one-shouldered fall of watered blue-green silk that clung to her lush form and changed colors with movement and light, just like her eyes. With it she would wear a peacock-eye plume mounted on a gold fillet in her hair, gold sandals, and gold silk gloves. If that didn't stir a declaration out of the sapskull, his doting mother vowed, she'd stir his brains with a footstool!

Sydney was too busy to worry about the viscount, but she knew what she knew, and smiled inside.

She was too busy for morning calls and such, but she made time for Bella, not wishing to appear to slur old friends, even when the duchess said Mrs. Ott reminded her of a housekeeper at some Irish hunt party.

Bella thought a benefit ball an excellent idea, especially when she heard the name of the charity. "Why, it's a sure stroke of genius, dearie, seeing how you're an orphan and I'm a widow. Ha-ha."

"I know you're only teasing, Mrs. Ott. You don't think anyone will suppose I am keeping the money, do you?"

"Stealing from the needy? Lawks, dearie, who'd ever think a thing like that?"

There would never be another ball like Sydney's. Decorations were joyous, with holly garlands and white satin bows draping the succession of rooms. Food was lavish, not confined to one refreshments area, but set up on tables in each room, with servants constantly circulating with wine and lemonade and champagne and trays of stuffed oysters and lobster patties and sweets. Music was everywhere, an orchestra in the large ballroom, a string quartet in a smaller reception room where sofas and comfortable chairs were placed, a gifted young man playing the pianoforte in the corner of another parlor. There was a card room with no music at all. There were candles and mirrors and a lantern-strung balcony, footmen to take the wraps, maids to repin hems and hairdos, majordomos to call out the names of the distinguished guests.

All of Sydney's careful planning was coming to glorious fulfillment, not just the details of the ball. Winifred was angelic in her happiness, Bren looking like the cat in the cream pot as they greeted each guest coming through the receiving line. The general was resplendent in his full-dress uniform, sword, medals, and sash, as he beamed proudly from his wheelchair between Winifred and Sydney. Aunt Harriet stood next on the line, formidable in magenta taffeta and ostrich feathers, her nose only slightly out of joint at having to pay admission. Not even family was exempt. The duchess stood nearby with her duke for a brief while, gloating. And the viscount had sent Sydney a gold filigree fan.

Best of all, the huge punch bowl in the entryway was filling up. Willy and Wally flanked the bowl like handsome bookends in their new red and white livery, exchanging party favors for the admission fee, boutonnieres of holly and white carnations for the gentlemen, dance cards on white satin ribbons for the ladies. As the delighted guests wandered around the rooms, some of them strolled back to congratulate the Lattimores again. They often dropped a stickpin or an earring or a snuffbox in the bowl, for such a good cause.

And the Prince did come for a brief, memorable moment. His equerry handed Willy a check, which everyone knew would be generous and not worth the paper it was writ on. Prinny did toss one of his rings in the bowl for the benefit of the poor families of those who gave their lives for God and country—and for the benefit of everyone who gathered in the reception area to see him. He smiled and waved as all the ladies in the room went into their deepest curtsies. Sydney's knees turned to pudding when he stopped in front of her after saying a few kind words to the general, then a firm hand was under her elbow, helping her wobbly knees lift the rest of her uncooperative body off the ground. Forrest was there next to her, and she could do anything, even smile at the heavy-handed flirtation of the heavy head of state.

Then it was time to start the dancing. The general was enjoying himself so much, smiling at old friends and accepting the well-wishes of old adversaries that Sydney asked if he wanted to stay on to greet latecomers.

"Go on, go on," Aunt Harriet scolded, "I'm paying those musicians by the night, not the song. I'll stay and see the old tartar doesn't fall off his seat or stab anyone with his sword."

Leaving Griffith behind the general's chair ready to wheel him away if he got tired, Sydney and Winifred went into the ballroom. The newly engaged couple led the opening cotillion and the duke and duchess followed, looking more in charity with each other than anyone could remember.

"Must be the season for love," one old dowager commented.

"Stuff," another replied, "they just ran out of reasons for fighting."

Then Forrest held his hand out to lead Sydney into the dance. There was not much chance for conversation in the pattern of the steps, but the touch of his hand brought a tingle she felt to her toes, and his smile almost filled her heart to bursting. The ball, the world, was a lifetime away. Soon, his eyes promised. But too soon it was time to trade partners and get back to being hostess. Sydney danced with the duke, Brennan, her own admirers, and some of Winifred's disappointed suitors, even Baron Scoville. Between dances she checked on the refreshments and the card room and the general in the entry hall.

Bella and her party arrived late. She kept her cloak with her, saying she was leaving early. She was not surprised to see Willy and Wally still near the door, for they were to stand there all night, guarding the punch bowl now gratifyingly full of donations. Bella handed over the price for two admissions.

"She's my new Indian maid," she told Willy, nodding toward the small woman draped in fabric who walked behind her. "She ain't going in, so I don't have to pay for her. This is for me and the captain." Bella's escort also tried to walk behind her. She dragged him to her side when she saw the general and Lady Windham, whom she had not expected to be where they were, not at all. While she was thinking, she yanked off one of her rings and tossed it in the bowl. "For the starving children." Let them eat paste.

Then she jerked the Indian girl forward and told the general, "This here's Ranshee. She'll stand here and look decorative for the folks. You can ask her to help; she understands English fine, don't you, Ranshee?"

The girl salaamed to the general, holding the edge of her veil across her face. Her eyes were darkened with kohl; her skin with tea. Her sari was yards of silk; two coffins were going naked into the earth.

The general had seen many an Indian maid in his day. Some even had hairy arms. None, however, had green eyes and wisps of red hair beneath their headpieces. Few were liable to have knives tucked in their sandals either. The general made his growling noises.

"Hush up, you old lecher," Lady Windham hissed in his ear. Griffith turned the general's chair away in case the sight of the Hindu girl was bringing back bad memories.

General Lattimore was now directly facing Bella's male escort, whom she introduced as Captain Otis Winchester. One of the naked coffins belonged to an officer of the Home Guard who went out for pistols for two, breakfast for one. He wasn't the one. Bella sewed an old shoe buckle over the heart-high rip, like another medal. The captain walked with a limp and a cane and had a patch over one eye. He also had a full beard and mustache and muttonchop sideburns, which were not all the exact same shade, but close enough. Like the general, he wore an ornamental sword and a sidearm pistol.

"One of our brave boys wounded in battle," Bella told the general, who promptly saluted, even though he couldn't quite make out the lad's rank and medals.

Bella had to kick the captain and whisper, "Salute, you dunderhead."

So Chester saluted. Ah, the old bar sinister, Chester's inheritance from his true father, was to have its day. Chester saluted with his left hand.

The general's face turned red. He gurgled in his throat and started pounding on his chair arm. Griffith wheeled him closer to the door for a little fresh air.

The Indian maid Ranshee, meanwhile, having taken up a serving tray from one of the waiters, went to offer an hors d'oeuvre to Lady Windham. Unfortunately the poor girl tripped over her sari and spilled the tray of hot lobster patties right down Lady Windham's magenta décolletage. One of the Minch twins came running over when the countess shrieked. Captain Winchester, praying the remaining footman was Willy of the fragile mandible, hit the fellow a resounding blow. It was Wally and he hit back, sending Chester's mustache flying in the general's direction. Griffith wheeled him around in time to see Bella pick up Winchester's cane and whap Wally over the head a few times until the footman went down. By now the Indian girl had torn off her veil and headpiece and was holding a knife to Willy's throat, or as close as pint-sized Randy could get. If that was Wally, though, this must be the easy one, so toothless Randy hit Willy alongside the jaw with the heavy silver tray. They got it right that time.

Aunt Harriet was flat on the ground in a swoon, like a banquet table for sea gulls. Bella was holding open her cloak while a groggy Chester tipped the donation bowl's contents into it.

When the bowl was empty, Bella knotted her cloak and headed for the door, Chester limping at her heels, Randy not far behind. But there was the general, cutting off retreat, his dress sword stretched in front of him, one last battle cry on his lips, his faithful batman wheeling him into the fray.

So the O'Toole tribe retrenched and headed for another exit, through the ballroom and out the glass doors to the rear gardens. In making her plans, Bella had not counted on finding half the upper ten thousand between her and escape. Sydney was first on the scene, having been headed in that direction anyway. Randy grabbed her before she could cry out, and held her in front of him as a shield, the knife now pressed to *her* throat. Bella lugged the sack and Chester limped, followed by Wally on his knees, and the general leading his own charge.

The moment they reached the ballroom, things got even more interesting. Ladies shrieked and fell into the arms of whoever was close by, even poor, homely men. Winnie started sobbing. Forrest and Brennan ran forward, but slid to a halt when they saw the knife threatening Sydney and the pistol now in Bella's hands. The viscount cursed when he reached for a sword that wasn't by his side. Those guests who were not trampling each other in their efforts to leave made sure there was a clear path to the doors. Then the duchess, standing by the refreshments table, saw her typically inept sons at a standstill and took matters into her own hands. A punch cup in one hand, a saucer in the other. Soon she was joined by the duke in an artillery fusillade that could have ended the Peninsular

Wars years earlier. Bella's gun was shot out of her hands by a dish of raspberry ice.

"Good shot, my dear."

"Years of practice, darling."

Dodging and weaving, the trio with their burdens tried to progress. Hobble-footed Chester slipped on the broken crockery and went down under the barrage. He pulled himself up by his mama's skirts, even though she kicked him. She grabbed his pistol. The general and his faithful Sancho Panza finally made their way into the thick of things. The general's outthrust sword nicked Bella's cloak, sending coins and gewgaws all over the floor. Chester slipped again. Wally hurtled onto his back, followed by Brennan. Bella whipped around, the pistol in her hand and blood in her eyes. Forrest ran forward and Sydney shrieked "No" along with a hundred other voices.

"You. You're the one caused all this, you meddling bastard," Bella spat at him. "Now I'm going to kill you."

As cool as you please, Forrest held up a hand. "Just one question before you do, ma'am: Who the bloody hell are you?"

"I'm their ma, God help me," she snarled, and raised the gun. The crowd gasped. The duchess started heaving full cups, which only doused the onlookers cowering against the walls. Sydney, with a knife still to her throat, kicked and struggled and wept. And the general and Griff? They just kept coming. Not even the general could skewer a woman, in the back to boot, but he could boot her to kingdom come. He lowered his sword and raised his legs as Griffith gave a mighty shove.

The impact toppled the general and knocked Bella to the floor, but the gun went sailing. Everyone ducked and screamed, except Forrest, who fielded it neatly. "All right, you bastard, let her go."

Randy kept twisting and looking over his shoulder, making sure no old geezers in wheelchairs were coming up behind him. His arm around Sydney's neck, he dragged her closer to the doors.

"You god id wrong again, Mayne. Chedder'd the bathtard. And you won'd shood, nod when I've shtill god the girl."

"How far do you think you'll get?" the viscount stalled. It took Randy so long to say his piece, anything could happen.

Sydney was getting a little tired of people pointing guns at her beloved, to say nothing of having a little redheaded man in a dress and no teeth hold a knife to her throat. So while he was busy trying to answer Forrest and watch his back, she put her head down and bit his arm as hard as she could. Then she turned around and practiced Willy's lesson in self-defense. Not the one about using a closed fist, the other one, which caused the seams of her gown to split at the knee. At the same time, the duke let fly with the half-full glass punch bowl, which missed Randy since he was already on the floor, and caught Forrest full in the chest, with bits of orange and lemon decking the halls along with the ivy.

Baron Scoville was heard to declare the whole thing a disgrace. Trixie replied with a slap that sent his toupee flying toward the orchestra, which immediately began playing *God Save the King*.

No, there would never be another ball like Sydney's.

27

Endings and Interest

"Dash it, Mischief, I didn't get to do anything! You saved yourself."

"Nonsense, you were very brave."

"No, I wasn't. I was terrified, seeing you in danger."

Sydney felt a sudden chill go through her at the thought of his facing Bella's pistol. She shuddered, but luckily she had something warm to fall back on, namely Forrest's chest.

They were back in Park Lane and it was nearly dawn. Her dress was changed, the vegetation was combed out of his hair, the O'Tooles long gone. They were most likely going to be transported, according to Bow Street. The reward money, it was decided, would go to the Minch brothers to open their inn. The duke and duchess were so in accord with each other and the world, they decided to match the ball's profits with a charitable donation of their own, which should scotch any rumors of misappropriation. Lord and Lady Mayne were so delighted with themselves, they even left Sydney and Forrest alone together, after getting a full explanation of events right back to Brennan's involvement.

The duke winked at Sydney on his way out, but told his son he better get a shrewd solicitor to handle the settlements. Sydney blushed, for nothing had been said about—

"Go on, you old windbag, let Forrest do things his own way," the duchess admonished, shooing her husband out the door. She was content now that Forrest would do it, but couldn't resist adding as she left, "Just one thing, my dears. That little dog of Sydney's? She's one of the best Pekingese in all of England, with a pedigree fancier than the Prince's by half."

"We really are not interested in dog stories, Mother. Not now." Forrest was just a trifle impatient.

"Of course you aren't, dear, but Sydney may be. I believe Princess Pennyfleur is breeding. The pups should fetch a pretty penny indeed."

Sydney's eyes lit up, and she would have followed the duchess out the door, except for Forrest's hand on her arm, pulling her back to the sofa.

"I still cannot believe that of Bella," Sydney mused while Forest added another log to the fire.

"I don't see why you don't believe it. I would never call you a fine judge of character, Mischief. Just think how you used to believe I was the lowest scum on earth." He sat next to her on the couch, pulling her closer.

She went willingly, but complained, "Well, you used to think I was a hopeless hoyden."

"But I was right, Mischief," he told her, blowing feathery kisses on her curls, "you are."

Sydney giggled. "Do you think I'll ever be invited anywhere again?"

"They'll never refuse a someday duchess." Now he was kissing her ear and the side of her neck.

"A . . . someday . . . duchess?"

"A current viscountess will have to do, then. A marriage will stop all the gossip instantly, you know. Will you?"

Sydney sat up and drew away. "Just to stop the gossip?" she asked indignantly.

"No, you goose." He laughed, pulling her into his lap. "To stop my heart from breaking. I have loved you from the first minute I saw you, despite myself, and I cannot bear to be without you a day longer. If I offered you my heart and my hand, do you think you could return my affection just a little?"

"Just a little? Is that all you want?"

"No, sweetheart, I want you to love me as I love you, with my very soul."

"I always have. I'll love you back with my heart and my soul, forever and ever, a hundred times over for all you love me. No, a thousand."

Which is a pretty fair rate of interest on any loan.

The Luck of the Devil

This one's for all my heroes, but especially Steve for all the years, Skip for all the roses, and Gene for no reason I've ever understood.

Chapter One

"*H*eavens, child, you are as nervy as a fox on opening day of the hunt season. I do not understand you, Rowanne. It is not as if you were some green girl never out in society before."

"Yes, Miss Simpson." Her governess-turned-companion was correct, of course. Rowanne Wimberly had been hostess for her widowed father for two years before his death and for her older brother Gabriel during the year of mourning since. The younger woman nodded, but still she remained at her mirror, twitching uncertainly at the tendrils of soft brown hair framing her face.

"Do you think all these curls make me look childish, ma'am?"

"Gracious, Rowanne, *Monsieur* Henri assured us they were all the crack. You wouldn't want to appear as a matron, would you?" Before her charge could start tugging up the décolletage of her gown again, a neckline cut lower than any Rowanne had ever worn, revealing more of Miss Wimberly than anyone but her maid had seen, Miss Simpson reassured her on that score also. "No more would you want to be considered one of the infantry. Now come, my dear, this is not like you. Your gown is superb, your hair is charming, and your brother is waiting."

Rowanne stood, however reluctantly. "We mustn't keep the horses standing, not after all it took to convince Gabe to accompany us." She gathered up her beaded reticule, her fan, and her courage, and headed for the door. "But are you sure about the pearls?"

Miss Simpson clucked impatiently. They had discussed the

pearls twice too often for her taste. "Yes, dear, the pearls are eminently suitable for a young lady in her first Season. Even if you are above the usual age, all of nineteen, your mama's diamonds would appear coming and the emeralds would make you look like a painted woman, with the color of your gown." The deep-rose satin was far more attractive to Miss Wimberly's honeyed coloring than debutante white would have been, if she were indeed a giddy seventeen-year-old. The ivory lace overskirt kept the gown from being too sophisticated for one not officially out. "The pearls are just the thing. Now shall we leave? Remember, they close the doors at eleven."

Miss Simpson was talking to Rowanne's back. "One minute more," Miss Wimberly called, rummaging in the velvet-covered chest atop her dresser. "There," she declared triumphantly, coming up with a small brooch, a pink coral cameo, which she held out to her ex-governess. "Mama gave it to me when I was barely six or so. See, it has her miniature inside." Rowanne flipped the tiny catch to show Miss Simpson the portrait that could have been Rowanne herself, so similar were her looks to her deceased mother's. She closed the locket and fixed the pin right at the vee of her neckline. She touched the cameo. "For luck. Now I am ready."

"Fustian," declared Miss Simpson, straightening her own gray silk gown and checking the neat bun at the back of her head. "Luck has nothing to do with it. You are the granddaughter of an earl and sister to a rising Parliamentarian. You are a substantial heiress, a charming-looking and well-figured young woman with, if I may say so who shouldn't, an excellent education and pleasing manners. Now do cry halt to all of these vaporish musings, Rowanne, before I get the headache in truth. After all, we are only going to Almack's."

"Only Almack's," Miss Wimberly echoed, trailing her companion down the hall.

There were three major hurdles in the frenzied steeplechase of a young girl's comeout: her curtsy to the queen, the most lavish ball her family was able to provide in her honor, and her acceptance at Almack's.

Miss Rowanne Wimberly sailed over the first fence with ease. Hadn't she been trotted around foreign courts all her life in the wake of her parents, when her father was with the diplomatic corps? She had been dandled on the knees of many an eminence, and Prince George himself had once carried the brown-eyed moppet on his shoulders, neighing in horse fashion to her childish delight. Her brother Gabriel had only to present Rowanne's name to Prinny's secretary and Miss Wimberly was summoned to the queen's next Drawing Room, hooped skirts and all. Rowanne neither blushed, stammered, fainted, nor fell over, so she was declared a pretty thing, whose parents would have been proud. Prinny pinched her, which Gabe assured Rowanne meant she was a success.

The debutante ball was another minor obstacle to overcome. The Wimberlys had no close kin in Town to demand a major crush to puff off the family's latest bud. Their uncle Donald, the Earl of Clyme, never came to London, so his niece and nephew had free rein with Wimberly House, Grosvenor Square, where they made their home. Most hopeful parents invited as many of the upper ten thousand as they could fit in their homes to their daughters' comeouts, and then some, in an effort to impress the ton with the family's financial worth and the chit's possibilities as a bride to some equally as well-born and well-breeched scion. Most times these crushes resulted in long waits on the carriage lines, no room to dance, insufficient refreshments, and too much noise for conversation. Instead, Rowanne and Gabriel invited only a select hundred or so guests and treated them lavishly. Feeling the awkwardness of being hostess for her own comeout, Rowanne invited mostly her parents' closest acquaintances and Gabriel's political associates.

She did write to Uncle Donald, just as she dutifully wrote him every second month, plus Christmas and his birthday, informing him of the event. Lord Clyme declined, to no one's surprise, but he did send her a small diamond tiara to wear, and a check to underwrite the expenses. Rowanne thought she could like her uncle very well and regretted the estrangement that had kept her father and Uncle Donald apart. As she later wrote to the earl, her ball was a grand success. The supper was delicious, the orchestra excellent, the talk elevating and intelligent. Even the prince regent stopped in for a moment and kissed her hand, then her cheek. Rowanne's reputation as a discerning hostess was secure.

But the third hurdle was Almack's. Now that was going to be a rough ride.

Rowanne had no intention of making a splash in polite society. She hadn't the least desire to become the Season's Incomparable or even a Belle. Her looks were passable, she knew, her fortune respectable, her ambitions modest. She decided she would hate the butterfly existence of her parents, flitting in constant travels, filling every moment with the social rounds. Miss Wimberly saw herself more as a humble inchworm, all feet on the ground, finding pleasure in small things, moving at a much slower speed. Occasionally she thought she might be happier in the country than in the city, although she hardly knew the rural life since her parents had disdained it so well. But her brother Gabriel was fixed in Town, scholarly, dedicated Gabe, waiting to take his seat in the Lords when he came into Uncle Donald's title. Meantime he was working with the Under Secretaries, researching policies, polishing speeches. Even Lord Castlereagh had commented that the boy had a good future ahead of him. Rowanne could not leave dear Gabriel to fend for himself, even if he was her elder by five years. The bookish Gabe would forget to eat if left to his own devices, and would certainly have no idea of making the right connections for a political career. Rowanne might picture herself off in Dorset tending roses, but she could never see Gabe, spectacles and all, rigged out as a country squire among pigs and sheep and cows. So here she was in London, a debutante at nineteen, about to make her first appearance at Almack's.

The problem was that while Miss Rowanne Wimberly did not seek to cut a dash through the ton, neither did she wish to be a wallflower. Vouchers to the sacrosanct Marriage Mart were easy to come by, with a morning call to her mother's friend Sally Jersey, but attendance alone at the assembly rooms in King Street did not mean acceptance in the *belle monde*. Only if she was seen to be popular would the other invitations and introductions follow. If a girl did not "take" at

Almack's, her social life hit a rasper. Gabe's learned associates were not likely to be found dancing on a Wednesday evening, nor would her father's cronies be looking over this year's crop of debutantes, and she certainly could not count on Prinny himself coming or singling her out in the squeeze. So who would dance with Rowanne? She had no mother or aunt to make introductions to mothers and aunts of likely young men, nor even any girlfriends likely to share their extra beaux. What friends Rowanne had managed to make in her early unsettled life were either abroad or married, retired from the lists.

Rowanne did have Gabriel, of course, who was just as liable to forget her existence if there should be an interesting discussion about the trade embargoes. And she did have Miss Simpson to lend her countenance. Even if that dear lady believed her duck to be a swan, however, she knew even less members of the ton than Rowanne and was, in fact, only a paid companion. So who would dance with Rowanne?

No one, that's who. After the first quadrille with Gabe, who had to be turned twice to get the figures straight, Rowanne was presented by Lady Jersey with a partner for the next set, a spotted youth who could neither dance nor converse and who, furthermore, was a good two inches shorter than Miss Wimberly. When the contra danse was mercifully ended, Rowanne limped over to where Miss Simpson had found them seats on the edge of the dance floor and gratefully sank into the little gilded chair. There she sat. And sat. She smoothed her long white gloves; she examined every spoke of her fan. She wished the ground would open up and swallow her. No such luck. A rough ride indeed.

Chapter Two

As the evening progressed, excruciating minutes dragging by into endless hours, Almack's became more crowded and the seats around Rowanne and Miss Simpson filled with other unfortunates. A bloated dowager claimed the chair on Miss Simpson's side, her purple turban fixed with a diamond the size of a robin's egg. Next to her she installed two giggly dumplings of daughters, swathed in tiers of white lace like matching wedding cakes. A frowning matron dressed entirely in black and smelling of camphor took the seat next to Rowanne. Obviously some more popular miss's duenna, the older woman surveyed the overdressed dowager near Miss Simpson and muttered what Rowanne interpreted as "jumped-up merchant's mushrooms." She sniffed, nodded at Rowanne and her companion, and promptly took out a book to read, ignoring the music, the company, and the other social misfits relegated to the spectators' seats. At least Rowanne could listen to the chatter of Mrs. Fitzwaller of Yorkshire, who was quick to make the introduction.

"I told Mr. Fitzwaller, I did. We'd be ducks out of water in London, I said. But would he listen? Is there ever a man who does? No, ma'am. His sister danced at Almack's and his daughters were blessed well going to appear here too. No matter to him that his stiff-rumped sister bespoke us vouchers and then left town to visit an ailing friend. Ailing, my aunt Ada. No matter, my girls are seeing London and they'll have plenty of tales to take back home to Sparrowbush. Have you and your young lady seen those Greek marble things everyone is raving about? Perishing bits of potsherds, if you ask me. Mr. Fitzwaller wouldn't let me set one out in the garden, you can be sure. Missing arms and noses and all, why, the neighbors would think we couldn't afford to replace the broken ones."

Rowanne bit her lip but Miss Simpson politely concurred, which was all Mrs. Fitzwaller needed to continue. "Town bronze, that's what Mr. Fitzwaller calls it. Town soot is more like it. But no matter, my girls can go home soon and marry good solid Yorkshire lads, boys not afraid to get their hands in the dirt. Why, I wouldn't have one of these London coxcombs for my girls, no, not even if he came with a title and twenty thousand pounds a year. Just look there, that chap's coat is so tight he couldn't do a day's work, and his shirt collar stiff enough to poke his eye out, and him acting as lost as a motherless lamb. If that's another prime example of London manhood, don't you know, I can take my girls home tomorrow." Mrs. Fitzwaller poked Miss Simpson with a beringed sausage-shaped finger. Miss Simpson turned away, coughing, so the other woman applied to Rowanne. "What do you think, missy?"

Rowanne stood up and smiled for the first time that evening. "I think that fribble is my brother Gabriel, Baronet Wimberly, come for his second dance." She also thought she heard a snort of amusement from the dark-clad woman on her other side, and a murmured, "And only ten thousand a year."

Rowanne did not release Gabriel after the dance, keeping a firm hold on his arm lest he disappear into some alcove again to discuss government policies. When she hissed in his ear that he absolutely had to introduce her to at least one dancing partner, Gabriel looked around vaguely, then drew his spectacles from his pocket.

"Ah, there's Lord Quinton. Fine fellow. Knows all about the Acts of Council."

But Rowanne wanted to dance, not listen to a lecture by a prosy old bore with snuff stains on his shirtfront and creaking stays. Finally she took Gabriel's arm again and towed him toward the gilt chairs and the Misses Fitzwaller. At least one of the wallflowers should have a dance.

"My brother is in politics," Rowanne told Mrs. Fitzwaller, after the two girls giggled and blushed and shoved each other over who should have the treat of being Gabriel's partner.

"That's all right, dear," Mrs. Fitzwaller commiserated, "I had a cousin who was a Captain Sharp."

Gabe danced with the other Fitzwaller daughter next, demonstrating he had at least a modicum of awareness of how to go on in polite society, to Rowanne's relief. His behavior, or the entertainment value of the interlude, served to thaw the black-garbed woman next to Rowanne into conversation with her and Miss Simpson.

Miss Sophronia Grimble was, as Rowanne had suspected, companion to a young woman of the first consequence, Lady Diana Hawley-Roth, a Diamond who was sure to stay un-seated the entire evening. Now in her third successful Season, Lady Diana could look as high as she wished for an eligible *parti* and she wished to look for a duke, perhaps an earl. A baron at the very least. Meantime, and as part of her job, Miss Grimble knew everyone in the ton.

Miss Grimble did not know the *haute monde* in the sense of acquaintance; she knew them more in the way a confirmed gambler knew every racehorse, each one's stable and stud. Just so, the austere Miss Grimble knew the families and finances of all those present at Almack's that Wednesday, their ancestors and incomes, their aims and eligibility. None of the young females, of course, could hold a candle to her lady; none of the gentlemen was quite up to Miss Hawley-Roth's weight. Miss Grimble was pleased enough to expound on the gathering for Rowanne's edification, flaunting her knowledge of which sprig was below hatches and hanging out for an heiress, which miss was hoping new ribbons would disguise last year's gown. Rowanne was more entertained than she had been all evening. At least the clock's hands were kept moving.

At the stroke of eleven, when Rowanne thought it must be quite one o'clock and nearly time to go home, there was a stir at the entry. Just as Almack's doors were closing to the last arrivals, three young men, each tall, well built, and dark-haired, two in the regulation dark coats and white knee breeches and the third in a scarlet-coated uniform, strode under the arch to be greeted by the lady patronesses. Polite conversations changed to outright gossip as everyone nearby noted the presence of the newcomers, and Rowanne was just as curious as the rest about three such obvious Corinthians. Miss Grimble did not fail her.

"Delverson's Devils, they are. Though what three such hey-go-mad rogues are doing in Almack's of all places is beyond me. Setting the cat among the pigeons, for sure. Look at all the hopeful mamas. They don't know whether to scoop their daughters out of harm's way or push them forward hoping to be noticed."

"Are the young men not acceptable then?" Rowanne wanted to know. From her seat they seemed elegant and animated, with healthy outdoor coloring and broad shoulders. What a shame if they should be asked to leave.

"Oh, they are good ton when they choose, which is rare enough. That's what all the fuss is about. The three of them are more usually up to some hell-raising or other, instead of doing the pretty out at parties and such. Wherever there is a wild bet or scatterbrained scheme, an unbroken horse, unbeaten pugilist, or comely serving wench, that's where you'll find Delverson's Devils."

"Devil's?"

"Aye, that's what they've been called, since birth, I assume. Old Cornelius Delverson, he was the Duke of St. Dillon then, raised them up, such as it was. St. Dillon was a sporting-mad gambler and a rakehell himself, with no time for motherless lads who were wild to a fault even then. St. Dillon passed on and Harry, he's the heavyset one, came into the title and fortune early. Once he reached his majority there were no holds on any of them anymore. The youngest one is Harry's brother Joss Delverson, who they say can ride anything with four legs. The third, the scamp in the uniform, as if he needed a uniform to turn all the girls' heads, is a cousin, Harmon Carrisbrooke Delverson, I believe. They call him Carey so there's no confusion with his cousin. Word is he never got on with his step-mama or her sister when she moved in—Selcrofts they were—so he made his home at St. Dillon Abbey in Somerset. None of the Devils are used to petticoat government, that's for sure. The county must have run out of foxes and virgins both, to send the Devils up to London. Pardon, Miss Wimberly."

Miss Simpson was scarlet-faced and the Fitzwaller girls

were tittering. Their mother was scowling at the very thought of three such libertines near her precious chicks. "Mr. Fitzwaller shall hear of this, you can be sure," she declared.

"I never heard of any real harm in the boys," Miss Grimble protested, "just wild oats. All young men go through that stage."

Rowanne thought of her own brother, who had to be of an age with the Delverson trio, and smiled. Gabe wouldn't recognize a wild oat if it sprouted in his porridge. She was still smiling as she turned back to the door, where only the uniformed gentleman still remained with Sally Jersey clutching his coat sleeve. The other two must have escaped the wily patroness's efforts to get them onto the dance floor, and the young officer was shaking his head and laughing. It was all very amusing for Rowanne until she realized Lady Jersey was leading the unwilling victim in *her* direction. The smile left her face.

"I think I'll go see about something cool to drink," she announced, rising and turning to leave. Unfortunately Miss Simpson grabbed her wrist and Miss Grimble on her other side muttered, "Oh, no you don't, missy. This is just what you need."

Just what she needed? Having her hostess find a sacrificial lamb to partner her? No, Rowanne corrected herself, not a lamb. This was no innocent, stammering youth coerced by his mother into attending the stuffy balls; this was a rake, a devilishly handsome rake with black hair and dimples and twinkling eyes of a clear blue circled by black rims. Good grief, the last thing an unprotected young female needed was the introduction to a rake!

Perhaps Lady Jersey intended him for one of the Fitzwaller girls, Rowanne prayed. Yes, and perhaps the orchestra members would turn into spotted cows before the next dance.

"Miss Wimberly," Lady Jersey was saying, "I am sorry to have neglected you so long. Your mother was a dear friend of mine and I had meant to see you established before this. The press of people, don't you know. But here, Lieutenant Delverson has just arrived and I know you will make him welcome."

While the patroness completed the introduction in form,

and to Miss Simpson, Rowanne was aware that the officer was grinning at her, well aware she had no more desire for his company than he had for hers. She raised her chin in dignity and made him a perfect curtsy. He bowed—and winked! No wonder the man had such a reputation! Rowanne smiled in spite of herself. She rested her hand on his arm and walked with him along the edge of the dance floor, waiting for the music to begin, trying to pretend that every eye in the place wasn't on them. Well, at least she was being noticed.

The lieutenant's older cousin approached them when they neared the far door, and Rowanne's partner made the introductions.

"B'gad, if you're Gabe Wimberly's sister, I won't ask you to dance. Bound to be much too bookish for a dunderhead like me. You'll do better with m'cousin." St. Dillon had the same twinkling black-rimmed blue eyes and the same good nature that made her want to smile back.

"Were you looking for a partner, Your Grace?" she teased. "I could introduce you to two perfect widgeons, if that is what you require. And I think my new acquaintance, Miss Grimble, is about to leave her seat to find her charge. Perhaps you know Lady Diana Hawley-Roth?"

The lieutenant laughed, a pleasant sound, Rowanne noted, but his cousin ran his finger around a suddenly too-tight collar and shuddered. "No, no, ma'am, not Diana the Huntress. I, ah, didn't come to dance, you know. It's m'cousin's last night on the town before joining his regiment. Carey's father thinks the army will settle the lad. I think the governor bought his commission to get him away from my dangerous influence." Harry laid his finger alongside his nose. "So Joss and I decided we had to make a special going-away for Carey here. We had this knacky idea of, ah, helping him gather fond memories. That's it."

"And Miss Wimberly shall be one of the fondest," Lieutenant Delverson vowed, his hand to his heart, his dimples showing.

Rowanne looked at the cousins with suspicion, took a deep breath, and wrinkled her nose at the whiff of spirits mixed in with lemon and spices. "Why, you're foxed!"

"Devil a bit," denied the soldier, "but St. Dillon might be a little above himself."

"What, me bosky? Why else would anyone come to such a shabby place as this? Gads, here come your Miss Grimble and the Mantrap. And looks like Mrs. Drummond-Burrell has a platter-faced chit in tow. It's like vultures circling a wounded deer. Ah, do you think I might have that dance, Miss Wimberly?"

"Oh, no, you don't, Harry," the lieutenant contradicted. "You'll not throw me to the wolves. Find your own partner, boyo. You're the one whose title and fortune are drawing them in for the kill."

"Only thing to do in that case is keep moving. Think I'll find the refreshments room. Devilish thirsty work, this doing the pretty. Servant, ma'am." St. Dillon bowed, fumbled with something his cousin handed behind his back, and left just as the music started.

Carey Delverson was an excellent dancer, naturally, with his athlete's smooth coordination, lean, muscular body, and firm—No, Rowanne checked herself. She would *not* be impressed, not even with the black curls that tumbled over his forehead. "Is His Grace always so . . . ?"

"Graceless? No, he was on his best behavior tonight. What were you doing over there?"

The abruptness of his question caused Rowanne to miss her step. "Sorry. Over where?"

He jerked his head toward the gilt chairs. "Over with the dragons and the antidotes."

"Goodness, there is a strong family resemblance among the Delversons, isn't there?" Rowanne asked to cover her embarrassment. They both knew she didn't mean the dark hair and blue eyes. Carey just grinned until she was blushing in earnest. "Wretched man. If you must know, I was sitting there because no one asked me to dance, of course. I do not have many acquaintances among the younger set and no one to introduce me, and I suppose I am not distinctive enough to attract anyone's notice."

To Rowanne's dismay, the maddening creature across from her subjected her to a careful scrutiny, right on the dance floor.

His lips quirked up appreciatively as his gaze drifted from her soft curls to her high cheekbones, now permanently pink-tinged, to the full mouth and down to her provocative figure in its exquisite high-styled gown.

"Gammon," he pronounced. "Totally charming. You've got the most beautiful brown eyes I've ever seen. Like a fawn's, all soft and dreamy, with tiny green and gold flecks."

Rowanne tripped again. "You must be in your cups, sir. This is highly irregular."

"Your dancing will improve with practice. That's the only fault I can find. You're not the ordinary English beauty, I'll grant them that, not some washed-out, insipid blonde they consider fashionable. The nodcocks must be blind."

Rowanne's heart was pounding, and not from the exertion of the dance. She looked around to make sure no one else could overhear this improper conversation. It was no wonder at all to her that innocent maidens were locked in their rooms when the Delversons were in town. "Please, Lieutenant. You mustn't . . ."

"Zeus, ma'am, I cannot very well let such an exquisite rose languish among the wallflowers. No, I'll introduce you around myself after the set. Mind, it's only that I am off to the Peninsula in the morning, otherwise I'd never let the other chaps near you. Just promise me you won't smile at any of them until I get back from the war."

"You, sir, are a complete hand. You won't even remember me tomorrow, much less when you come home."

"Ah, you wound me, fair one, doubting my constancy already. Have I ever lied to you before? I'll prove my devotion, you'll see. I know, I'll bring you a gift home from Spain. My stepaunt wants a mantilla and my stepsister wants a Toledo blade, bloodthirsty little hoyden that she is. Tell me your wish, Miss Wimberly, and I shall give proof of my memory when Bonaparte is defeated. Just don't ask for the moon and the stars. I'm only a junior officer, you know."

"And we've just met. Come home safely, that will be enough."

"Ah, a woman as gentle-hearted as she is beautiful. You see, Harry spoke truer than he knew. I shall have wonderful thoughts of English womanhood to warm my heart at lonely campfires. But come, my dear, surely you can name me a trinket to bring home. A fan? An ivory comb?"

"Miss Simpson would have my hide for saying it, sir, asking chance-met gentlemen for gifts, but I do collect miniatures."

"Small portraits?" he asked, turning her in the figure of the dance.

"No, small furniture and such. You know, for dollhouses and scale models and the like. My mother started the collection on her travels, and my father continued whenever he was posted somewhere out of England. I would be interested in seeing what Iberia has to offer, if it's not too much bother and you don't think it too forward of me."

"Not at all. Now if you had said you collected snuffboxes, that would have looked dashed peculiar. And pressed butterflies would have disappointed me. But there, I knew you were not the common daisy."

"And you are not the usual Tulip. But I thank you for the dance and the pretty compliments. Miss Grimble was correct: You were what I needed. See the gentlemen around Miss Simpson? I don't doubt they are following your lead, now that you have brought me to their attention."

"And Miss Grendel will be sure to inform them of your worth. You do have a handsome dowry, don't you? Then your Season is assured. Miss Wimberly, you are now a Toast. I have only one bit of advice to guarantee your success."

She laughed, waiting for another outrageous statement from this silver-tongued rogue. He twirled her about one final time, bowed, and left her at Miss Simpson's side while the entire assembly strained to hear the parting love words he whispered for her ears only:

"Don't drink the punch."

Chapter Three

$\mathcal{R}$owanne was breathless and her throat was dry. Besides, she was thirsty. The refreshments at Almack's were insipid and meager, but surely a young miss whose senses were reeling could hazard a sip. Here was Lord This begging for a dance, and Sir That asking if he could pay a morning call, two plain misters rushing to fetch her soothing glasses of orgeat—and she shouldn't drink it?

The whole situation was as inexplicable as that dashing officer finding Rowanne appealing, as improbable as the whole wicked conversation. Still, Rowanne handed the cups of punch over to the Misses Fitzwaller, along with the two plain misters.

After a boulanger with Lord Fotheringay, condemned as having his wealth founded on the family's being In Trade, according to Miss Grimble's asides, and a strenuous Roger de Coverly with Lord Pilkington ("Punting on tick until a wealthy aunt sticks her spoon in the wall."), Miss Wimberly was parched. She gladly accepted a cup from Lord Hightower ("Ten thousand but a passel of brats from a first marriage.") and raised it to her lips. Before she took a sip, though, she felt eyes boring into her. Sure enough, Carey Delverson was staring at her from across the room, shaking his head no.

"I'm sorry, my lord, I find I do not care for something cool," Rowanne said, handing the glass to Miss Simpson. Hoping no beads of perspiration on her forehead would give her the lie, she told her next partner, Sir Ambrose Harkness ("Well-to-pass, but the mother is a despot.") that she felt somewhat chilled. "Do you think we might take tea in the refreshment room rather than having the contra danse?"

211

Thoroughly used to a female's odd crotchets and complaints, Sir Ambrose patted her arm and led her off. They had to thread their way through the happy, laughing couples waiting to make up their sets on the dance floor, and Rowanne could not help feeling that despite her new popularity, everyone else at Almack's was still having a better time than she was.

The room set aside for the sparse supper was noisy and crowded, and Rowanne gulped her tea before it could be jostled out of her hand. When her eyes stopped tearing from the scalding liquid, she took a better look around. The youngest of the Delversons seemed to be presiding over the punch bowl, with that same rascally grin, while other youths shoved their cups forward to him for refills and their young ladies giggled so hard they had to hold each other up from falling.

Her eyes narrowed, Rowanne hurried Sir Ambrose back to the dance hall. The younger Miss Fitzwaller was asleep and like to fall off her little gilt chair, while the other was hitching up her stockings! Miss Grimble frowned awesomely at her charge, who was off in a corner, nearly cuddling with a skinny youth in a lavender waistcoat. ("Hell and tarnation, a second son.") and Miss Simpson—Great Heavens, Miss Simpson was on the dance floor, being tossed about in gay abandon by Gabriel's middle-aged political friend, Lord Quinton. ("Prosy old bore with an expensive French mistress.") Even Gabe was wearing a silly smirk, as if he'd just found a fallacy in an opponent's argument or a spelling error in the newspaper.

As soon as the dance ended Rowanne herded her brother and her companion toward the exit. She was too late.

Princess Esterhazy was dragging the youngest Delverson out of the supper room by his ear, and Mrs. Drummond-Burrell and Maria Sefton were prodding the other two grinning Devils ahead of them. Countess Lieven was screeching and Lady Bessborough was laid out on a narrow lounge, a flurry of turbaned dowagers waving fans, vinaigrettes, and shrill complaints under her nose. So much for the starched-up dignity of Almack's, where only the *crème de la crème* of polite society was invited, where only the highest sticklers issued edicts of proper decorum, where the youngest innocents of the ton could get thoroughly castaway on orgeat and smuggled gin.

Countess Lieven was so angry, smoke might have poured from her ears if she weren't a true lady. She couldn't birch the three miscreants, though her flailing arms indicated her fondest wish. Instead she could flay them with her tongue.

"How dare you bring your reckless pranks here, you miserable excuses for English gentlemen. Gentlemen, hah! You are nothing but nasty little boys. Where is your sense of honor, your duty to your name, your loyalty to your fellow noblemen?"

When the Russian ambassador's wife paused for breath, Harry put in: "Old Carey's off to war. That must count for something." He was grinning, his arm around his cousin. The lieutenant didn't look a whit abashed either, only raising his arm in a salute "To King and Country."

"You see, ma'am, fellow's going to be a regular hero, we couldn't do less than give him a proper send-off."

"There was nothing proper about this at all," Countess Lieven squawked. "You should have taken your hell-raking to the stews and kennels."

"Don't worry, ma'am, we still have all night. Carey's not leaving till tomorrow."

The countess turned from Harry in disgust. She scowled at the youngest mischief-maker and demanded, "And what about you, Master Joss? Are you going to plead that your big brother and older cousin led you astray? What do you have to say for yourself, sirrah?"

Joss straightened from where the wall was propping him up. "I think, ma'am, begging your pardon, that if you'd give your guests more food, they wouldn't get foxed so easily. Stale cake and toast ain't no supper. M'brother taught me never to drink on an empty stomach. Best of good fellows, St. Dillon, and old Carey too, don't you think?"

What Countess Lieven thought would only be known by those speaking Russian, but Rowanne could guess what the muttered words meant. She was an unwilling witness to the inquisition, unable to get past the group in the hallway or return to the larger rooms because so many people were pressed close behind her trying to see. She also couldn't keep herself from a barely muffled giggle, which earned her at least five censorious glares and one insouciant wink. The scarlet-coated scoundrel wasn't the least repentant. He and Harry were humming the hymn "Love the Sinners, Hate the Sin," while the lady-patronesses conferred.

Emily Cowper, who was truly the least starchy of Almack's governing board, struggled to keep her lips from twitching as she announced the committee's decision. "For the havoc you have created here this evening, and the damage done to the reputation of the institution itself, I regret that we are forced to banish you from the premises."

Harry took out a handkerchief and pretended to weep into it. Lady Cowper shook her finger at him, like a nanny scolding a little boy. "You, Your Grace, may return to Almack's when you are engaged to a proper female, not before."

Harry clutched his heart. "What, miss this place till I am forty?"

Lady Cowper ignored the histrionics and turned to Joss. "We have decided to be lenient with you, Lord Delverson, because of your age. You may return when you have graduated university."

Harry and Joss almost fell on the floor, laughing. Their cousin agreed: "Hell is likely to freeze over first! But tell me, ma'am, what is to be my sentence for the heinous crime? How long shall I be exiled?"

Lady Cowper smiled. "We shall be pleased to welcome you back into our midst, Lieutenant, as soon as the Corsican upstart has been conquered."

Harry and Joss—and some of the men behind Rowanne— were figuring odds and shouting out wagers for the betting book at White's, over which of the Devils was likely to see the inside of Almack's first.

"Out, you barbarians, get out while there is still the hint of civility about the place," Sally Jersey ordered, while the other dowager-arbiters of polite London pointed to the door and shouted "Begone" like so many exorcists in ostrich-feather headdresses.

The young Duke of St. Dillon and his brother made wobbly

courtier's bows and turned to leave, but Carey crossed his arms over his broad chest and said, "Hold. I bespoke another dance with Miss Wimberly and I refuse to leave with the promise unfulfilled."

Rowanne gasped as every eye turned to her. It was no such thing! She checked her dance card to be sure, for more peculiar things had happened this evening, then hissed, "You cannot go back in there, you gudgeon, everyone else is too jug-bitten to stand, much less dance."

Mrs. Drummond-Burrell nodded approvingly. "Good gel, don't encourage the scoundrel."

A beruffled debutante with pink satin bows in her hair stepped out of the crowd and lisped: "I'd be pweased to danth with the offither." Her mother boxed the chit's ears and dragged her off.

Carey grinned and held his ground. "At least someone feels sorry for the poor soldier on the eve of going off to fight his nation's battles. Never say, my good ladies of Almack's, that you are going to deny a condemned man his last wish."

"You haven't a prayer, Carey," Joss told him. "Only the good die young. Besides, you're embarrassing the young lady. Let's go."

"You are right, Joss, and my apologies to Miss Wimberly. If I cannot have my dance, however, I still insist on a token to carry with me to bring to mind the noble cause for which we are fighting. You know, English womanhood and all that. Every knight got to carry a lady's favor for luck in battle, and I demand no less."

Princess Esterhazy stepped forward and held out a lace-edged handkerchief. "Here, you wretched boy, take it and leave."

Delverson reached for the cloth and held the princess's hand, bringing it to his lips. "How kind, Your Majesty, but not what I envisioned."

The princess snatched her handkerchief back and everyone laughed, including a few of the other patronesses. The delighted spectators waited in expectation of further entertainment, and one or two of the dowagers smiled indulgently. Once again everyone seemed to be enjoying themselves more than Rowanne! Drat the man anyway. She supposed he would never go away until he got what he wanted, whatever that might be. Goodness, he couldn't expect a kiss as forfeit for a missed dance, could he? Never! Well, at least never in front of her brother, Miss Simpson, and half the ton. And why was he grinning so widely, with his even white teeth and dimples, as if he could read her mind? The lady that she was, the lady that she would be, certainly did not make bywords of themselves in public!

Rowanne quickly glanced from side to side, fumbled to unpin the cameo brooch at her neckline, and dashed forward. With her cheeks burning, she handed the pin to Lieutenant Delverson and whispered, "For luck," while Harry and Joss cheered.

Carey bowed, blew her a kiss, and left, thank heavens. The hostesses shooed the onlookers back into the ballroom and signaled the band to begin again. Rowanne sent Gabe to fetch their cloaks and have the carriage brought round. For a moment, waiting in the foyer and hoping her cheeks had finally cooled, Rowanne thought her Season was over before it had begun. Mrs. Drummond-Burrell fixed her with a Gorgon's stare and declared that she was sorely disappointed.

"I had been impressed with you, Miss Wimberly, because you were not as giddy as the other harum-scarum young females. I was pleased to see you not succumb to the loose behavior that threatened to turn Almack's into an undignified romp for the first time in memory. But association with that young man cannot do your credit any good. To be frank, if Carey Delverson was not leaving the country tomorrow, I would vote to revoke your voucher."

Even kind-hearted Lady Cowper gave Rowanne a sorrowful look that told her that she was in disgrace, although none of the contretemps had been of Rowanne's making, and she had done the only thing possible to end the bumblebroth and send the muddle-headed Delversons on their way. A lady simply never made a spectacle of herself in such a manner. Never.

It was Sally Jersey who reassured her. That lady put her arm around Rowanne's shoulders and spoke loudly enough for the passing company to hear. "It was not at all the thing, my dear, but I vow any woman here would have done the same."

Chapter Four

Some members of the ton suspected Miss Wimberly of being fast, others held that she was firm under fire. No one forgot her first appearance at Almack's. The highest sticklers might have disdained her company at their select affairs, but Rowanne might not have accepted anyway. Miss Wimberly had quite enough invitations to keep her busy, thank you.

The first weeks after the Almack's debut, London beaux wanted to meet the paragon who could attract such a noted connoisseur as Carey Delverson. The young ladies wanted to become acquainted in case the elusive St. Dillon came to call. A great deal of wildness can be excused in a twenty-five-year-old bachelor duke with a handsome face and a fortune at his command. Harry and his brother, though, traveled to South-ampton with their cousin, saw Carey onto his ship, and then decided to go hunting on the Isle of Wight. Then there was talk of a new Irish stud up for auction, grouse season in Scotland, a luscious set of twins with a traveling players' company.

Rowanne's popularity continued despite the absence of the Delversons. As her notoriety wore off, Miss Wimberly came to be appreciated for her own charms, ease of conversation, quiet dignity, gentle warmth, and a dowry not to be sneezed at. She had a steady court of gentlemen, a comfortable number of lady friends, and an ever-widening circle of admirers among the ton.

On clear days Rowanne went for rides in the park at nine, morning calls at eleven, Venetian breakfasts after noon, waltz

217

parties at three. She was back to be seen in the park at the fashionable saunter at four, then off to a dinner party, followed by the theater or opera, assembly, rout, or drum, sometimes two or three an evening. There were also jaunts to Vauxhall and picnic expeditions in the countryside, masquerades and musicales, card parties, and poetry readings. With so many functions Rowanne's wardrobe constantly needed replenishing, so she had to figure in time for shopping and fittings. Then, of course, she had to hire a dresser, in addition to her abigail.

Miss Simpson accompanied Rowanne, as did Gabe when she could drag him from his meetings and papers, but even without her brother Miss Wimberly was never without a male escort. Any number of bucks and blades, fops and fribbles were anxious to be at her side, some of them forever. Being of an elevated mind, Miss Wimberly did not keep count of the offers she was able to discourage, or the ones Gabe rejected on her behalf. They were considerable and, despite Gabriel's begging her to have one of the chaps so he could get back to his work without those awkward conversations in his library or tripping over the mooncalves in his drawing room at tea, Rowanne was not even tempted to accept a single one.

She was a success, and saw no reason to trade her pleasure-seeking freedom for the fetters of matrimony. There had been no scandals, no further missteps, and no grand passion, either. Her steady callers ranged from callow youths cheerfully following the fashion to plausible basket-scramblers more interested in her assets, with enough intelligent and sophisticated men-about-town thrown in to keep Rowanne entertained—and heart-whole. Of course she continued to read the journals for news of the war and the dispatches for the progress of Sir John Moore's troops, but so would any loyal Britisher, she told herself.

As the London Season waned with the coming of hot weather, so too did Rowanne's enjoyment of the frenetic pace. Conversations did not seem so witty, changing clothes four and five times a day grew to seem an absurd waste of time, and one ball was much like every other one: *on dits* served with the lobster patties, warm rooms, and warmer-blooded

218

swains hoping to lead a young lady to a balcony or garden or indiscretion.

Rowanne wrote to her uncle in Dorset that London was growing hot and thin of company as the *belle monde* retired to their country estates and house parties. The old curmudgeon replied with the suggestion that she visit Lady Silber in Bath; Rowanne must need the restorative waters if she was finding London dull.

Lady Silber was Rowanne's great-aunt Cora on her mother's side, a fragile old woman, or so she said whenever Rowanne had asked her to come to London to lend the Wimberlys countenance. She was a tiny birdlike woman with the thin bones and neck of a scrawny sparrow and the nose of a parrot. Aunt Cora had a tendency to tipple and a firm belief that age bestowed the right to speak one's mind, which she did loudly, due to her own deafness and refusal to use an ear trumpet. Aunt Cora also had one favorite question: "Why ain't you married yet, gal?"

When Rowanne was a gap-toothed moppet and her parents sent her to summer at the shore, she could giggle and reply, "Because I'm just a little girl."

Later Rowanne could grin and say she wasn't even out yet.

Last year she had smiled and reminded Aunt Cora that she was in mourning.

This summer the question was not amusing. She was hardly unpacked and seated in the yellow drawing room in Laura Place when Aunt Cora shouted, "I hear you turned Almack's on its ear, girl. Why ain't you married yet?"

"There's no hurry, Aunt. I am only nineteen."

"Close on twenty, 'n I miss my guess. I was married at sixteen and a widow at twenty-one, missy. Nothing wrong with that."

Rowanne saw a great deal wrong with it, but knew Aunt Cora grew deafer with disagreements. She sipped her tea. "I haven't met anyone who suits me and I see no reason to contract an alliance just for the sake of being married."

"That's a hen-witted notion, girl. Every woman's got to get married. Marriage is a lot like medicine: They all taste bad, but if you take it sooner rather than later, it might work. If something better comes along after, well . . ."

"Aunt Cora!" Rowanne put her cup down with a thump.

"Don't you go all niffy-naffy on me now, miss. Don't think I didn't hear all the gossip from London, and how you almost blotted your copybook. Only a married woman can smile at all the handsome rogues she wants, if she picks her husband right."

Rowanne took a deep breath. "That's not the kind of marriage I want. I don't want some man to marry me for my looks—and have him keep looking. And I don't want to become any man's chattel either, or have some wastrel play ducks-and-drakes with my inheritance."

"Hoity-toity, miss."

"That's right, I am a managing kind of female. You know how I have been running Wimberly House and taking charge of Gabriel. I am too used to being my own mistress to let any man ride roughshod over me, and I would not respect any man weak enough to let me hold sway over him."

"Poppycock. What about children? If all you young bubble-brains thought the same the human race would die out and rabbits would take over the world. Biggest regret of my life, it is, not having more nieces and nephews to boss around."

"Then why did you not remarry and have children of your own?"

Aunt Cora cupped her hand to her ear. "Merry and half-chilled what? You know I can't hear when you mumble, girl."

Rowanne smiled. "I think I should like to have children, but there is still no rush. Perhaps when I am an ape-leader at twenty-five I shall consider a marriage of convenience. Meanwhile I am independent, comfortably established, and I have Gabe for protection."

"Pshaw. Some protection. The boy forgets he has a sister half the time."

"Yes, but he could not very well get along without me. Can you imagine Gabriel overseeing the servants and keeping household accounts?"

"Then he should get him a wife of his own, not keep his sister as chatelaine. And you can't humbug me, missy. Your brother is way more than nineteen and I hear no rumors of him dropping the handkerchief either. What's the slowtop about anyway? He owes it to his name. I know that rackety father of yours never spent any time with either of you, but didn't he at least teach his son to carry on the line?"

"I don't know, Aunt Cora." And she really didn't. Somehow it never occurred to her that Gabe would marry. She had to threaten to burn his papers to get him to socialize, and he never danced more than duty required or took a female out for drives, to her knowledge. But of course he should marry.

After Uncle Donald, Gabriel, Viscount Wimberly, would be the Earl of Clyme, an ancient title that must not die out because Rowanne's brother forgot to find a bride the same way he forgot to eat dinner when there was an interesting debate at the House. Well, Rowanne had seen to his needs for the last years, she would just have to play matchmaker for him too. Hadn't she just told Aunt Cora what a good manager she was? Her girlfriends had always found him attractive, she knew, and they were always wistfully asking if Gabe was coming along on any outings, so finding a wife for him should not be difficult. On the other hand, finding the *perfect* wife for her dearly loved brother would take a little more thought.

That evening, when Rowanne could not fall asleep due to the unfamiliar bed, the early hour Aunt Cora insisted on retiring, and that lady's snores echoing through the walls of the little house, she thought about a bride for Gabe.

And her own future.

A milk-and-water schoolroom chit would never do for Gabe. He needed a woman who could anchor him to the world outside his library, oversee his career, and guarantee his comfort. In other words, he needed an organized, managing female, just like Rowanne, one who would resent an interfering sister-in-law. Miss Wimberly could never see herself living as a maiden aunt in such a woman's household either, so she would have to leave Grosvenor Square.

Perhaps she could move in with Aunt Cora permanently, sip sherry, and raise pug dogs. Maybe Uncle Donald would finally invite her to Dorset, to keep him company in his old age. Maybe pigs would fly. Or Rowanne and Miss Simpson could set up housekeeping somewhere by themselves. Now *that* would cause a dust-up even Gabe would notice. Rowanne had the financial means, but she didn't know if she had the back-bone. Ah well, there was always marriage.

She tossed the pillows to the floor and rolled over.

Rowanne had been looking forward to a relaxing month or so with her elderly aunt in Bath after the bustle of the London Season, walking on the strand, strolling in Sydney Gardens, catching up on her reading. Aunt Cora had other plans, and she was about as fragile in her determination as a red-eyed bull. Lady Silber was going to snabble her wayward niece an eligible *parti* if it killed both of them. In Aunt Cora's estimation, eligible meant any male between seventeen and seventy. She dragged Rowanne off to the Pump Room daily, to the Upper and Lower Assembly Rooms, and to as many other entertainments as she and her ancient cronies could devise. She made sure Rowanne accepted the multitude of invitations from the many other London visitors in Bath for the summer, and especially from the local great houses. Aunt Cora was positive a gentleman meeting even Rowanne's demanding standards could easily be found.

Every evening, when Rowanne came home and only wished to kick off her slippers and sink into bed, Aunt Cora would call out, loudly enough to wake all the servants, if not the next-door neighbors, "Well, did you find Prince Charming? Why ain't you married yet?"

Chapter Five

*R*owanne was delighted to be back in London, vowing this Season would be different. There would be no more junketing around, burning herself to the socket with no higher goal than filling her dance card or finding the most outrageous bonnet. Now Rowanne had a Mission. First she would reconnoiter, then plan her campaign.

She cornered her quarry in the breakfast room on the day following her return. The servants had finished serving and Miss Simpson had not yet returned from her month's vacation to her brother's family in Kent. Gabriel was reading the morning papers over his coffee and kippers.

Rowanne buttered her toast. She had not been able to imagine any graceful way of bringing the topic she wished to discuss into a conversation so she simply came out and asked: "Gabe, have you ever considered marrying?"

Her brother did not even put down the papers. "Poor puss, you *have* spent too much time with Aunt Cora, haven't you?"

"Quite, but surely, though, isn't it time you thought of taking a wife?"

Gabe laid the newspaper aside and boosted his spectacles back up on his nose. "I know what it is, you are finally going to take one of the coxcombs who are forever littering the place. Good. Which one shall it be, so I'm sure to make myself available to hear his declaration in form?"

"Don't be a goose, it is no such thing. Besides, my friends are not coxcombs, just because they are not all as serious-minded as you are."

"Not even Clifford Fairborn? I swear he composed an ode for every day you were gone. And yellow pantaloons, my dear."

"Very well, Lord Fairborn is a coxcomb, but I was talking about you." She poured him another cup of coffee.

"If you are worried about leaving, Ro, don't be. I really can manage, you know. You've trained Mrs. Ligett to natter at me quite competently, and Hinkle would never let me be seen in anything less than prime twig. You have been gone a whole month and Wimberly House is still standing. The bailiffs are not even pounding at the door."

"Housekeepers and valets are all well and good, but I am speaking of a wife, a helpmate, heirs, someone to carry on the title. You *have* to wed."

Gabriel opened the paper again. "Did you read today's news?"

"You are changing the subject, Gabriel Wimberly."

"Oh, I just wondered if you saw that St. Dillon's cousin was mentioned in the dispatches again, promoted in the field for bravery. I thought you'd be interested. Perhaps I was wrong."

Rowanne tore the newspaper out of his hands, knocking over the cream pitcher. Gabriel muttered into his coffee cup, "Perhaps not."

Despite Gabe's lack of enthusiasm or cooperation, Rowanne was determined to try her hand at matchmaking. She believed that if she could just bring the proper female to his attention, in a quiet, comfortable setting away from the mad crushes he disliked, Gabe would be quick enough to fix his interest.

Therefore, instead of coercing Gabe into escorting her to grand society balls, she accepted invitations to literary salons, where a well-featured bluestocking might appeal to him. Gabe refused to listen to one more dilettante spout one more opinion. Instead of attending Almack's, where two bewigged and liveried footmen still guarded the punch bowl every Wednesday evening, Rowanne cultivated some of the Whig hostesses at their political suppers, seeking a woman who shared Gabe's ideologies. The men stayed all evening with their port and cigars, never joining the ladies after dinner at all, and Rowanne was so bored she took to bringing her needle-work along. She was petit-pointing cushion seats for a tiny dining set she had found in a furniture showroom in Bath, left there by a journeyman cabinetmaker. At least her miniature collection was coming along, now that she was not keeping such a rackety pace, even if she was no closer to seeing her brother settled in wedded bliss.

Not being a hen-hearted female, Rowanne did not give up, even when the winter Little Season was half over. She crossed out intellectuals and politically oriented ladies from her mental list, along with brittle belles who made Gabe's hands perspire, twittery debs he confessed a desire to throttle, and country girls who only spoke of fox hunts and rootcrops, foreign languages to her citified brother. Maybe a more mature lady? But Rowanne was not about to consign her brother to any spinster at her last prayers. In all of London, with so many women on the lookout for a husband, surely there must be one to appeal to a lovable lobcock like her absentminded brother.

Rowanne started having small at-homes at Wimberly House. She invited her own admirers to keep Gabe unsuspecting, fellow bureaucrats like Lord Quinton to keep him in attendance, and every unattached young lady she could find. She had no trouble finding a great many, once her at-homes became noted for her collection of eligible bachelors, not the least of which was Gabe, heir to an earl and possible cabinet post. Miss Winslow played the pianoforte very prettily, Miss Castleberry was a dab hand at chess, Miss Ashford's father was an African missionary. Gabe listened and lost and asked questions, and never mentioned the girls again. He was the perfect host, or a perfect dolt, in his sister's eyes.

She kept looking through the winter and into spring, considering the merits of every girl she met. Heavens, Rowanne feared she was beginning to resemble Miss Grimble with her research. She even invited that redoubtable woman and her charge, Lady Diana Hawley-Roth, even though Lady Diana made Rowanne's knees quake. Poor Gabe almost developed a stutter before the evening was done, under the basilisk stare of the companion and the calculating appraisal of the Beauty.

If informal gatherings were too general—and too easy for Gabe to escape by getting lost in a debate with one of his gentleman friends—Rowanne would throw intimate dinners, before a ball, after the theater. With less than ten people at table, conversation had to be general, and maybe a heretofore unappealing lady would shine in Gabe's view. Rowanne was desperate for even a glimmer. She hired a new chef.

She couldn't have only females sit to dine with Gabriel, herself, and Miss Simpson, of course, so Rowanne kept inviting loyal members of her court. She was as popular as ever, perhaps more so for being less accessible and for having one of the finest chefs in Town, but she did not wish to give any of her admirers false hopes. Therefore she alternated Corinthians with Tulips, Town bucks with green boys, a lovesick Clifford Fairborn with a married schoolmate of Gabe's, and the persistent widower Lord Martindale with her brother's mentor Lord Quinton, to even the numbers with her prospective sisters-in-law.

At last her efforts were a success! Just when Rowanne feared another summer with Aunt Cora with nothing to report, wedding bells were in the air, a proposal was made and accepted. Unfortunately, it was Lord Quinton straining his corset to lay his heart at Miss Simpson's feet, those feet that had once danced the reel so merrily at Almack's.

At least a summer wedding was planned. Rowanne insisted on helping with the preparations and the trousseau and seeing the bride safely to her brother's house in Kent for the ceremony, so naturally she did not have time to travel to Bath at all.

"Shall you mind, Rowanne?" Miss Simpson asked her.

"Not going to Bath? Devil a bit. Of course I shall miss you after all these years of having you as my teacher and my friend, but I should feel like the veriest beast if I put my own welfare above your happiness."

"I never thought to marry after all these years, you know. I hope I am doing the right thing."

"I'm sure I hope so too. I cannot help worrying over what Miss Grimble told us about Lord Quinton's *cherie amour*. Won't that bother you?"

"Yes, it would," the proper ex-governess answered, "if I intended to let him keep the connection. He'll be too busy though."

"Why, Miss Simpson, I never!"

"Me neither, dear, but I hope to start."

Early fall brought another marriage, but Rowanne took no credit for this one at all. All of London was reeling from the shocking news that Lady Hawley-Roth, heiress and Diamond of the first water, had run away with a knight of the baize table. Diana the Hunter had bagged herself a weasel. Word had it that her parents were so furious they turned Miss Grimble off without a reference.

Rowanne found herself in need of a companion, lest doubts

about her adherence to society's strictures reflect poorly on Gabe, or keep any available females from being seen in her company. More important, she needed Miss Grimble's wealth of information if she was ever to find her brother the ideal spouse. At this point Rowanne would have settled for a less than ideal female, so long as she could make Gabe come up to scratch. She sent a letter to the Hawley-Roth address, telling Miss Grimble that she would be welcome at the Wimberly House at her convenience. There was no reply, and Rowanne wondered if the irate parents had even forwarded her letter.

A few months later it hardly mattered that she was unchaperoned, for Rowanne was losing her taste for the gay whirl of society. The newspapers were reporting casualty lists from the Peninsula daily, and the tolls were staggering. It seemed inconceivable to her that the ton could continue with their endless revels when so many of their sons and brothers were being cut down in their youth. Captain Delverson had been reported wounded at Oporto.

Rowanne was content with fewer parties, smaller dinners, old friends, throwing only the occasional female at her brother's head. She enjoyed quiet evenings with her projects while Gabriel read aloud or worked on his papers. Rowanne and the household staff had converted part of the smaller sitting room into a workshop for her miniature collection, with chests for supplies and an oilcloth-covered table for her messier ventures. The other half of the sitting room was filled with comfortable chairs and sofas, a cozy fireplace, and plenty of good working lights—and of course the collection itself.

Rowanne's miniatures were more than dollhouse toys by this time and were displayed cabinet-style on shelves in specially designed cupboards with glass-paneled doors. Some shelves were divided into complete room settings, others just held special objects as curios. Rowanne had model chairs from Mr. Chippendale and inch-wide dishes from Spode that her mother had commissioned when ordering new tableware for Wimberly House. Two room settings sported thumbnail family groupings painted by Lawrence as a favor to her father when he was doing the viscount's portrait, and palm-size brass beds were covered with sheets painstakingly embroidered with the family crest by her old nanny. Last Christmas Gabe had presented her with a silver tea service he'd had made for her, the whole thing, tray and all, no longer than her smallest finger. She had tiny gold filigree chairs from Russia, a carved cradle from Germany, and replicas of marble statues from Italy. There were working clocks, if one was careful about winding them, and wooden bowls of porcelain fruit.

Rowanne herself contributed tapestry weavings and painted-velvet rugs, little watercolors in locket frames, papier-mâché flowers—and whatever else she thought to try her hand at. It was taking her most of the winter to string Austrian glass beads into a crystal chandelier.

Miss Grimble arrived finally and, after assessing the house, the kitchens, stables, and attics, decided to stay while she wrote her memoirs. No mention was made of her previous position.

"I wouldn't take on just any young lady, you know. But yes, I can see where that brother of yours would be a challenge." Miss Grimble did not say that getting Miss Wimberly fired off would appear much more likely, and much better for her own tarnished reputation. The chit had to be nudging twenty-one. Time and past for a wealthy miss to be leg-shackled. They got strange notions after that. She nodded. "Getting a male settled would be a new twist for the book."

"I would hate to see my family named in a publication, Miss Grimble."

"Yes, yes, I can see where you would. No matter, I have enough material for several volumes. I can write while you are involved with your hobbies." The forbidding dame had been impressed by the collection. "Shows a serious turn of mind. At least you're not likely to chuck it all and go haring off to the Continent with some ivory-tuner. Now about Lord Wimberly. Your brother is known to be high-minded and dedicated. Dull."

"But he is the dearest creature in existence. He just does not like to make small talk or listen to gossip."

"He's a misfit in society, with no bark on it, but he's rich and titled, and there are a lot of widgeons wanting nothing more than a house to manage. We'll find a peagoose who will take him."

"That's no problem. Women like Gabriel. It is he who has no interest."

"Not peculiar, is he?"

"Peculiar?" Rowanne colored, then remembered that book of memoirs. "Of course not, and if you are going to go on like that, I don't think—"

"You never can tell. There's Lord—"

"Miss Grimble!"

The dragon recalled that she really did need this position, if only until the manuscript was completed. "I daresay we can find him a suitable wife in jig time."

"But he has to love her."

"That will take longer. My book might be done before then, but we can try. It will mean Almack's every week to look over the new crop of debutantes, and the major crushes where everyone and his uncle comes and brings his sister. A lot of tea parties and shopping expeditions, places where females gather. Are you ready for that, Miss Wimberly?"

Rowanne was ready to face society and enjoy herself doing it. Captain Delverson was mentioned again in the dispatches, back in the thick of things, but of course that had nothing whatsoever to do with her change of heart.

Chapter Six

Some men were fortunate in combat. They could come through whole battles without ever seeing the enemy. Others considered themselves blessed that they were still alive after the bloodiest confrontations. The battered survivors could look around at their fallen comrades and in dark humor declare, "Things could have been worse."

"Things could have been worse" became the motto of the men serving under the Honorable Harmon Carrisbrooke Delverson. Carey got his troops into—and out of—more scrapes than any other junior officer serving under Sir John Moore. Sir John wanted to put the bold hellion on the general staff, to make use of his daring strategies and lightning decisions, but the lieutenant preferred to stay in the field. "The men appreciate when their commands come from someone they trust."

"Aye, and someone willing to die alongside them. Loyalty's worth more than the few shillings we pay the poor sods. The men need you. See that you stay alive for them."

Carey did, rising to captain at Coruña. He took a musket ball in one shoulder and a saber slash in the thigh, and still stood to rally his men and get them back to the lines. As he rode to the rescue of one besieged recruit who found himself holding a piece of his ear in his hand, Carey called out, "Things could have been worse. The frog who did it is missing part of his skull." He rode on into one skirmish after another, in remarkable displays of horsemanship and sword-work, with a smile at the end for the troops gallant enough to follow him.

The men adored him and considered Carey some kind of talisman. From being one of the Delverson Devils, he became the Lucky Devil. He might get lost behind enemy lines, but he came back, with a sack of fresh-killed chickens. The replacement drummer may have beat *charge* instead of *retreat*, but the Frenchies were just as confused, and fled.

Delverson's legendary good fortune was quirky, never without cost. A cannonball at Oporto that missed him by inches would have taken his head clean off, if his favorite mount had not just got shot out from under him, leaving Carey with a knee wrenched so badly he used crutches for a month.

The left-handed luck extended past the battles, in escapades that made the captain's name a byword in mess tents and officers' clubs, such as the night an irate Madrileño *esposo* went berserk and shredded every item in Captain Delverson's tent. He would have shredded Carey too, if the Devil had been sleeping in his own bed. Instead he was busy having his nose broken by another irate husband coming home unexpectedly. Another time Carey foolishly sat in at a high-stakes card game at a local *taberna*. He'd had too much to drink to pay attention to his hand and went down heavily, losing far more than he could afford. So did the winner, who was found the next morning with his throat cut, victim of a neighborhood scheme to rebuild the local economy.

As for women, ah, the Spanish women with their dark eyes and red lips were nearly Carey's downfall, luck or not. The daughter of a *grandee* almost had him trapped into marriage, her *duenna* screeching when her mother rushed into the room and hysterically claimed El Diablo Delverson as *her* lover. All three women turned on him, with vases, chamber pots, and crucifixes. It could have been worse, of course. He could have been married to one of the shrews.

Such exploits kept the men in spirits, if anything could on the hard, hot drive across the Peninsula. The marches were dusty, the landscape painted in barren ocher tones. Insects, diseases, and Spanish *banditos* made conditions hellish; Soult's tactics of dividing up the British troops, separating them from their slower supply trains, made commands near impossible, ambushes likely, hunger and thirst daily companions. It could have been worse, the captain reminded: They could have been in the navy.

Sometimes it couldn't get any worse. Between battles, when the furious action left no time for thought, and after the victory celebrations to forget the losses and the exhaustion, sometimes Captain Delverson did not feel lucky at all. He reread his cousins' infrequent letters of races and wagers months past, and his father's missives about crops and country neighbors. Lord Delverson wrote that he was proud of his son, but missed him too, especially now that his young wife Eleanor had succumbed to an inflammation of the lungs. At least Lord Delverson had his and Eleanor's daughter Suzannah for company at Delmere in Dorset, and Eleanor's young sister Emonda too, while Carey had his men and madcap antics miles away and lifetimes apart, with his letters and a cameo brooch to remind him of home.

Sweltering in a musty tent, with no water to wash and only his coat for a bed and a flickering candle to see by, Carey would flip open the locket and take heart from the woman who smiled back at him. He thought she must be the Wimberly chit's mother, for the girl in the tiny portrait had her hair powdered, but they were close in appearance from what he could remember. No matter, the lady in the locket was sweet and perfumed and floating on some gallant's arm at Almack's; she was England and home, and she smiled at him and wished him luck.

"Bloody generals cannot get enough rations or ammunition here. You'd think the least they could do is deliver the mail! Look at this, Rudd. I get no correspondence for months on end, and now a blasted avalanche of— Oh, God, no."

"Cap'n?" The batman looked up from where he was polishing Carey's boots. Delverson's tanned face was ashen and the hand that was clutching a tattered, black-bordered sheet was trembling. Rudd searched out the last bottle of Portuguese brandy he'd been saving. "Bad news, sir?"

"My father. His heart gave out, the solicitor says, last March. Bloody hell, that was five months ago! Damn, I should have been there!"

Rudd put a glass in the captain's hand. "If it were sudden-like, you wouldn't of known anyways, even if they could of sent for you. Is the man handling things for you?"

Carey drained the glass and held it out for a refill. "Yes, I suppose. I don't know. He wants me to come home and decide about the tenants' roofs, of all the cork-brained ideas. What does the bastard think I am doing here? Having a picnic with the *señoritas*, that I should just pack up and leave, saying 'Sorry, I recalled another engagement'? Blast, the general is set to take a stand at Cifuente; I cannot ask for leave just days before an engagement."

"I'm thinking roofs can wait. They waited this long, ain't

they? Or send the bloke your dibs, if you trust him." Rudd pulled out the loaf of bread and slab of cheese he was hoarding for the coming battle, in case the supply lines were cut again. He didn't trust the commanders any more than he trusted the French. Captain Delverson, now that was another matter. Hadn't the captain hired him on as his personal servant when the surgeons declared Rudd unfit for battle? What was Rudd going to do in England with a wooden leg and a patch over one eye? Starve, that's what, and he may as well starve in Spain. Wouldn't do to let the captain drink on an empty stomach.

Carey absentmindedly cut a slice of cheese. He too had learned to eat whenever he had the chance. "I trust old Hayes, but he's in London; Delmere is in Dorset. Besides, there's more. It seems I am now responsible for two females, my stepsister Suzannah and her mother's sister."

Rudd thought about that one for a while. "Sounds like the second female is your aunt."

"Emonda Selcroft my aunt? The chit is barely seventeen, I'd wager. She was a timid little wren when she came to live at Delmere, much younger than her sister Eleanor, who was considerably younger than my father. Even then Emonda was the biggest goosecap you'd ever find, a watering pot afraid of her own shadow. If a chap should even suggest that the wind noise in the chimney sounded like one of the ancestors, she'd shriek for days."

"Bedeviled her, did you?"

Carey had to smile. "Not me so much as Harry. He couldn't resist. And Joss was always fond of snakes and toads. We were invited to take school vacations at the Abbey, one county over, after Emonda came to live with Eleanor and the governor. What in bloody hell does old Hayes expect me to do about Emonda?"

"What about t'other female? Your stepsister?"

"Suzannah's worse in her way. Last time I saw her, before I shipped out, she was a thirteen-year-old hoyden up in the trees with the local squire's son."

"Time cures a lot of high spirits, I'm thinking."

"It didn't do a lot for Harry and Joss. Damn, females and farming!" He had another glass. Rudd cut a slice of bread and shoved it near his hand, where Carey was sorting through the rest of his mail. "Bunch of condolences. What in hell do I care if some old harridan's got nothing better to do than write about her sympathy for my loss? He was my father, blast it!" Carey threw the glass across the tent and stormed out.

"Waste of good brandy, if you ask me," Rudd muttered after him.

When Captain Delverson returned some hours later—how far could he go with French troops behind every other hill?—he finished reading the letters. The scrawled envelope had to be from Suzannah; what had his father been about to get the chit so little schooling? Carey's stepsister wrote that she was distraught at the loss, but Carey should not worry about her, only about killing all the Frenchies he could find. She could come cook for him if he wanted, otherwise she hoped he would send his permission for her to marry Heywood Jeffers, the squire's son. So much for hopes that Suzannah was maturing into a sensible female.

The next letter brought him even less satisfaction. Emonda wrote in a thin, small hand, twice crossed so he could barely decipher the words. She too would miss Lord Delverson, who was a fine man to have taken in a homeless orphan like herself and even set aside a small dowry for her. Emonda did not mean to be a drain on Carey, she wrote, because she was no relative of his whatsoever and would not like to be a burden. Emonda went on to explain that she would go out for a governess as soon as Carey sent instructions as to which relatives she should send Suzannah. Unless, of course, he meant to let Suzannah wed the neighbor's boy.

Let his sister marry at fifteen and his seventeen-year-old stepaunt set out in the world to make her own living? Carey would sooner help Napoléon cross the Channel. Furious, he took out pen and paper.

You stay right where you are at Delmere, he wrote Emonda, *and make sure that Suzannah does the same. Seeing that she doesn't go off on some jingle-brained start is the least you can do for my father's memory. If you wish to be an instructor of young ladies, I suggest you start with your niece. I shall be in touch with Mr. Hayes concerning the estate since I am unable to return to England until after the next campaign. Yr. obed. servant.*

Then he wrote to the solicitor and to Harry, hoping the letter would find his scapegrace cousin wherever he was: *Cousin, please do not let me down. Get to Dorset posthaste, make sure the bailiff is honest, and, above all, find some respectable woman to oversee the girls. Yrs.* He added a postscript: *And keep your hands off Emonda. She's family.* Carey didn't think his mousy little aunt was in Harry's style, being a tiny dab of a washed-out blonde with die-away airs, but it never hurt to be careful where his cousin was concerned.

Having done what he could about family matters—hell and blast, he was head of the family now!—Captain Delverson pulled out another sheet and wrote a letter of appreciation to the only condolence note that made any sense. Miss Rowanne Wimberly had written how sad he must be to learn such news at a distance, and how helpless to change anything. She understood because her own parents had died when she could not be with them and she missed them still. She wrote in an elegant copperplate that she was sure his father must have been proud of him, and then she wished him Godspeed.

In the middle of his sorrow and Emonda's hysteria, in the chaos of war, Miss Wimberly was like a safe harbor. On the eve of battle, Carey took out the cameo and wrote a letter to the girl in the locket.

Some two months later, after a bloody battle at Talavera that had turned into more of a rout than a retreat, Captain Delverson lay on a cot in a deserted, bug-infested farmhouse, feverish from a saber slash across the palm of his left hand. The field surgeons were all for amputation, but the captain could still walk, and walk he did, right out to his horse and Rudd and this abandoned *hacienda* where he would either recover or not, without suffering worse at those butchers' hands. Rudd was able to bring him food and medicine and mail from head-quarters. The batman was pleased to see the letter with the crested seal, for now maybe the captain would rest easy, knowing his cousin was looking after the lasses.

Carey ripped the envelope awkwardly with one hand and eagerly read Harry's scrawl.

Not to worry, cuz, Harry wrote. *All at first oars. You've got a good steward, land's in good heart. And Joss and I found a likely widow in the village, hired her on to move into Delmere. Good-looking woman too, this Mrs. Reardon. Now you've got nothing to worry about except learning the* fandango *and keeping all the* señoritas *happy.*

Carey fell back on the bed, groaning. Things could be worse, he told himself. Harry could have installed Harriet Wilson, the most notorious courtesan in London, to chaperone the innocents. Instead he'd only hired Mrs. Reardon, the late Lord Delverson's mistress!

Chapter Seven

*L*ord Wellesley himself called Captain Delverson into headquarters concerning his request for leave.

"You could sell out, boy. No one could fault you for that, now that you have duties at home. You've given your pound of flesh, aye, and accounted for more French losses than half a battalion of Home Guard."

"No, sir, the job's not done. I'll come back, if I can just take care of family matters. I'd like to see a proper surgeon about my hand too, while I am in England. These quacks here tell me to keep it in a sling, that I'll never have use of it again, and it's liable to cause blood poisoning. I've been rubbing in horse liniment, though, and I think it's loosening up some. Oh, and with your permission, sir, I'll need to take my batman Rudd. It's deuced hard dressing with one hand."

Sir Arthur stacked some papers on his desk. "You go take care of the family business, lad, but I am not sure about Rudd or the physicians." He looked down his grand beak and smiled. "If you smell like a stable and you cannot get your pants down, maybe you'll stay out of trouble."

Carey's first stop in London was Delverson House, the St. Dillon town residence. Even with only one working hand, he was ready to strangle Harry. Every gentleman worth the name knew and honored the ancient tenet about not fouling one's own nest. A man did not introduce his mother to his lightskirts, he did not bring his bits of muslin to tea with his aunts, and he did not set up his uncle's mistress two doors down from his cousin's schoolroom! Harry had a lot to answer for. If he knew about Mrs. Reardon ... No, Carey decided, not even Harry could be so skitter-witted or so lost to convention. If he did not know, he damn well should have made inquiries before throwing Emonda and Suzannah into such a devilish coil.

Strangling was too good for Harry. Captain Delverson decided he'd make his cousin accompany him to Dorset instead, to face the hysterical scene bound to be waiting at Delmere. Harry could have the task of explaining to Emonda that she had been living with a demi-rep for months. For himself, Captain Delverson would rather face Marshal Soult again.

Unfortunately for Carey's plans, Delverson House looked and smelled like an abandoned barracks. Which was not to say Harry was not in residence. The only housemaids willing to work for St. Dillon were more familiar with his bedroom than his broom closet, and a little grease and grime were beneath Harry's notice as long as the stables were spotless. Harry was as liable to be down in the kitchens dicing with the footmen as sleeping in some hell in a barmaid's embrace. Fortunately for Harry, the old butler Turvey hadn't seen the master in months and had no notion as to his whereabouts.

The house might be falling down around Turvey's white-haired ears, but the stables behind the mews were ready for a riding party. Carey borrowed one of the sleek beasts and set off for the Surgeon General's quarters at the War Office.

Three physicians poked and prodded, stuck pins in his fingers, and nodded gravely.

"It looks healed, but it may putrefy. Best to resign the commission now."

"Not much movement," said the second. "You'll never have the use of it, be a hazard in battle."

"Regard the amount of pain," the third medico advised his colleagues, stabbing Delverson with a wickedly pointed instrument.

In one minute Carey was going to teach the learned doctors a thing or two about pain with his good right arm. "Devil take it, man, that hand is attached to a living person, not a cadaver."

"Quite. To continue, I would say the muscles are not permanently severed. The wound itself should remain salutary, without more trauma. With proper exercise, the digits might regain some mobility."

Which was precisely what Carey wanted to hear, so he forgave the surgeons and bought himself a large-size snuffbox to manipulate in his hand on the way to Dorset in one of Harry's carriages.

Carey and his man Rudd spent the night in Winchester and proceeded to Delmere, at Blandford, Dorsetshire, early the following morning.

If Captain Delverson had any hopes the situation was better than he surmised, or the county was ignorant of the bumble-broth, those hopes were soon quashed like a beetle underfoot.

Their first stop was the stables where Ned, the old groom who had set Carey on his first pony, welcomed the captain home by spitting in the straw and saying, " 'Bout time you got here. Ain't what a body likes, seeing such a one as that in your mama's place."

Pofford the butler, another longstanding employee, greeted Carey with a doleful shake of his bald head. "Now maybe the vicar will come to call."

Before seeking out the ladies, Carey sent for Mrs. Tulliver, the housekeeper and best baker of gingerbread a boy ever knew. She was no longer on the payroll, Pofford informed him.

"What? Tully would never leave the place. Her mother was housekeeper before her."

"Indeed, but the new ah, mistress, found her outspoken and 'uppity,' I believe was the word. Fortunately his late lordship remembered Mrs. Tulliver in his will. She was able to take rooms in Widow Vane's house in the village."

"Get her back. Before you go, have a carriage wait outside, won't you? Oh, and take one of the housemaids, one of *our* people, upstairs and see about helping Mrs. Reardon pack. She will be leaving within the hour, with every item she came with."

"And none else. I understand, milord. It will be my pleasure. Shall I announce you now?"

"What? In my own home? But yes, if we are in for high melodrama, let us have all the fanfare."

It was more of a farce. Emonda jumped up like a snake had crossed her foot, and her look gave no doubt that she considered Carey a viper indeed. She was swathed in stiff black bombazine, making her pale complexion and light hair even more colorless, and she was even scrawnier and more pinch-faced than he recalled. She clutched her needlework to her unprepossessing bosom and fled the room.

Mrs. Reardon, by way of contrast, wore gold tissue silk, much too fancy for a morning gown, cut much too low and tight to conceal her nearly over-abundant charms, and a topaz necklace, much too similar to one Eleanor had worn. With her reddish-blond hair and vibrant lips, her languid motions as she raised her plumpish self from the loveseat to lift her hand for Carey's kiss, Regina Reardon was everything Emonda was not—except a lady. Nor did she take her dismissal like a gently bred female, even though she was planning to leave soon on her own. A harborside alehouse doxy could not have expressed herself more loudly or more colorfully, with shattering punctuation. Luckily Carey had never been fond of his stepmama's grouping of china shepherdesses along the mantel. He sat at his ease while Mrs. Reardon stormed on, concentrating on turning the snuffbox in his left hand's fingers. When the dramatics wound down, Carey smiled and in a tone of voice bespeaking reason and firm resolve asked, "How much?"

The French might think love was the universal language; the British knew better. Mrs. Reardon licked her ruby lips and smiled back. "St. Dillon assured me a year's employment; I have only been paid for the quarter."

Carey waved his hand. "A contract is a contract."

"And I had to give up the lease on the cottage. A new place would cost dearly."

Carey studied the snuffbox. "I should think you might find a change of neighborhood to your liking."

"But I quite like it here. Of course, if I could afford London prices, I might consider moving away from my dear friends."

"I think you'll enjoy London. All the new sights and entertainments." Damn if he couldn't almost flip it open with his left hand.

"Do you think your cousin will be in London soon?"

So St. Dillon had stirred another pie. Carey shrugged, toting another debt in Harry's column.

Mrs. Reardon sighed. "I am not as young as I once was. Making new, ah, friends will not be so easy."

Carey gallantly stepped into the breech, as she knew he would: "Exquisite women like yourself only ripen with time, like fine wine. The Town Beaux are true connoisseurs, but I would naturally not expect a rare sherry to go for lowest price at auction."

"Might you consider bidding yourself, to see such a precious bottle protected?"

Carey picked a speck of lint off his jacket sleeve. "I regret that it was my father who was interested in keeping the cellars stocked, not myself."

Mrs. Reardon regretted it too; the handsome captain would have suited her to the nines, as generous as he was being. She had one more arrow in her quiver. No, she had two, counting the one reserved for bigger game. She patted her stomach. "You know, my lord, your father did not die quietly in his bed as we gave out."

Carey raised one eyebrow in question. "You begin to interest me, ma'am."

If that was a slur, Mrs. Reardon ignored it. "Well, he died in bed. I sent for his man and we brought him back here with no one the wiser."

"I owe you for that, ma'am."

"I rather thought you did. A woman needs a carriage of her own, to get around in London."

The coach and four was reduced to a chaise and pair, and the final price for Mrs. Reardon's departure and silence was ultimately agreed upon. Her leaving was not as quiet as Carey had hoped, once he insisted on getting the topaz necklace back, despite the fact that Suzannah was much too young for jewels and Emonda would have no use for it, being in mourning. Another tirade ensued when Mrs. Reardon saw her bags being carried out and loaded in a waiting carriage, without even time to change her gown. Only a particularly ugly vase on a hall table suffered the lady's ire as Captain Delverson escorted her to the coach by means of an iron-hard grip on her upper arm.

Carey wiped his brow, winked at the gaping footman in the hall, and asked if his sister and Miss Selcroft could attend him in the library.

Emonda slunk in, clutching an already-damp handkerchief. Hell, Carey thought, and poured himself a brandy. Emonda's eyes widened, almost as if she feared he would overindulge, lose control, and go on a ravening rampage after her virtue. "Oh, sit down, Emmy. I am not about to eat you." She took the seat as far from him as possible and perched on the edge of her chair, ready to run. Carey went on. "I am deuced sorry about this hobble. How did you let such a thing happen?"

"How did *I* let it happen?" She gazed at him as if he'd sprouted another head. "You ordered me to stay here to see about Suzannah, and you told St. Dillon to find a woman to keep us company. I tried to tell Harry, but he said I was always finding bogeymen under my bed. He hired that woman, and she said only he could fire her."

It would have been too much to expect Emonda to grow a backbone in the two years he'd been gone. She was so damnably weak and feather-headed. "I'd have thought Suzannah would have shown more spirit. Ah, would have kicked up a dust."

Emonda wiped her eyes. "She thought it was a great joke, just another one of Harry's pranks. And since Mrs. Reardon never interfered with her, Suzannah could not care one way or the other."

"She's still a hoyden then?"

"I am sure you are going to blame me for that too." She sniffled into the cloth.

"Will you stop that blubbering, Emmy! We'll come about."

"Fine for you to say. You'll go back to your silly war, and Suzannah is just a child, but I am ruined. I shall be tarred by the same brush as that woman, and no one shall ever hire me as a governess."

Now she was sobbing in earnest, and each sob added another knot in Carey's stomach. "Will you get that pea-brained notion out of your head? You are underage and I would never let my ward go into service."

"I am not your ward" came as a muffled cry from the handkerchief.

Carey handed his own linen over, thinking Lud, she must need a fresh one by now. "You were my father's ward, now you are mine," he told her firmly. "Surely he would have made some provision for seeing you settled."

"We were going to go up to London when Suzannah was a little older. He set aside a dowry for me." The weeping started anew.

Desperate, Carey promised, "We can still go. That's years away. You'll see, you'll make a fine match with your good lineage, a handsome portion, and your pretty looks. Blondes are all the crack." He tried to avoid looking at her red-stained eyes and splotchy face.

"No, I won't make any kind of match," she wailed, jumping out of her chair. "Who would have me after the Delverson Devils visited here, and then that . . . woman moved in? I am ruined!" She rushed past him, down the hall, and up the stairs.

"I should be charging you admission for this," Carey told the same footman before inquiring into his sister's whereabouts.

"I couldn't find her, milord, Captain, sir. Miss Delverson is usually out and about the countryside at this time of day."

Carey headed toward the ancient oak where he and his cousins had spent hours building forts and playing at Robin Hood. Suzannah and her playmate Heywood Jeffers had taken over the old climbing tree so Carey thought he'd look there first.

Suzannah and Woody were not climbing, and if the brat's interpretation of Maid Marian was correct, Nottingham Forest would have been a safer place for rich folks.

The two youngsters sprang apart at Carey's bellow and Suzannah, her dark hair, blue eyes, and aristocratic scowl a perfect match to Carey's own, stepped in front of her red-haired, red-faced swain. "We are going to be married," she announced, "and you cannot stop us."

"Watch me" was all Carey said. He'd had an unpleasant enough day with nowhere to vent his frustrations. Young Heywood was the perfect place. Sixteen and stringy, poor Woody could only dangle when Carey picked him up by the collar. Suzannah meanwhile was pounding her brother on the back with a fallen branch and screeching about cutting out his liver and lights. She was a flea to Carey's mastiff, and poor Woody was the rat being shaken into oblivion.

Ned was already bringing Woody's horse around from the stable so Carey booted the squire's son ahead of him. He stopped when they reached the gravel and turned the lad until Heywood could see death staring him in the eyes.

"I suggest you see about finishing your education, Master Jeffers, else I shall see to it for you, and I promise I shall not be such a lenient schoolmaster next time. Do you understand?"

Woody could barely nod, his bony Adam's apple bobbing up and down over Captain Delverson's fist. Carey tossed the boy over the saddle. He made sure Woody had the reins in his hands—Carey wasn't a bloodthirsty barbarian, despite his sister's caterwauling—and swatted the horse on the rump.

"And as for you, miss," Carey started, turning to his wayward sister, who was halfway through the door the grinning footman held for her. Suzannah brandished the umbrella

243

stand, shrieking about evil, black-hearted guardians, bullies boiling in oil, and True Love.

Carey wiped his hands on his trousers and strode off for the stables. There, that was a fine day's work. Three hysterical females and one quaking halfling. He felt as if he'd just taken on the whole French army.

Chapter Eight

$\mathcal{A}$ man cannot outride his troubles. They follow along, echoing with the rhythm of the horse's hooves. Suzannah was a hoyden and Emonda was ruined.

Suzannah would go to a proper school in Lyme Regis, if Carey had to get her there kicking and screaming about kidnappers and star-crossed lovers, which he fully expected. And Emonda was ruined.

Captain Delverson was a master at weapons and wars and even women—but not the kind of woman one could neither banter with nor bed. The chit was too old for school, too young to live alone, too innocent to ship to the Abbey as St. Dillon's problem. Besides, she was right: She was even less Harry's relative than Carey's, and so far her name was blackened only in Dorset. Association with St. Dillon could make her a byword in at least three other counties.

His horse was in a lather and Carey was miles away from home. He had to rejoin his unit, he knew no respectable females, and Emonda was still ruined. He looked around to get his bearings and realized he was looking up to the prospect of High Clyme, seat of his father's good friend and chess partner, Donald, Earl Clyme. Lord Clyme could not be a help now, since the gentleman was at least sixty and had never been

wed. What could he know of women? Then again, the earl
hardly ever permitted women in his house, which indicated to
Carey that Lord Clyme knew all about the creatures. He rode
toward the house, knowing at least Lord Clyme's hospitality
would save him an hour's worth of wailing and whining.

"It's a bad business, my boy," Lord Clyme told him after
greetings and condolences when they were seated comfortably
in the elderly nobleman's study. Lord Clyme's leg was
propped up on pillows and a globe of brandy was in his hand,
two not altogether unrelated facts. Carey stared into the fire
and sipped from his glass as the other man went on. "You
know what they say, a woman without reputation is like a
goblet with a hole in it. Pretty, but no one is going to be fool
enough to try to drink out of it."

Carey nodded gravely. He knew how cruel society could be.
He also knew the only solution, although he had refused to say
the words even in his mind, like old superstitions about not
naming the Devil, lest you call him forth. The captain loosened his collar. The heat from the fire was making him uncomfortable, Carey told himself, not the feeling of a noose
inexorably tightening around his neck as his lordship uttered
the fateful phrase: "She'll have to be married."

Carey took a gulp of the brandy. The liquor managed to get
past the lump in his throat and he was even able to speak ratio-
nally. "Yes, then she would be able to bring Suzannah out
when the time comes, and be a respectable chaperone over
school vacations and such until then."

"Aye, nothing quiets clacking tongues like a wedding."

Still reigned, except for the crackling of the fire. At last
Carey broke the silence. "I should make Harry take her, for
creating the scandal-brew, but they would both be wretched. It
would be like yoking a ewe lamb to an oxen. Harry would
have more tolerance for an untrained hound than for such a
watering pot, and Emonda is even more afraid of St. Dillon
than she is of me. There's always Joss, but he's too young to
even think of leg-shackles. Besides, he might mistake her for

245

one of his fillies and pat her on the rump. She'd have the vapors for sure."

"She's a delicate female, boy, that's all. She was raised up quietlike, not like you rough-and-tumble lads."

"She hates me," the younger man clarified. "She makes me feel overlarge and unkempt, as if she will shatter into a billion pieces if I speak too loudly. And of course I only want to shout at her for being such a henwit. Now there's a marriage made in heaven," he said dismally, then brightened. "Of course I could be killed in the next battle. That might sweeten the pill for Emonda, if I swear to do my damnedest to make her a widow."

"You know, lad, I was betrothed once myself."

"No, sir, I didn't." The old boy's mind must be wandering, Carey thought, but he was willing to follow the earl's direction. Anything was better than thinking of a parson's mousetrap and Emonda in the same breath.

The earl struggled out of his seat and opened the top desk drawer. He took out a framed portrait, stared at it a moment, then handed the picture to Carey.

Odd, Carey had one just like it, only smaller. "Rowanne Wimberly. I'd forgotten you were related to the Wimberlys, my lord, but what has she to do with—"

"No, it's her mother. Know my niece, do you? It must be true then that she's the image of Amalie."

"If the painting is of Amalie, she is. Miss Wimberly's hair is unpowdered of course, a soft brown, and cut in curls around her face. Haven't you seen her for yourself? Pardon, my lord, my own difficulties make me forget my manners. You cannot wish to discuss your family with me."

"You are wrong, I do. That's why I showed you the portrait. To answer your question, no, I don't know the chit. I always heard she took after her mother and I never thought I could bear to see that face again."

Carey studied the picture, and his memories. "It's a lovely face."

"But Amalie was not a lovely woman. I thought she was, at one time. I thought she was the moon and the stars too. I was the happiest man alive when she agreed to be my wife. Then she ran away with my brother Montgomery."

"Did she give you a reason?"

"She was courteous enough to send a letter with my ring. She never wanted me, it turned out, but her parents wanted the money and the title. They pushed her into accepting. When she found out I intended to devote my life to the estate, Amalie had second thoughts. By Jupiter, I was born to the land. I was brought up knowing High Clyme would be mine and every inch my responsibility. I had no interest in the glitter of London, and thought my precious bride would share my love for the country. More fool I.

"Amalie and her mother came to High Clyme to see about renovating the countess's suite. It was harvestime and there was flooding and a hundred other things that required my attention. And there was Monty, back from Russia, off to India or Persia, I don't know what outlandish places, with his tales of travel and receptions at every high court, the latest gossip from London, the latest fashions from Paris. They left together. I never saw either one again."

Carey could read the sorrow on the old man's face. "I am sorry, my lord. What a crushing blow that must have been to a young man's pride."

"Pride? I loved her. Pride came later, when I refused to see them. I never married, of course, and with Monty providing the heir, I never had to. That would be my nephew Gabriel, a likely lad, so I am informed."

"I've heard him spoken of highly in political circles."

"He knows nothing of agriculture."

"He's bright. He can learn."

Lord Clyme poured another glass. "When I'm gone, when I'm gone. But I have a few good years in me yet, more if I skip my port and cigars if the quacks are right. And nothing but my pride for company."

"Miss Wimberly?"

"She's a Toast, just like her mother. She follows the *beau monde* from London to Bath. She'd never be content in a rural backwater like Blandford, and I would never ask it of Amalie's daughter."

"I wonder if you misdoubt her, my lord. But . . ." Carey began to see where the conversation was leading and had a small glimmer of hope. Could salvation lie with a gouty old peer? "Emonda?" he asked in hushed tones.

Lord Clyme nodded. "I could see she is taken care of, and make a handsome enough settlement on her that she would never have to worry again. It wouldn't be stinting the heir, for there's enough blunt to keep him and his sister forever, without even counting Monty's legacy to them. Gabriel is a sober type of fellow by all accounts, not like to run through his patrimony in a year, so he won't notice the expense. When I stick my spoon in the wall, Emonda would be an independent woman, or Wimberly's responsibility at least. Meantime I could help look after Suzannah too, until your return."

"You'd do all this, for company?" Carey was incredulous.

"And for Emonda. She needs a husband and she deserves better than what you can offer. Your stepaunt is a sweet child who could brighten my days."

"And your nights?" The captain could not quite stomach the idea of timid little Emmy in an old man's bed, not even if it meant he could taste a hundred fellows' wedding cakes before he had to choke on his own.

Lord Clyme was affronted. "What, at my age? You would want heirs and so would Harry, who would likely frighten a fragile creature like Emonda half to death. No finesse, your cousin. I can promise a marriage of convenience only, so your conscience doesn't have to prick you."

"Very honorable of you, my lord. But are you sure?"

"It must be Emonda's choice, mind, but you go put it to her. I'd ride back with you, but the blasted leg won't let me. So you tell her how it has to be: you, me, or Harry."

You, me, or Harry, and Heaven alone knew where Harry was. So Emonda's choice was to be nursemaid to a rich old man in a sterile marriage, or wife in fact to a virile young hero, an out-and-outer, a practiced wooer of women with a silver tongue and a gleam in his blue eyes, a handsome rogue on every woman's wish list.

She chose Lord Clyme.

Captain Delverson had never considered his appeal for the ladies. It was just there, like his cleft chin and dimples. On the other hand, he never had to beg a woman for her favors, so he was astounded at Emonda's decision. Carey had added Lord Clyme's offer to his own almost as an afterthought, hoping to dam the flood of tears after his announcement that Emonda would have to be wed to save her reputation. She perked right out of an incipient swoon when Carey added the courtly earl's name to the lists, and Carey had to laugh at his own conceit.

His pique at being rejected was mixed with a huge dollop of relief, of course, and Captain Lord Delverson was sure he was the happiest person at the wedding.

It was a small ceremony with a special license, proper for a family in mourning, a comfort for the community. At Carey's insistence, Emonda put off her black and wore a lavender gown that added a bit of life to her insipid coloring, and the white lace *mantilla* Carey brought back from Spain. At least she wouldn't frighten the old gent into a heart spasm by appearing as Death walking at his side. Carey gave the bride away—and what a pleasure that was!—and Suzannah, deep in the sullens, was her aunt's attendant. Squire Jeffers was groomsman, and the earl himself looked pleased as punch with flowers in his buttonhole and a chaste kiss to his bride's cheek.

After the finest wedding breakfast Mrs. Tulliver could contrive on short notice, the happy couple repaired to High Clyme and Carey packed Suzannah off to school in Lyme Regis.

He did not have to resort to gags and handcuffs, for a short conversation with Squire Jeffers saw young Heywood off to university, to prepare for his future and to ensure that he lived long enough to have one.

Carey threatened to extend his stepsister's sentence if he heard a single hint of misbehavior. "When you are older, I'll ask Lord and Lady Clyme to sponsor you, locally at least. By then maybe the cursed war will be over and we can set up housekeeping in London. You'd like that, puss."

At least he wasn't promising to incarcerate her in some silly girls' school until she reached her majority—almost ten years away! "But what about Woody?"

"The next time you see Heywood, you'll be such a grand lady you won't recognize your old friends."

"I would never forget Woody. We are Pledged."

Carey leaned back against the squabs and pulled his hat over his eyes. "You'll see, poppet. Pretty soon you'll have suitors falling at your feet like autumn leaves. You'll wonder what you ever saw in your freckled Romeo."

"That's hateful, Harmon Carrisbrooke Delverson, and you have no tender emotions. I wouldn't repudiate my love for Woody if you tore my tongue out, if you kept me in the darkest dungeon and fed me moldy bread and water with insects floating in it, if—"

"If I tore up all of your Minerva Press novels. Go to sleep, poppet, you'll need to save your energy to put on a good act for the Misses Snead. I wrote them I was bringing a young *lady* to their school."

Carey had one more chore to complete before rejoining the army. Lord Clyme, honorable gentleman that he was, had charged Captain Delverson to inform young Wimberly about the wedding. The earl did not want his heir reading the announcement and thinking he was being cut out of the inheritance. The land was entailed, of course, but Donald wanted no more rancor in the family than need be, for Emonda's sake later.

Delverson did not resent this final task at all, even if it kept him from his men and accurate news of the battles for another few days. As he rode to London Carey wondered if Miss Wimberly was the empty-headed society belle her uncle made her out to be, or if she still had that tender look in her eyes and the calm good sense he admired. He told the driver to pick up the pace, curiously anxious to find out.

Chapter Nine

"$\mathcal{I}$ begin to think no woman will ever catch Gabriel's eye."

"He danced twice with the Winthrop chit last week."

"Yes, but that was because the forward miss cornered him in the orangery. It was either dance with her or chance being found alone with her. For all his absentmindedness, my brother is too downy a bird to be trapped that way."

"Or your way, it seems."

"What, would you have him forced into marriage with some scheming girl? No, we simply have not found the right bait."

Miss Grimble frowned but went back to studying the *on dits* columns and her lists. "Miss Parks seems an accommodating female. She comes to dinner Tuesday next with her brother. Perhaps she will do."

"Perhaps if she lost a stone and dressed in anything but yellow and did not agree with whatever anyone said. And the brother is as big a bore, although Gabe seems to feel his last speech to the Lords was well received. I am not looking forward to the dinner."

Even Miss Grimble was discouraged by now, after the hordes of women Rowanne had cast in Lord Wimberly's path and the scores of gentlemen Miss Grimble had earmarked for her protégé. It seemed to that strong-willed woman that she had met her match; the Wimberlys were the fussiest pair alive. Either that or they were determined to stay unwed. Fools, the *duenna* thought, knowing how depressing it was to have naught but one's memoirs for company.

Rowanne did not appear cast down at her single state. She

seemed quite satisfied in fact, sitting at her work table with scissors and glue pot, attempting to create tiny flower arrangements out of scraps of silk and green-dyed feathers. She had her brother's looking glass propped up in front of her, and bits of feather clinging to her simple blue round gown. Multicolored silk threads stuck to her fingers and in her hair when she pushed a wayward curl out of her eyes. Rowanne would be content if it were not for her desire to see Gabe settled before he grew into a reclusive old woman-hater like their uncle.

"What are the prospects for tonight?" she asked her companion in the search.

"We go to the Worthingtons' ball, for the debut of their eldest daughter. There are two others in the schoolroom so they are hoping to pop the gal off this Season. The grandfather has sweetened the pot with a handsome dowry, and Lady Aldritch, who knows the family from Hampshire, says the chit is prettily behaved, well educated, and comely. Lord Worthington, recall, is on the Fiduciary Council, which is why your brother agreed to attend. The gal has good connections."

"A paragon indeed. I'll bet she squints."

"Mayhaps Viscount Wimberly won't notice. He did not even recall meeting Maria Sefton's niece at Almack's last week and had to be introduced to her again in the park yesterday. Lady Sefton was not well pleased."

"The girl had spots. But no matter, you are right, I had better go remind him that we are pledged for this evening or he is liable to forget altogether." Rowanne put her materials aside for another day and wiped her fingers on a rag as best she could. She opened the door to leave, but called back, "If I am to be at all presentable for the Worthingtons' ball, I shall need extra time to prepare myself, in addition to Gabe."

She shut the door, took two steps into the hall, and walked smack into a scarlet-coated chest. "Oh!"

Oh indeed.

Those dark-rimmed eyes she so vividly remembered were laughing down at her. "You are charming as you are, Miss Wimberly," he was saying.

Rowanne looked around in confusion. Her daydreams had

never called him into being before. A footman stood down the hall, pointedly glancing the other way. She held out her hand, then recalled her sticky fingers. And her mussed gown and her hair coming down, oh dear! She pulled her hand back and bobbed the most awkward curtsy of her twenty-one years.

"Lieutenant, no, Captain Delverson. You are here. That is, in England. How, ah, kind of you to call."

His smile broadened at her addle-pated dithering, as if he was used to women literally throwing themselves at him. "Pardon me for not waiting for an invitation," he said, "and for picking such an awkward hour, but I was hoping to find Lord Wimberly home from Parliament. I could not help but overhear that you have accepted for the Worthingtons' this evening. May I have the pleasure of the first dance? And the supper dance also, if you have not already promised it? No, even if you have. I leave again for Spain tomorrow; that should give me some prerogatives."

"Certainly. That is, I would be delighted to save the dances for you. Did you say you came to see Gabriel?" she asked uncertainly. Whatever could Carey Delverson have to do with her brother?

Carey nodded toward the footman, keeping a discreet distance, waiting to escort him to Wimberly's library. "But I was hopeful of seeing you after, so that I might give you this. Perhaps I should wait and explain, but Lord Wimberly is expecting me. Here."

With that he reached into his uniform's inside pocket and pulled out a small box with a tooled leather lid and pressed it into her hand. He started to bow and turn when Rowanne called out.

Now that Rowanne's heartbeat had slowed enough for her to commence breathing again, and thinking, she took a better look at the captain. He was not quite as handsome as she remembered, with his nose a bit crooked and a scar at his jawline, and lines of weather and seasoning around his eyes. Not as handsome, perhaps, but infinitely more appealing, the way a statue of Adonis in a museum was admirable, but a flesh-and-blood man was— She caught herself and forced her mind to work. He held himself stiffly and fiddled nervously with an ornate snuffbox in his left hand.

He was ill at ease, here to see Gabe, and had just handed Rowanne a box the perfect size to hold a ring. Oh my! "Please wait."

He turned and she nodded dismissal to the footman, then glanced back to make sure the door behind her was firmly closed. She only wished her blood wasn't pounding so loudly in her ears she could not be sure of her own words.

"Please do not bother Gabe, my dear sir, for it would never do, and he only finds these interviews distracting and embarrassing. Many of the gentlemen are older than he and more worldly, and what can he tell them, after all? It is my choice alone, and I have decided not to give up my independence for a while yet, certainly not until my brother is comfortable." Rowanne knew she was blathering, but the captain was grinning at her and her tongue was still not following her brain's commands. She tried again. "I am highly honored, of course, but we hardly know each other, and I doubt I have the character needed to follow the drum. I realize that there is much to recommend you, the bravery and dedication they mention in the dispatches, despite your reputation. And please do not think that I would hold a man's prior, ah, experiences against him, for I am not such a milk-and-water miss."

It was all Carey could do to keep from laughing. Never again would he consider himself a ladies' man. Here he'd been rejected again—and this time without even offering!

Rowanne saw he was struggling under some strong emotion. Well, so was she! She had to end this dreadful conversation before the poor man chewed his lip clean through. She held out the little leather box. "Please, sir, let us both forget this meeting and remain friends."

Carey couldn't resist. He placed his snuffbox on the buhl table behind him, took her hands in both of his, and raised them to his mouth. "Tell me I haven't offended you and that I can put my luck to the touch in the future."

Rowanne could have bitten her own tongue when she heard herself say, "I hope you do."

Carey threw back his head and laughed out loud. Gads, the

chit was a delight, he thought, watching the emotions play across her lovely features. What a fool the Earl of Clyme had been, denying himself the pleasure of knowing this vibrant creature. It would have been a shame to hide Miss Wimberly's light in Dorset though, for if she was not a classic beauty, she was certainly an Original.

Rowanne watched him laughing like a Bedlamite. "Then you are not disappointed?"

Now if Carey were a true gentleman like the old earl, for instance, he would have begged her pardon, placed his trust in the future, and gone on his way. Captain Delverson had earned his reputation for deviltry, however, he had not just inherited it. Besides, she would know as soon as she opened the box.

"Devastated," he told her, lifting the tooled lid of his gift. He shook out onto her palm a tiny set of terra-cotta tableware, plates and cups and bowls, all cunningly painted with tiny flowers. "Do you remember my promise? I did. These were from an open-air market in Madrid." He saw her eyes widen and her mouth drop open as enlightenment dawned. "And now I really must see Gabriel about a message from your uncle." He kissed her hand again, the one with the dishes, saying "Until tonight," and turned to go before she could scream or cry or throw things. He gave one last chuckle and a softly murmured "Thank you," then knocked on the door to Gabriel's library.

Rowanne thought she might recover from her mortification, if she lived another hundred years! Meantime her face was redder than his coat and her body was shaking, except for her feet, which seemed anchored to the hall runner with the weight of her idiocy. How could she? How could he have let her? How could she chance him coming out of Gabe's study and finding her rooted to the same spot?

The thought of ever facing the captain again sent her fleeing to her bedroom, where she locked the door as if his knowing laughter could have followed and furiously kicked the dressing table chair. Then she hobbled to her bed, clutching her toes. Good, she thought, maybe they were broken. Now she could not attend the Worthingtons' do. For all she cared, Miss

Hillary Worthington was Gabe's one true love and he was doomed to a life of misery if he did not meet her this evening. So be it, he was doomed. Rowanne was not going to give that . . . that dastard another chance to laugh at her. Gads, what a complete and total cake she had made of herself then! And he had laughed!

"The miserable muckworm did what? He married his aunt off to Uncle Donald to wash his hands of her and cut you out? That swine!"

Gabe pushed his spectacles up and looked at his usually calm and even-tempered sister in amazement. "It was nothing like that at all, Ro. I just explained, Uncle Donald asked him to call specifically so I would not suspect such a thing. The entailment is sound and the estate in good heart."

"Wait till the new countess gets her hands on it. Who else but a conniving harpy would marry an old man for his money? You'll see, she will bleed the estate dry and leave you nothing. She won't be content in the country either, mark my words, now that she has a title and money. We'll have to give up Wimberly House to the shrew, see if we don't. And you cannot be fool enough to think she won't move heaven and earth to bear him a son and push you out of the succession altogether. I'll wager she is just like her nephew, the cold, unfeeling blackguard."

Gabe neatened his desk. "I, ah, thought you admired the captain."

"I was deceived in his character. He is a heartless care-for-naught and likely a glory-seeker in the wars. That must be why his name is mentioned in the news so often. He is not even attractive anymore, with all the signs of dissipation he exhibits, and I swear the man grows positively foppish, twiddling with his snuffbox in an affected manner."

"I understand you agreed to have supper with him this evening." Gabe's tone held the question.

"Did he say so? He must have misunderstood. I find that I do not care to attend another insipid comeout ball. I am sure you will be relieved to have a quiet evening at home."

"I would, quite, but I had to call on Lord Worthington

yesterday and he specifically asked me to dance with Miss Hillary. She is shy, but now that we have met he feels she might be easier with someone she knows. I cannot send my regrets at this late date. Won't you reconsider?"

Rowanne reflected that it was even more important than ever for Gabriel to find a wife, and a rich one at that, now that he could not count on the Clyme inheritance. Besides, why should Miss Wimberly allow any rag-mannered, scapegrace savage to keep her mewed up in her rooms? She would show the cur that the Wimberlys were not to be trifled with. She would go to the Worthingtons' ball and cut him dead if he had the gall to approach her. Then Gabriel could dance with his one-and-only true love and Rowanne could come home and have a good cry.

Chapter Ten

*M*iss Worthington neither squinted, stammered, nor had the spots. What she had was a severe case of debutante jitters. The chit was so shy and nervous she cast up her accounts right on the receiving line before the Wimberly party arrived. Rowanne need not have come after all. She expressed her polite sympathy to the unfortunate miss's parents, meanwhile wondering if she and Gabe could leave before the orchestra started tuning up.

"Don't worry about my gel," Lord Worthington advised, cornering Gabe. "Her mother'll see the lass comes back. Like getting up on a horse after being thrown, what? You have to do it sooner or later, and sooner is better, if you ask me. She'll be back down in the blink of an eye, so you can have your dance. Better make it the supper dance, if you please, to make sure the chit has someone she knows to go in with. D'you mind?"

Gabe was too polite to say if he did, of course, so they moved into the ballroom. Rowanne had no more gotten Miss Grimble settled on a chair in dowagers' row and seen Gabe off to find a crony for another endless debate, when there *he* was. For a second her stomach wished to take a page from Miss Worthington's book. She turned her back.

Carey took a moment to admire the stiff spine and delightful rear view of her clinging primrose silk gown and the soft brown ringlets trailing down a graceful neck.

"Good girl," he said. "I knew you had too much backbone to stay home. And a charming backbone it is too."

Who knew what other outrageous statements the cad would make right there in front of the matrons and maiden aunts? For all Rowanne knew they were each taking notes for their memoirs. She turned around and hissed, "Go away, you odious man."

He wore an injured look. "But you promised the first dance only this afternoon. Never say you are so fickle."

Rowanne checked the women behind her. Yes, they were all as avid as starlings on fence posts waiting for the farmer to sow his grain. Miss Grimble was frowning. "I do not care to dance this evening, Captain Delverson. I have injured my foot." Rowanne's foot was perfect, and by denying him she committed herself to a whole evening of sitting on the sidelines, but it would be worth the boredom.

"Fine," the wretch answered. "Then we may sit over here for a comfortable coze and become better acquainted."

"On second thought, my foot has recovered remarkably, sir."

"I thought it might," he said with a laugh.

The set was a quadrille, with the complicated figures of the dance making conversation unnecessary. When Rowanne and the captain did come together in the movements, she looked pointedly at the black armband on his uniform and announced, "You are in mourning; you should not be dancing."

"I am a soldier, Miss Wimberly. Friends die every day and I have to go on living. Besides, a wise person once wrote something about how we pay most honor to our loved ones by

258

keeping their memories alive in our hearts, not by the outward trappings of grief."

Rowanne nodded curtly. Those were the words *she* had written to comfort a soldier who could not attend his father's funeral, when she thought Carey Delverson deserved her sympathy.

After that, she granted him only monosyllables in response to his mindless prattle.

"The weather was lovely today."

"Yes."

"It is unfortunate Miss Worthington should miss part of her own ball."

"Yes."

"You're wishing me at Jericho."

"Yes."

"Would you like me to explain to Miss Grimble and the other dragons who are staring at us why you are scowling so fiercely?"

Rowanne instantly curved the edges of her mouth upward, and kept them there until the end of the dance, when she thought her cheeks would melt from the effort. Before the orchestra's last chord was finished echoing, she curtsied and rudely turned on her heel in Gabe's direction.

"I know you shall be busy with your admirers, Miss Wimberly," she heard from behind her, "but I pray you will not forget the supper dance you promised."

Gabe was rapt in a discussion of the Enclosures, but Captain Delverson's words were loud enough for Gabe's companions to hear, so now Rowanne could not accept another offer, pleading confusion. Nor could she claim a headache and go home, for Gabe still had to have his duty dance with the guest of honor. Drat that man! Rowanne turned a radiant smile on Lord Fairborn. She would show the bounder she could have a good time with a real gentleman, even if that coxcomb Fairborn was wearing a puce waistcoat and red high-heeled shoes.

Rowanne danced and laughed, conversed and flirted—and watched the captain. He danced once with Lady Worthington, bringing a girlish blush to that lady's cheeks, and once with

Lady Chiswick, a dashing widow in dampened skirts who tapped him with her fan when their dance was done. It was all of a piece. Then he stood near one of the windows in discussion with a group of War Office dignitaries. At least the cad would not be making Rowanne's ignominy public, would he?

"I say, Miss Wimberly, you look pale. It is stifling in here; perhaps you would care for a stroll on the terrace?"

"Thank you, Sir Stephen, that would be lovely." When they reached the open window Rowanne could hear Wellesley's name being mentioned, not hers, of course. Not even one of the Delverson Devils could be so lost to decency. Yet some night, she thought, in his cups maybe, or just out of boredom, or for one of those dreadful wagers with his reprobate cousins . . .

If Captain Delverson was surprised that Rowanne came so willingly into his arms for their dance, he hid it admirably in a delighted smile that widened further when the orchestra struck up a waltz. The waltz suited Rowanne's purposes very well also, enough that she could ignore the firm pressure of his hand radiating warmth to her waist. So what if she could feel a tingle in her hand, touching his hand, through her glove, through his glove? They could talk without being interrupted or overheard.

"You wouldn't tell anyone, would you?"

He stumbled. "The deuce. Pardon. Miss Wimberly, if you were a man I would call you out for that insult to my honor."

If she were a man she would have run him through that afternoon, but wishing got her nowhere. "What if you should be foxed, among your officer friends on the Peninsula, say?"

Now his remarkable blue eyes turned to ice, staring down into hers. Rowanne was not a small woman, but she had to look up; she was not a meek woman either, but she shivered at that cold gaze.

"Men do not become animals when they put on a uniform, Miss Wimberly, despite the barbarism of war. And I, for one, would not drink if I could not do so and remain a gentleman."

Rowanne looked away. "Thank you, you are right, I should not have mentioned the issue."

The pressure at her waist increased, but she would not look

at him again, not even when he said, "And I should not have laughed this afternoon."

"I am sure it was quite amusing."

"Only to my deplorable sense of humor. Do you think you could ever forgive me?"

"The dishes were lovely, thank you. They will be perfect in a vignette I am working on for a woodsman's cabin. My groom carved some wood into plank tables and rough-hewn shelves. I thought I might—"

"You haven't answered."

"You married your aunt off to Uncle Donald."

"They neither had anyone else. It was their choice."

Now it was her turn to fix him with an angry stare. "You let me make a fool of myself."

He swung her around and around in a senses-stealing twirl as the dance came to an end. "You were so adorable at it."

They sat down to supper with Gabriel and Miss Worthington. Miss Hillary was almost at ease, for no one could be afraid of Gabe, with his spectacles and vague manner and boyishly inept dancing style. The girl was pretty in a china-doll way, petite and fair. Rowanne had no doubts Miss Worthington would show to better advantage out of the debutante white gown, and began to wonder if the sweet little thing might not be Gabe's destiny after all. Rowanne tried to draw her out over the crab cakes and oysters, chantilly crèmes and raspberry ices. If light chatter with Miss Worthington helped her avoid conversation with her dinner partner, so much the better. Rowanne needed quiet time to think before she could take on Captain Delverson again.

The captain was doing his part to entertain Miss Worthington, telling amusing tales of his army life until they were all laughing merrily and the chit even added a comment or a question of her own.

Carey was joking about how one of his fellow officers managed to trade one of Sir Wellesley's own brass buttons for a chicken to a hero-worshipping *señora*—one in each town. The buttons were engraved with Arthur Wellesley's monogram and the officer, Alexander Warburton, kept having his mother send boxes of them. "There wasn't much we wouldn't do for a proper meal," Carey concluded, lifting his second iced cup. "I would trade my best pair of boots for one of Gunther's confections out in the field on those hot, dusty days. Instead I intend to eat as many as your mama will allow, Miss Worthington."

He turned to Hillary, the spoon in his right hand, the raspberry ice in his not-entirely reliable left hand, just as Miss Worthington waved her arms in the air to show how huge a delivery had been made. Their hands collided and the dessert cup went flying past Carey to land smack in Rowanne's lap. She jumped up, catching the attention of the diners at the neighboring table and sending sticky red droplets toward Captain Delverson's white pantaloons.

Servants came running, and Carey apologized profusely because his blasted hand could not be trusted. Miss Worthington, however, looked in horror from the stains on Rowanne's elegant primrose silk gown and the spatters on Captain Delverson's uniform, to the ogling crowd and back to her own plate, where reposed a solitary oyster she could not bring herself to eat. The slimy mollusk was the last straw. Hillary turned green and lost her dignity again, this time on Gabe's foot.

"No, Miss Wimberly," Lady Worthington chided, "you must not fret over the silly child. You have been more than gracious, you and your brother, having to leave the ball this way. My lord's valet should have him fixed up in a wink. I've sent a footman after your Miss Grimble and your wraps, and the carriage should be out front in a moment, though it's not what I would want, keeping you hidden away in the butler's pantry."

"Please don't fuss, my lady. I am sure my dresser can remove the stains. And do reassure poor Hillary that I hold her blameless. I should have realized she was not well-enough recovered for crab cakes and champagne."

"Lord Worthington always did say you Wimberlys had good blood and good breeding. I thank you, but it never was your responsibility to watch what the ninny ate. I should have known not to pitchfork such a retiring chit into the ton, but her fond papa did want to show her off. He had hopes that your brother . . . Well, can't cry over spilt milk. Or raspberry ice, heh-heh. The gal will do fine going back to the country, and next year she'll have her sister beside her. The ton will have forgotten all about it." The motherly lady did not think she need mention that the rumor mills were likely to make more of Miss Wimberly's two dances with the rakehell captain than they did of an unknown and undistinguished young miss's gaucherie. She merely clasped her hands and looked around nervously.

"Please go back to the party, my lady. Miss Grimble or Gabriel shall be along shortly, and you must be anxious to see to your guests."

"Are you sure? You have been everything that is kind and I cannot think what I am about to leave you like this, but someone of the family has to be in the ballroom."

"I'll be fine. Thank you for your attention, and for a, ah, an interesting evening."

The older woman hurried off, muttering about good lines and what a shame it was about the brother, but no one was *that* kind. When Rowanne heard footsteps a few minutes later, she left her hidey-hole and stepped out to the marble-floored hallway.

A scarlet jacket. She darted back, but not before Carey spotted her and followed her into the closetlike room.

"Captain, you forget yourself! My brother will be here . . . and Miss Grimble."

"I can deal with your brother. He's got no aptitude for swords or pistols. But you are right: It's that fire-breather of yours who has me quaking. I shall leave in a moment—my carriage must be waiting—but I have to know that you are all right."

He stood close, too close in the little room, and looked into her eyes. For some reason Rowanne's cheeks felt warm as she answered, "I am fine. Nothing that a bath won't cure. Please go."

"I need to talk to you. I can hear if someone is coming."

Not over the thundering of her heart, he couldn't. "We have nothing to say to each other."

Carey went on as if she had not spoken. "The first time we met I took something from you. I should have realized it was something precious to you, a picture of your mother, and returned it."

Rowanne waved dismissively. "I have many paintings of my mother. She enjoyed sitting for her portrait, and the locket was a trumpery piece I had not worn in years."

"Yet you wore it to your debut at Almack's. I should have sent it back. Now it means more to me. May I keep it?"

What was the snake trying to do, turn her up sweet? Rowanne was not about to let any practiced flirt cause her one more ounce of anguish, not even if her fingers itched to push that black curl off his forehead. She took refuge in anger.

"What is the difference if you have one more thing that belongs to me? You have stolen my dignity."

He raised one eyebrow. "How is that, Miss Wimberly? No one knows, no one shall ever know, and I'll be gone tomorrow. Meanwhile you were the perfect lady in there, helping that silly chit and then walking out as imperious as a queen while they all stared. No one has robbed anything from you." Then a different kind of light shone in his eyes. "But since you have accused me, I am minded to steal another memory to take back with me to cherish."

Rowanne hurriedly looked about her person. A ribbon? Her fan? Dear heavens, she did not want Gabe coming upon them and having to challenge this unprincipled libertine to a duel. She did not want another scene, and she did not want him staring at her with that devilish gleam that made her toes curl in her slippers.

"It's only a kiss I want to steal," he murmured, matching action to words like the military man he was, taking her gently in his arms and bringing their lips together. It was a moment of such bursting radiance that Rowanne forgot her toes, forgot her brother, forgot that she was spreading more raspberry stains on his unmentionables where they were touching her body in the most interesting manner.

Only a kiss?

Chapter Eleven

*V*engeance is mine, sayeth the Lord . . . and every woman who thinks her affections have been trifled with by a handsome rogue. Carey's left cheek was as red as the stains on his pants, but if Rowanne had known it, her revenge would have been that much sweeter, for Carey was as stunned by the kiss as she was. What he meant to take by thievery became instead a gift, and the warm memory he thought to carry away became a firebrand searing itself into his very being. Captain Delverson was shaken. Either that or she had permanently addled his brain with the resounding slap before leaving the little room.

Carey stayed where he was for her reputation's sake, if not the five-fingers mark on his face. Hell, he'd received worse wounds with less reward. He searched out the butler's private stock and settled back to wait.

Miss Grimble thought Rowanne was still upset about her gown and their dashed hopes for a match between Gabriel and Miss Worthington, so did not get alarmed at her charge's lack of color or conversation. The companion was too busy trying to work the evening's rump and riot into chapter twenty-seven.

Gabriel thought it was oddly ill-tempered of his sister to hold an unreasonable grudge against Delverson; the chap had been everything amiable, as far as Gabe could see. Delverson had taken command of the awful situation, giving orders to the servants, organizing a tactical retreat that would have made Old Hooky proud. But Rowanne was still in a swivet on the carriage ride home, Gabe could tell, and he knew enough about his sister's megrims to keep his own counsel on his own side of the coach.

To say Rowanne was upset was to say a monsoon was damp. On the way back to Wimberly House, all that night and more than a few nights and days after, Rowanne relived that kiss. It was a good thing the blackguard was out of the country, she thought, for she did not know what she would do if she saw him again, strangle him or aid wholeheartedly in her own seduction!

Those were thoroughly unacceptable notions for a maiden lady, as she well knew, but they would not go away. Uncomfortable thoughts had that knack about them. When she worked on her miniatures, she saw the little terra-cotta dishes he had brought. When she danced, she recalled the waltz in his arms, and when she lay awake for hours in her bed she wondered how it would be to—

She went down to the library for a book of sermons. Absolutely, positively refusing to consider that she was close to throwing her cap over the windmill for a hell-born here-and-thereian who was, moreover, *there*, Rowanne decided to try harder to find Gabe a wife and then get herself a husband. Such feelings as were disturbing her rest and muddling her senses were permissible in the married state, and she was not getting any younger. In addition, Aunt Cora's letters were growing more and more condemning of the Wimberlys' failure to provide her grandnieces and -nephews; living with her as an ape-leader after Gabe married held as much attraction as going to the tooth-drawer. Rowanne could no longer consider raising roses in Dorset now either, though she had contrived a cunning trellis for a scale-model patio out of a broken ivory hairpiece. She fashioned climbing vines out of painted string and silk, despairing that she would never get much closer to the real thing.

"Why don't you take over from the gardeners here, then, if you are so eager to get your hands soiled?" Gabe asked, after her third sigh finally penetrated Plato's *Republic*. "We have ample room out back, you know."

"Yes, but that would almost be like growing things in tubs in a conservatory. I have always wanted a real garden, one that would blend into the landscape and look natural despite the planning. The London garden is lovely but can only look as contrived as my silk roses, with its walls and terraces and spouting-dolphins fountain."

"Then why don't you accept Aunt Emonda's invitation to go visit at High Clyme?"

They had just received a pleasant letter from their new relation, thanking them for their kind congratulations and the gift of a Wedgewood tea set. The gift had taken a great deal of discussion, for Rowanne's first answer to the question of what to get the new bride was a younger husband. Then she thought to send a family heirloom, one of the ugly ormolu clocks or the silver epergne that seemed to depict Hannibal crossing the Alps, elephants and all. The heirlooms already belonged to Uncle Donald, Gabe reminded her, so they settled on the tea set, which suited admirably, judging from the warm thank you.

"I am sure she would let you dabble in the mud," Gabe went on. "Lud knows there is enough ground."

Rowanne put down the magnifying lens. "But it would not be mine."

"Still, she seems an all-right sort, trying to mend the family breech."

"And she hasn't thrown us out yet, nor sent word of a coming happy event. Likely she wants an unpaid companion."

Gabe wiped his spectacles with a lawn cloth. "That's not like you, to be so judgmental without evidence."

"You forget, brother, that I do have evidence, in an incorrigible rake. If she is anything like that nephew of hers . . ."

"Gammon, Ro, they are not even blood relatives, and I am not sure Delverson's wild reputation is entirely deserved."

Rowanne murmured to herself, "Trust me, it is."

"What's that, my dear? Never mind, you have been resty lately. Maybe you have been trotting so hard you'd benefit from a month or more in that clean country air and all that nice dirt."

"What, a month in someone else's household? Last week's halibut would be more welcome. Besides, you yourself know how awful house parties can be, with no solitude, no familiar servants who care about your comfort, and no choices. A female guest has to sew when the hostess feels like sitting quietly, entertain when she invites company, even retire for the evening when the lady of the house is tired!"

"But you would not be such a guest, you are family."

"And a stranger to both our uncle and new aunt. No, Aunt Emonda may enjoy her teapot in peace—and her honeymoon too. I am too busy to leave town now anyway. Did you see the pile of invitations? No one goes to the country in the middle of the Season."

Especially if they want to shop at the Marriage Mart.

Rowanne did not read purple-covered novels from the lending library. Not often enough, at any rate, to have her heart set on a storybook romance. Storybook heroes were all well and good—in the pages of books. In real life heroes tended to act outside comfortable conventions or, worse, go off to war. No matter, Rowanne was all too practical to wait for love to sweep her off her feet. She had been born to the principle of marrying well and had no doubt that if her father were alive, he would already have arranged an advantageous marriage for her. The gentleman would have been wealthy, titled, and well connected, whether she felt affection for him or not.

Rowanne reassessed her requirements. She was wealthy enough in her own right to consider a man's fortune of little concern, as long as he was not marrying her for the money, and expediency meant less than comfort, although she was not about to run off with the footman or anything. She wanted a man she could respect and the kind of life she was used to living. If he had a bit of property somewhere, all to the good. Now she added another factor: He had to answer the new longings that toad Delverson had aroused. To this end Rowanne started experimenting over the next few weeks.

Miss Wimberly's most persistent suitor was Lord Fairborn, whose self-esteem was as high as his shirt collars. With some little effort, Rowanne happened to lead their steps away from the bright lights at Vauxhall onto one of the infamous Dark Paths. Fairborn's kiss was wet and pulpy, reminding Rowanne unpleasantly of Miss Worthington's oyster. Rowanne had the dandy back in the lighted areas before the cat could lick its ear.

Sir Allerby, who gambled often and won less often, according to the omniscient Miss Grimble, was permitted to escort Rowanne to the balcony at Lady Haight's rout for a breath of air. His kiss was as dry and lifeless as yesterday's toast. Rowanne decided she needed a cool drink instead of the night's breeze.

Squire Farnsworth was next. ("Country gentleman, in town one month a year, but a good portion of Lincolnshire in the family. Pigs.") Rowanne wondered if Miss Grimble meant the cash crop or Farnsworth's manners. His kiss in the bushes of Hyde Park left her breathless all right, but only because he crushed her ribs so tightly.

Surely a Frenchman knew how to kiss! Le Comte de Chambarque was a newly arrived emigré. ("*Ancien Regime*. Lost the land, saved the money.") He was elegant in his manner, draping Rowanne across his arm, whispering French love words. The languid kiss would have made Mrs. Radcliffe weep, but his mustache tickled.

Lord Cavendish ("Good ton, gazetted rake.") tried to stick his tongue in Rowanne's mouth, so she bit it, garlic breath and all.

Weeks became months and Miss Grimble was hard-pressed to come up with new men to bring to Rowanne's attention. Hostesses began to look askance at the popular Miss Wimberly, and her dance partners were sending raffish leers her way. Miss Grimble's hair-ridden upper lip was pursed, and even Gabe wondered if females were accustomed to sowing wild oats. He did not ask what she was about; he just kept nodding and smiling at the chits she dragged home, listened to them batter the pianoforte, watched them simper over tea, danced with the required number of wallflowers—and hurried home to his books and speeches.

Then it was nearly summer, with Aunt Cora's querulous demand that Rowanne attend her at Bath and explain precisely what she was doing, making micefeet of her reputation. Aunt Emonda wrote again, inviting Gabriel and Rowanne to High

Clyme for the warm months. Rowanne was almost tempted, until Lady Clyme's next letter mentioned that her niece Suzannah would also be in residence for the summer. Perhaps Miss Wimberly recalled Suzannah's stepbrother, Captain Delverson? Miss Wimberly needed no reminders. She would not go to Dorset if the Holy Grail was buried there.

Happily they received another invitation, to help make up a house party at Lord Quinton's country residence in Suffolk, where Rowanne's ex-governess/companion, Miss Simpson, was slowly establishing herself in local society. Her standing in the community would be raised no end, Lady Quinton teased, if she could attract a Toast like Miss Wimberly to her little gathering of Whig gentlemen and their wives. Gabe would be content with Lord Quinton's company, and near enough to town for quick trips back. Rowanne accepted. After all, Suffolk was a whole new county of gentlemen.

Despite her thoughts about house parties and staying over-long in other people's homes, Rowanne was delighted to reestablish her friendship with the older woman, improve her riding, go for long walks on the downs, read forgotten treasures from Lord Quinton's extensive library. She finished a set of needlepoint firescreens, one for Wimberly House, one for the dollhouse. She learned to fish and she kissed more than a few local squires. Kissing the fish might have been more rewarding.

Gabe did not tumble for any of the local belles either, so fall saw both of the Wimberlys reestablished in Grosvenor Square, Gabe with a healthy tan and an eagerness to resume debates in the conference rooms at Whitehall, Rowanne slightly freckled and more than slightly disgruntled at having to face yet another Season on the catch for an eligible *parti*.

Then Miss Grimble's book was published.

Chapter Twelve

$\mathcal{A}$ *London Life*, by a Ladies' Companion, said one review, was a titillating glimpse into the ton and its denizens by a keen observer of human nature in its party clothes.

The first volume was into its third printing within a week. Common readers bought the book to laugh at their so-called betters, caught with their pants down and their hair in curl papers. The polite world rushed to see who could be identified in the unnamed characters, and pray it was not themselves. Entire evenings were given over to unraveling clues to the characters and possible authors, instead of charades or card parties. The consensus was that the book had to have been written by a committee, there being so many precise details. The tome held the usual scandalous tidbits, but young, unmarried girls of good repute were never mentioned. *A London Life* dealt primarily with the ages-old conflict between women trying to get men to the altar and men trying to get women off in the dark.

Members of the ton thought the book either hilarious or outrageous, usually depending on whether they thought they were mentioned in it or not, and sales continued brisk. A second volume followed in a few months and was equally as well received, especially when this one chronicled the little-known occasion of a certain rotund gentleman who bent down to pet the lapdog of a young lady when his unmentionables gave up the fight and ripped from back to front. The lady, no wandlike sylph herself, laughed so hard her corset snapped and slid down around her knees. They were married by special license, as soon as her father caught sight of them in their disarray.

Unfortunately, the young bride had only confided the tale to one person, her best friend, Lady Diana Hawley-Roth. Lady Diana was known to have had a companion, a dark specter of a Beldam with the mind of an accountant. Where was this silent spectator now? Living with that fast Miss Wimberly, that was where. If the upper ten thousand did not outright accuse Rowanne of co-authoring the books, most believed she had knowingly harbored a viper in their midst.

"I do wish I had understood the nature of your memoirs a trifle better," Rowanne complained to the viper. "Not that I did not enjoy the book, but Lady Sefton gave me the cut direct today in the park."

"No, Miss Wimberly, she cut our carriage, not you personally. I was also in the chaise."

"Yes, but *I* have almost no invitations for this week, except dear Lady Quinton. Whatever are we to do, Miss Grimble?"

"*We* shan't do anything. I shall leave, then the silly geese will forget all about the connection and you will be society's pet once again."

"But where can you go? I fear no one will hire you again. I can give you excellent references, of course, but I cannot think my word will hold much weight. Careful parents would worry their daughters' suitors will be scared off lest they be the object of your jibes. In addition, your last lady made an unfortunate marriage and I have made none, despite your valiant efforts, so you have no great record to cite."

"Very kind of you to be concerned with my future, I am sure, Miss Wimberly, but you need not be. I had a small sum set by and invested which, together with the book advance, would have seen me through in any event. The books are doing very well, you know, and Mr. Kenton, the publisher, wishes more and is willing to pay an even higher price. I shall be taking up residence in a respectable boardinghouse for ladies of genteel birth in Kensington before the end of the week. There I may concentrate on my writing. Of course I shan't be collecting new tales, but I have a wealth of material on which to draw. After that I think I shall try my hand at novels."

"How, ah, fortunate for you. Do you really think people will stop wondering if I helped write the stories?"

"Certainly. Next month's volume will have my own name inscribed as author."

"Next month's?"

It was time to visit relatives, as far from London as possible.

Aunt Emonda wrote that Lord Clyme was not in prime twig. His gout was bothering him, with the cool weather coming on, and perhaps Rowanne could put off her visit for a few weeks. Rowanne was pleased to see the woman seemed to have some care for Uncle Donald. On the other hand, if Emonda was indeed a money-grubbing harpy, she deserved to be tied to a crotchety old man. Either way, Rowanne was left with the choice of being considered no better than she should be in London, without even a chaperone for respectability, or Aunt Cora. It was a hard decision.

"So you're here to visit your dear auntie, eh? For the first time in three years, and in the middle of the Season, and with only your maid along? Cut line, girl, what have you done now?"

When Rowanne explained about the books—news of the authoress's identity had not yet trickled to Bath—Lady Silber called for a restorative. "You see," the old woman said after a hearty swig of brandy, "I told you to get a husband! All this niminy-piminy business of playing with toys has addled your brainbox. You need a man, Rowanne, then you can write blasted exposés yourself."

Rowanne looked away. "I have not found a man I can like. I am thinking of putting on my caps."

"What?" her aunt shrieked like a parrot with its foot stuck in the cage door. "I must be harder of hearing than I thought. You did say you couldn't find a pen that writes and you were taking a nap, didn't you? No niece of mine could be so totty-headed. Downy thinkers run in the family, girl, just look at your brother. No, he's not leg-shackled yet either. Well, speak up, missy. Why ain't you married?"

"Give over, do, Aunt Cora, I doubt any man would have me now."

"What, because you flirted too much or because that harridan wrote too much? Stuff and nonsense. You've still got your mother's fortune and her good looks. I hoped you didn't have your father's brains too; they weren't enough to go around the first time. Looks like I'll have to take things in hand if I ever want to see you ninnyhammers settled. Fine thing it is, when a woman my age has to start playing Cupid for a pair of clunches. Well, maybe the flap about the memoirs will die down in the spring and we can go to London to see about that brother of yours."

"Spring? That's months away. I thought—"

"What, that the ton had memories like fleas? They do, unless things are written down for them, like your Miss Grimble's name on every reading list. You did say there would be more coming, didn't you?"

"Yes, but did you say you were going to London with me?" Now Rowanne was only a curiosity; with Aunt Cora's outspoken ways she would be a laughingstock.

"Of course. You can't go alone, can you? I should have been there to chaperone you in the first place. You'd have been wed for years now. Of course if you wouldn't be so hard to please about the Bath gentlemen this time around you could save an old lady the trip. You can make yourself useful meantime. Take Toodles for a walk in the park."

Toodles was her aunt's French poodle, a miserable, snappish, yapping canine with an absurd haircut. He looked more like a sheep shorn by a blindfolded bank clerk than a dog, with tufts and wisps and little pom-poms at his feet and tail. Rowanne shuddered. It looked like she was going to see a lot of Toodles.

Captain Delverson was also seeing more of the French than he wanted. The wars in Portugal and Spain seemed to go on forever, with no end in sight. Wellesley pushed the French back, they regrouped and advanced. The British retreated, rallied, and called another victory—at unimaginable costs in English soldiers' lives. The men were disheartened, sick, tattered. They wanted to go home. So did Captain Delverson.

War was not a game anymore. Carey had another scar

across his cheek, a piece of shrapnel imbedded in his shoulder, the start of graying hair at his temples, and an aching desire to stand on his father's property and watch things grow instead of seeing them ground into dust. He would no more quit and sell out than he would desert any friend in need, though, so he stayed through skirmish and engagement and siege, and managed to survive them all, a little more ragged, a lot less devil-may-care.

His men still loved him and his odd luck still held.

Helping to lead Graham's first charge at Barrosa, Carey took a piece of the very first cannonball in the leg. He was off his horse and half conscious, waving his men onward. They marched ahead valiantly, "for the cap'n," leaving him bleeding in the dust to wait for the medics or his man Rudd to find him. The French had other ideas. In a maneuver typical of Napoleon's armies, another, smaller column of French moved behind to crush the British between the two pincers of enemy forces. The only thing between this new detachment and the unprotected rear flank of Delverson's men was the captain himself. Listening to the rumble of the oncoming soldiers, Carey thought he had perhaps ten minutes to live. There was not even a tree to hide behind, nor so much as a hillock for cover, if he could have reached it, leaving a trail of blood behind him. He could have lain unmoving, pretending he was dead, but he still had his pistol and his saber. He could keep at least one or two of the bastard's off his men's tail. Carey said his prayers, touched the talisman in his pocket, and took aim.

His men were not as resigned to death. When their second in command went down and they were left with a very green junior officer and a mess of frogs ahead, the troops fell back. The youngster could not rally the men, who turned and ran, straight to Captain Delverson and the oncoming second wave. The outnumbered French were not expecting to come face to face with grinning, whooping, fresh forces, and went down quickly. Carey turned his now-buoyant men to face the original target, but General Graham, wondering where the hell Delverson's company was, sent a squad from the left flank, and the baggage train was approaching from the right with the medics and supplies, so the French retreated. Captain

Delverson was promoted to major, right there on his back in the dust.

"The men like you," General Wellesley told Carey in the Spanish hospital when he came to make the promotion official and pin more bits of ribbon and metal on Carey's uniform. "And you've got more between your ears than a pretty face. Besides, we are running out of young officers. You take care of yourself, we need you back on the lines."

The leg was healing, the fevers passed, and the nurses fought over who would care for the handsome officer—and two of them were nuns! Best of all, with Carey in one place for a few weeks, the mail caught up with him.

I hate you, I hate this school, and I wish I had never been born, his sister Suzannah wrote. *It will serve you right when I die of a broken heart. I swear I will come back and haunt you all your days.* Her next letter, noticeably more grammatical and legible, was full of her new friends Angela and Denise and the touring company production of *Romeo and Juliet* the entire school got to attend. Carey moaned. Just what his sister needed, another dose of high melodrama and romantic twaddle. Nor was he pleased when Suzannah included young Heywood's progress at university along with her news.

Woody made the cricket team and might try rowing unless he is sent down on account of his marks. Isn't that capital? Which, Carey wondered, that the looby was a good batter or that he might be home again in Dorset?

Emonda's letters were less disturbing to a man laid up miles away from doing anything about wayward dependents. *Lord Clyme goes on well,* she wrote in her neat hand, *except for the gout, which he will not blame on the port he drinks. The vicar calls regularly, and I have begun to teach Sunday school. Mrs. Jeffers thinks that Heywood will be sent down shortly. Lord Clyme says the boy is no scholar and you should have encouraged his father to buy his colors instead. With your permission I shall allow Suzannah to spend the summer with her friend Angela's family in Brighton.*

Carey was astounded at the chit's good sense and wrote back immediately, having his bank add handsomely to Suzannah's allowance so she might have a new wardrobe for the trip, anything to get her away from Dorset. He also wrote to Emonda that the army life was not all it was cracked up to be and he hoped young Jeffers would not enlist, not even if he was a skinny teen-aged gigolo. Emonda seemed content with her life, and Carey was relieved.

Carey's last letter was a scribbled note from his cousin: *I've done it! Am getting hitched to Phoebe Allenturk. Capital horsewoman, don't you know. The wedding's not for a year, thank goodness, so plan on being here. Your turn is next.*

So old Harry was getting married. Carey laughed out loud, sending Rudd for the laudanum in case the fevers were back. "No, my friend, we need that aged sherry! M'cousin's getting leg-shackled and the illustrious line of St. Dillon will be secured for another generation."

"Good match, is it, sir?"

"The best. Phoebe's a sturdy countrywoman with no die-away airs, the only child of Harry's neighbor, with marching lands and the second finest racing stable in Somerset. Harry's is the first. She used to be a tomboy in britches, so she'll suit Harry to a tee, not cut up stiff about his hounds and his ram-shackle manners. Best of all, her father has been a lusty old goat for as long as I can remember, so Phoebe might even believe a husband's infidelity is part of the marriage vows. I cannot picture my cousin confining himself to one woman. Trust Harry to find himself a rich, complacent bride."

Carey smiled over his sherry. He liked Phoebe, and she would make Harry a comfortable wife. That wasn't the kind of marriage Carey would want, of course, if he ever wanted to jump the broomstick. He saw himself head over heels with a graceful, spirited beauty—she might have wavy brown hair and look up at him with doe eyes alight with intelligence and humor—not a riding companion or partner in landshares! They would love each other so deeply, their passion so strong, neither would think of taking another lover. Memory of a certain kiss was quickly suppressed as Carey laughed at himself, for now he was beginning to sound like Suzannah. Then he sobered. Suzannah was growing up, Emonda was growing wise, and even Harry was settling down! Only Carey stayed still, where his future was no further than the next battle. He could not afford to dream of a bride; he had to rejoin his men.

Chapter Thirteen

The battles went on and on, in sweltering summer heat, in torrential rains of the damp season. They marched through deserted towns, towns where they were welcomed as heroes and towns where they were spit on for the havoc in the people's lives. Some days the supply wagons kept up with the march, and other days there was nothing to eat but what the men carried in their packs or could buy, catch, or steal.

At the siege of Albuera, Carey's hair was singed and his jacket caught fire from the lighted powder kegs tossed down on the British. He stripped the coat off and fought in his shirt-sleeves, taking a lance in the shoulder, but he made it over the scaling ladders to help in the British victory. Victory be damned. So many men were lost, they said, that Wellesley cried. If there was not already a term for Pyrrhic victory, that hellhole would have been it. Major Delverson was not the only man in the injured officers' commandeered quarters to wake sweating with nightmares. His hair grew in more gray than black, but Rudd was able to find his master's coat and prop the cameo locket open next to Carey's bedside.

The British suffered more losses at Salamanca when they faced Marmont, and the major was concussed from being knocked off his horse twice. Confused, he got lost during the retreat. He managed to come to his senses that night somewhere behind the French lines, so he liberated a mount from a suddenly incapacitated sentry and a bottle of wine from an unguarded supply wagon. He made it back to the British side with information on the enemy's troop strength and position, and a severe headache.

Wellesley was in retreat toward Ciudad Rodrigo, with the retrenchment taking enough time that supply trains could reach the troops with a new batch of letters. Emonda's letter was all about Lord Clyme's health, his leg, his chest, his heart. For a moment's self-pity Carey wished someone cared that much for him, then he worried she was fretting the old gentleman to an early death, but Clyme had wanted a comfort in his waning years and he had it.

Suzannah was full of her plans for the coming year. *You must know I shall finish my studies next semester. I'll be seventeen and ready to be presented! My best friend Angela said her mother would sponsor me, if Lord Clyme is not well enough to travel to London. Emmy would never leave him, so do say I may go, so I can be there for Harry's wedding. Shall you be home?* Joy of joys, there was no mention of forbidden love or Heywood Jeffers, and Carey was tempted to let his little sister get a taste of the metropolis if Emonda endorsed the plan and this Angela's family. Suzannah might be ready to try her wings, now that she was over that calf-love. Carey was not sure London was ready for her.

His bailiff wrote, and his man of business. All was in train. Harry scribbled a message on the back of a betting slip, about a new Thoroughbred he was racing, called Lucky in Carey's honor. *Your horse came up lame on the way to the meets in Darlington, so Joss sent the nag home. That night the track's stables caught fire. Can you believe it?*

Why not? Here he was quartered in a Spanish *estancia* with three exquisite *señoritas* to cater to him and five other young officers, and he had to turn down their favors. He had an ague. The other fellows didn't; they all ended up with the pox.

The battle for the town itself was another bloodbath, with the French coming from three directions, but Wellesley had finally learned Napoleon's tactics and was prepared. The British held and claimed the victory.

At one point late in the battle Carey stood over a fallen officer who lay wounded while two French troopers sought to finish them both off. Delverson was exhausted, his sword arm throbbing, his impaired left hand barely able to hold the dagger. But he stood, holding the Frenchmen at bay, exhorting his comrade.

"Come on, Runyon, try to get up. Help is on the way, man. Just lift your sword and show them what the British are made of."

The mounted reinforcements arrived to rout the attackers, just in time to see Runyon raise his saber and take a slice off the back of Delverson's trousers, showing more British than usual on the field of battle. The slash also took a cut off Carey's posterior, so he marched on with the men to Badajos while Rudd led his horse. They all had a well-deserved laugh and agreed it could have been much, much worse for the Lucky Devil and his descendants.

Badajos was the worst. Five thousand British soldiers died there, and Carey took a rifle ball in the thigh. The war was over for him at last and he could finally go home, if he lived long enough.

The wound was grievous. It did not fester, but it would not heal, and only his faithful batman kept the surgeons from amputation. The major was weak from loss of blood and fevers, delirious half the time and near unconscious with the pain the rest. In one of Carey's rare lucid moments he made Rudd swear not to make him an addict, so the batman kept the doses of laudanum to the minimum, no matter how it hurt him to see his master's agony. The doctors shook their heads.

Carey recovered slowly, still too troubled by fevers to face the sail home, even after the leg started to heal. It would never be perfect again, the doctors told him, between bouts of chills and tremors; no amount of willpower or exercise could repair shattered bone. Carey's too-bright eyes remembered his fallen friends, then looked at Rudd, hobbling on his peg leg, and knew he must not be bitter. Things could have been worse. He would walk as soon as the fogs lifted from his head, and he would walk up the gangplank of the first ship headed to England. So what if he could not dance at Harry's wedding?

While Carey was fighting the army's battles, Rowanne was having a few skirmishes of her own in Bath.

"No, Aunt Cora, I shall not marry Sir Tristan. He has fat lips."

"Cat nips? By Jupiter, girl, you try my patience. How many times do I have to tell you it don't matter if the fellow is bald and bilious, he's richer than Golden Ball." Aunt Cora flailed her skinny arms in the air, dangling bracelets. Her beaked nose quivered in indignation. "And just what was wrong with Lord Harberry? I was sure I gave my permission for him to pay his addresses."

"Moth balls."

"Moist halls? I heard his pile was very pretty, newly renovated. That's why he's looking for a bride."

"No, he smells like moth balls, and it is not just his clothing."

"And I suppose you are going to say you turned down Rodman and his twenty thousand pounds because he has sore gums."

Rowanne looked at her aunt in puzzlement. "Could *you* live with a man who constantly picks his teeth?"

"Oh, get out of here, you wretched creature. Go walk the dog or something. I need to think."

Toodles and Rowanne had come to an understanding. She stopped laughing at the dog's haircut, and Toodles stopped snapping at her ankles when she passed in the hall. They still cordially disliked each other, grumbling and growling at each other's company, but they both enjoyed the walks in the park. As soon as they were out of Aunt Cora's sight, Rowanne slipped the dog's lead and they went their separate ways. Rowanne got to stroll among the flowers or bring her book to one of the benches, while Toodles harassed the squirrels, dug holes, and rolled about in every kind of muck and mire a dog could adore. A half an hour or so later Rowanne would whistle, the poodle would grudgingly return, and Aunt Cora would exclaim over her pet's condition. Rowanne was not ordered to exercise the beast for at least another week.

If only it was as easy to get out of the daily visit to the Pump Rooms Miss Wimberly might be more content. Aunt Cora took the waters and the gossip as a daily ritual and insisted on her niece's escort. One never knew who would be there, she declared.

Rowanne knew very well who would be there, at the height of the London Season: octogenarians and invalids and ladies of a certain age—and the Captain Sharps who came to prey on them. She thought there must be more fortune hunters in Bath than there were doctors, unbelievable as it seemed. When there was a healthy young man, or even one not so young anymore, as Rowanne reached a more mature age herself, the gentleman was less likely to be paying a duty call on his ailing mother than to be looking out for a wealthy widow. The men visiting relatives looked at her with relief; the others gazed at her speculatively. They all rushed to gain an introduction through Aunt Cora, and that little martinet was in her glory. Rowanne gave the boredom-sufferers cursory inspection, the basket-scramblers short shrift. Aunt Cora got madder and madder, and Rowanne more depressed.

Rowanne was disgruntled at herself for being in Bath in the first place, anxious because she was indeed nearing her own deadline for matrimony, and furious at her aunt for throwing unsuitable men at her. To Aunt Cora, suitable meant any gentleman not in a wheeled chair. However would Rowanne stand having Aunt Cora's meddling when they went to London in the spring? And if Gabriel thought Rowanne's efforts at matchmaking were a nuisance, wait until their aunt got her claws into him! Poor Gabe.

At least his letters kept Rowanne informed of the happenings in Town. Papers reached Bath's lending libraries days late, so Rowanne was pleased with any other communication from what she considered the real world. Not the gossip—Aunt Cora's cronies took care of that—but Gabe wrote of the doings in the Lords, the progress of the war, the newest books. Miss Grimble's latest volume was published and she was appearing at literary salons, he said, but the book's popularity was overshadowed by Byron's newest work being snapped off the shelves. Gabe was sure no one remembered Rowanne's connection, or cared. She could come home anytime, as long as she had Aunt Cora to lend her countenance. Little did he know!

The war news was not good. The British seemed to be winning, but the casualty lists were appalling. Captain Delverson's name appeared frequently, on the injured lists, on the commendations dispatches. It was just like that bounder, Rowanne told herself, to be in the thick of things. She did not care about him at all, of course, he was just another Englishman fighting for his country, nearly giving up his infuriating, immoral, impossible life! He was a major now, and would likely be home for his cousin's wedding in the spring, by all accounts sure to be the affair of the Season. Rowanne would have to make good and certain that Aunt Cora never got sight of the handsome makebait.

As the warm weather gave way to late fall and winter, Bath became even drearier. Wind sent raw drizzle through the thickest cloak and walking became uncomfortable. Fewer visitors came to the spa, and fewer of her aunt's older friends dared brave the weather to venture to the Pump Rooms or pay morning calls, so Lady Silber became more cranky and querulous and Rowanne grew even more bored. If she wanted to become a recluse, she thought, she could have hidden out in the London house, where at least she had her hobbies. Here she had only been able to do some watercolors and a bit of needlework, the only occupations her aunt considered ladylike, besides reading penny novels. Rowanne even came to appreciate Aunt Emonda's letters, full of Uncle Donald's health though they were, and taking Toodles for his walk became the highlight of Rowanne's day, especially because she knew the dog hated getting his feet wet.

While Major Delverson lay drenched in sweat from the heat of his fevers and the airless room, with Rudd near to wearing out his wooden leg with changing the sodden linens every half hour, England was having one of its coldest winters.

Bath turned even more dismal, if possible. The cold rain changed to sleet and snow, which melted into gray slush that froze at night, making the sloped streets of the town more like sledding hills. The wind raged off the water, buffeting anyone foolish enough to poke his nose out of doors.

Aunt Cora was one such fool. She insisted on her glass of

mineral water each day for her rheumatics. Rowanne thought it was more in hopes of a new bachelor's appearance, but she was glad enough for the outing, so did not usually complain. She had a new gold velvet pelisse with ermine lining, and furlined boots to match, so was warm enough walking beside Aunt Cora's chair. One morning, however, the roads were too treacherous even for the chairmen. Rowanne told her aunt the men did not want to make the short trip.

"What's that? Two old mice?"

"Too cold and icy, Aunt. We have to go back in."

"Nonsense. Lady Turnbull is bringing her son. War injuries. You can be sure a veteran ain't afraid of slippery roads."

So they set out. Not two doors down, one of the chairmen lost his footing, skewing the poles so the other could not hold his grip. The chair tipped over, dumping Aunt Cora right out into a snowbank, luckily. Nothing broke, but Lady Silber was shaken, bruised, and sorely distressed. The physician had to be sent for, and she was even more distressed when that worthy man recommended complete bed rest, no excitement, and no spirits to elevate the blood.

For the next weeks Rowanne began to have pity on Lady Clyme, being nursemaid to a cantankerous old man. The woman must be a saint, if Uncle Donald was anything like Aunt Cora, for her letters never whined nor complained about her lot. Rowanne's own patience was wearing thin after the first whiff of brandy on her aunt's breath, the third call for lavender water, and the umpteenth refusal to take the prescribed medicines. Lady Silber's maid handled the invalid better, so Rowanne walked to the Pump Room to fetch Aunt Cora's glass of water, haunted the lending library, and exercised the dog when the weather permitted. No, she did not put his knitted sweater on Toodles.

Finally the roads were passable and Gabe came down from London. He did not come to relieve her in attempting to entertain their aunt as she supposed, which was a good thing, for Lady Silber was not interested in his dry-as-dust news and took to throwing pillows at Gabe for being a slowtop who refused to do his duty by the family. He was not in Bath to rescue his sister from exile, either, although she could not have left her aunt then, for all the good her presence did. At least she kept the housemaids from giving notice when Cora started pitching her gruel at them. Gabe had sad news of his own. Uncle Donald had passed away.

"The mails were so slow due to the iced roads that the funeral was long past when Emonda's letter reached me in London," Gabe told his sister. She could tell that he thought he should have gone. Rowanne had her regrets too, wishing that she had met her uncle just once. She patted Gabe's hand.

"He had been ailing for some time, Gabe, there was no reason to think he would not survive another winter. He could have sent for his heir and only blood relations too, if he wanted."

"Lady Clyme wrote that the cold weather brought on a chill which turned to pneumonia and carried him off. He died at peace, she said. Do you know what else she wrote? That he kept all of our letters, yours and mine, in a box near his bed."

Rowanne wiped her eyes. "I must write to—I suppose she must be the Dowager Lady Clyme now, Gabe, for you are the earl."

"Yes, hard as it is to believe. Lady Emonda says there are a great deal of papers to be signed, but that they can wait until the thaw. The property has been looked after by the earl's man for years now, so I need not be burdened with those decisions if I wish. Heavens, Ro, I don't know anything about crops and such."

"Yes, dear, but the bailiff must be competent or Uncle Donald would not have kept him on. What about Lady Emonda, though? The family owes her a debt of gratitude for caring for the earl these last few years."

Gabe looked at her through his glasses, his brows notched. "I thought you hated her."

"Well, that was before I had to care for Aunt Cora. And there was no child to come ahead of you, and her letters are all that's polite. Was she left well provided for or shall you see to the old lady's future?"

"Her settlements were generous, I recall. And she very sweetly offered to move to the dower house as soon as I wish to take up residence, as if I would throw the poor dear out in the snow. I thought perhaps I would invite her to return to London with me, if you don't mind too much, when I go to take care of the business. I'll wait for the weather to warm, naturally, rather than subject her to dangerous roads and winter storms."

Rowanne was delighted. "That would be just the thing! I am sure she needs a change of scenery, and I need a chaperone! Oh, not to bear-lead me or make introductions, you know that, but just for propriety's sake. We would all be in partial mourning by then, I suppose, so there could be nothing to offend her, although in all truth she does not sound a priggish female. We could see that she enjoys herself with the opera and card parties, quiet entertainments, you know. It's the least we can do. Then Aunt Cora would not have to bestir herself, or nibble me to death with her demands that I marry every twiddlepoop and cod's-head she finds."

"Fine, why don't you suggest the visit to her? It would sound more the thing, coming from you. Oh, by the way, speaking of your beaux, Major Delverson was wounded again. Seriously, I'm afraid, or he would have been shipped home with the other casualties. I say, Rowanne, are you all right? I thought you did not care for the chap?"

"No, Gabe, I am fine. It's just the . . . the news about Uncle Donald. How sorry I am we never knew him. Now it is too late."

During that same dreadful winter, while Carey lay swearing to walk again, when he was conscious enough to do so, his cousins were celebrating Harry's last days as a bachelor. There was a three-day-long party with brandy and Birds of Paradise, culminating in a curricle race on the ice-covered, rutted roads. Harry held the ribbons, Joss blew the tin. They never saw the mailcoach in the swirling snow. And Carey did not have to worry any longer about dancing at Harry's wedding.

The Iron General himself came to Carey's bedside to bring the sad news. By the worst stroke of hellish luck in creation, Major Lord Harmon Carrisbrooke Delverson, Bart., became His Grace, the new Duke of St. Dillon.

Chapter Fourteen

*E*verything he knew or loved was gone. His father, his cousins, his career, his friends. Carey was left with nothing but responsibilities. Even General Wellesley had seen fit to remind him of his duties before he left the Peninsula.

"You've been a good officer, lad. Had my doubts at first, I admit. Looked like you'd use your guts for brains. Wouldn't have lasted long at that fool's gamble. Now you have an onus, boy, a God-given burden to use those wits, yes, and the backbone, to serve the country in another way. Not speaking ill of the dead, but your cousin never took his seat, never cared that the lands and people who depended on him were cared for except by hired overseers, never made sure one of the proudest names in the land would not die out with that last ball you took. Go home, boy, see to your obligations, raise up more fine lads to serve their country and carry on the name, and see if you cannot beat some sense into those old fools at the War Office."

Carey was on his way, his hair white at the temples, his uniform hanging on his gaunt frame, his cane and Rudd supporting most of his weight. His heart dead inside him.

The ship docked in Southampton after a miserable crossing. Carey had to be half carried to the coach that had been sent down to meet them from Delmere, and the old stableman, Ned, wiped at his eyes with a checkered kerchief as he whipped up the horses.

They dropped the batman off at Delmere before going on to High Clyme, over Rudd's protests. "Whatever's there can wait another day, sir, ah, Your Grace. I didn't nurse you all these months to have you cock your toes up the first day in England."

"Sergeant, you are sounding like an old woman. As is, I am putting off Harry's solicitors and bankers as well as the War Office, in order to see about Suzannah and Emonda. That's where I am going. I rested in the coach, so don't go clucking like a hen with one chick. Go ask Mrs. Tulliver to take a few of the holland covers off so we have beds for the night and a hot meal. Wait till you taste her cooking, Rudd. Good, plain English fare."

"I don't see why you have to be traipsing back and forth, is all. Why can't we bunk at this High Clyme then, if your wards are there?"

"Emonda's a widow, Rudd. It wouldn't suit her notions of respectability to have a bachelor under the roof, even one with a game leg and a burning desire for a hot bath. Knowing my stepaunt, the peagoose would lie awake all night worrying that I was battle-starved for a woman, and lusting after the first female with blond hair and pale skin."

Rudd shook his head in disgust and tucked the carriage blanket tighter around the major, neither of them being used to the chill dank air after the heat of Spain. Carey tapped his cane on the roof of the coach for Ned to proceed.

The new duke looked back on the gray stones of his home that was home no longer. He would have to take up residence at the Abbey, he supposed. Carey loved that rambling old pile where boys could get lost for days without a tutor ever finding them—but he could not face that yet. He supposed Delmere would go to his second son, as it had come to his father. The deuce, he thought, sons.

The hatchments were up at High Clyme. Trust Emonda to get all the conventions correct. Carey struggled out of the carriage and stood on the gravel drive contemplating the marble stairs. Blast, there must be twenty of the bloody things. He shook off the footman who came down to assist him, feigning desire to look around while he caught his breath.

Before he started the long climb, a girl came tumbling out of the ornamental maze toward the left of the carriage drive.

Suzannah must have heard the coach pull up and, giggling, hurried to greet her long-lost half-brother with—hell and damnation—Heywood Jeffers by her side.

Suzannah stopped when she got closer and had a better look at Carey, and he thought he read pity on her face so he frowned. Her chin came up with a determined set as she took Woody's hand and moved forward. She was lovely, Carey thought, with her black hair curling down her back, a Delverson through and through. The cawker at her side was wearing striped pantaloons, b'gad, and he may have filled out some, but young Jeffers never had grown into his ears. As for that carroty mop and the freckles, Jupiter, but love was blind.

Then Carey opened his own eyes wider as the pair reached him at the bottom step. Suzannah's high-necked gray gown was misbuttoned at the bodice, and her lower lip was swollen. The major grabbed for the sword that was not by his side and cursed.

Woody stepped forward, offering his hand. "Welcome home, Your Grace. We have been waiting your arrival to ask your permission to—"

Carey sneered at his sister's gown. She blushed. "This is how you wait, you bastard?" He reached for Woody's outstretched hand with his right, pulled him forward, and popped him a hard left smack in the middle of his nose. Woody went down, his claret drawn, and Carey, as was inevitable, collapsed alongside him. Carey pulled himself up to a sitting position before the footman could get to him, but sat there on the bottom step waiting for the pain to subside, watching his sister use the gossoon's neckcloth to tenderly wipe the blood from the face in her lap. Carey sent the footman off for water and towels, and so no more of this Cheltenham tragedy need make the rounds of the neighborhood.

"What are you doing home from school?" he asked his sister in a quiet tone that would have had many a junior officer quaking in his boots.

Suzannah looked up, her eyes blazingly defiant. "I came to support Emmy in her hour of need and I will not go back."

"I see." Carey nodded curtly at the youth, now moaning in her arms.

"No, you don't see at all. You never have, you heartless bully! Woody is going to London and Emmy says I cannot go with Angela and her parents because we are in mourning, so I won't see him again for ages if you won't let us get married."

"I said when you are eighteen, after you have had a Season, when you know your own mind. That is not unreasonable, Suky."

"But all those other girls will be there, with their London ways and flirting looks. They'll scoop Woody up for sure."

Carey took another look at the gangly boy in her arms. Love must be deaf and dumb too, if Suzannah thought the Town belles were pining away until this jug-eared sprig of a squire's son came to sweep them off their feet. "Think, Suzannah. You are now the stepsister to a duke! You'll have one of the handsomest fortunes in the land and you can look as high as you wish for a husband."

That chin came up again. "I know my own mind and I have since I was four. You can keep your money and your titles. I want Woody, and I want him now!"

In an unconsciously identical manner, Carey stiffened his own resolve. "You *will* go back to school, you *will* have a Season, and you damn well will not give yourself to any rutting young jackanapes before then!"

Tears filled her blue eyes. "But I love him."

Carey wished he could reach out to her, across the stairs, across the years. "Ah, Suky, you're too young to know love."

"No I'm not, Carey," she told him, hugging her fallen knight more closely. "You are just too old to understand. I'll bet you have never even been in love."

"But I have," he told her with a smile, "sometimes three or four times a night."

"Really? Woody— That is, that's not the kind of love I meant and you know it."

"I do, pet, and no, I have never known that 'spiritual coupling of two souls.' "

Maybe once he could have, when there was no room in a soldier's life. And maybe now he could have found it, that dream, that glory, if he were not maimed in body and in spirit. All he had to offer in trade for her glittering London life was an empty shell of a man and the shambles he'd been warned he'd find at St. Dillon. He had the title now and money, more than he could spend in his lifetime, but so did she, who could have bought herself a husband anytime these past four years. He would not even subject her to the ridicule of the London fishbowl, watching the cripple go acourting. Asking for her hand would be like clipping the wings of a beautiful dove, binding her to earth and ugliness.

No, he would never know love, but he understood duty very well.

"You are asking me to marry you?" Emonda reached for her salts. She was prettier than the last time Carey had seen her, still with that pale coloring, but dressed in a fashionable gray gown with black velvet ribbons instead of the heavy black crepe he had expected. Donald had made her promise not to go into deep mourning, it seemed.

She had also competently managed the debacle on her front steps, sending for Lord Clyme's valet to tend to Woody, ordering Suzannah upstairs to change her spattered gown, and overriding Carey's own insistence on struggling up the stairs himself. She sent two strapping footmen down to aid him. They were used to doing for Lord Clyme, she announced, making Carey feel like an ancient. At least she had the courtesy to turn her back when the men half carried him into her parlor.

For all that, and a few pounds on her thin frame, she was still the vaporish female he recalled.

"Yes, I am asking you to become the next Duchess of St. Dillon. Forgive me for not getting down on my knee. I would never get up."

Emonda fluttered her handkerchief in the air. "But why?"

"That should be obvious." He studied his fingernails. "You are all alone in the world now, with no family except myself and Suzannah. Gabriel Wimberly will be coming to take over High Clyme, and you cannot wish to live with a stranger as his dependent."

"But Lord Clyme provided very well for my future. You

know that, you helped draw up the marriage settlements. So I never have to marry again if I do not wish."

"What, would you spend the rest of your days alone? Emonda, you are all of what? Nineteen? Marriage is the only option for a female."

"Is it? There is the dower house, you know, so I would not be in the new earl's pocket. He seems a pleasant gentleman, from his letters, at any rate, who I doubt would make me feel like excess baggage. Besides, he is enthused at taking the seat in Parliament, so would not settle here permanently. His sister invites me to London when I am out of mourning."

"I shall be opening Delverson House in Town," he said as if that took care of all of her objections.

"Carey, Your Grace, I am not a Delverson and never have been. I am not your ward, not your responsibility. I am a Wimberly, and not even Lord Gabriel Wimberly can deny my right to settle my own future. I have been handed from relative to relative my entire life like some heirloom that's too valuable to throw away and too ugly to keep. Never again. You do not have to offer for me out of your sense of honor."

"I am offering for you, damn it, because I need help with Suzannah and I don't have time or inclination to go paying suit."

It was not the most graceful of proposals, but at that moment, when Carey was sick and heart-sore, Emonda liked him better than she ever had, not that she could imagine spending her life with a reckless hero who would want her to take up the tonnish life and manage his vast households. "But you would want heirs," she said, thinking of doing *that* with this grim-faced stranger. She shuddered.

He understood. She could not bear the idea of making love with a disfigured man. "I see. I am sorry, ma'am, I did not mean to offend. I cannot offer you a chaste marital bed like Lord Clyme, for an heir seems to be what I need more than anything else." He stood awkwardly, his mouth twisted in bitterness. "I have to travel to the Abbey. With your permission I shall leave Suzannah in your care, with the understanding that if she blots her copybook one more time I shall strangle her. We shall discuss other arrangements on my return."

Emonda shrank back in her seat. He was as authoritarian, sneering, and bloodthirsty as ever. Look what he'd done to poor Woody. She could not imagine a worse husband. He would be forever giving orders and expecting instant compliance, with nary a thought governing his own immoral behavior. Just look at that lightskirt he was supporting. Blood rushing to her face, she asked, "Why do you not marry Mrs. Reardon, then? You would have a ready-made heir."

"Mrs. Reardon?" The surprise of hearing his father's mistress's name almost knocked him off his uncertain balance. He clutched the back of his chair for support. "I believed the woman to be elsewhere."

"She was, for a while after you left last time, just long enough to return with an infant. She has a nanny walk his pram up and down the village streets for everyone to see the child's black curls and dark-rimmed blue eyes, just like yours."

Carey's knuckles turned white on the chair while his mind raced. What rig was that Reardon woman running? The child was not his, of course, as his caper-witted stepaunt seemed to be implying, but his reputation was such that Mrs. Reardon would likely be believed if she chose to point to him with the evidence of his butter-stamp. Lord, what that would do for Suzannah's chances when she went to London!

"I don't suppose there is any Mr. Reardon, or Mr. Anything else?"

Emonda shook her head, still blushing. "She tells anyone who will talk to her that you were very generous."

"I was, to get rid of her." Carey did hasty arithmetic in his head and concluded the child could not have been his father's, even if the jade was increasing at their last conversation as she must have been. If the boy was indeed the spit and image of one of the Delverson Devils, by God, that left Harry or Joss. For all Carey knew, neither of them was above littering the countryside with by-blows. The timing would be right for when they came down and hired her, and Harry always did like voluptuous females. Zeus, but Suzannah's idiocy must run in the family. "Has the woman approached you?"

Emonda sniffed. As if she would have anything to do with

such a wanton! A lady was not even supposed to know of the existence of women like that. "Of course not. I think she spoke with Donald once, but naturally he never mentioned the matter to me."

"Naturally," Carey echoed dryly, "or you might be able to tell me what they said so I would know how to proceed. No matter, now that Harry is gone I am sure I'll be hearing from her myself. If by some chance the harpy does call, and you can bring yourself to utter the words, tell her Hell will freeze over before a bastard becomes heir to St. Dillon."

Chapter Fifteen

One was a hobbledehoy schoolgirl steeped in lending library romances; the other was a young woman so sheltered that she feared any male older than ten and younger than sixty. One was headstrong, the other meek. Neither wanted to stay in Dorset to wait for Carey's "other arrangements."

"I just *have* to go to London, Emmy. I can't bear to let Woody go without me."

"And I daren't stay here for your brother to demand I marry."

"I won't go back to school."

"And I won't be subjected to another insulting call from any of the muslin company. I had the butler tell that woman she must speak to Carey, but what if she calls when the vicar is here? Whatever shall I do?"

Suzannah nibbled a gooseberry tart. "Do you really think the little boy is a Delverson? I saw him with his nanny at Mr. Stang's apothecary, when I went to fetch those camphor pastilles for you. I swear Mrs. Stang's eyes almost swiveled right out of her head, she was goggling back and forth between me and the boy so fast. He did look just like that portrait of Carey with his mother that hangs in the gold parlor at home, except that Carey has a smile in the picture, and this little chap seemed to be in a pout the whole time, even when I bought him a licorice stick."

"Suzannah, you didn't!"

"Well, yes, I did. He might be my nephew or at least my cousin, even if he was born on the wrong side of the blanket. None of it is *his* fault at any rate." She took another bite. "Did you know that his name is Gareth? Gary, Carey . . ."

"Harry. Or even that other cousin of yours who came that time, Lawrence Fieldstone."

"Yes, but don't even mention him in my brother's hearing. The Irish branch is not recognized, you know, and he and Larry have always hated each other."

"Oh dear, then Mr. Fieldstone is another, ah . . . ?"

"Like the little boy, yes."

Emonda's cup rattled in its saucer. "And the whole village knows that too, I suppose. Oh, why did that wretched man have to go away and leave me to face all of this? I daren't even show my face on the streets."

Suzannah chewed her sweet slowly, thinking. A dangerous gleam came to her eyes and her dimples showed. Emonda reached for her vinaigrette, recognizing the signs. "You know, Emmy, how we talked about your going back to London with the new Lord Clyme after he comes to view the property next month?"

"Yes, his sister particularly wanted me to visit," Emonda answered uncertainly. "But I hadn't decided."

"From what I heard at school, Miss Wimberly is a great gun, not at all high in the instep. You'll like her. And her brother's name has never been connected with the slightest scandal or hellraking." Gabriel Wimberly sounded dull as ditch-water to Suzannah, but she knew what her stepaunt would want to hear. "Perhaps they would not mind if you came for a visit a bit earlier."

"Rowanne did invite me for any time I chose, now that she is back from Bath. I suppose I could write."

"There's no time, Emmy. Woody leaves in two days and

you would not want to travel without a gentleman to accompany you, would you?"

"Heavens no, but to just arrive . . . ?"

"It cannot signify. You are the Dowager Lady Clyme; they cannot turn you away at the door."

"No, but I should hate to be thought encroaching, dear."

Suzannah made herself swallow another morsel and her impatience before saying, "They *want* you to come, Emmy, and you cannot mean to wait for Carey's return. He might even have some cork-brained notion of moving us all to St. Dillon, you, me, Mrs. Reardon, the b—"

"I'll go. But what about you, Suzannah? I am sure Lord Gabriel will consider me rag-mannered enough, so my bringing them one more uninvited guest would not make much difference. But Carey would not stand for it, you know. You are his ward, in truth, and he would simply go to London to fetch you back."

"Not if he doesn't know where I am," Suzannah said, daintily wiping her mouth. "You'll need to take a maid along, won't you?"

Aunt Cora had come to Town with Rowanne after all, despite the lingering agitation of her nerves. No rustic widow was proper chaperone for a girl already bent on developing a hurly-burly reputation, nor could this untonnish Emonda Selcroft person, dowager countess or not, ensure that her niece made a proper marriage. Lady Silber also wanted to consult another physician concerning her condition, on the assumption that sooner or later she would find one whose diagnosis agreed with her own, and whose treatments would recommend the use of spirits to calm her palpitations.

Although Town was still somewhat thin of company, Rowanne was pleased to be home, even if Aunt Cora's demands kept the house at sixes and sevens. Rowanne welcomed her brother's companionship and intelligent conversation too, as much as she had of it, with him taking his meals at his club more often than not, to avoid Aunt Cora and prepare for his maiden speech.

It was with some trepidation, therefore, that Rowanne

stepped into the front drawing room when Pitkin the butler unexpectedly brought in Lady Clyme's calling card, with the corner turned down to indicate a visit in person. Here was another old tartar, Rowanne thought, who believed she could ride roughshod over Miss Wimberly.

Rowanne was not one whit relieved to find a small, frail old woman swathed in black, with black hat and veil, sitting rigid in an armchair in front of the Adams fireplace. Her maid stood behind her chair, snuffling into a large handkerchief, her huge mobcap pulled down almost to her eyes and her shapeless gray uniform obscuring the rest of her. Country quizzes, Rowanne concluded, making her curtsy and holding her hand out to her aunt. "My dear aunt Emonda, welcome to Wimberly House."

Emonda had lost all of her courage in the carriage ride through the noisy, dirty, crowded streets of the city. By the time she found herself in the imposing mansion, in the elegant room, in the presence of this modish creature, she was speechless with terror. Her maid had to pinch her shoulder, hard. "Ouch! Ah, that is, Miss Wimberly, please, please forgive me for imposing on you this way. I know I should not have, and would not have, except St. Dillon arrived and that awful woman and I shan't wish to marry him at all, and the baby, oh dear."

Oh dear indeed. Rowanne could make no sense of the woman's ravings whatsoever, except to realize she had another high-strung female on her hands, and Carey Delverson to thank for it. "Please, ma'am, call me Rowanne. I'll just ring for tea. I am sure you will feel more the thing after, and by then your rooms shall be made ready. My housekeeper, Mrs. Ligett, can show your maid upstairs where she can—"

"She's sick!" Emonda hurried to say. The tall, sturdy-looking girl behind her coughed for good measure. "And she has to sleep in my room."

After giving instructions to the footman who answered her call, Rowanne reasoned, "But, my lady, if she is sick, surely she should have a room of her own in the servants' quarters where she can be looked after. You should not be further exposed to her infections."

The maid cleared her throat and Lady Clyme blushed. "No, she is not contagious, and I really need to look after her myself. I, ah, promised her brother before we left." Now the maid's coughs sounded oddly like muffled laughs, as she followed Mrs. Ligett out of the room and up the stairs.

"There, my lady, here's tea. Wouldn't you like to take your bonnet off and be more comfort— Oh, my stars, you cannot be Aunt Emonda."

Stars or spider monkeys, this fragile young lady—her junior by at least three years—was indeed Rowanne's aunt. Rowanne had to bite her tongue to keep from laughing at her hopes of this Lady Clyme becoming her chaperone. Why, from the garbled account, the girl, for she was hardly a woman, had no more idea how to go on than a newborn kitten. It was a miracle she managed to get herself and that odd maidservant to London. It seemed Rowanne would have to put on her caps after all and play nursemaid to her aunt. She could hardly wait to see Gabe's reaction.

"Please inform my brother and my aunt that Lady Emonda Wimberly, Countess of Clyme, has joined us, Pitkin," she asked the butler. "And see if they cannot join us for tea."

Gabriel's spectacles fell off when he bowed to his aunt, then he ground them right under his foot in slack-jawed idiocy, causing Emonda to blush furiously and go tongue-tied again. Aunt and nephew stood mumchance while Rowanne went to the bell-pull and asked the long-suffering Pitkin for another pair of her brother's glasses. While she stood by the door, swallowing her laughter, Aunt Cora wandered into the room. For once even the old harridan had nothing to say beyond "That old dog, Donald," which brought color to *Gabriel's* cheeks.

Emonda did not seem to be offended at the comment, if she understood it, but was instead exclaiming over the last member of the family to enter the parlor. "Oh, what a beautiful dog," she cooed.

Toodles? The ill-tempered beast was even wagging his absurd tuft of a tail at the chit. Rowanne was convinced her new relation was a charming little widgeon, and tried to catch her brother's eye to share the silliness of the occasion. Even with his new pair of spectacles, however, Gabe was still in a daze, watching the little blonde curtsy to Aunt Cora and again beg everyone's pardon for her untimely arrival.

"No, no, my dear," Gabe told Emonda, patting her hand, "I don't know how we managed to get on without your charming presence."

Gabe?

Aunt Cora was soon charmed by Emonda's sweet solicitude in inquiring after her health, jumping up to fix pillows behind her back, offering to read to the older lady. "I was so sorry to hear about your accident, ma'am. I have the receipt for a tisane that Lord Clyme found most soothing. May I make some up for you, Lady Silber?"

"What a good child you are. Call me Aunt Cora."

"May I really?" Emonda asked, tears of gratitude and relief coming to her eyes. "You have all been so kind. You cannot know what it is like to have a family again after so long."

"But I thought you had a niece, Suzannah Delverson. You used to write about her, didn't you?" Rowanne asked, and was surprised at Emonda's blushes.

"Suzannah is, ah, back at school. That's why I had to leave, you see."

Rowanne didn't, quite, but she listened as avidly as the others to another, longer account of Emonda's woes and Lord St. Dillon's villainy. Wild youths, wicked cousins, lost reputations, and fallen women figured prominently, along with forced marriages. When Emonda finally reached the end, with Carey's second proposal, the illegitimate child, and her fears for the future, her blue eyes were again awash in tears.

Gabe awkwardly handed her his handkerchief. "Now, now, you are safe with us. There shall be no more talk of arranged marriages or wicked guardians. *I* am head of this household, and no one would dare make you a licentious proposal. You may stay here with us as long as you wish, or in Dorset, whichever *you* choose, and no one else can say you nay. I will deal with that blackguard Delverson, or St. Dillon as he now is, if he dares show his face."

Rowanne blinked. What would Gabe do, challenge the ex-officer to a chess match? Aristotle at twelve paces? Meanwhile her aunt was threatening to see the dastard drawn and quartered for what he had done to dear little Emmy, and making plans to show the girl a good time in London as recompense. She was likely planning to find her a husband too, if Rowanne read aright that martial gleam in Aunt Cora's beady little eyes. Just as likely, from Gabe's besotted expression, the effort would be unnecessary. Rowanne studied the little dowager all the harder, trying to discover what made such a milk-and-water miss so appealing to men. A proud man like Major Delverson must truly love the pretty ninnyhammer, to offer for her twice. And there was Gabe, ready to jump on his white charger and ride to the damsel's rescue, even if dragon-breath would fog his spectacles. Men were fools, every last one of them. No wonder Miss Wimberly could not find one worthy to marry.

Chapter Sixteen

The pain grew worse with every mile Carey drew closer to the Abbey. Not his leg, although that ached, but his soul. While the major was in Spain, or even in Dorset, his loss was a disjointed fact, separate from his life. For all he knew then, Harry and Joss could still be raising hell at Newmarket, tupping the barmaids at some East End dive. Now that he was in Somerset, on St. Dillon lands, when his cousins should have come whooping out of the trees, racing his carriage to the front drive, he had to admit they were gone. God, to drive through the home woods—with its forts and treehouses, past the old water hole, over the fields where winter-born Thoroughbred colts raced the wind with no one to watch, no one to pick a likely comer—nearly wrenched the heart out of His Grace, the owner of all this. And he had not even faced the old retainers yet.

He cursed Harry fluently for doing this to him. "I hope you're laughing, you old makebait," he muttered. "And I wish you joy, riding to foxes with the hounds of Hell."

Anger got him through the damp-eyed embrace of Skuggs, the ex-pugilist the old duke, Harry's father, had hired on to keep the boys in line. The boys had adored the huge man with his cauliflower ear and flattened nose and endless tales of ringside valor. He taught them the Fancy and sportsmanship and respect, if not for their elders, at least for the elders big enough to box their ears. Skuggs married one of the housemaids and she became housekeeper when Harry made the giant his unlikely butler, after starchy old Naismith and his crotchety wife could be pensioned off. Carey remembered when they had all gone to Bristol to have Skuggs fitted for uniforms, his chest so swelled with pride the tailor had to take extra measurements.

Skuggs was older, balding, but still strong enough to crush Carey's ribs when he half-lifted him from the carriage and helped him through the vast bronzed front doors. "Whisht, lad, we'll have to fatten you up some, get you back to fighting weight. You'll be taking on all comers soon enough, Master Carey. Pardon, that's Your Grace." His gravelly voice caught on the words.

Carey patted the bruiser's back. "I know, old friend, it sits heavily on my shoulders too." Before he lost all composure and showed the gathered staff what a pudding heart the new duke was, Carey cleared his throat and pointed his cane to a large dusty pile of fur littering the black-and-white marble of the entry hall.

Skuggs waved his hand, dismissing the servants to their duties of seeing to rooms, baggage, dinner for the new master. "It's an Irish wolfhound, Your Grace, Master Joss's dog." Skuggs explained as he escorted Carey to the library where a fire was laid and decanters stood ready. The animal unfolded itself into an enormous, scraggly hound with bristly face and doleful expression. It followed Skuggs and Carey down the hall, then flopped in front of the hearth, sighing.

"Doesn't anybody feed the beast?" Carey asked, sinking into a chair. "I realize it could eat the kitchen cat and two scullery maids if it wished, but, zounds, man, the thing is a sack of bones." He wrinkled his nose. "And none too clean either."

Skuggs poured out a glass of cognac and shook his head. "I know, Your Grace, but the poor blighter's heart's broke and he won't eat more'n a bite here and there, and he won't let anyone handle him close enough. The kennelman wants to put him down, but I says he's not hurting anything, as long as you keep your distance."

Carey swallowed the portion in his glass and held it out for more. "You say he was Joss's?"

"Aye, they fair doted on each other, ever since that other cousin of yourn, Mr. Fieldstone, brought the hound down from Ireland when he come last time."

Carey's hand tightened on his glass. "I did not know that Mr. Fieldstone was back in this country."

"I suppose no one mentioned it 'cause they knew you wasn't on terms. I haven't seen him since the, ah, funerals."

"Have no fear, he'll show up." Lawrence Fieldstone was the old duke's eldest child, and would have been St. Dillon now, if his mother was not a round-heeled actress from an Irish traveling company. The old duke had provided well for his baseborn son, funding his education, seeing that he had a generous allowance, even bringing him to the Abbey to summer with his legitimate sons and nephew. Whatever Lawrence had was never enough. He was a bully, greedy and resentful of his station. In later years he battened on Harry, encouraging all his worst vices. And good-natured Harry always pulled Lawrence out of River Tick, paid his gambling debts, financed his extravagant lifestyle. Carey would not, and he was looking forward to telling the bastard so. Meantime, "Do you think he'll take the dog back if he comes?"

"Hell, no, the animal hates him. Bit his leg last time he come so Master Joss had to keep the animal locked in his bedroom. Mrs. Skuggs wasn't best pleased, I can tell you."

"How is your good lady, Skuggs? Forgive me for not asking

sooner. Please send my compliments, and I shall visit with her tomorrow. Put off the steward and the secretary and everyone else too. I could not face all that today. For now I just want to sit in here a while without being disturbed. Just leave the bottle within reach."

"Right, Your Grace. I'll bring your supper in here, so you don't have to stir your stumps. Time enough to throw your hat in the ring tomorrow."

"Thank you, Skuggs, and see if you cannot bring something for the dog too. I like the mutt better already, if it bit Lawrence Fieldstone. Oh, and what's the cur's name?"

Skuggs shrugged his massive shoulders. "No one recalls it being anything but 'Dog.' Mrs. Skuggs calls it the Hound from Hell, but that's not rightly a name. It don't come when anyone calls it anyway, so one name's as good as t'other."

Carey settled back in his chair to stare into the flames of the fire, but the dog whimpered in its sleep. At least Carey had the Abbey and old friends like Skuggs and this fine aged brandy to dull his mind, if he drank enough of it. He was lucky; the poor dumb animal didn't even have a name.

"I have more names and titles than I can write on half a page, old son," Carey told the dog. "Do you want one of them? Would you like the baronetcy? Perhaps you'd accept the military rank now that I have to sell out." The dog perked one ragged ear, then rolled over with another sigh.

"No? Quite right, look how mangled Major got me. I would not burden you with a sobriquet like Lucky, for I do believe the Fates take their revenge on such arrogance. Shall you be Cerberus, then, sir, the real Hound of Hell, guarding the gates?" The dog's snores were his only answer. Carey poured another glass. "I'd like to name you after my cousins, you know. You'd like that. Put some fire back into you, to be named for those hell-babes. But I cannot." He swallowed another gulp of the cognac. "I have to save those names for my sons. My sons!" He tossed the crystal goblet into the fire-place. "Damn you, Harry!"

Skuggs brought dinner on a tray and a bowl of scraps for the dog. He said nothing about the fractured shards on the firebrick, just setting down his burden and frowning at the sinking level in the decanter. Carey waved him out.

The dog would not eat from the bowl on the ground, but he would deign to take food from Carey's hand. When the scraps were gone, Carey fed the mutt his own dinner, having no taste even for Mrs. Skuggs's game pie. He did nibble at some cheese, after wiping his hands as thoroughly as possible with the serviette and the water in his drinking glass. "I won't tell Mrs. Skuggs if you don't," he whispered to the dog, who was now folded up like a discarded bearskin rug at the side of Carey's chair. Soon the dog was snoring again, and every once in a while emitting vaguely sulfurous fumes, while Carey continued drinking and staring at the fire. "Whew," Carey said, turning his head away, "you even smell like fire and brimstone." The animal got up at the sound of his voice and frantically scratched behind his ear. Carey took over, rubbing just the right spot, and smiled. "That's it, Old Scratch. You'll be one of the Devils after all." Scratch laid his shaggy head in Carey's lap and gave a gusty sigh.

They stayed that way through the night, the duke and the dog, and if occasionally the hound felt a drop of moisture on his head, he sighed again.

The next morning, with a headache already making his eyeballs wish they resided elsewhere, the Duke of St. Dillon tried to absorb almost thirty years of information about crop rotations, lumber rights, corn prices, and sheep dips.

"Did Harry know all this?" he asked the steward, Canthorpe.

"Some of it, Your Grace. But I made sure you would want to be an informed landlord. His Grace, that is, his late lordship, always said you were the downiest one of the family."

"Thank you for the compliment, if that's what it is. I shall try to live up to your expectations and the late duke's also, but not all in one morning, if you please. You must carry on the way I am sure you have been managing on your own for years, Canthorpe, for if you try to tell me Harry cared which breed of milchcow did best on which graze, I'll know you've been pitching me gammon just to make a farmer out of me."

Canthorpe laughed and gave way to Harry's local man of

business, with his lists of cotton mills and tin mines and sugar plantations. Here the new duke had more definitive ideas:

"I know the estate is vast and the profits well invested. Later I would like to see the books and the accountings so I might help in those decisions, but for now I should like to rest easy in my bed, knowing my new wardrobe will not be paid for with the earnings of slave labor or children's blood or war profiteering."

"But, Your Grace, we derive a great deal of income from such sources."

"We?" With one word and one raised eyebrow Carey took on the stature of St. Dillon the aristocrat, his uncle, not his scapegrace cousin. The man of business bowed deeply and left, tucking papers into his case.

Carey asked the secretary to lunch with him, to save time. Over Mrs. Skuggs's excellent offering of braised venison, most of which Carey fed to Scratch, he quizzed Johnston about the household accounts and the shambles his cousins' personal affairs had left.

"I believe most of the gaming debts were paid, and any of the tradesmen whose bills were presented. There was never a question of outrunning the bailiffs, only a certain untidiness. Your cousins were a tad careless about such things, but we're coming about."

Carey kept thinking how fortunate Harry was in his employees. They were honest, loyal, and far more forgiving of negligence than he would be. "Make sure you give yourself a raise, old chap," he told the secretary, "for I am going to saddle you with a great deal more work, now that you have shown me how competent you are. There is Delmere to be considered and my wards, and the War Office wants me to write up some reports, and all those stuffy letters of condolence to be answered." When the secretary rose to leave, Carey asked if he could prepare an accounting, when Johnston got the chance of course, no hurry, of how much Harry paid out in Lawrence Fieldstone's behalf, for when he came to call. Carey paused in peeling the skin off an apple to add, "One more thing, has there been any communication from a Mrs. Reardon?"

Johnston cleared his throat nervously. "There has been, Your Grace, and I have not been sure what course to pursue. Your cousin read the first letter and consigned it to the fire, directing me to dispose of any others likewise. Which I did, of course. The latest missive in that lady's script is addressed to you, Your Grace. Shall I fetch it?"

"She's no lady and no, I think it will hold. This day already has enough treats in store."

After luncheon, and a glass or two of port on a nearly empty stomach, Carey ordered a curricle brought round. While the ex-officer listened calmly as Rudd and Ned argued about his taking the ribbons himself, refusing a groom and not leaving his direction, Old Scratch lunged up to the seat alongside the driver's and growled. End of discussion.

Carey's destination was Four Oaks, the Abbey's nearest neighbor and home to Squire Allenturk and his daughter Phoebe. Another glass or three would not have come amiss.

"Devilish business, Harry and all." The squire mopped his brow. He'd brought Carey into the parlor, moving a stack of racing forms to clear a comfortable chair. The fire wasn't even lighted, nevertheless Allenturk's face was turning redder and damper with each moment he faced this somber young man in his ill-fitted clothes. "Settlements signed and all, you know. Excellent marriage for both parties, 'pon rep. Girl gets to stay practically to home near her papa, with a title and a London house to boot, and St. Dillon gets all this"—an expansive wave of his sweaty hand—"when I pop off."

Carey nodded. Squire Allenturk stuck a finger in his suddenly-tight collar, deciding then and there never to play cards with the stone-faced fellow. He hopped up. "I know I can count on you to do the right thing. Gentleman and all that. I'll send in m'girl."

Like a recurring bad dream, Carey found himself making his second marriage proposal in less than three days. And receiving his second refusal.

"Thank you, Carey, but there is no need," Phoebe told him. "I would never hold you to the agreements."

Carey thought she was looking her best in a military-cut

riding habit. The feather curling on her cheek showed to advantage the healthy glow of an outdoors countrywoman. "It would not be a bad marriage, you know."

Phoebe turned away from him, her riding crop swinging against her leg. "Oh, it would be a fine match, the lands and titles and fortunes. And I expect you would make a more comfortable husband than Harry, now that you are done trying to get yourself scattered across the continent." She paused and fumbled in her pocket for a handkerchief. "But you see, I loved Harry."

"I'm sorry, Phoebe, I didn't know."

"Neither did he." Then she was crying into his shirt collar— Phoebe Allenturk was a big girl—and Carey was wondering if his bad leg would hold up both of them for much longer. He handed her his linen square and she apologized, saying "I am sure you don't need me playing Tragedy Jill, no more than you need a farm girl with a good riding seat as your duchess."

"I *will* ride again."

"What's that to do with— Oh, your leg. Don't be more of a clunch than you have to be, Carey. I do not wish to marry anyone now. In a few years I shall have to do my duty, just as you are doing yours. That will be time enough for a marriage of convenience."

"Your father will be disappointed."

"No, he was disappointed that I was not born a son. Now he'll be furious. Of course, he might be convinced not to sue for breech of promise if you'll sell him that new colt of Harry's. He's by Excelsior out of Sundance and already clocking the fastest quarters and—"

"Consider it a gift, my dear. A betrothal gift that came too late. Harry was very happy with his engagement, and very fond of you."

Of course, Harry might not have been as fond of Phoebe as Carey was at that moment.

The ride home was shorter. As he drove through the gates of the Abbey of St. Dillon, Carey pulled the horses over to view the prospect. The rose window of the original chapel glowed in the afternoon sun and the sprawling building looked homey

to his eyes, with the hodge-podge of architecture in mis-
matched wings added by successive generations to the old
monastery. It all blended together somehow, at least in Carey's
mind, a combination of gray stone from the estate's own
quarry and centuries of tradition. In the map room was a
record of each addition, with the name of each duke who had
commissioned it. *His* ancestors, *his* traditions.

Carey rubbed the dog's ears, got licked on the cheek in
return, and felt almost like the day he'd taken the arrow in his
shoulder. Once the arrow was out, he still had a deuced big
hole in his shoulder, but at least he didn't have a foot of wood
poking him in the ear.

He even took a little food with his dinner's drink, and
decided to give the dog a bath, so they *both* did not end up
smelling like a ferret down a rat hole on a rainy day. Then he
read Mrs. Reardon's letter.

Chapter Seventeen

The letter read: *Your Grace, we have a small matter to
discuss. I was sorry to have missed you in Dorset, and must
have misunderstood your message. Surely you wish to continue your cousin's line of generosity? I am certain you will be
in London shortly. Shall I call on your sister and stepaunt
there?*

Carey swore. The letter was masterful, insinuating much,
saying little that could be held against the author. There was
no outright extortion demand, simply hints about a small
child, the succession, and embarrassing his womenfolk. But
many families had conspicuous dirty linen without being bled
dry. Hell, the St. Dillons already had Lawrence Fieldstone.

And Emonda had already been mortified; she and Suzannah could not be shamed further, safe in Dorset.

Carey felt a shiver down his spine like the night before a battle. They were in Dorset, weren't they? By Jupiter, if those two innocents were capering about Town without a proper *doyenne* and the Reardon woman and infant started rumor mills grinding, Suzannah's prospects would be nil. She'd be lucky if that puppy Jeffers offered for her. His eyes narrowed. Now wouldn't that be just like his sad romp of a sister, to force his hand with a scandal? "Damn!" he said aloud. The dog looked up and padded over to his chair. "Damn all women, Scratch, they're nothing but a misery."

Now he was going to have to go haring off to London where his every limping move would be as public as an exhibit at the Royal Academy, and every conniving mama would have her gimlet eye fixed on his bankbook and her heart set on his title. That was assuming any gently bred female could stomach both his lameness and his besmirched name, after Mrs. Reardon left her little calling card at his door. Profligacy was one thing to the ton; discretion was all. Carey refused to consider the type of woman who could overlook a man's flaws and foibles in favor of his purse—he wasn't desperate enough yet to let one get her claws into him—so he was going to have to deal with the lightskirt and her brat instead of throwing the letter in the fire. He would have to come to terms with the shrew, and do it all in London at the height of the Season. "Blast!"

For a moment he was tempted to accept the boy as Harry's get and end this misbegotten need to look further for a cursed bride he didn't want, but there was no proof. He had too much honor, furthermore, to pay blood money, and too much dignity to let a by-blow, someone else's by-blow at that, wear the St. Dillon signet ring after him. Most of all he had too much pride to dance to any woman's tune.

"A pox on all of them!"

The dog wagged his tail.

Emonda settled in nicely in Grosvenor Square. Due to her mourning, she excused herself from balls and fetes, the crushes that would have overwhelmed her. She enjoyed sight-seeing and shopping and unexceptionable dinner parties and small musicales and visits to the opera. She *liked* walking Toodles! She was just as pleased to sit home reading to Aunt Cora or practicing the pianoforte or playing a surprisingly astute hand of cards. Piquet was Lord Clyme's favorite pastime, she blushingly admitted, and he had spent hours teaching her.

Aunt Cora adored the girl, who was always eager to sympathize with her complaints and who could be cajoled or browbeaten into pouring the old lady a glass of sherry when Rowanne's back was turned.

As for the young widow's relationship with Gabriel, Rowanne decided that even prickly hedgehogs must go about the thing with less roundaboutation. Anyone but the veriest looby could see the two were well suited, and they had not even progressed to a first-names basis.

Emonda was fascinated by Gabe's latest theories and did not seem to find his political friends' conversations tedious. She smiled and nodded and impressed all the old men, and one shy young one. Gabriel took time off from his new duties to show her Westminster and the Tower, with all its history.

"And he didn't have to refer to the guidebooks once," Emonda proclaimed with awe.

Rowanne wanted to shake the both of them. Otherwise Emonda was the perfect guest, except for her maid.

At first the girl Suky was declared too ill to wait on her mistress, so another abigail was assigned, to Emonda's almost stuttered appreciation. But no, Suky did not need a doctor; hers was a chronic condition. When a few days had passed and Mrs. Ligett reported that the girl never left her rooms and the other maids were grumbling about having to fetch Suky's meals up the stairs and wait on *her*, Rowanne decided she had better look into the matter, in case her sweet little peagoose of an aunt was being flummoxed.

She knocked on Emonda's door one evening after a family dinner and waited, impatiently tapping her fingers on the book she had brought along as an excuse. Not that she needed an excuse, she told herself, it was her house, and if anything untoward was going on she should know about it. She tapped again, and the door finally opened. Emonda was sitting by the chaise where the maid lay sprawled in her enveloping outfit, a damp towel over most of her face.

"I thought you might like this new book by Miss Austen, Emonda, but now that am I here, is there anything I can do to help?" She indicated the recumbent maid.

Emonda was scarlet-faced to the roots of her pale-blond hair, but she quickly denied any need for assistance.

"I really think we must have the doctor in, Emonda, just to relieve Mrs. Ligett. The other maids are wondering if there is some plague in the house."

"Oh no, you mustn't. That is, you mustn't go to so much bother. You have been too kind and Suky is . . . is just unhappy. That's it, she is not sick at all."

"Oh, the poor girl must be homesick. Don't you think we should send her back to Dorset?"

The maid groaned and Emonda hurried on: "But I need her company."

"But my dear, you have all of us now, and if the girl is so unhappy . . ."

"No, she cannot go back. If St. Dillon finds her—"

"He broke my heart" came a moan from under the towel.

"Yes, that's it, she is disappointed in love."

Good grief, Rowanne thought, was there no end to that man's villainy? Emonda had mentioned another love-child in her litany of St. Dillon's sins, and now he was seducing house-maids! Mrs. Ligett would have kittenfits if the girl was increasing, but Rowanne could not send her back to that libertine. "Don't worry, Emonda," she told her aunt, "I'll make sure that dreadful duke never has his way with her again."

"The duke? Have his way?" Emonda was sputtering, but the maid had fallen over in an hysterical weeping seizure that lasted until Emonda pinched the girl's arm.

"She'll be fine now," Emonda stated, "and this . . . indisposition should not last much longer."

Rowanne had her doubts, about nine months of them, but she left to have a few words with the housekeeper anyway.

* * *

A few days later Mrs. Ligett came into the sitting room where Rowanne was cutting up an old pair of thin kid gloves to cover tiny books. She had just begun to have more time for her own interests, now that Emonda was confident enough to go shopping with a maid or pay visits with Aunt Cora. This afternoon Rowanne had refused Gabriel's invitation to the ladies for a ride in his carriage, rare as such invitations were, so she might have this time to herself.

"It's that sorry I am to disturb you, Miss Wimberly, but you said to keep my eyes peeled, and that I have. It's the maid, miss. Our Jem caught her sneakin' down the back stairs, in her mistress's clothes no less, and carryin' a bandbox. If she's not up to something havey-cavey, I'll eat my best bonnet. Jem's got her in the kitchen. What should we do?"

When Rowanne got to the kitchen the maid was taking tea like a princess, the veil of Emonda's black hat pulled back just enough for her to wade through a plate of Cook's raspberry tarts set aside for tea. Rowanne dismissed Jem and the pot boy and the scullery maid and all the other servants gathered in expectation of a little excitement.

Taking a seat opposite the maid, Rowanne told her, "Your mistress isn't going to like this one bit, you know."

"And I am bloody well sick of it too," the girl said, removing the ugly bonnet to reveal shiny black curls and distinctively dark-rimmed blue eyes—and dimples.

For a moment Rowanne just stared, the tart in her hands falling back to the plate. The niece at school, of course. "Don't *any* of you Delversons have an ounce of decorum?" she finally managed to ask, which earned her a wide grin that was all too familiar, even after all those months.

"I told Emmy you were a great gun. And you must have met the Devils." A shadow crossed the lovely face, but she went on. "At any rate, my papa said we all grow into proper ladies and gentlemen in our dotage. My own brother is growing patriarchal at an early age."

"Then he does not seduce housemaids?"

The grin came back. "No, but he is a perfect beast."

"Don't tell me, he is trying to force you into marriage with a vile old man too, or else he's stealing your dowry. I wouldn't put anything past that scoundrel."

"Emmy is a trifle . . . highstrung," Suzannah said, as if that explained St. Dillon's baseness. "But it's nothing like that." Then she treated Rowanne to a highly entertaining tale of True Love being positively *fraught* with impediments and heartless guardians who refused to recognize *years* of devotion and the absolute *agony* of parting from her dearest Heywood. The farce at Drury Lane couldn't have done it better. Rowanne almost choked on her tart, trying not to laugh.

"But if your brother refuses to give you permission to marry until next year when you will be an old maid at eighteen, what do you hope to accomplish by coming to London?"

"I thought I could convince Woody to fly to Gretna Green with me." She took another bite as casually as if she'd just mentioned buying a new pair of gloves.

"Horrors, you really must be Carey Delverson's sister. Don't you know that would ruin you forever? The ton would never forgive such an escapade, and local society is even more straight-laced."

"That's what Woody says. His mother would be upset and she's ever so nice, but I didn't know what else to do." Tears started to fill those remarkable eyes.

Rowanne poured tea and offered a handkerchief. "Couldn't you wait? I am sure your brother only wants you to see more of life."

"But I want to see it with Woody," the girl wailed. "He says we can come back to London any time and do all the sights together and be ever so much gayer as a married couple. He's having a wonderful time now, while I sit upstairs reading."

"I have no answer to that, but you really cannot go abroad in London by yourself, even disguised as a maid. Your young man should not encourage you."

"Oh, he doesn't. Woody's petrified of my brother, you see. But I threatened to come to his rooms if he didn't meet me in the park, so he had no choice."

Rowanne almost began to feel sorry for the girl's guardian. She took a deep breath, wondering if she was doing the right thing. No, the right thing would be to tie the forward chit in the cellar and hire Bow Street Runners to guard her till either her brother came or she turned eighteen. But she liked the girl and saw no reason to worry over St. Dillon's approval, not since he had mismanaged the whole affair—and many others too numerous to bear.

"Very well, miss," she directed, "here is what we shall do. In one hour, your gentleman shall escort you, in a hackney, to the front door of Wimberly House. You have just returned from school and have come to visit your aunt, at my invitation. Your maid fell ill at the last posting house, but since you are nearly betrothed to Mr. Jeffers, no lasting harm was done. He shall call on you here and may escort you around, with a proper chaperone of course. If I hear one whisper, one inkling of indiscretion, however, I myself shall write to your brother. I am not the least petrified of him."

"You're not? I mean, you are a Trojan, Miss Wimberly!" She threw her arms around her hostess, laughing. "I shall never forget you! I'll be a regular pattern card, you'll see."

Rowanne had her doubts but she said, "My servants will forget Suky ever existed, but I'll have to tell my brother about you. He's the one St. Dillon will blame at any rate."

Suzannah put another spoonful of sugar in her cup. "Oh, no, Carey always knows it's my fault."

"Yes, dear, but this is London, and gentlemen here have odd notions. I am afraid Gabriel might think the honor of his house is at stake if your brother should, ah, cut up stiff."

"From Emmy's descriptions, Miss Wimberly, I know your brother to be a fine gentleman, but surely he's not one who . . . who . . ."

"Who seems ready for pistols for two and breakfast for one? You must have been peeping over the banisters, minx, but you are quite right, and that is why you must be on perfect behavior so we can squeak through. I am very fond of my brother, even if he is a mild-mannered scholar, while your brother, from what I am confusedly gathering, is a warrior-hero, a rake, a scoundrel, or a fool, possibly all of them at once."

It was on the tip of Suzannah's tongue to fly to her brother's defense. Carey was the most honorable man she knew, after her father of course, and Uncle Donald. He was the downiest, even General Wellesley said so, and the bravest. Suzannah's brother was perfection itself, a real out-and-outer according to Woody. He was just overprotective, stubborn, and blind to True Love's urgency. She could not say that to Miss Wimberly, naturally, not after she and Emmy had painted him the villain of the piece. Instead the girl reassured her rescuer that no one would be able to fault her behavior, not even Suzannah's black-hearted brother.

"By George, he is so mean he has clobbered dear Woody twice already, and Woody is ten years younger and half his size!"

Suzannah neglected to mention why, leading Miss Wimberly to worry if any of them would be safe when Carey Delverson came to Town, as come he must. Rowanne supposed she would be as safe as she'd ever been with him, which was to say not at all.

Chapter Eighteen

$\mathcal{R}$owanne felt cheated. She finally understood why the fans in the pit felt entitled to throw rotten fruit on the stage. The hero in every other romantic melodrama was dark and brooding or golden and godlike. Hers was a skinny youth with flaming red hair and ears that would make a jackrabbit blush. Heywood Jeffers just could not be anyone's *beau ideal*; he hardly shaved yet and his nose had a decided sideward tilt.

The nose, she was quickly informed by an enthusiastic Suzannah making the introductions, was thanks to St. Dillon, at whose name Woody's face lost all color, except for the freckles. The younster gallantly added that his prospective brother-in-law had the handiest pair of fives he'd ever seen.

Rowanne decided the boy's brainbox was too small to hold a grudge, and immediately concluded that, instead of the strong champion needed to keep Suzannah from her wilder excesses, she had another good-natured noddy on her hands—wearing baggy yellow Cossack trousers.

Emonda was tearfully thrilled that someone else was taking responsibility for Suzannah, and Aunt Cora declared she hadn't had this much fun in years. She beamed on the young lovers, together devouring a second batch of raspberry tarts, as the only sensible creatures in the house. "Nothing wrong with an early marriage. I like a gel that knows her own mind. What's that, Rowanne? Sad imps and immense whats? Don't mumble, girl."

"Admit impediments, Aunt. I was just recalling a sonnet."

"You'd do better to recall your age, missy. Look at the young'uns, gathering their rosebuds."

And all the raspberry tarts.

Gabriel could not understand how any gently nurtured female could be as hey-go-mad heedless as Suzannah, not with Emonda's delicate example. "And the chit chatters like a magpie. Really, Rowanne, do you have to fill the house with every stray female you come upon? And that . . . that school-boy. Doesn't he have rooms of his own?"

"Yes, but no cook. I am sorry, dear, that your peace is cut up with so many strangers and high spirits. Shall I pack them all up and send them back to Dorset? I'm sure Emonda would go if I expressed a wish to rusticate. Then you could have the house all to yourself again."

"No, no, wouldn't want to deprive the dear lady of her time in Town. Don't think of going during the Season, my dear, not with my maiden speech scheduled so soon." Gabe bit his tongue. What were a little peace and quiet, if he had more time with the delightful widow? What were one or two less rasp-berry tarts, even if they were his favorites and Cook made them just for him?

Rowanne decreed that Suzannah's first official public appearance, other than rides in the park, was to be at the opera at the end of the week, leaving just enough time for a month's worth of shopping. Rowanne's favorite dressmaker undertook the perfect dress, white satin, as befit such a young miss, but with an emerald-blue net overskirt strewn with pearls. Only shoes and gloves and a hairpiece and reticule remained to be purchased, along with day dresses suitable for half mourning, and boots, bonnets, parasols, and pelisses for warmer weather. Ailing Aunt Cora managed to pull herself off her sickbed for the spending orgy, so Rowanne was able to stay home the next afternoon, working on her miniature books.

She had a handful of real scaled-down books, including a Bible whose words could almost be made out with a magnifier, and a tiny edition of *Othello*, given out as a favor to commemorate a forgotten actor's benefit performance some thirty years before. These prizes rested on diminutive stands in the various rooms of the collection. She also had a tiny matched set of purple-bound volumes that an admirer had given her in her first year on the Town. She enjoyed the books far more than the admirer, who'd had the effrontery to write a dreadful poem to Rowanne's beauty inside each volume. The embarrassing works stayed on the bookcase in one of the miniature bedrooms. She still needed rows of books for the library room, hence her efforts with the leather and little blocks cut from her watercolor pad. Now she was adding gold leaf to the Lilliputian spines for a more realistic touch. Hating to stop even when the shopping expedition returned home, with Woody since it was nearly teatime, Rowanne called them into her workroom. She kept at lifting the hair-thin sheets of gold with a dampened brush and applying it to her new library, all the while enthusing over the purchases.

Aunt Cora took herself off for a much-deserved nap, and the others relaxed in the sunny parlor, considering whether a visit to Astley's Amphitheater would show disrespect for the recently departed of both families.

Rowanne was barely listening, concentrating now on transferring gold dust to the lightly glued surface of the top pages of the books, where they might be seen on the shelves. The job was not unlike sanding a letter, she considered, sprinkling the powdered dust, then shaking off the unattached glitter onto a clean sheet of paper. It was only infinitely more expensive. Two more books and she would ring for tea.

Then the butler came in with a card on a silver salver. "I cannot look at it now, Pitkin," she told him. "My hands are full. Who is calling?"

The august butler did not have to read the card; he had it memorized. "Harmon Carrisbrooke Delverson," he intoned, "His Grace, the Duke of St. Dillon."

Rowanne dropped the brush, the book, and the small jar, just as a cloud of gold dust rose around her when some fool suddenly opened the doors to the terrace, Woody having decided not to stay for tea after all. Suzannah looked to be following suit and Emonda could not choose between tears or a swoon.

"You stay right there," Rowanne ordered the younger girl, "and you, Emonda, get hold of yourself. He is not going to eat you." She sneezed. "You cannot leave me alone to face the ogre."

Neither of the others saw why not, and Suzannah saw an open door. "I'll be right outside listening. Please, please, Miss Wimberly, don't give me away!"

Emonda was too slow. Rowanne had an iron grip on her arm. "Show His Grace in, Pitkin."

"Gilding the lily, ma'am?" were his first words after a silence really too long to be polite.

God, she's still as beautiful, he thought, bowing over her hand, while Rowanne thought the duke looked much more vulnerably human than the soldier ever had. He was thinner, with fine lines at his face and a tired look to his eyes where she had used to see a mischievous glint. St. Dillon's hair was mussed and sprinkled with gray; his Bath superfine coat was too large for him. The Delverson dimples never showed, only one edge of Carey's lips quirking up when he saw the gold dust all over her, as if his mouth had forgotten how to smile.

"Not intentionally, I can assure you," she said, recalling she was hostess, not a portrait painter fixing his image in her mind for later study. "Welcome home, Your Grace, and welcome to Wimberly House. We were about to send for tea, but if you would prefer sherry or—" She led him to Emonda, who seemed to burrow deeper into the cushions of the sofa with each halting step he took closer to her.

Carey bowed to his stepaunt. "Nothing, ma'am, but I thank you, and I regret that once again I am an awkward guest. Would you mind terribly if I had a private word with Lady Clyme?"

"Not at all. If you'll excuse me."

Rowanne nodded and started to leave but Emonda squealed, "Don't leave me!" Then she turned to Carey and announced, "Miss Wimberly has stood my friend. She knows All."

"Then she knows more than I do," Carey muttered, but he nodded that Rowanne might stay if she wished.

She did wish, for curiosity's sake if none other, but going would have been hard in any case, with Emonda clinging to her arm like a barnacle, so she sat next to the pale girl on the sofa. Rowanne thought to wipe the gold off her cheeks with her handkerchief, but one glance at Emonda's quivering lip told her the lace-edged cloth would be better held in reserve.

Carey did not sit. He limped toward the shelves holding her collection and seemed to study the tiny objects there. When he spoke at last, just when Rowanne thought Emonda would go off in a faint after all, his words were surprisingly mild. "I suppose that I am sunk beneath reproach, Emmy, but do you think you might tell me why?"

"Why?" Emonda squeaked, nearly jumping out of her seat.

"Really, Emonda, what an impression Miss Wimberly must be getting. I have never beaten you yet. Not that I haven't been sorely tempted, but yes, my dear, dear Emonda, why?" His voice rose with each sentence, until he practically shouted: "Why the bloody hell couldn't you have stayed in Dorset for two more blasted weeks and looked after Suzannah as I asked you?"

Rowanne frowned at the nobleman's back and handed the scrap of linen over to Emonda. She clutched it like a lifeline and barely whispered, "You said you would . . . I was afraid that you might . . ."

He turned around slowly. "What kind of cockleheaded nonsense have you talked yourself into now? I said I would make other arrangements, open the London town house, hire a companion for the two of you or something. Hell and damnation, I should have hired a bloody keeper!"

"Carey, your language!" Emonda glanced fearfully at her hostess.

"Oh, Miss Wimberly won't wilt from a rough soldier's speech. She's got more bottom than that. And yes, Emonda, we have met before, three very memorable occasions to be exact. I only regret our fourth meeting is under these conditions, thanks to you and my stubborn, spoiled sister. I expected better of you, Emmy. I really thought you had grown into a sensible young lady."

He even sounded regretful, to Rowanne's ears. Emonda must have thought so too, for she tried to explain her precipitous departure from High Clyme. "That Mrs. Reardon came to call."

Carey sat down heavily, shaking his head. "But Emmy, Mrs. Reardon is a whore; you are a countess. Doesn't that tell you something? Doesn't it seem to you that you could have stuck your nose in the air and walked past her? Tarnation, Emonda, if she couldn't rattle you, she'd stop trying and we could have brushed through, instead of having our dirty linen hanging out for all of London to see. Devil take it, Emmy, I told you to tell her to go to hell."

Emonda sprang up from the sofa, tears pouring down her cheeks, her voice quavering on every word she managed to get out on her way across the room. "I cannot do things like that, Carey, and you always ask me! I cannot control your sister and I cannot face my friends knowing that . . . that what-you-said waves to me in church. In church, Carey!" She sobbed at the doorway. "And I cannot stand it when you yell at me just because I don't have b-b-bottom!"

And here Rowanne had been wondering how Emonda could turn down such a charming rogue.

Rowanne thought a glass of wine would be timely. Carey might need one too. He was staring at the gold head of his cane when she put the glass near his hand and said, "Very well done, my lord."

He grimaced, reaching for the wine. "I do have a fine light touch with your delicate fair sex, don't I?" He raised the glass to her in a toast. "My apologies again, Miss Wimberly. I am not always so cow-handed. Someday perhaps we shall meet without such high emotions."

But not today, Rowanne was sure, not after he found out about his sister. The longer she put off *that* discussion the better. She sipped her wine and smiled. "I wonder that you were surprised she ran away. Of course you are used to everyone obeying your every command, aren't you?"

"Do I detect a note of censure? I assure you my men never deserted under fire."

"Far be it from me to criticize, Your Grace. I'll just go fetch another dozen handkerchiefs or two, distill some rose water, perhaps burn a few feathers under her nose."

Carey ran his hands through his already disordered curls, then rubbed his injured leg. "Please forgive my wretched manners. Of course it is you who shall have to bear the brunt of Emonda's megrims, and I am in your debt for looking after the ninnies in the first place. I can only blame my heavy-handed treatment of Emmy on how frantic I have been to get here and make sure they were safe. They did not even take a maid, you know."

She knew better than he did, thank heavens. "I am certain you are also tired and aching from the drive and yesterday's rain," she stated matter-of-factly. "Perhaps you should find your bed and call again tomorrow. By then maybe Emonda will talk reason."

"And maybe pigs will fly. I'll stop cluttering your sitting room as soon as I have spoken with my sister."

"Ah, about your sister . . ."

He sat forward in his chair. "My word, she is here, isn't she?"

"What would you do if she is? Would you shout and send her flying to her room in tears?"

"No, I thought I'd have her burned at the stake. I begged my father to strangle the nuisance in her cradle. He should have listened."

"What if she is not here?"

"Then she's ruined." He stood slowly, with the aid of his cane. "You were my one and only hope. Now I'll have to track down that Jeffers whelp and shake her whereabouts out of him before I murder the poor beggar. A young cawker like him should not be hard to find in London. I simply have to inquire at every cockfight, horse race, and brawl, or check the dives where some ivory-tuner will be relieving him of his patrimony. People are bound to have noticed a carrot-top with a broken nose."

Rowanne ignored the more lurid promises of violence. "And when you find him?" she pressed.

"Then I suppose I shall have to let them get married. Set the puppy up as manager of Delmere, or call in some chits in the War Office and make some poor sod take him on as a secretary, if he can read. I don't care anymore, they can even live off her money. Lord knows I can spare more when they go through it. I just want my sister back!"

"You do?" cried a rushing swirl of draperies and sprigged muslin, hurling herself through the glass doors and into his arms. "Oh, Carey, you *do* care about me!"

The duke fell back in his chair, a lapful of radiant young female laughing and crying at the same time.

Rowanne had seen another facet of the duke, his own eyes suspiciously damp. Now she felt *de trop* and stood to leave the brother and sister alone.

"No, Miss Wimberly, you must stay." Carey's request was not quite a question. "I believe I have you to thank for this pretty little puss in her cropped curls and *à la mode* outfit."

"Do I detect a note of censure *there*?" she echoed. She would not crumble like Emonda under that icy stare. "Would you have preferred Gretna?"

"Touché," he acknowledged over Suzannah's giggles. He hugged her closer and tugged one of her black curls. "But what's to do, Suky? I would truly hate to see you wed so young. You could be having children when you are barely out of childhood yourself."

"Miss Wimberly says that an engaged lady has much more latitude than a debutante, and an affianced couple can spend a great amount of time together without lifting eyebrows."

"The inestimable Miss Wimberly! Will you wait a year, then, poppet, if we declare a formal betrothal?"

Suzannah almost cut off his air supply in her joy. "But you have to promise not to break Woody's nose again."

"Agreed. My future brother-in-law—Gads, Woody!—is safe as houses unless I find he is taking advantage." He spoke loudly enough to be heard by anyone out on the terrace. "In which case, he will not have to worry about his nose, his teeth, or his ability to propagate the human race."

"He won't! We won't! Oh, you are the best of good brothers," Suzannah shouted back on her way out the glass doors. "I told you he was, didn't I, Miss Wimberly?"

Well, no. Between Suzannah and Emonda, they had called Carey a heartless villain, an unfeeling brute, a vile seducer, and an unprincipled rake who wanted to marry the young widow. Now what was Rowanne to believe?

Chapter Nineteen

Rowanne's father had been with the Foreign Office. Surely some of his diplomacy must have rubbed off on her, that she could assemble her disparate group for a dinner party the following night. Then again, her mother's father had been a noted horse-trader.

"I still do not see why you had to invite that dirty dish to our table, Ro," her brother complained when she interrupted him in his study that evening. "He may be a duke now, and a war hero, but he is no gentleman."

"How could I not invite St. Dillon, Gabe, when it's an engagement dinner for his sister, who just happens to be staying with us? It is merely *en famille*, dear, to please Suzannah."

"If it's his sister, why isn't *he* throwing a dinner?" Gabe asked grumpily, tossing down his pen. Today there were no almond tarts left for his tea; for the second day in a row he had to make do with buttered fingers of toast. Furthermore, for the first time in his life, and at the worst time for his career, Gabriel was having difficulties concentrating on his work. He blamed it all on the intrusion into his life of that harum-scarum female Suzannah Delverson, and now her rackety brother.

"He will, dear, but he is a bachelor in mourning, and Delverson House is not yet in condition for guests. His Grace sent for the staff from Delmere in Dorset to come help, but until then he is putting up at Grillon's. He asked very nicely if we would mind entertaining Suzannah a bit longer, and naturally I told him no. It will not be for long."

"Good. Then he won't be making any improper proposals at my dinner table."

"No, for Emonda will likely leave with Suzannah."

That gave her brother pause. He polished his spectacles. "Hmph. We'll see about that. Lady Clyme belongs at Wimberly House, not some bachelor's barracks. In the meantime, Rowanne, I can tell you it's going to be deuced difficult being polite to a philanderer who sold his own aunt to a crotchety old man."

"You know, Gabe, you once accused me of condemning him without a fair hearing. Emonda tends to be the smallest bit oversensitive where St. Dillon is concerned."

"Lady Clyme's innocence and gentleness of spirit leave her unprepared for the attentions of a rake. She is everything that a lady should be."

Rowanne got up to leave. "Then we must show her that we are also everything polite, by extending our courtesies to her relations."

"Hmph." Gabe went back to his papers.

Emonda refused to attend the dinner if Lord St. Dillon was coming, Suzannah's engagement or no. "I'll stay in my room, then your numbers will be even: Woody, St. Dillon, and Lord Gabriel, you, Suzannah, and Lady Silber."

Rowanne pretended to consider the implications of an odd number. "No," she reflected out loud, "I think I must worry more for my brother's assuming that St. Dillon had offended you to such an extent you could not face him. I only pray that Gabe does not challenge His Grace to a duel. . . ."

Emonda gasped and pressed both hands to her cheeks. She would come.

"St. Dillon's a sinner? I know that, girl. I prayed for his soul just last night."

"No, Aunt Cora, he's coming to dinner."

Lady Silber lofted her parrot-beak of a nose and announced, "I shall not break bread with a profligate who goes around littering the countryside like a stray tom, and neither shall you.

"When are you going to have a care for your name, you cloth-head? Dallying with the likes of Carey Delverson won't get you an eligible *parti*, missy."

"Aunt Cora, I am not getting up a flirtation with the man, I am inviting him to dinner for his sister's sake."

Cora hadn't heard a word. "No, not even if he is as rich as Golden Ball and has to find a wife soon, he'll never make a good husband for you."

"Me?" Rowanne tried to laugh heartily. "Ha-ha. It's Emonda the duke wants. Ha." That was half-heartedly, the half that didn't feel a sharp pang at the idea of His Grace limping down the aisle with Emonda on his arm. Rowanne could not think the duke would be comfortable taking Emonda to wive, if she did not expire during the wedding service. Nor did their last dialogue seem loverlike. Rowanne had heard more affectionate conversation between Cook and a butcher with his thumb on the scales. Still, "The duke is liable to snabble Emonda right out from under Gabe's nose if you are not there. A practiced rake and all that."

"I daresay you are right. The chit is too sweet by half, and Toodles likes her too, but there's no getting around that she's got more hair than wit. And that brother of yours couldn't attach a female on his own if he sat in the glue pot. No, I'll have to come to your dinner, Rowanne. Pour me a cordial, will you, to make sure I'll have enough strength."

"It's not good for your heart, Aunt."

"What's that? Your part in it? Don't worry, girl, you're safe.

St. Dillon's high-flyers were always riper females than you'll ever be, and he'll never look in your direction, not if he's looking to marry a biddable girl like Emonda."

Ha.

Woody wanted to know what was for dinner, and Suzannah begged for champagne for the toasts. Rowanne had such a headache she thought she might cancel the whole thing.

And the subject of all this rumination? Leaning back in his soaking tub of hot water to ease his leg after spending the evening at White's, a cheroot in one hand, a brandy in the other, Carey, Lord St. Dillon, considered that life could be worse.

His sister's future was secure, even if it was not the future he would have chosen. No doubt those two would be as productive as rabbits, so Carey could even petition the courts to have Suzannah's first son succeed him if necessary. Hell, they wouldn't have to fly the ducal banner when Suzannah's brat was in residence; they could just let his ears flap in the breeze. And Emonda was actually welcomed to stay by Clyme and his sister.

Now there was a rare bit of luck, Carey reflected, lazily blowing smoke rings. His wayward wards had landed on the doorstep of the one gently bred young woman in all of London of whom he had fond memories.

Miss Wimberly was as lovely as he recalled, an appeal formed not just of her considerable quiet beauty but her intelligence and poise. He'd swear she was not given to high flights and fancies that could make a man's life a living hell, and she had a fortune of her own so there would be no question of cream-pot love. She had a sense of humor and varied interests. Carey had been fascinated by the collection of fragile little things that seemed to show so well Miss Wimberly's delicate touch and her good taste, beyond the elegance of her house and dress. More, she seemed to accept his handicap without looking on him with pity, or fussing over him with cushions and commiseration.

She had even graciously invited him to dinner, although he could sense her reluctance. Carey blew the smoke into the brandy snifter and watched it rise over the amber liquid. Devil take it, how the deuce was he going to sit through a dinner with Miss Wimberly, making social chit-chat? What he really wanted to do was throw her over his saddle bow, ride off into the night, and keep her captive with his kisses until she promised to marry him. He could practically taste her lips—no, not the brandy—as she met his passion with her own, agreeing to give up her glittering London life for marriage to a half-man, a rundown estate, and social calls from Mrs. Reardon. No, he acknowledged, taking another swallow, it would never work. He couldn't even sit a horse.

Nevertheless, it was an unbelievable stroke of good fortune finding Miss Wimberly still unwed while he was in need of a bride . . . even if she did look upon him as something that lived under a damp rock.

It was a very different gentleman who appeared at Wimberly House the next evening. The slightly seedy-looking ex-soldier had spent the day with his tailor, his banker, his superiors at the War Office, and various discreet individuals he set to making inquiries. He was now formally a civilian, wealthy beyond even his expectations, and every inch a duke. He wore black satin breeches and a black velvet coat stretched perfectly across his broad shoulders, tapering at his narrow waist where a white marcella waistcoat and white lawn shirt showed in pristine splendor. His neckcloth was tied just so, with a fine black pearl nestled in its precise folds. He carried a jeweled snuffbox, mostly to ensure the muscles of his hand did not tighten up with lack of use, and a silver cane with a quizzing glass mounted in the handle.

If looking back at a blue eye magnified twenty times did not scare Master Jeffers out of his striped pantaloons, nothing would. Woody tried to disappear into the wainscoting, as much as he could wearing a gold coat with padded shoulders, shirt collars so high they almost succeeding in camouflaging the ears and an orange waistcoat embroidered with goldfish and waterlilies.

Rowanne's lips twitched and she nearly applauded St.

Dillon's performance as an affected dandy. It was an act, wasn't it?

He was appreciative to Gabe for seeing to his ladies, and civil to Emonda, who snatched her hand back from his kiss and wiped it on her skirt.

Suzannah threw her arms around him again in her excitement, causing Carey to beg her, "Leave off, puss, the rig took long enough to get right. Rudd fussed so, I felt like a prize pig being readied for judging. Besides, I've brought you a gift." He reached into his pocket.

"What's that?" Aunt Cora wanted to know. "What's the mealymouthed coxcomb mumbling about, Rowanne?"

Rowanne tried to shush her aunt. "He is giving Suzannah an engagement present, pearls, I think."

"Prevent girls? The jackanapes is more of a fool than I thought. They ain't even shackled yet. 'Sides, that's an old wives' tale, how you can do anything to get sons instead of daughters. Just look at Prinny." Aunt Cora's voice was always loud enough for someone as deaf as herself to hear. Now it seemed as loud as the bishop's at St. George's on Sunday morning as she blared out: "Fellow must have been injured worse than we thought, if he's looking to his sister for the heirs."

Emonda shrieked and Suzannah giggled, but St. Dillon turned to Rowanne, who was sitting on the sofa next to Aunt Cora—and he winked. His eyes held the twinkle Rowanne had been missing in the urbane Exquisite in her drawing room and the careworn traveler of yesterday. She smiled back.

"My dear Lady Silber," he said, bowing outrageously in that lady's direction, "your concern for the continuance of my name, ah, unmans me. Rest assured, however, that while I may no longer take up sword in the country's defense, the proud house of St. Dillon shall ever be ready, willing . . . and able to answer the call."

Rowanne announced that dinner was served. Ten minutes early.

Dinner was not a total disaster. The food was good, when it got there. Rowanne had struggled with a seating chart for the small group in vain. There was simply no way to keep her one awkward guest apart from Gabe, Emonda, Woody, and Aunt Cora at the same time unless she seated the duke in the kitchen. Instead she put him in her usual seat, facing down the table to Gabriel. She placed herself to his right, Suzannah to his left, Emonda and Aunt Cora next to Gabe. Woody was on Suzannah's other side, where she could act as buffer in case the duke took exception to Woody's extravagant lace sleeves flowing in the turtle soup.

As the dinner progressed from sole in lobster sauce through roulade of beef and veal Florentine, conversation was general. That is, Suzannah chattered away about her sightseeing, Aunt Cora talked about weddings, and Woody ate his way through four courses and removes. Gabriel answered Rowanne's questions about the day's events in Parliament and St. Dillon answered her questions about news from the War Office. Emonda sat silently next to Gabe, pushing peas around on her plate and pleating her serviette. One would think they were serving poison, to look at the young widow. Rowanne almost wished they were, as Gabe grew more and more taciturn, seeing Emonda's distress, and Suzannah more loquacious with each glass of champagne. Rowanne was disgusted with all of them. She'd been hostessing brilliant dinners for years with scintillating conversation, gay repartee, informative discussions. This was not one of them.

Finally St. Dillon put a halt to Suzannah's prattle by nodding to a footman to take her glass away. He then gently asked Lady Silber to make a list of everything she deemed necessary for a proper wedding, for Heaven knew, neither he nor Suzannah had the least notion. Of course nothing need be done for a year, he told that lady, with Suzannah underage and the family still in mourning.

"Speaking of mourning," he casually went on, gesturing toward Emonda's gray gown, "I am surprised to see you still wearing widow's weeds."

Gabe was scowling even more ferociously, and Rowanne was wondering if she could suggest leaving the men to their port before dessert was served. It was chocolate mousse, her favorite, though, so she fixed a gay smile on her face and answered St. Dillon: "Oh, Emmy would be in black if we let her. She is everything that is proper. It is Gabe and I who bend the conventions. But I find black depressing, don't you know. And we never even met the earl."

She felt her leg kicked! Surely she did. She stared in amazement at Carey, but he was lounging back in his seat, still looking at Emonda. The widow's eyes were fixed on the ring her water glass had left on the table.

"Quite right," Carey told Rowanne, slurring his words as if he had had too much champagne also, although Rowanne knew he had not. He had barely touched the stuff except for the toast, and hardly ate enough to justify Cook's exertions, preparing all day for a wealthy, bachelor *dook*. "And your good fortune, never knowing the old curmudgeon. I'm surprised at Emonda, though, wearing the willow for that tough old bird I had to force her to marry. Kicking and screaming, she was. We even thought about pouring laudanum down her throat, but she agreed to behave if we didn't tie her up."

Woody's mouth was hanging open and Suzannah whispered, "Carey how can you?" Rowanne would have given anything to see the devil's eyes, but he was still staring at Emonda. "After a year or more I would have thought you'd be happy to see the last of the old nipcheese, now that you are free to spend some of his money at last. I suppose it's too much to hope you'd thank me for the favor I—"

Emonda had had enough. She threw her napkin, rather the worse for wear, on the table and shouted, "You know that is not the way it was! How dare you say one bad thing about Lord Clyme! He was the most wonderful, kind, and generous man there ever was in this whole world and I was proud to marry him. Suzannah can tell you how pretty the wedding was, even if we had to scramble through it so you could go back to your horrid war!"

Carey sat up straight, all traces of insobriety vanished. He nodded apologetically toward Rowanne, smiled gently at Emonda, and asked, "Then why is it that my host keeps looking at me like I sold you to white slavers and Lady Silber treats me like a leper?" He turned toward Gabriel. "Your uncle was a true gentleman, and I was honored to know him."

Gabe was red-faced when he turned to Emonda. "Is it true, my dear, that no one forced you to marry against your will, and my uncle treated you with respect?"

"He saved my good name," she whispered, "he and Carey. And then Lord Clyme treated me like a princess, like a best-loved daughter he never had." She looked at Rowanne, then back to Gabriel. "And you must never think he was a bitter old man who hated all of his relatives. He cared about you very much and made me reread all of your letters."

"But he never—" Rowanne started at the same time Gabe asked, "Then why . . . ?"

Emonda turned to Carey, who answered, "He loved your mother, but she chose your father over him. He was afraid that if he saw you, Miss Wimberly, looking so much like her, then his heart would break all over again."

"Oh, the poor man!" Then Suzannah and Woody had to tell how Lord Clyme was the most respected man in the county and loved by everyone, and Aunt Cora related what she knew about the old love story. Carey told about the portrait in the desk and about his father's friendship with the late earl. Soon it was a cheerful group at the table. The dinner was never going to be one of Rowanne's most brilliant, but it was a success. She wasn't tempted more than twice to throw the chocolate mousse in Carey's lap.

Chapter Twenty

So he was not an ogre. He was still a rake, and what a swath he would cut through the ton with his elegant new dignity and his romantic limp to remind the feather-headed chits of his heroism. They would be throwing themselves at his feet, Rowanne knew, positively smothering him with embarrassing adoration. To save the poor man that discomfort—he was Suzannah's stepbrother, after all—Rowanne made sure to invite him back to Wimberly House for tea and potluck supper, lest he be thrown to the wolves on an empty stomach. The man was too thin, she told herself.

She herself was not one of those impressionable misses, susceptible to a philanderer who coldbloodedly shopped for a wife while his mistresses popped up at inconvenient moments. Heavens, most gentlemen left their inamoratas with a parting gift, not a family. As used as she was to London morals, or lack thereof, Rowanne could not countenance such behavior, not in any man she would marry, should he ask her.

None of which stopped her from replying in the affirmative, however, when Carey asked if she would visit Delverson House in Park Lane with Emonda and Suzannah. The place had been let go so long, he complained, that he did not know where to start to make improvements and would appreciate their advice. He was staying on at the hotel until the place could be sanded, painted, and refurbished, but he begged the women's assistance in selecting colors, fabrics, and styles. Rowanne could not refuse, for Suzannah's sake.

Carey decided to make an occasion of the outing, repaying the Wimberlys' hospitality by hosting luncheon at his hotel, before they all went on to view the devastation. Aunt Cora cried off, having seen her fill of dirty old houses, but Gabriel accepted, just to make sure they were not mistaken about St. Dillon again, the fellow being as changeable as a chameleon. Woody went where Suzannah went, especially for meals.

The duke regretted that he could not even invite them for tea at the house, since the stove did not draw properly and the chimney man was not coming until the morrow. He did suggest Gunther's afterward, if they were not too tired. Luckily no one noticed that Rowanne's cheeks turned rosy, remembering the last time she and Carey Delverson had shared an ice.

Suzannah rattled on all through the meal about which style of home furnishings was more in favor in the ladies' magazines, the Egyptian or the Chinese.

"I think I prefer the Egyptian, with those cunning crocodile armchairs. They say Lady Poindexter has a real sarcophagus in her parlor! Doesn't that just make your scalp shiver, Woody? Can we get one, Carey?"

Woody looked up from his second helping of green goose and pigeon pie. He'd already had one unnerving experience that day, when he helped Suzannah out of the carriage. Lord St. Dillon was standing at the curb, frowning at Woody's new coat with its saucer-sized gold buttons. Perhaps Woody's hand had strayed a bit, but some dead pharaoh wrapped in sheets couldn't touch the duke for dampening a lad's ardor. Nearly put him off his appetite, it did.

Suzannah was off on another tangent. "The Chinese is very pretty too, with the silk hangings and lacquered cabinets and inlaid vases. We could have lots of colorful pillows on the floor for guests to sit on, and a huge brass gong, like Baroness Smythe's in the magazine's picture, with dragons all over it."

"On second thought, puss," Carey teased, "maybe you should stay back here instead of coming along to the house. When I asked for your advice, I meant color schemes, not settings for gothic romances. I don't fancy taking tea with a mummy or sitting on the floor or wondering if my chair is going to snap my arm off. I am sure Emonda will have better ideas for what's suitable for a gentleman's residence."

Suzannah stuck her tongue out at him, but Emonda blushed at his praise. They were never to know Lady Clyme's ideas, however, for when they arrived at the large house, set back on its property across from the park, a huge moth-eaten dog tore down the steps to greet them. Emonda refused to get out of the carriage.

"It's only Old Scratch, Emmy," Carey told her. "He won't bother you."

It was true, the scraggly mammoth canine had eyes only for St. Dillon, tearing around in an excess of joy until Carey was firmly on the ground, then jumping up to put his paws on the man's shoulders and give him a wet welcoming salute.

"Down, sir," Carey ordered before his leg gave out. He would have fallen to the dusty carriageway if Woody hadn't grabbed for his arm and steadied him. Woody blanched at his audacity—Jupiter, he'd actually touched the duke—then blushed furiously when Carey thanked him. "That was quick thinking, lad. Perhaps there's hope for you yet, if those starched shirtpoints don't rattle your brains."

Carey handed Rowanne out of the carriage and introduced her to the dog, who was now sitting decorously, wagging his tail and drooling happily. "He was my cousin's and he seems to have adopted me. I couldn't leave him in the country for he would simply pine away, according to the grooms, the house-keeper, and the gardener, all of whom were incidentally petri-fied of him. Did you know hotels won't accept dogs of his size?"

"Really? I wonder why." Rowanne was making friends with the shaggy beast, promising him Toodles for breakfast if he behaved. Not even seeing Rowanne shake hands with the creature could encourage Emonda out of the carriage, so Gabe nobly forbore viewing the house in order to keep her company in the coach.

"He never liked dogs much either," Rowanne confided to the others as they filed through carved oak doors under the St. Dillon crest, Scratch bounding in circles around them.

The huge entry hall was clean, at least. The staff had taken off the holland covers and started polishing. But the wooden banisters were splintered or wobbly, and the chandelier was missing many of its crystals. The portrait of some long-dead ancestor that hung in a niche between the double staircases had a gunshot hole through the forehead, and many of the black-and-white marble tiles had nicks and scratches. One appeared to have a hoofmark gouged in it. What furniture there was seemed to have survived from the Middle Ages, oversized dark trestle tables and massive carved chairs that looked as comfortable as a stocks. Rowanne wondered that Carey had disdained Suzannah's mummy, for two rusty, dented knights stood guard at the foot of the stairs.

Carey was correct: Beeswax and lemon oil were not going to set this place to rights.

Suzannah was thrilled with the double stairs, planning the engagement ball where she would come floating down the spiral to face the admiring throng below. "It's perfect, Carey! Can we have a grand fête when it's done? Is there a ballroom?

How many places can we set at the table?" She and Woody rushed off to explore for themselves.

"So much for my sister's advice. She'd leave the place as it is, most likely, only asking the staff to return the spider webs for better effect. Do you mind continuing? I really would appreciate your opinions. The repairs have to come first, naturally, but I should like to start ordering new hangings and such."

Rowanne was barely listening. They were alone. No, the dog was there, shedding brownish hair on her burgundy carriage dress. Her brother was just outside, the youngsters were dashing up the stairs, but she and the elegant duke were alone, and he wanted her . . . opinions. "Frog-bonnets!"

Carey was smiling at her. "Excuse me, is that another new fashion? I thought I might prefer maroon velvet. But come see the upstairs, if you will. I don't trust those two in the state bedrooms."

The rest of the house was in just as poor condition, and Suzannah and Woody quickly tired of dull inspection. They went outside to check the potentials of the grounds for al fresco entertaining.

By the time they had gone through most of the building and were back in one of the double-square drawing rooms, Rowanne's opinion of the departed cousins had slipped a notch. "How could anyone have treated a fine old home this way?"

"The stables are in excellent condition," Carey said in defense of what was indefensible. He was annoyed himself. "At least Harry had enough sense to roll up the Aubusson carpets and the Turkey runners and some of the tapestries before he turned the place into a kennel. Maybe he simply did not like them. Either way, there were a bunch stored in the attic. I've had them taken out for cleaning."

"Wonderful, that's your starting point. You decide which goes where, then select furnishings and colors to complement. I am familiar with a great many furniture manufacturers, from my days of haunting them for miniatures, and I am always poking around the fabric warehouses for new ideas. I would be glad to give you the names and whatever assistance I can. I have hundreds of suggestions as is, and I'm itching to hurry off and make lists for you."

"How kind of you. Do you really not mind?"

"Mind? Why, the place is one glorious dollhouse that I'd love to get my hands on to turn it into a showpiece. I'm a very managing female, you know. Of course I would never presume to make decisions for you, not knowing your tastes or habits."

He smiled and said, "I am sure I can trust your judgment," which pleased her far more than the flowery compliments she was so used to receiving from her beaux. She checked the condition of the curtains, chiding herself for being such a goosecap. He was *not* a beau.

St. Dillon casually inspected the carved acorn design on the drawing-room mantel. "It would take a great deal of your time, especially having to consult with me," he continued, as if that was not the purpose of the whole thing. Hell, he could have had his secretary hire a decorator and been done.

"That's no problem," she answered airily, picking up a chipped vase to see if it was worth repairing, as if she would not offer to refurbish a pigsty if it gave her the opportunity to spend more time in his company.

Carey touched the loving cup on the mantel, a trophy from some race or other. "I, ah, would not want your name to be bandied about Town, the gossips, you know."

He would not want their names linked, more like, she interpreted. He was carefully telling her not to get her hopes stirred; his intentions were honorable, just platonic. Rowanne set the vase down with a thud. Too ugly to bother. She waved aside his concern with as much nonchalance as she could muster. "I am beyond the age where such things are of paramount concern."

"Oh, yes, you are quite in your dotage." He laughed. It was a very nice laugh.

"It is not as if I would be calling on a bachelor," she went on quickly. "You are not even in residence, and a great deal of the decisions will be made at the warehouses or from lists at my home. I shall make sure to have Emonda or Suzannah along in any case, because they will need to consult about their choices too."

"I doubt you'll get much cooperation from Emonda, and Suzannah has already expressed her preference for the corner suite. Blue skies and golden cherubs." He shuddered. "Please do not consult *too* much with that minx."

Rowanne thought Emonda would like nothing better than to visit linen drapers and furniture showrooms, even if she could not be brought to put one foot inside the house if the dog remained. St. Dillon did not seem in the least surprised nor disappointed that Emonda showed no interest in her future home. Of course it had never been openly discussed, to Rowanne's knowledge, whether Emonda would actually move out of Wimberly House when Suzannah took up residence with her stepbrother. It was all very curious, and Rowanne had a great deal to think about, upholsterers being the least of it.

They did not particularly enjoy their ices at Gunther's. A baby kept crying. There were a great many children in the place, as it was a lovely day for an outing, and Rowanne thought nothing of the bawling toddler, sitting across the room with his nanny and a stunning woman with red-gold hair. Suzannah and Woody never noticed anything above the usual din, too busy planning their grand ball and enjoying their confections. Emonda developed a sick headache from the noise, though, and Gabriel hastened to escort her home. Carey simply let his ice melt in its dish. His leg must be bothering him from all the walking through the house, Rowanne thought, and now the crying was grating on his nerves, poor man. He must not even like children, she conjectured from the way he was scowling, and then tried to ignore her own keen disappointment in that fact. She hurried through her treat so they could leave shortly.

That evening a certain loose-tongued luncheon waiter at Grillon's was dismissed. "She said as 'ow she was 'is friend, she did," he whined to his mates at the Crown and Thistle. "If Oi 'ad a friend like that Prime Article, Oi'd not mind 'er askin' after me, not by 'alf. Thought Oi was doin' the nob a favor, Oi did." He spit on the floor. "Damned gentry. The Frenchies 'ad a point, they did."

Chapter Twenty-one

"*I* do not like it, Rowanne."

"Don't you, Gabe?" She was studying page seventeen of Ackermann's *Repository*, making note of a curio shelf that might hold the duke's growing collection of snuffboxes. "But you don't need a curio shelf. You don't have any collections beyond your books, thank goodness, or this house would be overrun, what with all of my accumulations."

"I am not speaking of furniture, Rowanne, and you well know it."

Rowanne looked up at her brother's unusually harsh tones. They were alone in the sitting room, the others having retired to their beds, and she thought he was content with his book by the fire. Her own eyes narrowed. "Do I? What exactly is it that you do not like, dear?"

"I don't like you living in that man's pocket, that's what. It's not seemly, your acting the errand boy for such a frippery fellow."

Rowanne turned another page, without looking at it. "But I am enjoying myself immensely." And she was, not just because she was getting to express her talents and tastes on a grand scale, but due to that very proximity to St. Dillon. The duke had excellent judgment, was decisive in his opinions, and vastly appreciative of her time and assistance. He seemed less tense and drawn, now that he was building a home for his family. She had even seen his dimples peeping out once or twice, to her delight, but she did not think Gabe would want to hear about *that* part of her enjoyment. "Surely my pleasure in helping St. Dillon counts for something, doesn't it?" she asked her brother. "And I thought you and he were getting along better now. You seemed to spend a great deal of time over your port after dinner, at any rate."

"I'm not denying he's interesting and intelligent. I was quite impressed, actually, when we talked about his taking his seat in the Lords. About time a St. Dillon did. He's got insight to the mess of the war supplies and munitions, and wants to make sure we do more for the returning veterans. Then he turns slippery as an eel and kites off with that young cawker Jeffers, to some auction at Tattersall's or a brutal exhibition of fisticuffs or a foolish curricle race where fortunes—and lives—are won or lost. No one should know better than he the cost of such frivolous pastimes."

"But he was used to being so active, so in the thick of things. Can you not understand his restlessness? Besides, I think he goes to some of the events just to watch out for Woody. You know what pitfalls a young man can find, alone in London without a steadying influence."

"But is he a steadying influence? You know his reputation, Rowanne. That's why I am concerned. The old tabbies will be lapping this up, you and the last Devil."

"And that devil take all gossip. I am not worried." She turned another page of her magazine to prove her point to Gabe, if not to herself. She was, in fact, midway between anxiety and panic. She could not give a tinker's damn for the gabblemongers linking their names, but what had her in the boughs was the thought of the gossip to come when Carey started looking over the crops of debutantes. Worse, and she believed it even more inevitable, would be the talk when he started squiring barques of frailty around Town. She did not know how she would live through his loving another woman, and she did not have the least idea of what to do about it. Maybe her scholarly brother would have an answer. "Do you think he will offer for Emonda again?"

Gabe swallowed wrong and started choking. Rowanne leapt up and pounded his back, sending his glasses flying across the room. That answered one of her questions.

"Emonda would make Delverson a fine wife," Gabe pronounced when he could see and speak again. Then he blushed, spoiling the solemn effect. "And I mean to see she don't."

"Then what are you waiting for? Why haven't you put it to the test?" Rowanne asked herself if she could possibly be so base as to promote a match between Gabe and Emonda just to have the pretty little widow out of Carey's way. No, she answered quite firmly, she merely thought that Emonda's retiring ways suited Gabriel much better. Gabe was still flustered by his own declaration, so she went on. "I think you would appreciate Lord St. Dillon's finer points a great deal better if you were not jealous."

"Jealous? Me? That's absurd."

As absurd as Rowanne being jealous of Emonda and every other woman in London, Somerset, and Spain. "Then why don't you offer?"

"It's too soon. We've known each other such a short time and we're in mourning. Furthermore she's living under my roof. That's not good ton."

"Would you rather she lived under St. Dillon's?"

"Heaven forbid. I mean, his sister is one thing, but he and Emmy aren't even closely related. Here at least Aunt Cora is in residence.

"So?"

Gabe grinned sheepishly. "I've been trying to decide if I have to ask St. Dillon's permission to pay my addresses. He'll either darken my daylights or laugh at me."

"He'll laugh," she said, her fingers crossed. "And rightly so, you looby. You may as well ask yourself, for you are head of the family. Then you can give yourself your blessing."

There was pleading in Gabe's brown eyes behind the thick lenses. "Then you think there is hope?"

"For you to become an impetuous, passion-maddened lover? None. But I wish you would try."

They set out for the park the next afternoon in high spirits, four women in their new spring gowns. Aunt Cora sat in the forward-facing seat with Emonda beside her, for Lady Clyme tended to queasiness if her back was to the horses. Aunt Cora's poodle sat between them, a silly bow in his topknot matching the lavender ruching of Aunt Cora's bonnet. Rowanne and Suzannah sat across, the latter twirling her fringed parasol in excited disregard for Rowanne's well-being, exclaiming over the notables on the fashionable promenade, the stylish ensembles, the high-bred horses. Rowanne smiled and moved farther along her seat.

Woody Jeffers rode alongside, showing off his new bay hack, the yellow turned-down cuffs of his high boots, and a boutonniere of yellow primroses as large as the nosegay Rowanne carried to her first ball. She could not decide which looked more absurd, the ginger-haired sprig of fashion or Toodles. At least Woody's mount appeared to be more substance than show, which Rowanne noted to Suzannah.

"Isn't he beautiful? The gelding, I mean, not Woody," Suzannah said with a giggle. "But Woody cannot take the credit. He was all set to buy a roan from Lord Arkwright, but Carey steered him off it because Arkwright crammed his horses, and its mouth was likely ruined. Woody says he's a real downy cove, my brother. Of course he dresses too soberly, but Woody says all of the fellows think he is top of the trees."

"Woody says" being Miss Delverson's favorite phrase, Rowanne all but ignored the animated description of Woody's horse that followed, until she heard Suzannah's next words: "Woody says it's a secret, but Carey bought himself a horse. He's going to try to ride again."

"Oh, dear," Emonda exclaimed. "That cannot be wise. He could be permanently crippled. He should not take such chances."

"Oh, pooh, you'd have him in a Bath chair next," Suzannah told her aunt, and Rowanne had to agree, although she also felt a stab of apprehension. Suzannah continued. "He must hate not being up and doing all the time, and Carey can do anything once he sets his mind to it."

"And there never was a Delverson yet with a ha'penny's worth of good sense," Aunt Cora put in, glaring at Suzannah. She had come down early for the carriage ride to find Suzannah and Woody seated at the pianoforte playing a duet, with the instrument closed up tight.

"But horses are so . . . large and unpredictable, Suzannah." Emonda drew her shawl tighter around her slim shoulders.

"Woody says that's why Carey bought a new mount. Everything in Harry's stables is too high-spirited by half, to start." Suzannah noted Rowanne's heightened interest in the riders on the bridle paths, to Rowanne's chagrin, and smiled knowingly. "Oh, he won't practice out in the park where you—ah, the crowds—could see him. Woody says Carey and his man Rudd will likely hire an indoor ring at one of the stables, with lots of sawdust on the ground, just in case."

The drives were more crowded and Woody had a difficult time staying abreast of their carriage. Ladies in coaches and gentlemen on horseback stopped to greet Rowanne and be introduced to her guests. The carriage was barely moving along in the press of traffic, so they decided to get down and stroll a bit, except for Aunt Cora, who had their driver pull alongside Lady Brierly's chaise in the shade for a comfortable coze. Woody tied his horse behind the carriage and proudly escorted his three pretty ladies down the less-traveled paths.

Woody and Suzannah were walking a bit ahead of Rowanne, Emonda, and Toodles, who had to stop at every bush, so Rowanne nearly bumped into them when the young couple paused suddenly and turned back along the path.

"Mustn't leave Lady Silber alone too long," Woody explained, while Suzannah claimed a twisted ankle, hopping artfully.

Rowanne could not see ahead beyond Woody, but Emonda could. "Oh, heavens," she cried, throwing her hands up to her cheeks and dropping the dog's leash as she too turned to hurry back to the carriage.

It was too late. Toodles was off, growling and grabbing a biscuit from the hands of a small dark-haired tot on leading strings. At the other end of the strings, Rowanne could see now, was the ravishing strawberry-blonde from Gunther's, and she was waving merrily.

"Why, if it isn't Lady Clyme," she called gaily, "and Miss Delverson too. And Mr. Jeffers, I would recognize you even in all your finery. Isn't it lovely to meet old friends from Dorset?"

Rowanne was bending down trying to sooth the screaming child, so she did not notice her companions' distress. Emonda was rooted to the spot and Woody's face was bright red. Suzannah knew they should turn and cut the woman dead, but there was Miss Wimberly, wiping the brat's eyes.

Clear blue eyes with a dark rim around them and black eyelashes and—Rowanne straightened to take a better look at the woman. She wore a burgundy muslin gown that concealed few of her lush charms, and the vivid color of her cheeks and lips could never be found in nature. Carey's mistress, for it could be no other, was just now effusively greeting her, without an introduction. "You must be Miss Wimberly. I have been hearing delightful things about you, my dear. So kind to put up Carey's relations, don't you know. You have already met my dearest boy Gareth. Gary, precious, make your little bow to the nice lady as Mama taught you."

Gareth bent on his stocky little legs, encased in burgundy velvet shorts to match his mother's outfit, and picked up a handful of pebbles, which he tossed at the dog.

"Vicious little beast," Suzannah muttered, grabbing the dog's leash as Toodles ran past.

Now Emonda might be too much of a mouse, and Suzannah and Woody simply not up to snuff, but Miss Wimberly had been on the Town for years and was every inch an earl's granddaughter. She well knew how to depress pretensions from vulgar, encroaching mushrooms. She nodded curtly, turned on her heel, gathered Suzannah and Emonda on either arm, and said, "I do not believe I have had the . . . pleasure, ma'am. Good day."

"Good show," Suzannah congratulated when they were out of earshot. "I swear I thought I would sink into the ground." Emonda was clutching her handkerchief to her mouth and Woody was still tongue-tied. Rowanne was simply too angry to speak, so when Aunt Cora wanted to know what they were doing back in the carriage so soon—she and Lady Brierly had hardly begun to discuss their ailments—Rowanne mumbled something under her breath.

"What's that," the old lady shouted, "a rabid wild boar? Here in the park?" which started a panicked exodus toward the gates.

"No, Aunt," Rowanne ground out, giving the driver the office to start. "A bastard child and a whore."

In the ancient parable of the three blind men and the elephant, each of the men had different bits of knowledge, different interpretations, and different conclusions. So too the members of Rowanne's party.

Emonda thought the child must belong to one of the Delverson cousins and did not care which. All she knew was that the scandal would horrify a fine upstanding gentleman like Gabriel Wimberly. With his hopes for a Cabinet position, Lord Clyme could not afford to let such filth touch his name. Emonda wept softly into her handkerchief.

Woody, who knew about as much of infants as he knew of mathematics, assumed the child was the elder Lord Delverson's, Carey and Suzannah's father. Everyone in the village knew who was keeping the high flyer when Mrs. Reardon moved to that little cottage. Woody's major concern was whether or not Carey St. Dillon would murder him for allowing the encounter. He wondered if Suzannah was still interested in an elopement.

Suzannah thought the child could well be her handsome brother's. No woman could resist him, naturally, and the boy did have the Delverson coloring, even if he seemed to be a bad-mannered crybaby, which Carey would never countenance. The meeting was unfortunate, but her invincible stepbrother would guarantee that it never happened again. The only difficulty Suzannah saw was the anger flashing from Miss Wimberly's brown eyes. Suzannah knew all about such things, of course—they were a part of her growing up—but Miss Wimberly must be more straitlaced than she'd thought to be so furious. Which was too bad, for Suzannah'd had such great hopes.

Aunt Cora hadn't seen the woman, hadn't seen the child. She only knew she wasn't going to get back to her comfortable life in Bath any time soon. "Devil take all men," she muttered.

Last but by no means least, Rowanne added, "Amen to that." How could she ever have hoped to compete with a stunning woman like Mrs. Reardon, who already had his child and his affection, if he brought her to London? How could she have been so stupid and naive and blind?

Like those other blind men and their elephant, the party returning to Wimberly House were agreed on one conclusion: Whatever else it was, the situation stank.

Chapter Twenty-two

"Dragons?"

"Yes, dragons. Your stepbrother can have fire-breathing dragons all over his bedroom, with blood in their eyes and gore dripping from their talons so he has nightmares every night. I do not care."

"Then you won't come down to tea and discuss the master suite with him?"

"He's here for tea? I hope the milk curdles and the tea is so hot it burns his tongue. I hope he chokes on Cook's macaroons. And what's to discuss? *I* am never likely to see the inside of his bedroom," Rowanne raged. "What should I care what colors he chooses? Purple and orange, magenta and puce, bilious yellow and mildew green, it's all the same to me. I would not put one foot in that libertine's house, and you can tell him for me, Suzannah. Why doesn't he stop being a cad and marry that woman? Then *she* can decorate his blasted house. Naked nymphs and satyrs should look lovely in the master bedroom, with red satin sheets."

"Miss Wimberly has the headache," reported Suzannah, ever the optimist. "She told us to go ahead without her."

Only Woody and Lord St. Dillon were in the sitting room when the butler brought the tea tray. Gabriel often missed tea if a session ran late. "But what about Emonda?" Carey wanted to know.

"Oh, she *definitely* has the headache."

Woody snorted.

"And Lady Silber?" Carey asked, curious that his sister would not look him in the eye and Woody kept edging his chair farther away. "Another headache? I don't even see the dog. Don't tell me Toodles has succumbed."

"Well, you know how Lady Silber is about her dog and proper company. . . ."

"No, I don't," he answered silkily. "Perhaps you might inform me."

Suzannah looked to Woody desperately. He came to her rescue by passing the macaroons. "Devilish good, Your Grace. Why don't you have some?"

Carey stood. "I would not feel right stopping in a house of illness, nor sitting in the parlor with neither host, hostess, nor member of the family present. Very bad ton. Come, Woody."

"Me too?" Woody squealed, his voice cracking in dismay.

"Of course. You don't wish to be guilty of bad manners, I am sure. Furthermore, without my presence you and Suzannah have no chaperone. Shall we?"

Suzannah hurriedly bundled some macaroons into a napkin for Woody, trying to hide a sniffle. "You will remember about tomorrow night, won't you, Carey? You promised to come to the opera with us for my very first visit there." Sniff. "I wanted everything to be perfect."

"I'll try, puss," Carey told her, picking up his cane, "if I do not develop a headache after my conversation with young Lochinvar here."

* * *

It was worse than a headache, a lot worse. "I'm really in the suds, aren't I, Woody?"

"Up to the eyeballs and sinking." Woody's tongue moved freer than usual when in the duke's presence, partly due to the French brandy St. Dillon ordered, partly due to Woody's excitement at finally being invited inside the portals of White's, even if the porter sneered at his spotted Belcher neckcloth. Besides, Woody could afford to condescend: The hero might have fists of iron, but he had feet of clay just like every other mortal man.

"I don't suppose you could have done anything to avoid the whole mess, could you?"

Woody came back to earth with a thud. "Me, sir? We were walking, like I said, and I tried to turn away, but the dog and Miss Wimberly and the screaming brat . . ."

"I didn't think so," Carey mused as if Woody had not spoken. "And after? There must have been something you could have done to ease the situation."

"I caught Lady Clyme when she started to swoon on the walk back to the carriage."

Carey poured them each another drink. "So I am back to being the barbarian at the gates of Wimberly House, just when things were going so well. Double damnation! I suppose courtesy dictates I should cry off tomorrow night's engagement so the ladies don't have migraines again, but deuce if I will."

Woody had had one brandy too many. "That's the ticket, Your Grace. You show those women they can't dictate morals to us men. I mean, a chap steps off the straight and narrow, you'd think it was a hanging offense."

The duke moved Woody's glass out of reach and eyed him coldly. "Jeffers, if I ever hear of your tomcatting, there won't be enough left of you to hang, is that understood?"

Woody understood the tone of voice and the intent. His Adam's apple bobbing, he swore eternal fidelity to his Suky. "True blue and honor bright."

"Good, then shall we order dinner?" Carey shook his head. Another foolish question.

* * *

Things could have been worse, Carey assumed, but he could not imagine how unless La Reardon had twins. Neither he nor his paid men had been able to locate the woman, and until he got rid of her, he knew, there would be no getting near Miss Wimberly. Rowanne would not even greet him the following evening when he called as arranged to escort the party to the opera. She floated down the stairs looking even more beautiful than ever in a gown of peach silk that clung to her graceful curves, with a garland of matching roses in her hair making her appear a woodland fairy princess. He burned with the heat of a Jamaican summer, and she was as cold as the Russian steppes.

Carey could not tell that she seethed inside, nor that she had spent all afternoon with potions and lotions and cucumber slices on her reddened eyes so she would look her best tonight, just to spite him. He only knew that his heart ached when she turned her back on him in the foyer of Wimberly House, pretending to give instructions to the butler as if Pitkin did not know to lock up after them or to leave a footman on duty.

The duke had also taken great pains with his appearance this evening, donning a shoulder-hugging midnight-blue swallowtail coat and skin-tight white satin knee breeches, with a tapestried waistcoat of blue and black stripes. He might have been invisible, for all the attention he received from the other operagoers. Emonda shrank away from his touch and Gabriel frowned at him. Lady Silber was busy telling Toodles to be a good doggie, mumsy would be home soon.

Only Suzannah welcomed Carey with any enthusiasm, showing off her new gown and the pearls he had given. Even she was more interested in the nosegay Woody handed her, a dainty little bouquet of white rosebuds and blue forget-me-nots that Carey'd had to remind the clunch to purchase.

This was absurd. Carey feared he would start prattling babytalk to Toodles if Rowanne continued to ignore him. When all the cloaks and wraps were fetched, therefore, and he spotted a maid with a peach satin cape matching Miss Wimberly's gown, he intercepted the girl. He carried the garment to Rowanne and softly said, "I am sorry."

She turned her back so he could place the cape around her

shoulders. Speaking low enough that no one else could hear, in the confusion of putting on shawls and buttoning gloves, she hissed, "Sorry for what, Your Grace? Sorry your mistress accosted me in the park in view of half the ton, or sorry you shall have to select your dining-room chairs for yourself?"

He lifted the brown curls that trailed down her back so they would lie outside the cape, feeling their silkiness run through his fingers. "I am sorry," he told her, "that my friends cannot have more faith in me." Then he leaned forward and gently kissed the back of her neck.

Rowanne spun around, her mouth open in an astonished *O*, her eyes wide. No one else saw how tenderly he adjusted the bow of the cape under her chin; no one else heard how sincerely he vowed, "I'll make things right."

Carey swore to do just that, track the woman down and get rid of her once and for all, even if he had to kidnap the jade and ship her to the colonies. By Jupiter, it was time and enough he got to enjoy being a civilian.

His luck held. Instead of spending another three or four days sending men to every haunt of the *belle monde* and the *demimonde*, or impatiently waiting for her next dunning letter, Carey found his quarry that very night. There she was, right in the box opposite theirs, waving at him so vigorously that the indecent neckline of her emerald-green gown was in grave danger of becoming her waistline. After the episode in the park, all eyes in the horseshoe theater were upon them, lorgnettes flashing in the glow from the crystal chandelier, the bucks in the pit calling rude encouragement. All eyes, that is, except Miss Wimberly's, which were staring determinedly at the stage. Rowanne had a faint smile on her mouth in enjoyment of the evening's entertainment, and her head nodded with the music. Unfortunately, the curtains were still down. The only performance was her own.

At the first intermission, with Suzannah nearly bouncing in her seat with excitement ("Did you see Giovanelli's swordplay? Who is that lady in the diamond tiara? Why must I not wave to Robin Westlake just because he is sitting in the pit?"),

Lord St. Dillon quietly excused himself. He walked out of their box and all across the back of the theater to the other side of the horseshoe, past knowing eyes and smirking lips, raised quizzing glasses, and raised eyebrows. It was a damnably long walk, for a man with a limp.

The door to Mrs. Reardon's box was ajar and he could hear laughter, both masculine and a high feminine trill. He cleared his throat and entered. Two Tulips scurried away instantly, lisping and bowing. One buck left a trifle more slowly, for his own pride's sake, but he left quickly enough after noting St. Dillon's set jaw and determined stance, arms crossed in front of his chest.

Mrs. Reardon laughed again, a high tinkling sound that grated on Carey's ears, and patted the seat next to her. "La, Your Grace, I have been expecting you."

Carey remained standing, somewhat in the shadows toward the rear of the box. He did not bow, nod, or salute her hand, a deliberate insult noted by the scores of watchers. Mrs. Reardon flushed slightly but laughed again. "You are looking very well, Your Grace. Are you enjoying the opera?"

"I am not here to flirt, ma'am. Why did you not tell me you were increasing?"

"Ah, a man who fences with the button off his foil."

"It would be wise to remember that I am a soldier, not a park saunterer who plays at deadly games. When I draw my sword, I have one purpose only." He leaned against the wall of the box, taking weight off his leg. This was not going to be a short interview. "I would have been even more generous, you know, if you had told me about the child."

Mrs. Reardon smiled for the spectators, then waved an ostrich feather fan coyly in front of her face. "Yes, I believe you would have been, but I had other plans at the time. Unfortunately . . ."

"You thought you'd get Harry to marry you?" Carey forgot where he was for a moment and threw his head back and laughed, adding to the speculation from the nearby boxes. "My cousin was a loose screw, Mrs. Reardon, but he would never have brought home a harlot's son."

Her mouth puckered in ill humor behind the fan. "Did you come here to insult me?"

"Would that get rid of you? We both know different. What do you want?"

"You carry bluntness too far, sirrah. But very well, I shall place my cards on the table also. I want my son Gareth named as your legal heir."

Carey raised his hand to the scar along his jawbone, considering. "Why? So you can take out post-obit loans on me?" He took note of the increased tempo of the fan's waving. "Somehow I doubt I would live long enough to sire a legitimate successor."

"Gareth could be," she protested. "I have proof—"

"No, if you had proof of marriage lines or even promises of Harry's intent, you would have laid them at my door long ago. You are no threat, ma'am, you are just a nuisance." He looked across the theater. "Admittedly an inconvenient and awkward one."

He came out of the shadows then and a few steps closer, so he could speak even more softly. "Whoever is behind your plan, Mrs. Reardon—and I have my suspicions—has been giving you bad advice. I *can* declare the boy my heir, and my ward. I can legally adopt the child, after I have you declared an unfit mother. I cannot think your fond heart will be broken, for I'd wager it's not mother's milk flowing through your greedy veins, but I could make it so you never saw the boy again. Or a dime of the St. Dillon fortune."

"You cannot do that!" she snapped.

"Oh, no? There are certain privileges to being a duke, but of course you knew that, didn't you? I would naturally insure the future of the estate by tying it up so tightly that you could never see a groat whether I lived or died. Especially if I died. Every banker and barrister I know would be trustee, and I would see that reliable men like the Earl of Clyme stood as guardian to the boy. You know how starched up he is; I cannot think you'd have greater luck with him. Now what say you, madam?"

"I say you are a cold-hearted bastard and a—"

"Ah yes, the nuisance value." Carey brushed off his coat

sleeve. "Shall we say a hundred pounds quarterly, for the boy's education and upkeep? Of course, that is provided neither you nor the brat are ever in my vicinity again, or that of my family and friends. The moment I hear of you or from you, the payments stop. Is that clear? You may send your address to my secretary for the first check."

He turned to go but the woman's screeching words stopped him in his tracks: "May you rot in hell, you arrogant bastard. You are offering us hundreds when the Delversons have thousands upon thousands!"

He bowed. "Ah, madam, but there's the point. The boy is *not* a Delverson."

Chapter Twenty-three

It felt good to be riding again. No, Carey admitted to himself, that was a lie. It hurt like hell to be in the saddle. But as it also hurt to walk, to sit, to clamber in and out of carriages, he might as well hurt while doing something he enjoyed. There were few respectable pastimes he could think of that would be more enjoyable than this: an hour or two on a beautiful crisp spring day, with the air smelling clean and the skies a clear blue, sitting a horse that was perhaps more well mannered than well favored but dependable for all that, and a lovely, gracious, *trusting* woman riding by his side.

He had come back to their box after the intermission just as the lights were dimmed and the curtains rose. He took his seat next to Rowanne and, in the cover of darkness, squeezed her hand.

Silent communication could say so much: the tingle of the touch, spreading from her gloved hand to the depths of her very being, the confident strength she felt in his grasp, gentled for her comfort and protection. And it could say so little.

That woman was gone from her box at the next intermission.

When Carey drew Rowanne aside after the return to Wimberly House, therefore, and quietly asked if they might ride in the morning, she said yes. She had to know what that touch meant, if it meant anything to him at all.

Emonda never rode and Aunt Cora never stirred before noon in Town. Suzannah would sleep in this morning too, after her dazzling evening, with supper after the opera at a private room in the Clarendon. It was Woody's treat, with St. Dillon's backing, and Jeffers made a great show of presenting Suzannah with the diamond engagement ring she'd spent days selecting. Champagne toasts and *flambé* desserts capped the occasion, with even Emonda smiling at the young couple's joy. Aunt Cora fell asleep after the second course and the third toast, and had to be woken for the ride home. "What's that about a dying king? Old Mad George gone at last?" which sent the hotel manager rushing to order black crepe for the windows.

So brother and sister breakfasted alone. Seeing no reason to brangle over the kippers, Rowanne never mentioned her morning's escort when Gabe looked up from his newspapers and noted her riding habit. It was her new one, fawn-colored velvet with gold buttons and a single gold feather in the matching hat. Gabe went back to his papers, idly reminding her to take her groom and enjoy herself. She thought she just might.

John Groom was small and wiry, an ex-jockey. He followed closely behind on the way to the park, where delivery drays and business traffic could have upset the high-bred horses. Once in the park he dropped discreetly back. Just as discreetly Rowanne observed the duke, to make sure he was managing the ride. He looked so at ease on his horse, in his tight buckskins and with the most carefree expression she had seen on his face since his return, that for a moment Rowanne let her own reins go slack. She then had to regain control of her cavorting mare like a rank amateur. Carey suggested a run to shake the fidgets out of the horses while the park was still thin of riders, and they set off at a gallop down one of the paths leading to the water.

Breathless, with her cheeks flushed and her hair coming undone, Rowanne was happy to agree to dismounting by the low stone benches along the water's edge, where a family of ducks was quickly lining up in case they'd brought crumbs. Carey lifted her off the mare, his hands firm at her waist, and John led the horses over to a nearby stand of trees.

"Shall we sit?" Carey asked.

Somehow Rowanne's tongue was stuck to her teeth so she just nodded. Then her legs went pudding-kneed and she would have stumbled except for his hand still on her waist, which was causing the problems in the first place. She did manage to sit on the backless bench without tripping over her skirts or blurting out some inanity like "I wish you would take your hand away because I like it too much." She fussed with a wayward curl and a hairpin, trying to regain her composure.

Carey seemed to be having his own difficulties. He knew what he wanted to say, had rehearsed it since dawn. With her there next to him, though, he forgot everything, his speech, his manners, his name. He just stared at her. He knew in his heart that Rowanne was not the prettiest female he'd ever seen, but guineas to goose feathers, she was beautiful to him! He longed to run his fingers through that silky hair she was repinning, to say nothing of how his hands ached when her raised arms stretched the fabric of her habit across her breasts. Her eyes were pansy-bright today, with gold flickers reflecting the sunlight off the water, and her smooth creamy cheeks were brushed by a fresh glow and that one silly golden feather. Damn, he thought, he just had to get hold of himself.

And Drat, Rowanne thought, more silent communication.

They both started talking at once: "About last night . . ." and "Did the carpenters . . . ?" when *Boom*, a pistol was fired and a ball whistled past Carey's head.

Before Rowanne recognized the noise for a gunshot, she found herself off the bench, on her back, in the dusty ground, with Carey half on top of her. "Shh," he whispered, when she would have squawked. She heard a horse being ridden hard—

354

away, not to their rescue—and could make out John shouting to their own frightened, plunging mounts.

Rowanne would have struggled to her feet but for Carey's weight. "Stay," he ordered. "There may be others." He was listening carefully and peering around the bench.

"Someone tried to kill you!" she whispered hoarsely, shock giving way to reason.

"No, I think not. We were sitting pigeons; he could have done the job easily. I think this was just meant as a reminder of my mortality. I thought I had taken care of that business last night, unless . . ." He did not finish, all too aware of his position—and Miss Wimberly's. He looked down at Rowanne, just inches away, and grinned.

She was outraged. "You're enjoying this! Someone tries to murder you in broad daylight and you can laugh! I shall never understand you, Carey Delverson."

He was still smiling, an impish gleam in his eyes. "I don't like being used for target practice any more than the next fellow, sweetheart. I'm laughing because I've still got the devil's own luck. I live through the Peninsula only to get shot at in Hyde Park. Then I end up not only alive and unwounded, but right where I have wanted to be for two lifetimes. Maybe three."

In the park? In the dirt? On top of—Rowanne gasped, which Carey felt through the layers of clothing between them. Before she could protest he bent his head and pressed his lips to hers in a moment so sweet, so tender, yet so stirring that the earth moved. No, that was the pounding of the horses' hooves as John ran them over to the bench.

"Miss Wimberly?" he called. "Your Grace? Be ye all right? Should I get the Watch?"

Carey helped her up, helped brush off her habit. "No, John, I doubt there is anything the Watch could do. The marksman is long gone. Did you see anyone?"

"No, milord, that sorry I am, but the horses was carrying on so, I couldn't do more'n see what direction he took."

"That's all right, John," Rowanne told the small man, who was looking as if he blamed himself for the whole thing. "There was no harm done and the horses did not run away."

355

St. Dillon glanced back at the trees. "Perhaps it was just some squire up from the country, coming home at dawn and mistaking our ducks for partridges."

Rowanne snorted and John scratched his head. "I don't know about that, Your Grace. I think the authorities had ought to be informed. A body should be safe here in the park."

"I doubt there will be any more such incidents, John, so I see no reason to cause a ruckus, do you?"

The look Carey gave the little groom had quailed whole regiments. John shook his head. "No, Your Grace."

"Good. I think we will give out that I had trouble with my horse, the blasted leg, don't you know. Not to fault your riding, my dear Miss Wimberly, but in your effort to come to my aid you dismounted a trifle precipitously. That should explain your, ah, dusty look and take care of any conjecture."

Rowanne had to agree. "Heavens, if Emonda heard about the gunshot she'd have the vapors for a week." And if Gabe heard about the kiss, he'd be issuing a challenge.

Carey looked from the groom to the lady, recombed now and remounted. "John, I am trusting you to keep a watch on your mistress. Rowanne, would you make sure Suzannah does not go off by herself? I do not think there could be a threat to either of you, but just be extra careful."

"And what about you?" Rowanne demanded. "If you won't go to the authorities, what will you do?"

He smiled, showing those roguish dimples. "Are you worried, Miss Wimberly? Don't be. I'll just have a talk with whomever is behind this, and then you and I can continue our own conversation." He winked. "Right where we left off."

Rowanne had to be content with that because St. Dillon would not reveal his suspicions. On the ride home John stayed so close she had no chance to quiz Carey about his intentions, or which conversation he meant to take up again. At the door, when John led Rowanne's horse away and a boy came to hold St. Dillon's, he only told her, "We'll talk more when this hobble is done. I am just an old-fashioned warrior who cannot wage two campaigns at once." He took her arm, removed her dirt-soiled glove, and kissed the palm of her hand. Smiling broadly, he declared, "And I intend to win both."

Before going upstairs to change, Rowanne went through the house to the kitchen door and out to the mews, where John was rubbing down the horses. The ex-jockey scratched his head when he heard what she wanted, then nodded and called one of the stable boys to finish with the mare.

John nodded again when she left. So that's the way of it, he chuckled to himself, hurrying to the kitchen to up his wager with that stick Pitkin, who never could pick a winner.

On her way back Rowanne passed Emonda in the hall. There was Rowanne in all her dirt, her hair straggling down her back, the feather on her hat sadly broken, and Emonda cordially inquired, "Did you have a pleasant ride? That's nice," before drifting off down the hall in a blissful haze. Rowanne's suspicions were confirmed when Pitkin disclosed that Lord Clyme had left for Whitehall much later than usual, after partaking of a second breakfast with Lady Clyme.

Nodcocks and ninnyhammers, both of them, Rowanne decided as she finally reclined in her bath. Gabe and Emonda were obviously besotted with each other, and must have come to some kind of private understanding at last. Of course neither would mention it until the proper moment, as if propriety had anything to do with love or affection or that delicious feeling that made one's bones turn into *blanc mange* and one's mind into butter. She must be hungry.

Rowanne stepped out of the bath and sat by the fire to dry her hair, sipping cocoa and nibbling on a sweet roll. She felt warm and glowing, and neither the fire nor the bath was responsible. At least one thing was clear now: All those practice kisses were for naught. All the experiments with young men, old men, practiced flirts, and green boys, all had been doomed from the start. She was never going to find a kiss to match Carey Delverson's, not that stolen moment of tenderness at Hillary Worthington's ball, not the sudden rush of passion this morning in the dirt. It was the man, not the kiss, who stirred her. Only Carey Delverson could make her wonder whether she walked on water or drowned. Of course. She knew that.

Rowanne smiled, a chocolate mustache on her lips, dreamily thinking of the wonder of it all, the magic that St. Dillon wrought.

If he lived.

John's report the next day was distressing. John's condition was dismal. The small man had a split lip and a blackened eye and a broken rib.

"John, are you all right? No, I can see you are not. Shall I call for the doctor? John, what about His Grace . . . ?"

"Don't fatch yourself, Miss Wimberly, the duke never got into the rowdy-dow. A fine set-to it was too, I can tell you. Why, I whopped that vermin something fierce. He'll never hang around outside Lord St. Dillon's house again, I swan."

"You mean there really was someone following his lordship and you caught him? Good man!"

John scratched his head. "Well, it was more like he caught me. Wanted to know what *I* was doing thereabouts. So one thing led to another, and here I be, but the gallows-bait is in no better shape, my lady. Why, I clobbered that one-legged son of a—"

"One-legged?"

"Yes'm. Broke my rib with his wooden limb, he did, when I was down. But I got up again, Miss Wimberly, you'd be that proud, and made kindling out of the blasted stump. Old Cyclops picked up a tree branch but I tipped him a leveler, I did."

"Cyclops?"

"And uglier nor an alley cat from Hell with that patch over one eye. Don't worry, he won't be bothering His Grace none for many a day."

Nor shaving him, nor laying out his clothes nor looking after him like a mother hen. Poor Rudd.

Poor John. His life was likely worth less than a brass farthing. "I think you deserve a vacation, John, so you can recuperate, a paid vacation of course. I know you have not seen your mother in the country since last Christmas. Are you well enough to leave soon? Tonight?"

John nodded. "That's right generous of you, Miss Wimberly. But what about the duke?"

Poor Rowanne.

Chapter Twenty-four

To flee was the act of a coward. To remain, to explain to Lord St. Dillon that yes, she was a managing female and yes, she had been meddling where she had no business, that no, she did not trust him to have proper concern for his well-being—and why his well-being should possibly matter to her—would have been the act of a hero. Or a fool. She fled.

"I thought we were to meet Carey at the house to look over wallpaper patterns this afternoon," Suzannah reminded.

"We were, but I forgot I had promised Lady Quinton that I would stop in at her literary salon today. She used to be my governess, then my companion, and I would hate to disappoint her. I believe she is having a Herr Doktor Wurthemburger come to discuss his paper on the new science of phrenology. That's where a person's character is determined from the lumps on his head. I was sorry to have missed last week's lecture by a Cambridge professor who spoke on the music of the spheres in Shakespeare's dramas. Should you like to accompany me, Emonda? I know you do not like to visit Delverson House."

Suzannah hid a chuckle behind her hand while Emonda fluttered. "Oh, dear me, no, ah, that is, I have another engagement. I, ah, promised Gabe, oh my, Lord Clyme, to listen to the first draft of his speech."

The silly widgeon was scarlet to the roots of her hair so Rowanne took pity on her and turned to invite her aunt. Lady Silber had discovered Suzannah's gothic romances from Hatchard's and was ensconced in a comfortable chair by the fire, Toodles on her lap, a box of bonbons on the table by her side. "Germs on tits? I should think not! What is this world coming— Oh, a German scientist, why didn't you say so?" She went back to her book.

Rowanne straightened her bonnet, a very fetching affair with silk buttercups sewn to the brim and a yellow bow tied at her cheek. It really was a shame to waste such a confection on a bunch of bluestockings, but safer in the long run. Perhaps Lady Quinton would invite her to stay for dinner.

"You really do not need me to pick the wallpaper, Suzannah, dear," she said on her way out, "just take your maid and avoid cabbage roses."

Emonda wandered off in her rosy haze to plan the perfect ensemble for hearing a speech, and Lady Silber was drowsing over the book, so Suzannah was thoroughly bored when the letter came.

Pitkin brought her the note on his salver, his wrinkled nose expressing disapproval of Very Young Ladies receiving private communication. Suzannah twirled her engagement ring as she removed the folded sheet. If the tiny diamond did not blind him, her blasé yawn should prove her worldliness.

The message on the white sheet read: *Dearest, we must meet. Green Park, south gate, in an hour. Please don't fail me. Yr. devoted servant, Heywood.*

Suzannah clapped her hands in excitement. The letter was certainly not from Woody; he couldn't spell that well. He would never call her dearest, never sign his name Heywood, and he would never, ever tempt Carey's wrath by meeting her privately. He knew she would never go either, not after giving her word. Therefore the message had to be a ruse to involve her in whatever it was Carey and Miss Wimberly and that strange battered little groom weren't revealing. Good, then she could go.

She'd do it for Carey's sake. He really was bang up to the mark and deserved better than another scandal to give Miss Wimberly a disgust of him.

Complimenting herself on her foresight and good sense, Suzannah collected all of her pin money in case she needed to pay off some extortionist, a hooded cloak so she would not be recognized, and a heavy paperweight to stuff in her reticule as a weapon. She did not even think of having such a glorious adventure without her best friend, so she took the time to send a footman round to Woody's rooms with a note telling him where to meet her. Of course, in typical Delverson fashion, she did not wait to see if Woody got the message. She just made sure that no one could accuse her of impetuous or clandestine behavior by nudging Lady Silber awake enough to tell the old lady she and Woody would be going to Green Park.

"Wed in Gretna Green on a lark? And you just let her go, Emmy? I don't believe it!" Carey was furious. Aside from his valet being battered and his agents still failing to locate a certain address, he had been waiting half the day for Rowanne to show up at the house, and now this! He had to believe it, though, when Suzannah's maid returned with Woody's note. "I'll shred him to pulp. I'll grind him to sawdust. I'll—"

The trembling maid also delivered the information that Miss Delverson had taken all of her money, a heavy cloak, and, peculiarly, a glass paperweight, the one with the winter scene that you could turn upside down and make snow.

"Damn, my father gave her that. She's not coming back." He struck his cane against a chair and the maid fled without being dismissed. "She gave her word," he thundered, "and I believed her."

Lord St. Dillon had sticking plaster on his chin where he had cut himself shaving, dog footprints on his coat, and new gray hairs for him to run his hands through in outrage and anxiety. "Fiend take all women. How could you have let this happen, Emmy?"

Emonda squeaked that it had been Lady Silber who took the message. That lady was passed out in her chair from the Madeira she had consumed, for her nerves. The dog was eating the bonbons. Emonda had been resting, she told him, and Miss Wimberly was at a literary salon, to which he muttered "Pudding heart." Emonda took this last to mean herself and started weeping all the more.

"Will you cease that infernal whimpering, Emmy? I have to think." He stomped around the sitting room, downing the remains of Aunt Cora's glass and idly taking one of the sweets. Even Toodles knew better than to growl at the irate nobleman.

"They cannot have been gone long," he finally declared. "We'll have to go after them."

"We will?"

"We cannot let our family bring any more disgrace to Miss Wimberly. She was sponsoring Suzannah; the scandal will be laid at her door. Get your cloak, Emmy. You have to come along to say you were with Suzannah and Woody the whole time. There cannot be that many posting houses on the North Road and no one could forget Woody's hair, so we ought to be able to track them down before dark. I'll need you to hold the horses since I don't even have Rudd. I don't want to take any other servants to add to the gossip."

Now Emonda would rather have gone to Hell in a handcart. Delverson on one of his good days—and this was assuredly not one of them—but whatever scandal fell on Miss Wimberly would also shadow her brother. Lord Clyme's speech, his whole political career could be in jeopardy. For Gabriel she would even—if she did not faint—hold the horses.

Rowanne decided not to stay at Lady Quinton's for dinner after all, not when the sausage-fingered savant expressed particular interest in examining *Fraulein* Wimberly's hollows and extrusions. She arrived back in Grosvenor Square in time to find Woody arguing on the doorstep with Pitkin.

"High-britches over here wouldn't let me in, Miss Wimberly. Says no one is receiving. I say, Suzannah ain't with you, is she?"

"Why, no, I thought she was going to look at wallpaper with you." Rowanne untied her bonnet strings.

"I was a bit late getting to the house. Carey—he said I may call him Carey," the boy put in with pride, "had sent me to his own tailor. Devilish long time it took, fittings and all. When I got to the house, Suzannah wasn't there. St. Dillon's man Rudd said she'd never been, and Carey had gone off in a pet. 'Pon rep, you don't think the duke would maul his own valet, do you? Rudd wouldn't say."

Rowanne said a silent prayer and handed her bonnet and gloves to the butler, who was desperately trying to get her attention about something. "What is it, Pitkin? Woody is practically family, you can say whatever you think I should know."

"It's Lady Silber, Miss Wimberly, she's carrying on something fierce. She claims the Duke of St. Dillon has run off to Gretna Green with Lady Clyme."

On second thought, Rowanne wished Pitkin had kept his information to himself. She felt all the blood suddenly drain from her head and wondered if she was going to swoon for the first time in her life. But Woody was accusing the prickly butler of checking the wine cellars once too often, and Pitkin was adding that Lady Silber suspected the duke of poisoning the dog too, so Rowanne decided to get the facts straight, *then* have the vapors.

Aunt Cora was moaning and Toodles was writhing on the floor at her feet. Rowanne took one look at the empty box of sweets and ordered Pitkin to take the dog outside, quickly, for the sake of the carpets.

"Now, Aunt, what is this about Lord St. Dillon and Emonda?"

"What I'd like to know," Woody put in, "is where's Suzannah?"

"You!" Aunt Cora looked with loathing at Woody and immediately threw her book at him. "You are the cause of this whole hubbub, you hot-blooded young jackanapes. If you'd been thinking with what the good Lord put in your head instead of what He put in your pants, we wouldn't be in this coil!"

"But where's Suzannah?" repeated Woody, easily catching the book, although a letter fell out of it to the floor at his feet. "What!" he exclaimed when he picked up the page and glanced at it. "I never—"

Rowanne snatched it from him and read it quickly. The letter may or may not have had anything to do with Emonda and Carey's flight to Scotland, but it obviously took priority, especially after the gunshot in the park yesterday. Rowanne decided against giving Woody that news; he was pale enough as is, freckles standing out like raisins in gruel. "Buck up,

Woody, we'll find her. She can't have gone very far, even if there has been an abduction, and we know where to start."

Rowanne ordered up Gabe's curricle because it was faster than her chaise and needed less attendants. The fewer servants who could carry tales the better. If only she hadn't sent John on that fool's errand, but no use crying over spilled milk, or blood. Rowanne took the reins after another look at Woody's pale face and shaking hands.

They were fortunate. A group of nursery maids and off-duty footmen were still gathered near the park entrance, discussing the kidnapping. The Watch had just left to make his report, scanty though it could be, since no one recognized either the young lady or her captor.

"Hired coach, it looked to be," one of the footmen volunteered when Rowanne asked about her missing "sister" and Woody jingled some coins in his pocket. "With job horses."

A fat nursemaid pushed her pram closer to Rowanne's carriage. "The driver was a good-looking nob, dark like the little gal. We thought it could have been her brother at first, so didn't say nothing when they started having a real argle-bargle."

"Then 'e snatched 'er up an' tossed 'er in the coach," a chestnut vendor took up, "but your little miss, she put up a good fight. A real game 'un, she looked. Got the snabbler a smart 'un with 'er ridicule, she did, popped 'is cork."

"We tried to give chase, miss, honest we did," the footman said, "but we was on foot and lost them. But they was headed out of town, all right, on the Richmond road. Should be easy to trace, with the driver dripping claret down his shirt front."

Rowanne and Woody set out on the chase as soon as they had distributed largesse and sent the footman back to Grosvenor Square with a message for Gabe. They stopped at posting houses every once in a while to make sure they were on the right road, following a hired coach whose driver had a bloody nose.

Carey was not as lucky. None of the ostlers he interviewed recalled a red-headed sprig or a dark-haired wench. It was growing late, his leg was aching from getting up and down from the curricle so often, and Emonda had wept herself into such a limp rag that he did not see how she could hold on to the seat much longer. Defeated, he turned back.

When Pitkin announced that Lord Clyme was home, Emonda gasped, "Oh, no, I couldn't," and ran up the stairs. Carey limped on down the hall.

Now Gabriel had come home from a long day of political harangues, expecting a serene household dedicated to his comfort and an admiring little audience of his own. He did not expect his house to be in an uproar, his aunt raving that his own intended had been abducted.

Not even St. Dillon would go so far, Gabe mourned, sinking into a chair. She must have gone willingly. He did not understand what Rowanne hoped to accomplish by chasing after them, for if Emonda preferred the dashing duke with his vast fortune and practiced charm, there was nothing anyone could do. Gabe poured himself a brandy and tried to drink to Emonda's happiness. He couldn't quite do it, so he tried again.

Thus when Carey Delverson staggered through the door, Gabe's first intent was to slap him across the cheek in the accepted manner of issuing a challenge. "Vile seducer," he shouted. "I'll meet you on the field of honor, if you have any."

But more than his judgment was clouded. Gabe's aim was off, and bitter resentment lent strength to his arm. He struck Carey a heavy blow to the chin. The suddenness of the attack combined with the weakness in his leg sent Carey to the floor. Before he could say "I haven't even *seen* your sister today," Aunt Cora started beating him about the head with her book. Now that Carey was down, Toodles bravely waded into the fray, snarling and savaging the duke's leather boot.

That's when Rudd lurched in, looking like the remains of a carriage wreck.

Chapter Twenty-five

"*B*loody war was safer'n civilian life, I reckon, Major." Rudd was brandishing a makeshift crutch and a large pistol.

"And made a damn sight more sense," Carey noted, accepting Gabe's hand to get to his feet. Rudd moved the barrel of his weapon until it was trained on Toodles, still gnawing at St. Dillon's boot. Lady Silber quickly snatched her pet out of Rudd's vicinity, though the valet was tempted, seeing the gold tassel swinging from the mutt's mouth.

"I didn't intend to knock you down, you know," Gabe apologized. "Can't be good form, but I've never done this before. Sorry." Then he realized whom he was addressing. "Oh, Lud, what have you done with the woman I love?"

Carey brushed himself off. "Blister me if I even know who— Is that why Emmy's upstairs crying her eyes out about dragging your name through the mud?"

"She's upstairs? Oh, my precious darling, to think of me at a time like this. I must go to her at once."

He started to dash from the room, but Carey cried "Halt!"

Gabe was not a soldier, had never been a soldier, and even if his befogged mind recognized that tone of authority, it was not listening. If Gabe was disguised enough to throw caution to the wind and challenge one of Delverson's Devils, he was surely enough above himself to ignore a direct order in his own house. So Rudd extended his crutch as the gentleman tore past, and Gabe went flying.

"Civilians," the ex-batman muttered in disgust.

It was Carey's turn to offer the other man a hand. "A word before you leave, my lord, if you would be so kind. I believe it

366

is possible that my sister has been abducted from this house. Do you have any knowledge of her whereabouts?"

"It was your *sister*?" Gabe cast a dark look at his aunt. "That must be why Rowanne and Jeffers took my curricle."

"The deuce you say, now she's gone missing too?" Carey took the snuffbox out of his pocket, just to have something in his hand.

"No, thanks, I don't indulge. Messy habit." Gabe was pouring two glasses of wine. "Rowanne sent back a note that they're setting out on the Richmond road. I couldn't make head nor tails of it, for Gretna Green is in quite the opposite direction."

"I know, I've already been halfway there. Damn, I wish I knew what sent Rowanne south."

Rudd cleared his throat. "Pardon, Major, but you know the man you had looking for the female and her brat or that other cove? He reported back while you were out and the address he gave was in Richmond. I got it here. That's why I come, and brought the pistols. The dog too, in case we need to be tracking."

Carey didn't have the heart to tell poor battered Rudd the dog was a sight hound and couldn't follow a scent any better than Toodles. He smiled and said, "Good man! Damn if I don't recommend you for a medal, but I suppose you'd rather have a raise." Carey was happier now that he wasn't merely chasing shadows. In fact he was almost lighthearted, eagerly looking forward to the coming confrontation. As in any battle, the waiting was the hardest part. Now he simply had to set fresh horses in the traces, drive like hell, and commit a little mayhem. Of course he wasn't thrilled that Rowanne was involved—and neither, it turned out, was Gabe.

"Do you mean you knew someone was going to attack you? And now my sister is going there, where you need pistols? You are all Bedlamites, and I am coming with you."

"Have you ever shot a man? I thought not. Rudd and I can handle it; you'll stay here." It was simple and direct, and an insult to Gabe's honor. He started to bluster but Carey tempered the order: "I think there will be a ransom note by morning. If I am not back, I need you here to answer it. I'll leave you a blank draft for my bank."

Gabe nodded, satisfied. He really would rather comfort Emonda, as long as his sister was not in danger. "That won't be necessary. I can lay out the blunt until you get back with Rowanne."

"It could be considerable. The swine knows how much I am worth." They shook hands and Carey solemnly told the other man, "I'll bring her back." Then he smiled and added on his way through the door, "Of course, you might offer the kidnapper double if he'll keep Suzannah. The chit's always been more trouble than she's worth."

Rowanne and Woody did not drive quite as fast as Carey was wont to. Only a handful of madmen did. Nor did they have any definite destination. They knew they were on the right road because various farmers and tradesmen had seen a carriage fitting their description, the driver holding a bloodied cloth to his nose, but they were running out of funds, daylight, and well-trafficked road.

"They could have turned off anywhere without our knowing it," Woody fretted. "These lanes could go on for miles, with Jupiter knows how many abandoned farms or crumbled manor houses."

"You've been reading Suzannah's gothic romances again, haven't you? We'll just have to stop at every likely place we see and hope someone recognizes the man's description. If he is staying around here, the locals will know him, although without the bloody nose he is just a dark-haired, well set-up man. There's an inn up ahead so we'll start there. I for one could use some food too. We drove through teatime, and heaven knows when we'll get dinner."

Woody brightened, as she knew he would, and the innkeep was more friendly than the others they had consulted along the road. He turned positively talkative once he found out they were a respectable brother and sister, trying to return a purse the gentleman had left at a posting house where they had sat together. "You must mean Mr. Fieldstone. It's my carriage he's hired at that. Gone to London to fetch back his cousin, he is. Not that I should be gossiping about the customers, but the chit was set on marrying a fortune hunter."

Woody jumped up and would have given the game away, except for a sharp kick under the table. "I, ah, have a cramp in my leg. Sitting too long in the carriage, don't you know. I hope this Fielding person lives nearby so we can deliver the purse and head home."

Rowanne smiled at him. There was hope for the boy yet. She passed the boiled potatoes.

"That's Mr. Fieldstone, and he's renting the Turner place, him and his missus and the boy. You can't miss the house, it's up the hill from Endicott's farm and the third drive on your left, or is it right? Anyways, it's got a big oak out front. Maybe an elm."

They found the house eventually, then drove on past to hide the curricle and horses in the woods and make plans. Woody was all for knocking on the front door and demanding Suzannah's release. Rowanne suspected that someone who had gone to the trouble of abducting a female in broad daylight was not going to be quite so easily convinced to give up his prize. She had no better plan, however, since neither she nor Woody had thought to bring a weapon or reinforcements.

"Perhaps we should creep up to the house and peek in the windows to see how many accomplices he has," she offered. "Or we could set fire to the barn and grab up Suzannah when they run out to check. Or maybe we should go back to the inn and get help."

The discussion was ended before it began when a scream pierced the air. Woody charged the door, yelling "I'm coming, Suky!"

Rowanne had no choice but to follow him, and burst through the entry on his heels, just in time to look down the barrel of a pistol in Mr. Lawrence Fieldstone's left hand. His right held a second weapon trained on Woody.

The Reardon woman was across the room, holding still another gun to Suzannah's head. "I told you we should have gagged the chit," she snarled at Fieldstone, "but no, that was too rough for your little cousin. Now look what we've got."

"What we've got is more hostages and no one skulking around outside. Come in, come in," he invited Woody and Rowanne, his gesture with the guns making it clear they could not refuse.

Woody rushed to Suzannah's side. "Are you all right, Suky? They haven't hurt you? Why were you screaming?"

"I'm fine, just hungry. I thought I heard a carriage go by and hoped it would stop, and it was you! Oh, Woody!"

"How sweet." Fieldstone was cut from the Delverson mold, just as Woody had explained, but his eyes were hard and cold, and his mouth wore a sneer instead of Carey's ready smile. His nose, of course, was red and swollen. "The gallant knight coming to rescue his lady in distress. Unfortunately, Sir Galahad, you forgot your lance," he taunted, before turning to Rowanne. "But here is a treasure indeed. Here, if I am not mistaken, is my dear cousin's light-o'-love. My, how the luck seems to fall, Regina."

Mrs. Reardon was not as pleased. "There's too many, Larry. We can't keep them all here without the neighbors seeing something. Their coach must be somewhere nearby, and what if they stopped at the inn for directions?"

"Astute as always, my dear. No, we shall have to make other arrangements. We cannot just release them, not this veritable plethora of hostages begging to be ransomed, although I doubt the country turnip can fetch much. I should think the lady"—he leered in Rowanne's direction—"would fetch a pretty penny from her brother. At least her disappearance should cost dear Carrisbrooke untold anguish. I'll enjoy that."

Rowanne did not think she would, not the way Fieldstone was running his eyes over her and licking his bottom lip. Suzannah was wide-eyed, while Woody's gaze was darting to the fireplace poker. She herself had noted a heavy pewter pitcher on the table nearby and was calculating odds. Three against two was good, but the two had three pistols, and that was very bad. In addition, Suzannah was tied and had to be counted a handicap. Maybe she and Woody should have done a tad more planning. Rowanne was not really frightened, for the two abductors were obviously interested in the money. Not even Gabe would be nodcock enough to pay ransom for a dead sister. Still, Fieldstone was looking at her as if she were naked before him. She could not like it.

Neither could Mrs. Reardon. "We have to get them out of here, Larry, soon."

He brushed her away. "I wonder what we can get for the lot?"

Then a deep voice from behind him answered: "A one-way trip to Botany Bay, if you are lucky."

Carey!

Then the dogs of Hell were loosed, or Old Scratch at any rate. The big animal rushed past Fieldstone, setting him off balance. Mrs. Reardon screamed. Fieldstone recovered and turned. Rowanne grabbed for the pitcher, Woody dived for the poker, Suzannah screamed. The dog barked, shots were fired, a baby screamed. More shots, more screams, more smoke than a body could see through to discover who stood, who lay fallen. Then came almost silence, except for a child's whimpers, somewhere upstairs.

And Rudd, coming through a back door, disgusted. "Dash it, Major, you didn't leave me nothing to do."

Fieldstone was on the floor, a ball in his shoulder, a hundred-pound dog on his chest drooling in his face. Carey had a streak of blood across one cheek, and an armful of Rowanne dabbing at the scratch with her handkerchief. Hearing Rudd's voice and recalling the others present, she leapt away. Carey grinned and reloaded. Mrs. Reardon was rubbing her arm, and an exultant Woody was holding her pistol while Suzannah cheered.

Rudd nodded at the youth approvingly. "Guess he's smarter than he looks."

To which Carey mumbled for Rowanne's ears only, "*Toodles* is smarter than Woody looks." Aloud he congratulated the young man on his quick thinking. "Although I think we shall discuss later precisely what you intended by bringing Miss Wimberly into danger, without even a proper weapon."

Woody looked abashed, but Rowanne claimed it was all her own fault, for she would insist on rushing off without a groom, in hopes of protecting Suzannah's name. Unfortunately that

371

reminded Carey of his sister, being happily untied by Woody, now that Rudd guarded the Reardon woman. "You and I, miss, shall certainly have a conversation about traipsing off on your own." Carey spoke slowly, fixing the girl with a cold stare that promised he would make up for whatever lapses in her education an indulgent papa had allowed. "Hell and tarnation, Suky, don't you *ever* think of your reputation?"

She just grinned at him, that same Delverson smile, dimples and twinkling eyes. "But the wife of a country squire does not have to guard her name so closely, Carey. Who's going to care, back in Dorset, that the soon-to-be Mrs. Jeffers went to visit her noble relations and took a walk without her maid? It wasn't as if I were going to be a duchess or anything, you know," she added slyly, bringing roses to Rowanne's cheeks.

Carey grinned back. "Minx. By the by, how come neither you nor Emonda told me that Fieldstone had visited Delmere with our cousins after the governor passed away? That would have saved a lot of pother, Suky."

"Because you'd ordered us never to mention his name again, remember? And I always try to obey orders, Major," she answered with a giggle.

Carey looked at Woody, pityingly. "Are you *sure* you want the brat?" Woody just smiled, ear to silly ear. Carey shrugged. "Suzannah, why don't you and the hero go upstairs and see about the child, while I take care of some loose threads here."

"He's hungry," Mrs. Reardon wearily told Suzannah. "We sent the nursemaid off for the day."

"Good. Come on, Woody, let's go practice. And see what else is in the kitchen." The two skipped out as if there had never been any shots fired, never been any danger. Rowanne sank into a chair.

"Poor puss," Carey sympathized, coming behind her to quickly grasp her shoulder. Then he kissed the top of her head—and put a pistol in her hand.

Carey whistled Scratch away and bent to heave Fieldstone onto another chair. He tore away the man's coat and shirt, wadding the latter to press against the wound. "You'll live, unfortunately."

"No thanks to you, you miserable—"

Carey pressed a little harder. Fieldstone bit his lip and sub-sided. Carey removed his own neckcloth, none too fresh after the day's events, but better than Fieldstone deserved. As he wrapped the makeshift bandage, he asked, "Why, Larry? I offered Mrs., ah, Fieldstone, I assume?" The woman nodded. "A fair deal, and you had ample funds from Harry. Why did you have to be so blasted greedy?"

"It wasn't just the money, damn you. It was you, the way you always treated me like dirt because I was base-born."

"You were mistaken, Larry. I never disliked you for being a bastard, I despised you for acting like one."

He tied the ends of the bandage off in a knot and stood back. "Now what would you have me do? Welcome a kid-napper, extortionist, near murderer to the family fold? I think not." Carey touched the new mark on his cheek, then turned to the woman who was his father's mistress, his bastard cousin's wife. "My offer still stands," he told her, "with minor varia-tions. I have some unwanted property in Jamaica. The slaves have already been freed, but the land is profitable. It is yours, along with passage there for you, the boy, and this piece of trash. An account for the boy shall be opened in Kingston. In two days' time there shall also be a warrant issued for your arrest, both of you. If you are found, if you ever set foot in England again, it will be served. You may take your chances with the law, but I do not suggest that course. I have money, witnesses, your forged letters, and a definite limit to my compassion."

It was better than she hoped. The woman agreed.

"We'll stop at that inn and have them send for a doctor. I'll see you get the proper papers tomorrow." He called for Suzannah and Woody, and shepherded his valiant troop out the door. Then he turned back. "One last thing has been bothering me. Tell me, was there ever a Mr. Reardon?"

She threw a candy dish at his head. Carey laughed.

Chapter Twenty-six

*E*veryone was chaperoned for the ride home. Rudd led off driving the Wimberly curricle, with Suzannah and Woody on the seat with him. It was a tight squeeze, but neither Woody nor Suzannah complained.

A bit behind, Carey held the ribbons of his own equipage with one hand, Miss Wimberly with the other. Old Scratch played dogsberry, balanced on the tiger's bench behind, his tongue tasting the night air and only occasionally drooling on his master's shoulder. His ears caught the breeze and the fond words as the carriage dropped farther and farther behind the other vehicle.

The words did not begin quite so tenderly.

"If you ever put yourself into danger like that again I'll thrash you to within an inch of your life. Do you know how I felt, seeing that gun pointed at you?" Carey squeezed her closer, as if to keep her from harm.

Rowanne felt safe and warm, warmer indeed than the cool evening warranted. "I couldn't very well just sit around and wait, not when Suzannah might need help. And I did tell you I was a managing sort of woman."

"Good," Carey told her, looking into her eyes, seeing stars reflected in their depths. He smiled, that heart-stopping smile that made her toes curl. "I need managing," he went on. "Rudd cannot do the job alone."

"Ah, about Rudd . . ." She fussed with the blanket across their laps.

"Don't worry, sweetheart, he understands. Of course I had to promise him the new ivory leg he's had his eye on, as a wedding present."

"Oh, is he getting married?"

Then the curricle came to a halt altogether, while Carey demonstrated to Rowanne exactly who should be getting wed and why. Scratch had time to jump off and visit a bush before the horses were moving again.

"You will marry me, won't you, my dearest Rowanne?" Carey begged when he could speak again. "I have loved you so long, but things kept getting in the way. Wars, wicked women . . . It seems I have been wanting forever to ask."

"And I have been waiting forever. I think I loved you from our first dance," she told him, which required another long halt and a few deep breaths afterward.

"You were so graceful, like a swaying rose in my arms." Carey sighed, clucking the horses to motion. "Do you mind that we'll never have another dance like it?"

"Why, silly, because of your injury? The memory of our first waltz will be that much sweeter."

"You remember, then?"

"Everything. Every word, every smile, even that first night at Almack's when you were so gay and dashing." She watched him now as he watched the horses, memorizing every inch of his splendid profile, thinking he was even more handsome now, if that was possible.

"And you were so sweet and lovely. I still have the cameo, you know. I carry it always."

"For luck?"

"No, for love."

Scratch was getting tired, jumping on and off the vehicle. They were going so slowly, when they moved at all, that he could just amble alongside.

Carey had other things on his mind. "You do understand it will mean giving up some of the Town life you are used to, don't you? St. Dillon's has been neglected far too long, and I mean to learn to be a responsible landlord. Shall you mind very much?"

"May I grow roses?"

He looked at her in surprise. "Do you know how to grow roses?"

"No, but I mean to learn, and daffodils too. It's what I've

always wanted, to watch things grow, not just ferns in tubs and oranges in the conservatory, but real things, from seeds."

Carey hugged her and chuckled. "My precious, we shall learn together, but even I know daffodils grow from bulbs. Besides, you'll be busy fixing up the Abbey. It's in much worse condition than the London house."

Rowanne laughed delightedly. "Wonderful, I cannot wait to start!"

"When?" he asked, nuzzling her ear. "When will you start? Tonight? I know the way to Gretna Green, we could just keep going."

"But, Carey, think of what Suzannah would say! A runaway marriage would not suit your dignities, and a duchess must think more of propriety." Right then she was finding it difficult to think at all.

"Devil take propriety and dignity both! I'll give you three weeks for the banns to be read, not one day longer."

"Why?" she teased, feeling his breath stir her hair. "Are you afraid I won't love you anymore, after all these years?"

"No," he answered, knotting the reins around the railing to keep the horses from bolting while he convinced her. "I'm just afraid my luck will finally run out."